BOXED IN

J. DAVIS

BOXED IN

J. Davis

Cover Design by Wren Taylor

Published in the United States of America by

DLG Publishing Partners

www.DLGPUBLISHINGPARTNERS.com

I'd like to thank my wife, Brinley Widerman. Far before I ever dreamt of writing a novel, she was by my side and helping me navigate life. This book is hers, too.

I'd like to also thank my sister Luciana. She selflessly immersed herself in this business, guiding me through all the "behind-the-scenes" stuff I had no interest in tending to.

Finally, I'd like to thank my students at Conniston Middle School. If not for your interest in my story (and phenomenal 4th-quarter projects), this book would still be half-completed on a flash drive collecting dust.

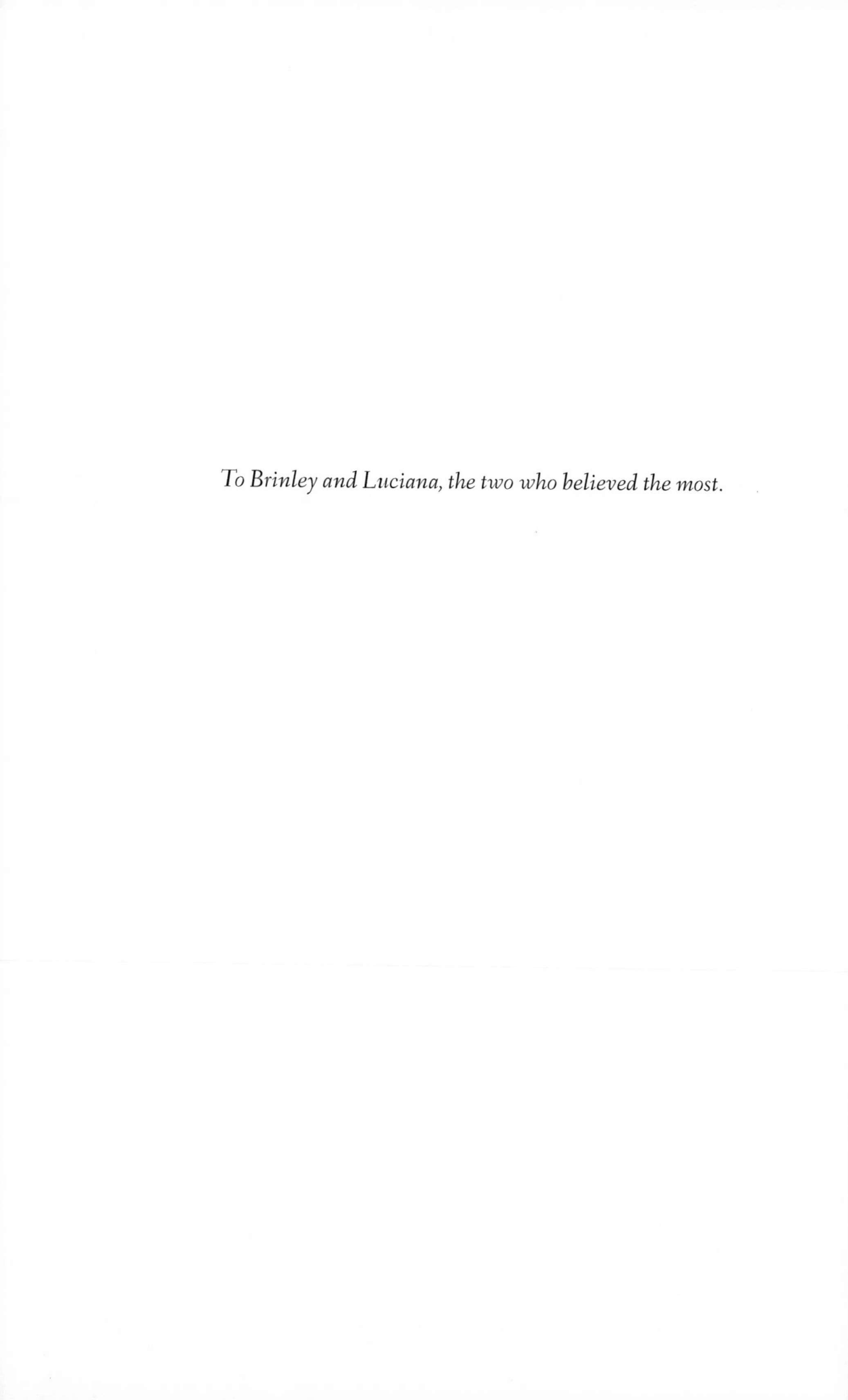

To Brinley and Luciana, the two who believed the most.

A decrepit, sinister town…

A young boxer who wants to escape…

A mafioso with a solution….

Salvador Purelli has been watching Richie Frezza and likes what he sees. When the mob boss makes contact, the offer is simple: represent the Solano Crime Family or find a new market.

When enemies muscle in on the boxing trade and an ambitious police officer begins snooping, the Family must preserve its grip on Ridgemont Cove's underworld and silence former Solano fighter Timothy Vietta.

Soon, Richie learns commitment to the Family is more about sin and less about boxing.

Can Richie escape the inevitable carnage, or does Salvador Purelli have a plan of his own?

It's the twelfth and final round, but who is in Richie's corner?

CONTENTS

CHAPTER ONE

The cement of the Imperial Fish & Game locker room chilled the soles of Richie Frezza's feet. Remnants of a lukewarm shower dripped from him, splotching irregular circles to the floor. Street clothes from before the double shift hung from a wire in a rusting locker.

A cheap Timex, its strap worn to the point of tarnishing, dangled on his left arm. It read 6:42 P.M. Each payday he told himself he'd get a new one. But every two weeks, the paycheck came and went, and the same watch remained on his wrist.

A yawn escaped from within and he brushed damp bronze hair from his forehead. The square mirror sagging from the top shelf reflected a wind-burned face and glossy blue eyes—far too haggard and worn to belong to a nineteen-year-old.

Clyde Storey, the night supervisor, trudged in accompanied by offcuts of the frozen night.

Chunky and tan, the man embodied the salty-dog persona. Rough red patches crossed his cheeks. Graying stubble matched the breaking crests of incoming waves. A white sailor cap and the butt of a cheap cigar jammed between dry and flaking lips completed the caricature.

"Good job out there, young man. Tuesdays are tough, you know. All those asshole captains trying to sneak in every last bit before quotas are up." Clyde unbuttoned his jacket. "I appreciate you pulling the overtime."

"Not a problem. I need the scratch." Richie stood and snagged faded sweatpants from the locker. They were a rare gift from his mother, who, at present, was no more than an acquaintance. With some caution, he slid into them, ignoring the pops and aches of his body.

"I worked the double shift for three years, Monday through Friday." Clyde sat beside him. "We'll make a man out of you yet."

The aroma of burned tobacco wafted from his mouth. Outside on the dock and loading bay, the decay of the sea filled nostrils. In the employee locker room, body odor and fading smoke perfumed the air.

"I can handle the job." Richie forced the lids of his eyes to climb. "Tired today. Trained hard this morning with Joe."

"At Knuckles Up?" Clyde gummed the unlit cigar. "What time you get there?"

"Four or so, most mornings. Workout, grab coffee at Ms. May's, and then jog here."

"Jesus, that's like ten miles. You're going to run home, too?"

"I clocked it. Three and a quarter from stoop to stoop. It's good training." Richie shrugged the clean shirt on and fought another stubborn yawn. "Besides, I don't have a car."

"Why the hell not?"

"You giving out raises soon?"

"Don't sell yourself short. I packed every day for twelve years. Now, I don't need to take a shower when I leave.

With your work ethic, you'll be foreman and running a crew."

"I don't have twelve years."

"Good money at my level. Not a lot of places in Ridgemont Cove offering overtime and retirement."

"No offense, but this"—Richie pointed to the Imperial Fish & Game logo on the stained long sleeve draped over the locker's bottom shelf—"isn't my future."

"Oh, I forgot, you're going to be world champion one day." He rose and threw a few shadow punches in the air, bobbing and weaving as he did so. "Let's grab a beer, Tyson."

"Can't. I have a date. I need to get home and change." He plucked a tester vial of cologne from the front pocket of a backpack sandwiched next to tomorrow's rubber overalls and boots.

"Careful, pal. Too much of that'll make you stink like a French whore." Clyde heaved a mesh bag of soiled shirts and gear over his shoulder, walked to the end of the locker room and dropped the sack in the over-sized commercial laundry hamper. "By the way, what kind of respectable young woman is dating a bum with a bus pass?"

"A sexy waitress. I do love redheads."

"And where does this unfortunate soul live?"

"A few miles from here. Why? You interested?"

Clyde fished a key chain from his coat pocket. With thick and calloused fingers, he removed one of three vehicle keys and tossed it to the bench. "Dating? That's a young man's game. Tell you what, Richie. Borrow the pickup if you want. We won't need it tonight. Bring it back after the redhead. You can still get in a run afterward."

"If the date goes right, I sure as hell won't be dropping her off." Richie licked his lips and spanked the air.

"Oh, to be young." Clyde returned the remaining keys to his pocket. He snatched a newspaper from an open locker and perused the front page. He eyed the headline. "If the Dodge is back in the lot before your shift tomorrow, nobody has to know it ever left."

"Overtime pay and now this?"

"I reward effort, youngster. Keep it up."

CHAPTER TWO

Knuckles Up resembled the stereotypical hole-in-the-wall gym. A stretching area lined the majority of floor space to the left. Two rows of punching bags bolted to the ceiling dangled from eye hooks on the right. Mounted in the middle, a regulation-sized sparring ring encompassed much of the remaining real estate.

A scuffed and failing door cut into the wall of the training area. The steel plate at the bottom now tarnished with etched streaks of rust running its length like claw marks. That entrance led into a small shower room with lukewarm water and sweat-scented rubber flooring.

At the opposite end of the thousand square foot gym, just behind a mirrored half-wall and dumbbell rack, Joe Gallant's office hid from it all.

When Vietnam ended, Joe turned the anguish and unspeakable horrors from his time in "the shit" into fuel for fighting. From his first amateur bout, Joe "The Giant Killer" Gallant teemed with swagger and the innate ability to break bones with his bare hands.

An unblemished amateur record of fifty-seven wins and

zero losses led to promotion from the now defunct RC Boxing Academy. He then compiled a twenty-seven-match win streak and reached number three in the professional middleweight rankings.

And then it ended. Curtains drawn. Game over.

They were to blame, and one day, they would pay, he told himself. But thirty-three years later, *they* still owned the town, and he kept counting pennies.

Between his exit from the professional ranks and the grand opening of Knuckles Up—a business opportunity that fell into his lap—Jim Beam-fueled stupors took their toll on his health, career, and wallet.

Now sober with ten years of Knuckles Up ownership behind him, the hazy recollections of guilt-ridden nights lived in parts of his brain impossible to retract. The urge remained. It always would, according to a plethora of AA sponsors throughout the years.

Physically, a clean bill of health, according to an overpaid doctor in Sharpton, left him wondering if all the bad he'd done to his body somehow canceled each other out. Despite a two-pack a day habit of cancer sticks and thirty years' worth of bourbon, his lungs and liver held no worrisome diagnosis.

That a fact? Then why the hell am I losing weight and pissing blood?

One area of his past life still teetering on the edge of pathetic remained financial stability. Sobriety and exercise didn't stuff the wallet. And, as he knew too well, vultures from all walks of life, some avoidable and some not, inched in with hands outstretched.

He tapped a scratch-off nestled in the front pocket of his hoodie. It hadn't won a damn cent. *They rarely did.* But Joe still bought them in droves, elated when the final dust presented a winner and ticked when the last scratched slot revealed a losing bet.

Losses piled up as of late, and that didn't count protection payments due each week. For all he'd endured and accomplished, the mighty dollar seemed to be a problem.

The kid could change it all, though.

Richie Frezza, often the only person in the dank of the gym lifting metal and throwing punches, ripped shots into a duct-taped heavy bag.

Joe surveyed the young fighter's stance. Like usual, the kid displayed pristine footwork and guard.

Clean movement and brute strength were enough to knock out a few clowns, but that alone wouldn't assist a fighter in climbing the ranks.

Richie possessed the greatest trait a fighter could. *Brains.*

No matter the amount of money you handed a trainer or coach who promised the world, if you lacked the ability to identify tendencies of your opponent and exploit them, you'd never reach the pros and the paperbacks had been better spent elsewhere.

The kid, though? A genius, as far as boxers were concerned. Three steps ahead, and he had the physical talent to capitalize on opponents' mistakes.

Joe trotted Richie out in front of every sparring partner he could find. All gained early momentum, but then Richie's mind defeated them. Every. Single. One.

When he hits the ring for real, the money will sort itself out. Hopefully.

Sweat splashed off Richie's body with each swing.

"Keep your left up. Jab. Jab. Jab. Duck. Hook," Joe yelled, clutching the handle of his cane.

Richie circled the punching bag and obeyed. It

swooped in circles from a rusted chain attached to the low ceiling. Each landed shot reverberated within the gym—three resounding *thwaps*, a pause, and then a crunching *pow*.

He performed the sequence six times with no rest.

Joe pressed forward. "Your shoulder hurt?"

"No, sir."

Beads of sweat streamed from Richie's dampened hair. The kid's face flushed red, and even in the early morning, with little sunlight penetrating the small window carved into the front door, Joe could see him growing redder with each punch.

"If I see that left glove drop again, you'll get the cane, youngin'." Joe shook the mahogany stick inches from Richie's rising left hand. "You want the bright lights?"

"Yes, sir," Richie replied, bobbing and driving three straights to the bottom half of the bag.

"You want the headlines?" Joe screamed, his voice a mix of rising phlegm and sandpaper scratching across gravel.

"Yes, sir."

"Then focus. Release your thoughts. That shitty job of yours. The broad from two nights ago. Clear it all, ya hear?"

"Yes, sir." Richie popped up from a feigned duck and centered a shot to the upper portion of the bag.

"Any Goddamn thing in this world you want you can have. But it won't be handed to you. You earn the right to take it. You remember that?"

Richie's mouth opened, but the words evaporated, and Joe realized the kid had been full-go for the better part of fifteen minutes. The dripping sweat, now an avalanche of water, splattered—landing hard enough to echo.

"The pain you feel"—Joe brought the cane to Richie's ribs with a slight jab—"is just weakness leaving the body.

Let it go. Again. Keep your left up. Jab. Jab. Jab. Duck. Hook."

The front door opened, breathing frigid air into the musty gym. Dim daylight crept forward, illuminating Richie's training shoes in a soft yellow haze.

A shadow emerged in the doorway. The silhouette morphed into a man. His belly burst from within a buttoned suit jacket. Men flanked each side, and the trio walked in unison.

From behind the bag, Joe eyed the lead man, Benny "Beans" Bianchi. A Solano Crime Family member and no stranger to the headlines, he visited Knuckles Up weekly.

The effect of the mobster's presence never changed. Reading about him in the paper kept the evil and danger at bay. But much like seeing a car crash in person as opposed to on television, witnessing the Solano underboss in real time channeled anxiety through each nerve in the body.

The mobster fished a ringing cell from within his suit and pressed it to his ear. He breathed into the device. "Yeah. I'm here now."

Joe yanked the chain of the heavy bag and slowed its spin. Training was over.

Benny slipped the phone into his pocket, brushed the mop of greasy hair to the side, and ambled towards the office door.

"Give me a minute, kid," Joe said, his voice now glass and broken.

Richie, thankful for the reprieve judging by the audible sigh escaping his gaped mouth, shrugged and shook the sweat from his leaking bangs.

Benny's two bodyguards stood at the office door, their heads swiveling to and fro like spectators at a tennis match.

Joe limped forward. "That time again?"

"Clockwork, old man." Benny tapped the chunky gold timepiece peeking from the cuff of his shirt. "You're my first stop every Thursday. Tick-Tock, my old friend."

Joe flung the door open, and the four men corralled inside.

CHAPTER THREE

Richie knew when the brute and his lackeys entered, the day ended. That was why, he supposed, Joe ran his ass into the ground earlier. On any other morning, heavy bag training preceded aerobics. Then, based on available time, light yoga and stretching followed.

However, Thursdays were payday, and not the kind Joe liked.

On most paydays, Joe screamed with an arm slung over the top of his mahogany cane and watched Richie unleash combinations and power punches. Then the pep-talk began, a rendition growing stale like the smoke of Joe's budget-buy cigarettes.

It'll come, kid. You're close. Any week now, and we'll book a real one.

His eyes returned to the bag. Sweat dripped from his hair and painted the flooring with splatters of wet spots. He threw a few quick jabs, then his eyes roamed to the closed office door.

Thursdays.

Collection day. Joe called it rent, but Richie knew

better. Men like Benny Bianchi and his boss Salvador Purelli didn't manage property.

The gym, a hand-me-down Joe said he initially considered a burden, had no loan attached to it. But these men built the town, and not many people argued when levies were collected. The cash—men like Benny would remind the citizens of Ridgemont Cove—guarded those unable to protect themselves.

This wasn't something Joe needed, but Richie imagined refusing to drop a few bucks into Salvador Purelli's pockets could cause far more damage than good.

Richie untied his gloves and then sat on the edge of the ring. Muffled voices leaked from beneath the door.

It swung open, and Benny emerged with his entourage.

"He's gotta profound sense of humor, fellas." A smile painted the round man's chubby, pockmarked face.

Neither of the bodyguards replied. They walked ahead to the entrance, the smaller clutching an envelope.

They rob another soul and walk away. Give me money I don't deserve. Thank you so much for the contribution.

Joe limped out of the office. A lit cigarette pinched between his lips. His liver-spotted hand brushed through his hair, once blond and full but now thin and straw. The ragged hooded sweatshirt he wore draped over his slender frame like the shroud of a corpse.

"That's why I love you, Joey." Benny wheezed. His belly protruded over the black designer slacks.

Smoke seeped from the orange ember of the cigarette, masking Joe's gaunt countenance in a film of gray. He took another drag and chewed at his lip as if uninterested in the compliment and then plucked the cigarette free, smashing the butt into his worn and calloused palm.

Richie retracted.

Ash embedded in Joe's hand. The smell of dead skin fizzed, but his expression did nothing to sway the indifference painted on the older man's face.

"Hey." Benny slapped Joe's back and jeered, the rolls of his chin gyrating in unison. "We should get a line on the fights tomorrow. You ever going to let this kid go? I can make a call to one of my guys."

Richie picked at the hand tape wrapped on his knuckles. Beneath his fingernails, leftover gunk emanated the decay of rotting fish.

Jesus, this smell. No matter how many showers, Richie thought, continuing to pluck the tape, forcing his mind to zig zag Benny's statement.

Remembering what Joe had told him a few months back, he fought the impulse to acknowledge the mobster. *Never look these guys in the eyes, and never speak unless they speak to you.*

Joe didn't answer at first. Then a muttered phrase followed the flick of the dead cigarette butt, and the hooded shroud sauntered toward the office.

"We're looking for talent, old man." Benny's words followed Joe's retreat. "My guy Lorenzo has the contacts, and we've got the promotion."

"Let me worry about my fighters." Joe turned in the doorway of his office, planting his feet at the threshold.

"Suit yourself." Benny's footsteps faded toward the entrance, and it took every ounce of self-discipline for Richie not to tilt his head.

Light from outside of the gym shrank behind the closing door.

Richie glanced toward Joe. "Can I ask you something?"

"If you want me to lend you money, the answer is no."

The wrinkles of the old man's eyes became more prominent when he smiled.

"No, it's something else. Why do you deal with those guys?"

"Long story."

"I just don't get it."

"You don't need to. It's nothing for you to worry about, okay?"

"I'm not stupid."

"I didn't say you were."

"Then talk to me, man."

Joe tucked the morning paper beneath his arm and limped to Richie's punching bag, grimacing with each left stride. "The world ain't fair." He picked at a duct-taped portion of the bag until a strand peeled off. He rolled the discarded tape into a ball, then tossed it into a metal can sitting near the ringside. "Just read the newspaper on any shitty Ridgemont Cove morning."

The paper flew into Richie's lap. He flattened it out and read the headline: *Search for Prominent Businessman Continues. Foul Play Suspected.*

"The news is never good."

"That's my point." Joe snatched the paper. "When's the last time the front page had a happy story? Always so-and-so raped in an abandoned building, teenager robbed a store and killed the clerk, or a little girl's body found off Route 9. If I gotta deal with these assholes, so be it. I get by."

Each time, Benny's routine was the same. He glided in with an entourage of muscle-headed goons, flashed the gold jewelry living on his fingers, and pocketed some of Joe's hard-earned money. It was tough to care for guys like Benny. Thugs in suits weren't likeable, but their command of the town and stream of cash built by gorging the innocent, as despicable as it was, demanded attention and respect.

They were assholes. No question there. *Rich and powerful assholes.*

People all over town knew Benny "The Beans". You didn't have to like the business model, but you sure as hell needed to respect the process. Here Richie was, grinding away in the gym every day for an ever-elusive shot at the bright lights, and this chunky prick pranced around like the CEO. *Power. Money. Trouble.*

"I don't get it. Why are they picking on you?"

"They own the whole Goddamn town, kid. As long as I've been here, they've had their hands in everybody's pockets. What am I gonna to do? Am I supposed to stiff Salvador Purelli? He says, '*pay*', and I ask, '*how much*', right?"

"What if you said no?"

Joe shrugged and drew a glare to the paper in his hand. "A lot of people try. I'm not that stupid."

"I didn't mean anything by it. I'm just trying to look out for you. You know this is all I've got. Trying to have your back."

"I've been alive longer than you and your momma combined. I don't need a babysitter. Worry about your training. Leave the rest of the town alone. Got it?"

"Yeah. Speaking of training, am I ever going to fight?"

"Think you're ready, hotshot?" Joe's cane fell to the floor, and the old man barreled toward a bag. As if the arthritis subsided, and the years melted in an instant, Joe struck the bag with sharp, successive shots. It swayed back and forth. Dust particles floated from the eye hook screwed into the ceiling.

"When? Been busting my ass." The words came out shallow and Richie regretted them.

Joe gathered his cane from the floor and looked up. For the first time this morning, the expression on the weathered man's face had character. The neutral scowl of indifference disappeared, leaving an annoyed frown.

"You remember our conversation three months ago?"

"Yeah."

"What did we agree on?"

"I know. I know." Richie's confidence now dwindled like the brightness of Joe's eyes. "I think I'm ready, don't you?"

"If you can't beat an old man like me"—he bobbed and weaved, throwing ghost jabs—"how you gonna take on a contender?"

Richie put his hands up in a defensive position and forced a chuckle.

"Besides, you want to end up like Vietta?" Joe patted Richie's clenched fists.

Memories of a time he'd like to forget rolled in like a thick fog blanketing the incoming tide outside of Imperial Fish & Game.

Vietta's head had cracked the mat with a popping scream after Mitch Mahomes leveled him with a nasty hook. His motionless body, strung out in in the middle of the ring, resembled noodles on a grotesque plate of spaghetti. Beneath his head, red poured, the result of a clean flow from the unconscious man's left ear, eye, and mouth. A thin, but deep, cut on the crown of his head added to the growing pool of red.

Guys got flattened out all the time, but the ferocity of the punch and sickening thud of bones crunching beneath canvas proved unsettling. Richie had forced the vomit back into his stomach.

Other fighters and spectators hollered and cheered like the crowds of ancient Rome, thirsty to see a gladiator's head chopped off. But not Richie, no. He had said nothing and turned from the carnage.

You can't unsee a sight like that. Richie willed the memory to recede. *Timothy Vietta's head split open and draining.*

"Kid, the time will come, and you'll get your shot. Hell, I may need you to make me some cash. With the wise guys hassling me every Goddamn week, it'll be you handling the Solano fee."

Joe retreated to the office, his left leg dragging just behind the right. The door closed and Richie brought a glare to the ceiling. Silence and emptiness. Another morning gone and wasted.

Wise guys or not, they're not starving like us.

CHAPTER FOUR

Standing in a walk-in freezer inside of The Tango, Lorenzo Cantu filled his lungs with the joint scents of preserved meats, frozen fruits, and an earthy hint of blood. He shot a glance to his bronze-colored boss. A gray mustache arched over the man's thin lips and matched a receding mop of salt and pepper hair.

"Hold him up." Gold-rimmed glasses sat high on the tanned cheekbones of Salvador Purelli. Slight but muscular, he wore a three-piece silver suit with black wingtip shoes. "I want to look into his eyes."

Roger Cranswell whimpered in the corner of the freezer. His arms wrapped over bony knees. Each exhalation produced tornadoes of fog.

"You heard the boss." Lorenzo tugged at the husk of the man's shoulders, then slapped him. "Get up."

Cranswell moaned and drew back. An impulsive yelp filled the freezer, though this utterance lacked courage. Lorenzo drove a knee into him. The whimpering ceased, and the man rose.

"We should try this again." Salvador's thick, raspy voice forced smoke to the center of the box. "The money?"

"I'm n-not—" Cranswell stuttered like an elementary school kid attempting a new word. "I don't know. Y-you gotta believe me."

With both eyes blackened, and a deep split at the arch of his nose, a whistling sound seeped from his exhaling nostrils. A small bulb of black blood had dripped from the brow and froze in place.

"We're wasting time here, boss." Lorenzo tapped his watch. "Fridays are busy. The staff will be here soon."

"I am well aware of my business." Purelli then nodded to Cranswell. "Proceed."

Lorenzo dropped the helpless debtor with a right hook. The vibrating and tingling pain never lost its luster. An onslaught of stomps followed, producing spurts of blood from the man's head. His mouth and eyes swelled like balloons at half strength, and crimson droplets dripped onto the plastic sheeting taped to the floor of the freezer. It crystallized and hardened into a dark maroon.

"Enough. Enforce my word, do not overstep."

"Sorry," Lorenzo offered, feeling honor and embarrassment all at once.

The title of enforcer had long since stuck with Lorenzo Cantu, and as a wise guy attempting to earn his street credentials, he reveled when given the opportunity. He stooped to inspect Cranswell's damaged body. "He'll live. Maybe a little brain damage."

"I hope not." A light haze blanketed the lenses of Purelli's glasses. He removed them and exhaled. His breath climbed like smoke swirling from a cigar. "There is still much work to do."

Lorenzo rose, massaging the throbbing sting of the hand. Vibrations of monotonous pain traveled his knuckles. Roughing pricks up came naturally. Hell, it was fun, but this knock-out in the Kolpak walk-in was a first. He used the chilled interior wall of the freezer to thwart the aching of his hand.

Purelli clicked the handle and forced his shoulder into the door. It lurched open, revealing a window-view of the sleeping kitchen.

Lorenzo's eyes wandered to Cranswell. He stepped over the motionless mass and followed the boss through the opening. *Another issue handled. Time for breakfast.*

Now at the chrome industrial sink, Purelli flicked the faucet on. He whistled *One Fine Day* by The Chiffons; a tune Lorenzo recognized from past summer father-son road trips. Like Mr. Purelli, his dad was a hard-nosed Italian immigrant, though the similarities ended there. Ronnie Cantu died penniless and nobody seemed to care.

You can't respect that legacy.

He forced the thought to the base of his brain, unwilling to allow distracting memories to flow.

"You believe him?" Lorenzo glanced at Cranswell, who moaned incoherently.

If you can't handle the spanking for being naughty, don't show your ass. Take your lumps like a man.

Purelli ignored the question and continued whistling. He washed blood spurts from the cuff of his shirt. The red drips morphed into pink and circled in the sink.

"What's next?" Lorenzo asked, cautious of speaking out of turn. He'd elevated his status in the hierarchy without question, but a man of the code never forgot that holes in the ground were ready to swallow the bodies of the disobedient.

Purelli dried his hands with a dish towel and turned

toward Cranswell. His onyx eyes lingered on the man's shivering body as if to capture every tremor the freezer and beating had created. "It's ten past six. The staff will be here in two hours. They must not know we were here. It is bad for business. Let him sit in there for a little longer. The cold may unlock the truth."

"If not?"

"Call Frankie to clean up the mess and take him to the farm." Purelli picked a stray piece of lint from his pants and flicked it to the floor. He slammed the freezer door in place, drowning the pathetic utterances of the condemned man. "Benny is coming to get you."

"Are you sure *you* don't need me?"

"I can manage just fine. Do as you are told."

"We've put a licking on that guy, boss." Lorenzo jabbed a thumb toward the Kolpak. "If he won't or can't talk, what do I tell Frankie to do?"

"Feed the pigs."

CHAPTER FIVE

Mommy dearest, an ardent member of Ridgemont Cove's sinister scene, passed out most nights. After training, Richie made an effort to check in. Many mornings, but especially Fridays like today, Richie swung by to ensure the metamorphosis from addled junkie to comatose hibernator transpired. If the train was still chugging early Friday, then it would charge off the tracks by Sunday and no amount of fish guts or frigid temperatures would squelch his anxiety.

This training session ran later than usual. Richie's Timex read 6:25 AM. And though Clyde's praises a couple nights back added a few inches of leeway, arriving late could act as the scissors that cut the leash altogether. Today's trek to work would be more sprint than trot.

The bait packing job wasn't the future, but it remained a necessity in the present. Besides, rerouting himself home meant less time with *her*. Mom's whereabouts took second place today.

"See you Monday, kid?" Joe limped beside him, stride-for-stride.

"Where else would I be?" Richie nudged the old man with an elbow and pushed the door open.

Car horns and radios from balconies blared in the distance, but the neighborhood slept in for the most part. A raging fiesta last night—like most nights—shook the brains of Ridgemont Cove, forcing it to pull the covers up for a couple more ticks of the clock.

A few stragglers accompanied Richie this morning. Blurry-eyed beggars shook paper cups, loose change clanking their piercing songs. An attractive woman with a yapping dog hurried past, her eyes down and posture defensive. Richie ignored them all.

He crossed over Madison Blvd. and slowed his stride. An old Buick meandered through the intersection. Its driver honked and Richie flipped the middle finger.

Another beautiful day in Ridgemont Cove.

The silhouette of Knuckles Up faded.

Rays of the sun fought to slice the early morning fog, and a few beams reached the diner a block ahead.

Glancing over a shoulder, the dog walker shot him a quizzical expression.

He blew her a kiss, and her pace quickened a beat.

We're not all thugs and thieves, lady.

Ms. May swept the dirt off the steps and ignored Richie's approach.

"Morning."

"She's not here." Her eyes followed the broom grazing the concrete.

"Don't fib." He climbed the first step, but she pressed the handle of the broom into his chest.

"You stay away from her, boy. You keep gallivanting with my girls, and I'll have nobody to tend this diner."

Richie swiped the handle to the side. "It's a wonder I still give you my business." A smirk tugged at his lips.

"Business? Humph. All you ever get round' here is coffee. Too busy staring at my girls. Boy, if you so much as look at Ruby." She stuck her fat pointer into his shoulder.

"Can't be eating pies and muffins." Richie pinched his abdomen. "I'm a middleweight. Gotta watch the calories."

"Yeah. Well, watch those. Not my girls."

"Promise." He drummed fingers against his chest.

"Really?"

"Promise I'll treat her right," Richie cackled, sidestepping her.

Her face morphed. The eyes spit fire, but the mouth couldn't help but grin. She pushed the door open. "Wise-ass."

He entered and crossed over the glossy checkered tile. A replica of a fifty's original jukebox played an old doo-wop song. The woman's high-pitched voice crooned about *One Fine Day*, and Richie chuckled.

Come check out Ridgemont Cove and then tell me about a fine day.

A man sat in one of the red booths lining the right side, a laptop and files took up most of the table surface. Steam hovered over the beige mug in front of him.

Behind the pearl-colored laminate bar top, Ruby washed dishes in the sink positioned in front of a wall-length mirror—a blockade of the patrons' view of the kitchen.

Richie plopped on a stool in front of Ruby, taking in the scene one frame at a time.

Her lower half bobbed to the faint music helping her plump ass gyrate like a buoy in the water. This show continued until the chorus of the song faded. He rapped his fingers on the countertop, jilting the performance.

She swung around in surprise. Her red hair twirled, fell a bit across her face and then dropped beyond her shoulders. The aroma of Ruby's lilac shampoo drifted across the countertop, masking the scent of baked apples and cinnamon.

"Hey, Richie."

"Hello, darling." Richie flashed a tooth-filled smile and straightened his posture. He dropped the hood from his head and ran his fingers through the disheveled mop of hair still slick from sweat.

Her pale skin flushed, and she reached below the counter for a coffee mug. "The usual?" She poured coffee to the brim. "No sugar, just cream?"

"You know me so well."

"Eating?" She dropped a laminated menu on the placemat in front of him.

"No, thanks." He rolled the sleeves of his hoodie to the elbows. "Hey, I had fun the other night. We hit it off, right?"

"Yeah," she replied, drawing her attention to the front door opening. The bell jingled, a slight tone beneath the doo-wop. "I don't know. I'm pulling a double. Not sure I'd be much fun."

"Doesn't have to be tonight. What about tomorrow? There's a new restaurant downtown. It's pricey, but you're worth it." He pressed forward and winked.

"I am? After one night you're willing to buy me steak and lobster?"

"Wait a minute, who said anything about that? You know I work at the loading dock, right?"

"I recall you talking about all the money you're going to

be making with boxing. So, which is it, am I worth it or not?"

Her pink uniform, with frilly white lace at the neckline and hem, clung tight to the curves of her body. His eyes wandered to her legs and then climbed upward to the tight stomach, pronounced breasts and finally the speckled emerald eyes. Those stared back.

"You're worth it. Tonight, at eight?"

"Maybe."

"That word isn't in my vocabulary, baby."

"You're crazy, Richie." She shook her head, drawing a glance to the floor.

"Don't be coy." He took a swig of coffee and flipped the menu toward her. "I want to see you again. You must be tired of eating food like this."

"Look, I had fun, but I'm not sure I should—"

"Why?" The muscles in his jaw tensed, and a rash of heat began its climb across his forehead.

"It's complicated. I'm not really in the market for commitment."

A man sat a few stools down the bar and offered a wave. She placed a menu in front of the new customer, but kept her eyes trained on Richie. "I have a lot going on."

"You're making excuses."

"I have to work. I'm sorry." She turned to the guest with a pad and pen and scribbled his order.

"Wow, I'm speechless." Richie crossed his arms and leaned back. A swiveled sneer crossed his face.

Ruby poured a fresh coffee for the new patron and then turned to Richie. "I'm not saying never. Just, not right now."

Richie's hands interlocked atop his head. "It's cool. No need to explain yourself. I'll be honest. I do like the chase. The hard-to-get thing gets me going, baby. When the little game here ends, you'll call. They always find their way back."

"I'm sure they do." Ruby wiped at the bar top then tossed the damp rag underneath. She flopped the check booklet to the counter. It smacked against the waxed finish, louder than the squeaky teens' falsetto now swimming from the jukebox speakers.

She then shoved through the kitchen swivel doors. Pots and pans tolling reverberated throughout the bar area behind her.

Finishing what remained of the coffee, the date reran in his mind. A stroll in the park, a few tacos from the food trucks, and a boring movie about a girl's struggle with infidelity. An attempt to caress her leg before the opening credits thwarted by a brisk swat of her hand.

She brushed him away with a mischievous expression. It said, *no rush*.

They'd kissed outside of her apartment before parting.

No rush, indeed. The peck was more maternal than sexy, and it blindsided him.

How could she not be interested? This one was different.

"Boy, I done told you to stay away from my girls." Ms. May, now behind the bar with a steaming pot of coffee and content expression of *I told you so*, poured some into Richie's cup. "It looks like you got yourself a fighter."

"I like a challenge." He sipped the blazing black sludge but relented. "Needs cream."

"Aren't you a cocky one? Can't win them all, hon."

"You know what Joe says?"

"What?" Ms. May slid a cream dispenser toward him. The bell above the entrance jingled, and her eyes shifted to the door for a moment. "Hey, Ms. Griffin. We'll be right with you."

Richie knocked on the countertop. "You're not always trying to take the round. Remember, there are twelve. Pick your spots and be patient."

Ms. May grimaced like Richie's words pinched her cheeks—exaggerated but a veiled truth seemingly behind it. She planted both of her palms on the countertop, driving her upper half over the bar. "I like ya, boy, I do, but don't be messing with my help, ya hear?"

Richie's hands shot upward, and he shrugged. "The heart wants what the heart wants, right?"

She eyed him pouring cream into the mug. "You ain't got no heart. My momma always warned me about boys like you. And you best believe I'll set my girls straight."

"As I said, I welcome a challenge. See you tomorrow." He dropped a crumpled pile of dollar bills and sipped again. "Jesus, you strain this with a blowtorch?"

"Plenty of places sell coffee." Ms. May waddled toward the kitchen's swivel doors.

"But yours is the best."

Music oozed from the jukebox. More fifties doo-wop, a ridiculous genre Richie couldn't stomach. Happy, lovey-dovey bullshit. He stood from the stool and murmured under his breath, "Blow the fine day out of your ass." With a glance back toward the bar he sauntered to the door.

He stopped on the sidewalk, adjusted a fraying disobedient left shoelace, and then sprung into a jog. He shook the cold from his aching thighs and the pace quickened.

A few cars dotted the landscape, but most slept in a thin film of ice. He passed a couple of vehicles he recognized. Myles Winslow's yellow cab parked in the handicapped spot in front of Suga Cones, an ice cream shop that struggled to the maintain business during summer.

How the hell are they making money in November?

Chad Parson's tires overstepped the parking lines outside of CCR Consignment. He'd spent some time in Knuckles Up a few months back.

Richie recalled he walked in with a bruised eye and swollen jaw, the result of a beating from a group of a tough guys outside the Stop and Save. He trained for a few weeks and then failed to show up again.

Apparently, fourteen days of Joe's training were either too hard or Chad felt he'd learned enough to deflect a future attack.

He'd need to be able to defend himself, too. The rumor mills churned out many a story in town, none more prevalent than Chad dipping his banana into Bianca Baker's fruit basket. She was married to Ronald Baker, an associate of the Irish fellas in West Ridgemont Cove.

Some people are too stupid for their own good.

Moving further toward the shaded tree line, the desolate street opened for Richie and the town evaporated. Now, controlled breaths and precision took over. The sounds of the street faded, and the sun's breaking haze widened.

Just focus on the run. Feel the aches and breathe.

He sped up and turned the corner to knife through the park, passing a black Cadillac parked on the shoulder. Smoke from its exhaust burped gray fog.

Its tinted windows and chrome wheels sparkled in the early daybreak. Richie traced back in search of a memory, unable to recall any car of real value idling in the street on his morning runs. The occasional pimp would swing by Skyline Apartments down the road, but this was different. It wasn't a sex salesman.

Far too clean.

He entered a shallow fog cloaking Rose Wood Park

with another glance to the odd vehicle, careful to not stare. The unknown in this part of town spelled trouble. Something unfamiliar acted like an alarm, blaring through the psyche of the Ridgemont Cove regulars.

With nothing new to gather from the little peek, he turned and charged into the park's belly.

Richie shadow boxed by throwing punches and feigning left and right.

Keep your left up. Jab. Jab. Jab. Duck. Hook.

Joe's words rang in his head.

The time will come, and you'll get your shot.

Fancy footwork tore through the terrain. Blades of grass and piles of dirt jumped from the ground. He dashed by an old beggar using a park bench for a bed. Burning calves and quads be damned, the pace intensified.

Keep your left up. Jab. Jab. Jab. Duck. Hook.

The mantra repeated, and each subsequent chant drew a speck more breath than the previous.

The fog broke in patches at waist level, and for a moment he seemed to be swimming in smoke. Ahead, the sign for Worthington Avenue reflected in the foreground.

Beads of sweat cooled by the air created tiny streams the length of his face. Sweat and salt covered his lips, counteracting the bitter coffee residual resting on his tongue.

Just a little further to go.

Worthington Avenue ran perpendicular with the park's trail, and a sharp right led to the snaking channel of water leading to the ocean. Another mile and a quarter uphill converged with Chaplin Trace, the back street that acted as an entry point to the reception bays where he'd spend seven hours unloading bait fish from circular bales lowered onto the dock from the commercial fisherman ships.

The familiar collision of salt and moistness set in. The

scent acted as a benchmark, and he knew six and half minutes remained in the hike when the pungent sea's breath invaded his nostrils.

He made the turn moments later, though his boiling calves remained unsupportive. As he crossed to the sidewalk stalking along the river, the Cadillac from earlier, the only car on the road, decelerated and shifted into the slow lane.

Far too clean.

Richie pumped his legs and panted. Salt mist from the channel sprayed daggers of frozen pellets across the sidewalk.

A bus stop sat ahead. The plastic casing on the near side panel, marked with various scribbles and gang-based tags, offered a hazy mirror in spots not desecrated with paint.

He reached it in seconds and found a portion of plastic undisturbed by vandals. In a yellowing but discernible reflection, the Cadillac trolled behind him.

The unfamiliar now stalked its prey. Richie *felt* the alarms blaring within.

CHAPTER SIX

The white room, a blinding view of nothing, whirred with the melody of various medical equipment. Monotonous beeps pinged every other second. An EKG monitoring machine emitted a vibrating thud.

Timothy Vietta attempted to swallow, but his tongue was sandpaper, and his throat tightened with every exhalation.

A pathetic eight-inch television, anchored to the wall across from his bed, showed the snowfall of static.

"Can't get much worse." It had been ten days of the same routine. Wake up, stare at the little box struggling to configure a picture, await the petite nurse with dimples to bring him food and medicine, eat and take the pills, and then sleep until dinner. If the painkillers hadn't melted his memory beyond repair, he was certain today was Friday and soggy meatloaf awaited tonight.

He had no visitors, no cards, and no flowers on the table. If this hospital visit was in the distant past, a stack of hall-mark 'get-wells' would topple over on the side table. Vases of colorful, sweet flowers would jockey for sunlight. And, *she* would be here.

This invading memory lived vividly when the lights shined above the ring's canvas and Timothy met an opponent in the middle. Each battle began and ended with her. She'd been the driving factor in all his choices for a long time.

Even after their split and the carnage eruption from the twist and turns in their relationship, his corner beamed and supported him. But with each passing match and deeper dive into the life, the 'well-wishes' and 'attaboys' faded.

Now, especially now, only true family remained, and that was a stretch.

He understood this setback would provide an overabundance of ammunition for the relentless preaching of why boxing wasn't a real career. It was though. To Timothy, it was the only career.

A gauze bandage wrapped around the upper portion of his head, obscuring his vision somewhat. He craned his neck in an emphatic yawn and caught an abnormality in the usual routine. Today, a visitor sat at the bedside.

He swiveled his head further. A man dressed in a three-piece suit flipped through the newspaper. Behind gold-rimmed glasses, the man's eyes flicked from word-to-word.

Timothy raised his right hand to the nape of his neck and allowed the fingers to climb to the crown. The staples secured his scalp—the cold and rigid steel a reminder.

He didn't remember much but did recall the ref screaming for a medic. His body had crumpled to the mat amid the vociferous cheering of spectators. *Had he passed out?* He still struggled to piece the events together. It was all hazy and insignificant now.

The far more pressing matter sat in a chair, mere feet

away. Salvador Purelli turned the pages of the newspaper once more.

"Thunderstorm Vietta." Purelli's voice was grinding and raspy—like tires screeching over asphalt.

Timothy said nothing. The healthy eye followed the visitor's movements.

Purelli placed the newspaper on the seat next to him and stood. The bottom of his shoes grated the floor, the noise humming across the room and over the dull patter of the EKG machine, now showing heightened activity on its screen.

"I imagine you know why I am here?" Purelli inched closer, his hands tucked within the pockets of his pants.

"No." Timothy scratched at the skin beneath the cuff wrapped around his bicep.

"What's your record now?" He snagged a white handkerchief from the breast pocket of his suit and wiped the lenses of the gold-rimmed glasses.

With the unobscured eye still trained on him; Timothy shivered beneath the cloak of the hospital sheet, unable to compute the relevance of such a question.

"Twenty and one."

He remembered what Benny had told him right before the bout.

Some important people are here tonight, kid. People with deep pockets and itchy trigger fingers.

Timothy shook the memory of Benny loose. Full concentration on the beast now a mandate from his brain.

"Ah, that is right." Purelli spun the ring on his pinky and then moved forward again. "Correct me if I am wrong, but were you not undefeated?"

"Yes."

"And please remind me, have I invested quite a bit of money into your training and promotion?"

"Mr. Purelli, I—"

The mobster wagged his slender finger with a tight-lipped scowl.

"You do not speak my name. Understand?"

Timothy glanced to the clock on the far wall. The nurse checked in around eight o'clock most days. It was 7:12. *All alone.*

"Yes, sir."

"You have put me in quite a difficult situation. I am at a crossroads. The choice is not an easy one."

"Please." Timothy's wobbling pleas bordered on pathetic even to his ears. Going strike for strike with some of the most gifted middleweights had been easy. Staring at death's own nightmare, a far more daunting fight.

Purelli frowned and inched closer. His thighs grazed the hospital bed's rail, and the cologne he wore drifted to Timothy's nose.

"I need another chance," Timothy squealed, now sure the EKG machine would short out and start smoking like a poorly written cartoon. "I'll win the rematch. You'll double your bets."

Ignoring the assurances, Purelli continued the same matter-of-fact tone. "This is business. In business, there are no rematches. Preparation and effort result in success. Were you not prepared? Did my men ensure you wanted for nothing?"

"It was me. I—"

"This I already know. Do you think I am a man to cower when I have failed? No, I stand tall regardless of the consequence. Now you will do the same."

"What consequences? Mr. Pur—" Timothy's mouth

closed. The severity of this little visit became clear. Now, beneath the sheets, he trembled. Uncontrollable fear hooked into him, squeezing sweat from his pores.

"We had a plan for you. You have failed us—me."

"But I." Timothy glanced to the door in hopes time fast-forwarded.

"Nobody is coming," Purelli hissed like a serpent circling its prey. "You will face this head on like a man."

Timothy relented. A litany of excuses rushed to his head, but he knew all were in vain. He'd been expected to win, but Mitch Mahomes' well-disguised right hook sent him to the canvas. The dregs of Ridgemont Cove had shelled out their Friday checks, children's college fund, or granny's nest egg when the golden betting opportunity presented itself. Purelli sold the dream, and the public devoured the possibility.

Unfortunately, Timothy's early nap complicated things.

"What happens now?"

"The debt must be paid. Honor restored." Purelli stepped back from the hospital bed, reaching into the coat once more.

"What do you mean?"

"As I have said, I am not in the business of second chances."

A glint of silver reflected from the fluorescent light above the bed, and Purelli's last words slipped like silk. The knife cut the air with a resounding whoosh. Before Timothy could move, the mobster drove its point through his bare hand still perched on the edge of the hospital bed.

Timothy's mouth opened, and the knife ejected from the hand—the slurping noise of steel escaping from liquid undeniable and as disgusting as the wound itself.

"Shh." Purelli's single word rustled into the air like a breath in the cold of night. "Honor restored, remember?"

The wound drained and throbbed—a thick stain formed beneath the gash. As if in a distant dream, Timothy's scream lingered for a few seconds then rested on the tip of his tongue.

Purelli brought the knife to his throat. "Shh." He spoke to him like a parent would soothe a newborn baby. "If you make another sound," he whispered, the faint scent of mint propelling from his mouth. "I will run this same blade through your daughter's neck. Do you understand?"

"Yes," Timothy gurgled, fighting the throbbing pulses of fire snaking through his left arm. "I'll do what you want. Please don't hurt her."

Where is the honor in this?

The screams festering in his throat traveled upward, but Annabelle's face surfaced in his mind before they could graduate to audible utterances of despair. She came to him in a dream-like slumber, and he was no longer at Ridgemont Cove Memorial.

They were at the farm tossing the chickens handfuls of feed. They laughed, and she ran among them, squealing in delight. Innocent joy between a father and daughter. The sun brightened the two pigtails bouncing on her head like Slinky's, and she chortled with a wide laugh, revealing two missing front teeth.

He was there, if only for a moment, and then the toddler's smile morphed into a sinister mask. Bella's pigtails grew into open-mouthed vipers snapping their jaws. The farm faded and broke its shape until black entombed the dream, and the mangled hand's pain reemerged.

He tried to ignore it. The knife pierced his hand again, carving a new hole in the flesh.

I'm with you, Bella, he screamed wordlessly.

He felt the flap of skin still hanging from his hand but declined to confirm the shredded flesh and open gash leaking.

I'm with you, Bella.

Purelli twisted his wrist, grunting from the exertion, and the blade sawed through the skin, widening the hole.

Timothy's lids blinked in rhythm with the whimpers he struggled to contain. Purelli's left hand clamped onto his throat, suffocating the utterances building within him.

A final grunt escaped Salvador's lips, and he pulled the blade.

Blood spurted, and soon its juices splashed color on the white sheets and Timothy's gown.

Purelli backed up and retrieved the white handkerchief once more. He dabbed at his face and then wiped the length of the steel.

Timothy's adrenaline now masked the throbbing covering his left side, and he grabbed hold of the bedsheet, rolling it over in a pathetic attempt to clot the bleeding.

The white fabric darkened into an ever-growing mosaic of red and purple hues. Scorching pain from the fresh cut traveled to his neck.

Purelli mopped droplets of Timothy from his suit with the handkerchief.

"Please don't hurt her." Tears fell now, but they didn't appear from the pain or trauma. They were preemptive drops of salted water at the mere thought of Bella facing the same blade.

He moved his fingers beneath the sheet but couldn't tell if they were all mobile or none were working. The fear of severed ligaments materialized. *Move your fingers.*

The sheet covering the hand didn't flinch.

Move your fucking fingers!

Purelli lifted the newspaper from the chair and isolated a page, folding it, so the intended article was crisp and easy to read. "It is your lucky day." He placed the paper on the ball of sheets entombing Timothy's hand. "I have found someone new."

He straightened his tie and adjusted the collar. With a final piercing stare, he walked toward the door, his shoes clipping the floor. Out of sight, his cheerful whistle in the hall echoed into the room.

Using the uninjured hand, Timothy reached for the newspaper and brought it to his unscathed eye. Page eight of the *Ridgemont Cove Gazette* presented his battered body sprawled out in the ring with his opponent's gloves raised to the sky. The caption below the picture read:

Local amateur middleweight contender, Timothy "Thunderstorm" Vietta, lies on the canvas after suffering a brutal knockout at the hands of Mitch Mahomes. Vietta's record now stands at 20-1, while Mahomes' improves to 2-17.

CHAPTER SEVEN

Richie shot hesitant glances over each shoulder. In his peripheral, the car neared. He sped up and cut left, tracking across the street and into a community playground.

A cluster of buildings to the west provided three alleyways. Behind Earl's Auto Stop, a rundown mechanic shop known more for marijuana sales than actual vehicle upkeep, a thin backstreet knifed through two major veins of road separating vacant lots and various industrial warehouses. At the northern tip of the alley, Landers Avenue ran perpendicular, and beyond the street, a three-tier gate stretched in each direction for a quarter mile.

Sprint, jump the barrier, and cut back toward work under the camouflage of sea grapes, he thought, still unsure if the plan mounting within him warranted action. *Or stop being paranoid. It could just be a granny trolling too slow, right?* Reaching the backstreet moments later, Richie swiveled his head to locate the Cadillac. *Let's find out.*

It was gone.

Richie ducked into the alley and slid his back to the far wall, out of sight from the oncoming traffic.

He kneeled and panted, fighting the frozen air stinging his lungs and shaking his body worse than the adrenaline manifesting from the unknown vehicle.

Get a grip and get up, he thought, slapping the asphalt. *Get up.*

He pressed forward. Richie spotted a stranger lurking at the opposite end of the corridor. Throttled by the realization a stranger blocked his escape, his feet stopped as if on cue.

A man with a face shaped like an anvil stood there motionless with hands shoved into coat pockets. Richie locked eyes with him, wary of the timing and intent.

He slipped balled fists from the pockets of his hoodie and bounced on the balls of his feet. The stranger advanced.

Experience taught a harsh lesson; fight first and ask questions later.

Living by this motto since Jimmy Mulligan pounced his ass in the fourth grade, preparation for a fight always took precedence over seeing the good in people. Back then, menacing glares led to insults, but Richie had slid away too afraid to confront the bully head-on.

Returning from the bathroom after recess, Mulligan jumped him from behind. Later, surveying the bloody eyebrow and swollen nose of his prepubescent face in a cracked mirror near the row of tiny urinals in the High Point Elementary cafeteria bathroom, Richie swore to learn to defend himself.

Now older, and perhaps a bit wiser but more likely just less afraid, it was clear fighting wasn't just a survival technique—it was a mandate in Ridgemont Cove.

"Stop," a voice from behind bellowed.

Startled, Richie pivoted to find another man. This one

sported black aviator glasses. Sunlight glistened atop his bald head. His body blocked the entrance from which Richie had just come. Now, with men at each end, Richie's heartbeat quickened, and sweat propelled through his pores.

"I'm not looking for trouble." He kept his eyes on Aviator and listened for the footsteps of the other thug. "What do you want?"

"We need to talk," Aviator grunted.

"No, we don't." Richie glanced behind to find the other man's progress now had him at arm's length.

Richie recognized the face but couldn't isolate the time or place he'd seen it before. Regardless, two men book-ended him, and the only course of action was to fight. Jimmy Mulligan happened once and would never happen again.

Shifting his weight, he spun and swung. The hook connected, sending tingling shards of pain racing up his arm. The man collapsed to the ground. Richie turned to face Aviator and felt a deflating blow to his stomach.

He dropped to one knee and raised his left forearm to protect from another strike.

Aviator shoved him against the brick wall of the alley and lifted him by the neck. "Just listen, you little son of a bitch."

With his feet dangling, and the hold on his throat intensifying, Richie drove an elbow into the man's face.

The thug's grip didn't lessen, and Richie felt the air moving through his lungs diminishing. With the remaining energy he could muster, he slung his knee upward and connected.

Stunned, Aviator released the hold and Richie slumped down the wall.

The original attacker stumbled and lunged forward.

Joe's drills had prepared him to anticipate, and the charge might as well have come with a blueprint. He weaved to his left and guided the man's unprotected head into the brick wall behind him.

The crack echoed within the secluded backstreet.

Richie turned from the wall, felt another stinging punch from Aviator, and stumbled to the ground again. Blistering beams of colored spots danced in his vision.

Massive channels of staggered, flickering light followed by seconds of darkness. He rose from the ground and felt a punch connect to his ribs. A subsequent kick launched him into the air. Landing hard on the gravel, thumping pain shot through his neck. The beams of color became probing stars and flashed with the melody of his choked breathing.

The man now hovered above with slanted, cracked sunglasses, and a steady drip of blood slipped from his mouth.

"I told you to stop." He slammed his fist into Richie's chest. "Not so tough now, are ya?"

"Enough," a third voice cracked, echoing in thick tones within the alley.

Richie rolled over to face the voice—though, now, only a silhouette of a man decipherable.

The original man, a cartoonish swollen Mario look-alike, stood on two uncertain legs. A dark circle of wet blood painted the brick a dark maroon behind him.

"Get Lorenzo outta here," the same distant voice yelled.

Lorenzo, Richie assumed, must have been the one with a concussion and losing pints of blood by the second.

Richie flattened and laid on his back, outstretched with his eyes on the morning sky. Clouds whipped through in gray and off-white patches.

The flickering of stars and darkness returned.

Adrenaline's vigor began its retreat and the tenderness of aches and strained muscles set in.

Then, footsteps neared, and Richie braced for another attack. He reached a crouched position and felt a force between his shoulder blades which sent him spiraling to the ground. Again, on his back, Richie gazed upward. He tallied his breaths—an old trick Joe taught him to avoid pain's insistent prodding.

Count the inhale, count the exhale, and forget that you're fucking hurt, he'd say.

A figure hovered over, silhouetted by the stark stars matching the pace of his temples.

The leader. The owner of the booming voice.

Sunlight rushed on the outside of his shadowy presence, but after a few seconds, Richie recognized the man. He felt sweat begin its steady swim down his swollen cheeks.

A sudden urge to run, asinine as it was unrealistic, overtook the adrenaline. Fight or flight? *Cradle tight and hope death's assault is swift and painless.*

"Kid." The leader grabbed Richie by the shoulders and forced him to his feet. "You got any clue how much trouble you're in?"

With his head down and loose pieces of gravel intertwined in his damp hair, Richie responded, "No, Benny."

"That's Mr. Bianchi to you."

CHAPTER EIGHT

The short walk to the parked Cadillac provided Benny a moment of silence. A swift and easy pick up now more complicated than it needed to be.

Young punks, these days. No fucking respect.

A harsh wind howled outside of the alley, brushing his face like a frozen sponge. On the street, pedestrians and cars began their inevitable commutes, ignoring the bloodied men approaching. Another day in Ridgemont Cove, nothing else.

"You don't have to do this." The kid yelped, struggling to break free from Benny's grasp. He shifted his shoulder and lunged toward the sidewalk. "What the hell is going on?"

Benny tightened his grip on Richie's limp hood. "Shut up, or I'll sick the dogs on you again. This time I won't tell 'em to stop." He shoved the little prick into the backseat and then eyed two men approaching on the sidewalk. "What the fuck you looking at?"

They said nothing, but both of them stared at Lorenzo

emerging from the alley. His swollen and distorted face leaked blood, splattering the different creases in his face.

"I said, what the fuck you looking at?" Benny repeated, now edging toward the two pedestrians. They looked away and their pace quickened a bit.

"Mr. Bianchi"—the kid laid across the backseat squealed in a cracked and subdued voice—"I'm sorry. I didn't know."

Benny turned after a five second stare bore through the backs of the nosy strangers strolling his town. "Oh, what a surprise. A teenager with shit-for-brains doesn't know something."

He slammed the door and circled around the car to Lorenzo, who now knelt over the car's hood grasping his head in a weak attempt to halt the red streaks from pouring down his face.

"I brought you along to make this quick and easy. Why are you fighting the kid?"

"He started it."

"What are you, seven?" Benny slapped the back of Lorenzo's head. "You do know who you represent?"

"He didn't give us a chance to explain." The wounded man peered up, revealing jagged lines of red zig-zagging across his forehead. "That little son-of-a-bitch is gonna get it."

"No."—Benny pointed to the kid—"he's not going to be touched because the boss says so, *capisce*?"

"But—"

"But nothing." He lifted his man's chin and examined the extent of the damage. "We need to get off the street. Head to Donnie's. I'll send for ya."

The mobster obeyed and staggered toward the alley, red

droplets following his footsteps like a macabre trail of breadcrumbs.

Benny then turned to Sonny. The bald brute stood near the driver-side door, examining his bent aviator sunglasses.

"You bleeding?" Benny asked, circling toward the opposite side of the Cadillac. "If so, I'll drive myself. This is a ninety-thousand-dollar car, and it don't need your blood all over."

"I'm all right." Sonny rubbed his jaw with a jewelry-filled hand. "Let's just get out of here. People are watching."

Both men popped their doors open and entered.

Benny slid into the backseat. His massive frame forced Richie to press against the opposite door.

"You want to tell me what that was all about?" Benny raised his hands and feigned utter amazement. "What the hell were you thinking?"

Richie looked at the floorboard for a moment then shook his head.

"Nothing to say, eh?" Benny's eyes grew larger. "You crack my guy's head into a brick wall and nothin'? For Christ's sake, now we gotta explain it to a hospital. There's no healthcare in this business."

"And what *business* is that?" Richie's eyes tracked toward the window.

"Sonny, you hearing this kid? Got some balls, eh?"

"Watch your tone, tough guy." Sonny glared in the rearview mirror. "Don't forget who you're talking to."

"This is my driver, kid." Benny leaned toward Richie and pointed to the front seat. "His name is Sonny Denardo, and I believe you owe him an apology."

"For what?"

"Attacking a member of our organization, you little shit." Benny swatted at the kid's face.

Richie drew back, hesitated and then massaged his right hand. "I'm sorry. I'm a little foggy right now. I didn't mean any disrespect."

"That happened already," Benny said, agitation laying the foundation of his voice. "From here on out, don't throw a punch unless I say so, *capisce*?"

A solemn nod from Richie.

"All right," Benny said, sensing the kid's apprehension. "You'll learn how this works soon enough. Now, explain yourself."

"I didn't know who they were. Thought they were trying to mug me. What was I supposed to think?"

"You kidding me?" Benny's cheeks rose and spittle misted the air. "Do you not see me and my guys nearly every fucking Thursday?"

"I didn't see *you* until after. I try to ignore you guys anyway. Joe said to, at least."

"Well, bad advice from your mentor there, pal. Real bad. We're the ones to know and respect."

Benny lurched forward and tapped Sonny's shoulder. The engine thundered on and the doors locked.

CHAPTER NINE

Daylight broke free from dusk and the skies bloomed blue and turquoise. Sonny shifted the car to drive and pulled from the curb running perpendicular to the alleyway still dripping in fresh blood.

"Benny, I mean, Mr. Bianchi, why are you doing this?" He grasped the right hand again—the knuckles tender and swollen.

"Head to the farm," Benny said to Sonny, pointing north toward the freeway.

The Cadillac angled to the interstate, and Richie contemplated how much it would hurt if he jumped from the vehicle.

Now would be the time. You got the balls?

He'd heard about the wrath of Benny Bianchi. A well-known story from a few years back came to mind.

A jeweler from Sharpton hawked a newly acquired batch of stolen diamonds for him. Not an expert in the field of gems, Benny took the man's word that the price was fair. Honestly, who would renege on a deal with the Solanos? For some reason, this guy shorted him eleven thousand dollars.

With the plot to swindle Benny uncovered, the Solano underboss did nothing. For two months, he continued other business dealings with the fraudster. After another heist by his crew netted pink champagne diamonds, Benny sent a few fellas to the jeweler again.

Police found the corpse in the jewelry shop, the tongue severed, and each finger hacked off with a crude instrument the forensic team never could identify. The body parts, totaling eleven, lay on the main glass case, each topped with a pink champagne diamond. Authorities contacted an appraiser, who after examining the stones' cut and clarity, determined the value of jewels left behind at the crime scene totaled over twenty-thousand dollars.

And so, the legend grew. Benny "Beans" Bianchi didn't give a rat's ass about the money. Respect and honor topped dollars. Message delivered.

Stories like this and the behavioral observations of any and all Solano members were perceived by the public as exaggerations. The media filling headlines. Silly ghost stories kids told at sleepovers.

Richie knew better. Newspapers misrepresented the misdeeds of the evil monarchs who held Ridgemont Cove hostage. Their payroll depth had reached into the media but reading between the lines took only minimal effort. These men were killers and sadistic, regardless of the facade they attempted to build.

And still, Richie's breathing confirmed something else. If Benny "Beans" Bianchi wanted him dead, the alleyway provided an excellent place to dispose of a corpse.

They'd thrown him in the car and insulted him, sure, but why go through the motions for no reason? Something he learned about the underworld's top players—in news reports and town gossip—involved one word: methodical.

They didn't act out of haste and planned everything to minute detail.

What's the plan for me?

Almost as if he had read Richie's mind, Benny said, "You don't work at the dock anymore, kid." He yawned like the fistfight, and subsequent abduction were just another day at the office, then lowered the window.

November wind bit Richie's face, cooling the thumping heat still present in his jaw. "What do you mean, Mr. Bianchi?"

"Sonny, toss me a smoke from my pack."

The driver followed the order without a word, and Benny soon exhaled gray tentacles of fog from his lit cigarette.

"You gonna kill me?" Richie's voice cracked, and for the first time since the car edged away from the alleyway, a gripping fear seized him. "For defending myself?"

Benny turned his gaze from the windshield. A sneer formed, lifting the bottom half of his face closer to his torpedo-shaped eyes.

"If I wanted you dead, you'd be dead."

"Well, then what? What am I supposed to think?"

Richie's fingers gripped the door handle, and he reconsidered a painful but satisfying jump from the Cadillac. Now they were cruising at eighty miles per hour, and the landscape was a blur of greens, yellows, and browns.

Jimmy Mulligan all over again.

"We've been watching you." Benny exhaled a cloud of smoke. It broke into strands and slipped through the cracked window.

The statement sliced the silence, altering Richie's plan.

"We?"

"Yeah, your new business partners, kid. Look, if we

wanted you in a hole, I wouldn't be wasting the drive out to Belleview. Relax." Benny dragged again, exhaling through his nose. Channels of gray dropped from each nostril.

The spectacle reminded Richie of a bull about to charge its matador.

Then, when the cartoonish image vanished within his mind, he remembered where he was, and who sat next to him. He faced the window, unable to connect his importance in the Solano's operation.

Belleview?

Early morning commuters' cars sped past in colorful blends. Ridgemont Cove was a populated area, but as evidenced by the rundown buildings and ever-increasing crime rate, scarce job opportunities headlined the business section of the newspaper.

The northbound freeway jammed up around seven. People embarked on thirty to forty-minute commutes. Many people lived within the city limits because of the low rent, but few found meaningful jobs. Those who wanted to earn more than minimum wage got in cars or took buses to cities like Sharpton.

Imperial Fish & Game had been a rare exception. At this moment, Richie wished he and Clyde were out on the icy dock packing cod into oversized Ziplocks. He'd trade fish guts and frostbite to get out of this.

A trio of cars slid up the right side of the freeway. Richie's eyes followed them, and his job, his safety net, became a singular thought.

They're heading to work, probably. Something I have . . . had.

Six months of languishing on a wait list and a probationary period of minimal pay wasn't the most appealing career choice, but at least Richie didn't hike forty minutes each way like the never-ending caravan of cars this morning.

Benny's words cut into the trance. *You don't work at the dock anymore, kid.*

Trees and mile markers whizzed by, and from the looks of things, his morning routine was anything but, today.

Why not?

"What's in Belleview?" Richie turned to the glass, afraid to endure another slap for a stupid question. None came.

He knew the name, sure. Northeast of Sharpton, twenty miles through desolate and dusty streets, the renowned town specked the map. Much like Benny's jeweler tale, people knew—almost without wanting to, it seemed—the demographic of Belleview.

What he didn't understand was why they were trekking there.

"You tell me, tough guy. What type of people live in Belleview?" Benny adjusted himself in the seat. The girth of his gut extended the seatbelt further out.

"I don't know." Richie turned from the window, sure that the answer was coming, regardless. "Farmers, maybe."

"And," Sonny offered from the front, his glassless eyes tracing Richie through the rearview.

Richie knew what to say, but he sure as hell didn't *want* to say it. Was he at liberty to refer to these men like the rest of the world did behind closed doors?

"Go ahead," Benny said, motioning his hand as if to say it was okay.

"Mafia."

"Ding, ding, ding," Sonny snickered from the front seat. His ice eyes now wide and glinting.

"Just us good old boys, kid." Benny sucked saliva

through a small gap in his teeth. "Us, the mobsters, the bad guys, right?"

"Yeah. I guess." Richie's glance shifted from the rearview to Benny. A stern face stared back.

"We claimed it in the 1920s. Back then, the dirt was cheap. The soil was soft, and the farmers saw opportunity."

"Listen up." Benny smacked Richie's chest with the back of his hand, and his ring-garnished fingers left a dull ache in their wake. "It ain't naptime. I'm talking so you're listening, *capisce*?" He paused long enough to drag at his cigarette. "The farmers weren't the only fellas hip to the scene though. We saw our chance and went for it. You know why?"

Richie's mouth opened and then he paused, rethinking his answer. Finally, he said, "County lines."

"Ding, ding, ding," Sonny shrieked from the front again. He slapped the steering wheel with his two massive hands.

"I'll be damned, Sonny. He ain't brain dead after all." Benny's cheeks puffed with a chuckle, and the acne scars widened and filled with color for a moment. "Can't beat it, kid. Right smack dab on the line between the Greater Belleview police and Navajo country."

"So, nobody bothers you guys." Richie said it aloud, but the statement was more revelation than conversation.

"Exactly." Benny flicked the cigarette out the window. "You see, the pigs and the Injuns muscle in for jurisdiction. What can I say? The whites don't like the reds and vice versa. So, while they squabble, we drop a few coins in either direction and let them chase their tails."

"Right." Sonny adjusted the rearview and changed lanes. "Too easy, right boss?"

"Gotta love this business." Benny's lips smacked together, a putrid sound to Richie's ears. "Neither of them wants to give control to the other, so we hand an envelope of cash to one and do a favor for the other."

"Play your enemies against each other." Richie sat forward and absentmindedly rubbed his throbbing hand.

"That's it." Benny pulled a phone from his pocket and flipped the screen. He jabbed at the display a few times with his pudgy fingers and then dropped it back into his coat. "Step on it, Sonny."

The car accelerated and weaved through a cluster of cars. They then cut off a semi, whose driver protested by laying on the horn.

"If he only knew who was in this fucking car." Benny fumed, swiveling his head to get a better look at the truck driver. He flicked the smoke out of the window. "Lucky the boss is waiting, or we'd stop and introduce ourselves."

Richie pieced the rest together. Belleview awaited because that's where Salvador Purelli lived. And, as crazy as it seemed, that's who anticipated his arrival. He didn't know why, but the mere thought forced acidic bile creeping up his throat.

The Boss.

"So, we're meeting *him*." Richie fell back into the seat, the wind knocked out of him harder than anytime during the melee in the alleyway.

"What do you know about *him*?" Benny turned and squared his shoulders.

"Just what I've seen on television. Lives in a mansion in Belleview. It's surrounded by an eight-foot iron gate. Armed guard in a golf cart patrols the lot."

Sonny and Benny both hacked in laughter simultaneously.

"Yeah." Benny slapped his driver's shoulder. "Sounds like he's been watching too much TV."

"Next, he'll say Mr. Purelli has a tiger in a cage like Scarface." Sonny cracked up again. Benny didn't join.

"No need to use names. Never know who is listening, ya hear?"

"Sorry, boss." Sonny wiped the grin away with his palm and switched lanes again.

"But that's where we're going, right?" Richie shrugged, pretending the news didn't send darts of anxiety from his head to his balls. "Leader of the Family. Handpicked by Freddie Solano, himself."

What do they want from me?

"Don't think too hard and hurt yourself." Benny's words interrupted Richie's mental seesaw. "We've got a ways to go. If I were you, I'd start working on my story."

"What story?"

"Why you bashed Lorenzo's head in. Payback is coming. How much is up to the boss?"

Richie's hand throbbed. *Jesus Christ, Lorenzo's face was hard.* He tracked the last time he hit someone without a glove on. Around the time he first walked into Knuckles Up, some guy spit a few derogatory comments about a girl Richie was banging. Words became punches, though there was no ebbing pain afterward.

"I was defending myself."

"Don't matter"—Benny glanced to the rearview and scoffed, as if communicating an unspoken joke to Sonny—"besides, from the look of your hand, we might not have any use for ya."

Richie turned to his window, drawing an exaggerated sigh. This morning he'd been slopping blazing coffee down and watching Ruby's ass bounce to the melody of doo-wop. *How did this all go so wrong?*

"You there." Benny slapped at Richie's face again, snapping the recollection, and drawing him back into the Cadillac.

"Yeah. This about me fighting? Like, a sparring partner or something?"

"It'll be explained." Benny snagged another cigarette from the pack sitting on the center console. "Get your story straight."

Low-lying hedges and field brush no longer hugged the interstate. The landscape shifted again. Hills outlined with oak trees divided sizeable gaps of land stretching for miles in either direction. Earthen scents floated into the car, overpowering the remnants of Benny's stale smoke.

"Not sure what I'm supposed to say."

Joe's warnings and incessant hatred for Benny and his buddies came to him. He wasn't sorry for defending himself. He'd not spent two years building *this* body and *these* skills to back down. *What kind of sense would that make?*

"Kid, you don't get it." Benny adjusted himself in the seat, using the armrest for leverage. The unlit cigarette dangled from his thick, pale lips. "We have business to conduct."

"And if I say no?"

"You're smart, right?" A smirk crossed Benny's face.

"If I say no?"

"We've buried far tougher than you." He unfastened his jacket to reveal the butt of a handgun.

The smirk disappeared.

CHAPTER TEN

After Purelli's visit, Timothy pressed the red call button but exerted earnest effort in doing so, falling over the railing of the bed. Moments later, the nurse, whose name still escaped him, shuffled in with her routine, pleasant smile. His last memory before losing consciousness was her cheerful expression transform into horror at the sight of his hand dripping black fluid onto the hospital's white and polished floor.

Then dreams overtook him.

Upon waking, he learned an MRI detected muscle damage only, and the ligaments and blood vessels remained intact. "You're very lucky," the technician had remarked.

Yeah. I'm headed to buy a lotto ticket now, asshole.

The hand required sixteen stitches, and then they rolled him back to the room with a cocktail of pain killers and anti-inflammatory meds to accompany a tetanus shot.

Now, a few hours removed from the ordeal, two men with badges clipped to their belts strolled in and fired questions Timothy had no interest in answering.

"Name is Detective Vito Marzetti," the port and

unkempt one said. He resembled an inflated budget store mannequin dressed in clothes from a time when Timothy had not yet mastered the alphabet. A faded blue dress shirt, half-tucked into wrinkled pants. Splotched sweat stains grew beneath the armpits. A badge clipped to the belt fought to preserve its shine. "I'm here to clear a few things up."

The partner, a younger and more presentable officer, walked past his bedside clutching a notepad and briefcase.

"Ya'll are here to help me, huh?" Timothy's eyes rolled and landed on the small television. Through the grainy picture, a news anchor relayed an update in the missing persons case of Roger Cranswell. Timothy pointed to the screen. "Your expertise is better spent elsewhere."

"One thing at a time, Mr. Vietta." Marzetti hooked thumbs through the belt loops of the fading slacks. The awkward stance pushed his gut over the waistline obscuring the gold badge. "So, tell us what happened?"

He examined the fat detective. Capillaries had exploded in his cheeks, sending winding streams of pink through the stubble of his face. Timothy first considered the man lived with a skin condition, but after second thought, arrived at the assumption Marzetti indulged in libations a bit too much.

Most lawmen in this town did, anyway.

"Nothing to go over. Fell out of bed and gashed myself pretty good." A streak of fire ripped through Timothy's hand, causing him to wince. No amount of morphine or denial masked the wound's ferocity.

"Cut it on what? The floor?"

"I guess." Timothy held the bandaged hand up. "Crazy, right?"

"That's not the word I'd use to describe this situation,

Mr. Vietta." Marzetti's tone teetered near annoyance. He glanced over to his partner. "Hey, little help here."

"Mr. Vietta, I'm Detective Campini," said the younger cop. His eyes remained trained on the notepad that he scrawled across with a pen. A five o'clock shadow covered his sturdy jaw and a small scar raised the skin above the left eye. Dirty-blond, feathered hair came close to hiding it.

He wore a tailored beige suit with cufflinks fastened into an ocean-colored shirt. A colorful pin depicting his support of some righteous cause stuck into the lapel. Timothy laughed inwardly at the thought of him transforming into Marzetti twenty years down the road.

"You don't need to fear Purelli." He capped the pen and slid a manila folder from the leather briefcase at his feet. "The man doesn't own this town like you think."

"Don't know what you're talking about." Forcing a yawn, Timothy pressed the button to release the morphine into his IV. His wound chilled from the influx of drugs beneath a pound of gauze and medical wraps.

With the good hand, he caressed his shaved head. The unexpected hairdo grew on him after a few days, and he was glad the doctor buzzed it for the staples and stitches required a week ago.

He caught a glimpse of himself in the small mirror on the opposite wall of his bed—a bandage across the upper left eye, sagging shoulders, and a deflated chest. He resembled a half-ass version of a mummy.

"Mr. Vietta, we're here to get answers." Campini stood and opened the folder. He leafed through a few documents then retrieved a stack of black and white photos. He dropped a pair to the bed. "These are surveillance photographs of this hospital wing. Taken this morning when you were attacked."

"I wasn't attacked, man. I fell from the bed."

"Excuse me. When you fell."

Ignoring the obvious sarcasm, Timothy glanced at the photos and then to the pompous police officer. "Are we about done?"

"Do you remember this man entering your room?" The detective pointed to a photograph time stamped at 7:06 AM. It depicted Purelli grasping the knob to Timothy's room.

Darting pain traveled the wound at the mere sight of the devil. With furrowed eyebrows, he did his best impression of a pensive eyewitness.

"Nope. Never saw him before. Who is he?"

Campini glanced to Marzetti, who scoffed and shook his head.

"And this photo taken at seven-sixteen?"—he shoved the new image inches from Timothy's unobscured eye—"is the same person. Salvador Purelli, a dangerous and powerful man, leaving your room. You don't recall any of this?"

"I must have been asleep."

"So, he watched you sleep for ten minutes?"

"I suppose. It's the only logical conclusion I can draw." Happy to trade sarcastic barbs, a sly grin crossed Timothy's face. An itch surfaced beneath the gauze on his head. He ran the unwrapped hand over the bandaged eye.

Each movement caused another part of his body to ache. Gauze and morphine, two new welcome buddies, helped the discomfort but didn't eradicate it.

"And in the same time frame, your hand gets mangled." Marzetti snarled from across the room. His skin grew redder, exacerbating the hue of the blood vessels on his cheeks. "Sounds like assault with a deadly weapon. Hell, that's attempted murder. The doctor said the wound is an eighth of an inch from your palmar artery."

"The hand is fine. A few stitches and some drugs. I'll live."

"This is bullshit." Marzetti stomped forward and tapped his partner's shoulder. "We're wasting our time."

Campini gripped the bed's railing. "You know Purelli, *Thunderstorm*. He attacked you but didn't finish the job. Why?"

Timothy ignored the question, too tired and woozy to continue the circular dialogue.

They don't believe me, and I'm not changing the story. Unstoppable force meets immovable object.

His eyes reverted to the mirror's reflection.

The door clanked open and the nurse entered with a tray in hand. Avoiding eye contact with the officers and hurrying to the bedside, she pulled the folding table back and placed the food down. "It's your favorite."

Timothy removed the plate cover. A pungent aroma of wild rice filled the room.

"Ugh, I thought we had meatloaf." Timothy adjusted himself in the bed but struggled to brace the flimsy pillow behind him.

"For dinner, Mr. Vietta. It's almost noon." She pressed a few buttons on the rail of the bed and it climbed upward. "Better?"

"Yes. Thanks." His lids closed hard then opened.

"If you don't have an appetite, it's okay." Her voice offered a layer of comfort.

She flashed a genuine expression, kind but not flirtatious, and propped a second pillow between the cushion and his shoulders.

"But try to drink the water, though. Doctor's orders."

"We've been tracking this asshole a long time." Marzetti stuffed the photos and notepad into the folder. "He's going down sooner or later. Which side do you want to be on?"

"You'll have to excuse my partner." Campini nudged Marzetti and displayed a weak smile to the nurse. "Too little coffee and even less sleep. Let's go, partner."

He pulled a card from his coat pocket and flicked it on the table next to the steaming bowl of soup. "Mr. Vietta, we'll be in touch."

"Looking forward to it."

The nurse followed the detectives toward the door and shut it. She returned a moment later and fiddled with the IV bag pole, adjusting the height causing the trio of clear bags to bounce into each other. "Pain meds working?"

"For the most part. Kind of feel numb. This hurts a bit." Timothy lifted the bandaged hand, aware of the shards of pain overtaking the novelty of the most recent morphine pop.

"You've been through a lot this morning. I'll up the dosage, hon." She jotted notes on the dry erase board bolted beneath the television. "So, pain level?" She pointed a marker to a circular frowning cartoon face taped to the whiteboard and dragged it forward to a similar face, though this one smiled. In between, the numbers one through ten were stenciled in. Each number sat below a description of varying pain levels.

"About a six."

"Okay." The nurse circled the six on the line and wrote the time. 11:56. "Let me talk to the doctor and see what we can do. I'll check back in an hour. Will you be okay until then?"

"Yeah." He extended his bandaged hand to the tray.

Three fingers slid out from the heavy gauze and grasped the cop's card.

"Detective Reese Campini, Organized Crime Division," he whispered to himself. "First card I've got in this place."

CHAPTER ELEVEN

The Cadillac veered onto a narrow dirt road beneath a canopy of elm trees, coming to a screeching halt in front of a barn suited for an Alfred Hitchcock film. A lot of horror stories began with an unlucky character in the woods with monsters. *This was no different.* Be damned what Benny said. Death was rushing to meet him.

He exited the car and looked around. A gripping hand squeezed his wrist, leading him to the door of the building.

"Put your ass in the chair." Benny Bianchi shouted.

Uneven rows of hay bales lined one side of the open space. A warped shelf nailed above them supported glass mason jars filled with an array of nails, screws, nuts, and bolts. On the opposite side, farm equipment hung.

Richie stumbled across the dirt floor, gripping his side with the swollen hand. He obeyed and slid into the single rickety wooden chair.

Abandoned barn with fresh-cut hay?

A far more vexing thought intruded.

Why am I here?

In the span of an hour, he had participated in a fistfight,

been abducted, threatened at gunpoint, and now, sat in this decrepit building without any justification.

"Don't touch a Goddamn thing." Benny walked out of the room. The door clanked behind him and then locked into place.

Faint voices outside murmured but were too jumbled to comprehend.

Richie scanned the interior of the barn. Periodic dashes of sunlight peeked through holes in the wooden frame, casting oblong yellow stains across the clean farm equipment. *Clean?* A weed whacker, chainsaw, sledgehammer, rake, and two hoes hung from rusted prongs nailed into the wood siding of the barn.

A hit room, should the need arise?

Richie presumed the meeting would take place at Purelli's home.

Then why the fuck am I here!

Above the door, a hexagonal window siphoned sunlight onto the dirt at his feet. Decaying rafters supported an aging, plank roof. Cobwebs plastered the corners where the roof met the frame. Behind him, a wooden staircase climbed toward a loft.

A scratching noise pinged in his ears. The grating sound gained definitiveness and then faded like the volume dial of a radio tilting upward and then dropping in succession.

Richie guessed a trapped varmint struggled to escape. Perhaps termites ate breakfast within the walls? *Or maybe it's all in your head and this is a dream because there is no possible way this is actually happening.*

He shivered and thought of Ruby. She'd materialized earlier when Benny and Sonny continued their childish, albeit intimidating, back-and-forth.

His mind's eye went to work painting an image. Fresh

paint slathered the inside walls of the barn. A puppy with black and white spots chased its tail on the hay bales. Ruby returned tools to the racks after a day in the garden. Specks of dirt streaked her forehead. They embraced, intertwining in a mound of haystacks. He felt the straw on his back and the wetness of her kiss.

A faint scratching noise from behind gnawed at his ear, forcing the make-believe pleasantries of his imagination to dissipate. He craned his neck as far as possible.

A closed-off area sat near the rear of the structure. The silver padlock clipped into the door's rusted handle caught a sliver of sunlight from outside and glinted like a string of lightning.

Maybe a raccoon?

Standing to investigate, he made it two steps before the hinges of the entrance door squeaked. Blinding rays of sun penetrated the barn, forcing him to cover his eyes. He struggled to adjust and retreated toward the wicker chair.

Shadows marched in, stretching the length of the floor, and snaking up the walls.

Sonny and Benny filled the doorway.

"I believe I said to sit your ass down," said Benny with shoulders back and posture erect, as if standing at attention. The pair pushed through the opening.

Behind them a man wearing gold-rimmed glasses strolled with his hands tucked inside the pockets of a crisp jacket.

Richie sat and squinted again. It was *him.*

Papers and newscasts flaunted pictures of the legendary man any time a lead broke—a black-and-white photo of him sliding into a car. High-priced lawyer, standing with him on the courthouse steps, celebrating an acquittal. Charity events he sponsored, grinning in the glow of awed spectators, no doubt, as he handed out hundreds to the parents of disabled children.

A celebrity. A bigshot. A wise guy.

But the media coverage didn't prepare Richie for the genuine encounter. The presence of Salvador Purelli swallowed the air in the room and sent tremors through his body. Their eyes connected. The man's onyx pupils bore through him as if a second-long stare taught the man everything there was to know about the young fighter. Richie flinched, remembering Joe's warning.

Never look these guys in the eyes and don't speak unless they speak to you.

Richie flattened in the chair, trying to appear relaxed, but felt the thumping of his heart could vibrate the rotting wooden rafters of the still barn.

Tally your breaths. In and out.

"Stand up, you little shit." Richie recognized Sonny's voice and obeyed.

Benny snaked by and made his way to the stairwell loft.

Over Sonny's shoulder, Richie glanced at Salvador Purelli. His slender frame leaned against the interior wall of the barn. The onyx eyes unflinching, zeroed in like a scope.

Without another word, Sonny threw a punch.

The thick fist crashed into Richie's chin, sending electricity through his lower jaw. He dropped to his knees and another blow to the side of the neck created fireworks of agony. Richie popped up and back stepped, assuming the boxer's stance engrained within the muscle memory developed over the past years.

Sonny pursued. "One on one. How it should have been earlier."

Richie flung a wild jab. It missed, slipping past Sonny's ear. The big guy countered with a knee to Richie's gut.

"Enough," a new voice rasped.

On one knee, Richie followed the unfamiliar voice. *Him.*

"That's it, Sonny." Benny's hoarse yell echoed in the barn. "Get up, kid."

Richie shook his head and rose, craning his neck to glimpse Benny seated on the first step of the loft. Welcoming the intervention, Richie massaged the lump surfacing in his jaw. His teeth moved during each swallow.

Sonny's got some bite with his bark.

"Sit. The. Fuck. Down." Benny pointed at the empty chair. Richie's eyes now followed Sonny, who shook his hand in the air and headed toward the entrance.

He whispered something to Purelli.

"*Chiamami quando e' finito.*" The mob boss smoothed out the thin mustache atop his lips.

Richie searched childhood memories. When his father got angry—which was often—he'd spit an Italian expletive or two. His mother endured the brunt of those verbal thrashings. She deserved it most of the time. On one occasion, dishes breaking against a wall birthed tiny projectiles, slicing Richie's shoulder. Back then, the scar was an angry purple and jagged but faint now.

"Sit," Purelli hissed, extending an open hand to the chair.

He tracked forward, stalking in elevated steps. Richie's stomach turned, and he obeyed. The throbbing in his hand and jaw now weak and insignificant. His ears picked up new sounds in the storage room. Meek yelps preceded the strengthening scratches.

"Do you know who I am?" Purelli stood flat. His arms draped forward.

Richie nodded.

"*Bene*. This will be less complicated."

The steps of the stairs creaked. Soon after, Benny placed an identical wooden chair in front of Richie.

"You should be dead." Purelli's thin finger jabbed forward and shook in a slight circle. "You never put your hands on one of my men. I am going to assume you did not know they were *my* men and meant no disrespect."

Benny shot a sneer toward Richie, who nodded and brought his eyes to the dirt.

"I believe you owe me an apology, Mr. Frezza." Purelli unbuttoned his suit jacket and sat.

Richie's initial inclination was to lash out.

What am I supposed to apologize about? I didn't start this.

The reality of his situation plucked the condescending attitude from his brain. A sequestering in Belleview's thick woods flanked by two men whose faces graced television broadcasts for all the wrong reasons required some level of humility.

Richie cleared his throat. "Sorry."

"I'm afraid you will have to do better. Do not make me ask again."

Another glance to Benny, and then Richie's brows arched. "I'm very sorry."

"Good. Now, this business with Sonny is over. You will seek no retribution."

"Understood."

"Benjamin has told me of your talent." Purelli leaned in and grasped Richie's swollen hand. "Is this okay?"

The mobster's soft touch tied a knot in Richie's throat. "It'll be fine."

"I imagine you are a bit confused." Purelli released the grip and leaned back in the chair. "As I said, Benjamin tells me you can fight. Do you feel you are capable of winning?"

"I'm still training. I've never fought in the ring for real."

"But you are talented, no?" The man's black eyes, unflinching and pure, widened. "I have seen what you have done to my men."

"Again, I'm—"

Purelli's hand rose like a teacher admonishing a student. "An apology has already been made. No need for another. A second reveals cowardice. Are you a coward, Mr. Frezza?"

"No."

"Good answer." Purelli offered a trivial smile akin to an embarrassed scoff reacting to an unfunny joke. He pulled a shiny metal case from the vest of his suit and opened it. From within it, he removed a cigarette.

Benny struck a match on cue and drew the flame near.

"Thank you, Benjamin." Purelli sucked in a substantial drag, and two gray snakes of smoke slithered from his nostrils. "So, you have talent, are not a coward, and are interested in fighting?"

"I guess."

"Do you guess, or do you know?" The mob boss pressed forward, clasping his slender hands together. The gold jewelry on each hand clanked together.

"I know, sir."

"I'm a businessman, young man. This city is my business." He dragged again; the smoke swirls leaped from his mouth. "It presents situations, and I react as best as I can. I do this by being open-minded and understanding of what works and what doesn't. For instance, you rough up a few of my men, and I must make a decision. Do I punish you, or do I embrace a new opportunity?"

Richie squirmed in the seat, unsure if he was supposed to answer Purelli's question.

"You are a fighter, and it just so happens, I am in the market." Purelli tapped the ash off the cigarette.

Richie rub at his swollen hand, willing the ache to recede.

Purelli snapped his fingers, twice, and Benny approached.

A series of hushed whispers ensued—the words out of reach—then the big guy left the barn.

"I'd like to offer a proposal." Purelli loosened his necktie and shrugged the coat off his shoulders. He draped it across his lap and smoothed the creases.

"What kind of proposal?" Richie leaned forward, resting his forearms atop his thighs.

"A business arrangement."

Richie said nothing. Sore and confused, he couldn't locate the right words. For the first time since the alley brawl, the true extent of his injuries surfaced. An aching hand. Wet cut beneath the eyelid. Jaw throbbing and pulsing, and ringing in his right ear.

"Would you like to hear more?"

"Do I have a choice?"

Purelli blinked, as if astonished by Richie's impotence. "Bravery is a quality I look for in a business partner. Stupidity is not. You may be walking the line."

"I mean no disrespect, Mr. Purelli. I'm a little out of it."

"Well, get with *it*. My proposal, like my time, is valuable."

"Yes, sir."

"You live at home with your mother, who from what I understand, is not much of a parent. She is more of a nuisance. Your father left six years ago, and you assumed the role few thirteen-year-old kids are ready for. High school ended at seventeen, but you kept your nose clean. No crime. No drugs. Just a job packing bait for minimum wage. Is that about right?"

"Yeah. I mean yes, sir." Richie's brows rose, creasing the skin in his forehead.

They're watching me, but for how long?

"Then you show up at Joe's gym. Trained hard. You are itching to fight and breakthrough. You go home at night and dream of the dazzling lights. The money. The women. The glory. It eats at you every day. And before your eyes close each night, you wonder things. Why can't I get a shot? What more will it take?"

"How do you know all of this?"

"Because I am Salvador Purelli." He leaned forward an inch from Richie's nose. The scent of tobacco and mint wafting. "This is *my* city."

Benny entered the barn with a bag of ice. "Catch." He chucked it at Richie then rustled with something and seconds later, he plopped on a chair next to Purelli.

"If you want to box, I'll promote you." Purelli flicked the cigarette into the dirt and smashed its corpse with the heel of his shoe.

Benny leaned in. "Relax." He crushed the ice pellets in the bag and then held it underneath Richie's hand. "Grip it."

Richie obeyed, fighting the sparks and throbs traveling like lighting beneath his skin.

Purelli's stare gave off the impression the man captured every movement and breath Richie made. Like a snake in a tree, stalking powerless prey.

Richie closed his hand, and the ice pellets collided and crunched.

"So," Purelli said. "Do we have a deal?"

"With respect and all, I've never fought before. Why me?"

"Opportunity. Do you want it?"

Richie remembered Benny's words during the drive. *We've buried far tougher than you.*

The scratching returned from behind the locked door but weakened. Whatever—or whoever—was responsible for it had tired.

Is it animals? Maybe some chickens had been brought in out of the cold? Or could be a rake swung in the breeze and grated the wall?

"I won't let you down." The phrase came out flat and scared, but it was the best Richie could do.

"*Bene.* From here on out, you will deal with Benjamin." Purelli patted his underboss's knee. "We have met now, and I have been clear about my intentions. That is a sign of respect from me, and I demand the same from you moving forward."

"Yes, sir."

"The young man is yours now." Purelli nodded to Benny and then rose, flinging the jacket over his arm. He strolled out of the barn as calm as his entrance.

"Think he likes you." Benny's grin inverted his mustache like a caterpillar dancing.

"What makes you say that?"

"You're still alive, kid."

Still alive.

CHAPTER TWELVE

Thunder clouds clapped over Ridgemont Cove Friday afternoon.

A cracking succession of booms startled Joe, who at present, puffed on a cigarette and reviewed bills and invoices.

The clunky radio on the corner of the wooden desk hummed. Static broke through now and again, but the soothing voice of Smokey Robinson filled the stagnant air as best it could.

A second thunderous roar echoed and shook the digital clock of the radio. It blinked. *Lunch time.*

He limped through the office and extended a hand for the knob.

His fingers traced the handle with a familiar touch.

The door muscled inward, the edge an inch from Joe's forehead.

He stumbled, took a few steps, and then planted a palm to the wall to reclaim his balance.

A bull of a man, shaved to the skin like a particular cleaning product sponsor, blocked the opening.

Sonny Denardo—another Benny "Beans" disciple. Great. Just fucking great.

"You ever hear of knocking?" Joe crossed his arms and almost tilted over without the aid of his trusted cane.

"Take a seat, old man. We've got a few things to discuss."

Joe brushed at his silver hair and turned toward the desk. Another day in Ridgemont Cove. The monitor bolted in the corner of the office displayed a few gym patrons working on the punching bags, but for the most part, Knuckles Up sat quiet and stagnant.

"Jesus, I already dealt with you guys yesterday." He stretched for the cigarette pack sitting on the desk. "You were here, remember?"

"I do." Sonny stepped into the room and closed the door. He pointed to the cancer stick with a bruised finger. "Those things will kill you."

"Yeah." Joe slid an ashtray closer. "I've survived worse."

Sonny waved a cloud of smoke away and glanced around the walls.

Motel art and degrading promotional banners for fighters long out of public view hung to the cheap plaster by thumbtacks. His eyes landed on a poster for a few moments and then targeted Joe.

"My name is Sonny."

"I know who you are." Joe circled around his desk and plopped onto the reclining office chair. Another crack of thunder ravaged the sky, though its vigor seemed more distant this time. "What brings you to my humble establishment?"

"I'm here on behalf of my employer." The man's biceps popped through a cream-colored silk shirt tucked into designer slacks running the length of his legs like vines swirling down tree trunks. On the shirt, faint but noticeable, a slanted streak of what appeared to be blood crept across the collar.

Joe tapped ash from the cigarette and let his left hand drop beneath the trim of the desk where a pistol hung on an eye hook. "What can I do for you?" If this mysterious beast charged, he'd have no choice.

"We want to use the kid."

"What *kid*?"

"You know damn well."

Joe's index finger traced the handle of the pistol. A quick snatch and pull of the trigger were all it would take.

Sonny brought his attention to the poster again and flattened a crinkle in the material with an outstretched hand, smoothing the face of a young Joe Gallant.

"I lost in the twelfth round." Joe's hand now gripped the handle of the gun hiding from view—a surging force urging to pull and pop.

"I know." Sonny scowled as if he'd just bitten into a lemon. "I was there. Saw the great Joe Gallant knocked out by a punk. Papers talked about it for days."

"Ah, he caught me by surprise. Tough guy, good boxer."

"There's more to it."

Joe ignored the accusation and extinguished the cigarette. A final cloud of smoke escaped into the air. "Why do you want the kid?"

"Orders are orders. I follow them and suggest you do the same."

"I don't own Richie. What do you need me for?"

"He trusts you."

"I can't make him do anything. You asking me to get him on board with you guys?"

"He's already agreed. This meeting is out of respect. We

want to promote the kid. And with your help, my employer believes he'll be successful."

"Can you stop talking to me like I'm an idiot? I know who your Goddamn *employer* is."

Sonny smirked and moved forward, leaning on the edge of Joe's desk. The force shook the top, sending a cup of pencils rolling. "If you agree, it'll make this arrangement easier for everyone."

"So, what do you want?"

"Your loyalty. You work for us now." He stood from the desk and crossed his arms. "Is that going to be a problem?"

Joe looked at the poster and that night returned to him.

Muscular and confident with an aura of bluster unteachable to many. The lights flashing in different neon bulbs, blinding and exciting the warriors. Then surging pain. Face planted on the musty canvas with sour sweat trickling into his gaped mouth. The metallic taste of blood filling the indentations from his vacated mouth guard. A roar of the crowd.

His body shivered at the recollection.

Sonny slapped the desk and Joe woke from the memory. "Do we have a deal, Mr. Gallant?"

"What do I get out of this?"

"As long as the kid is fighting, your rent checks are considered paid." Sonny started toward the door and glanced at the poster one more time.

"Where's Richie now?" Joe leaned back in the chair. Its spine squeaked.

"He'll be here tomorrow." Sonny stopped in the threshold. "Don't let us down, old man."

"We don't train on Saturdays."

"You do now."

CHAPTER THIRTEEN

"See ya soon, kid." Benny flicked ashes out the window then tossed an envelope.

"What's this?" Richie caught the hurled package. A flash of green peeked from under the unsealed flap.

"A little taste, kid." The mobster winked. "Report to the gym tomorrow. It's time to earn your keep."

"I don't—"

"Save it. Everything is handled. Tomorrow."

After the rumble in the alleyway, Purelli's cold but endearing showcase at the abandoned farm, and the silent weather-induced traffic jam-filled trek home, he was relieved to see Benny "Beans" drive away from his mother's apartment.

Richie's Timex read a few minutes before two—the middle school a few blocks away was about to end for the day, releasing a sea of pubescent mongrels.

His hand and jaw ached. Benny's few words during the drive home, regarding the next steps in the process, rattled his brain like the ghost of things *Yet to Come*.

Joe would continue to train him. Benny, acting as Purelli's eyes and ears on the street, would assume the role of manager. Richie had protested—the one time his lips moved during the ride—but it was made clear, he was in no position to negotiate.

Joe's involvement irked Richie. The old man maintained a fierce hatred for the mafia element. For him to agree, there'd have to be a lucrative deal on the table, or a sinister threat issued. Richie prayed it was the former.

He sat hunched in the cold on the damp steps of the slum his mother called home. The sun's heat touched his face but was no match for the November frost in the air.

The damaged buildings of The Trails faced inward like a prison cell block, offering a view of the other tenants. Though the street remained empty of passing cars, the balconies and porches rocked with frenzied activity. Some drank beer. Others shot dice. A trio on a third-floor balcony blared rap music. Still others huddled in denim and hooded sweatshirts. A cloud of rancid marijuana smoke, judging from the musty smell, levitated in the air above them. The pair on the second floor of the building across from Richie had passed out upright in their balcony chairs, bodies limp.

Cracks desecrated most windows. The resourceful, out-of-work tenants of the apartments duct taped cardboard pizza boxes from the inside to prevent water and clear sight from creeping into their devious worlds.

Spending the majority of his young adult life attempting to rip his mother from the clutch of The Trails proved to be one fight he couldn't punch his way through. The liquor and drug abuse, a prerequisite for renters in this complex it seemed, addled her mind and numbed the maternal instinct.

Excuses and lies poured from her mouth like soda from a fountain at the run-down movie theater, famous once for comfy chairs and hip movies, but now, nothing more than a drug-crazed orgy landing.

Look, kids. Dinner and a movie! Just watch out for needles and pedophilia.

Reluctance to accept she belonged with the parasites in the neighborhood waned now, as sad a realization as it was.

While contemplating these familiar issues, he clutched the small envelope from Benny. The mobster's words replayed in his head. *A little taste, kid. Time to earn your keep.*

Richie lifted the seal and thumbed through the stack. Twenty crisp one-hundred-dollar bills. Flush with excitement at first, the shivers surfaced.

Big mistake. This month's rent and a spoonful of shame, please.

Accepting the cash and moving forward with Purelli was thrilling, but gripping an envelope of dough from the mob felt wrong and dirty. *Kinda like the people in this neighborhood.*

He returned the stack to its paper vault and climbed the steps.

As was customary in a shit hole such as The Trails, he shot a quizzical glance over the shoulder.

Two months back, a little girl coming home from school had not followed protocol. She had turned the knob, and a masked man forced himself inside. He stole the innocence of the eleven-year-old, cracking her femur and future in the process. Then he lifted some valuables from the house and disappeared like the boogey man. *Any leads, detective? Hello?*

The quick peek revealed most of the tenants were engaged in their previous activities. However, a few had stopped and glared from a balcony across the street.

Relax, they didn't see.

Richie returned their gazes with a menacing scowl and entered the apartment. He latched the chain lock and deadbolt, turned the hall light off, and peered through the window near the door. The men lost interest and returned to their dice game.

He drew the blinds. They pattered next to each other, swiveling in faint semi-circles. Beams of light ebbed and flowed over the yellowing tiles of the foyer. Beyond the landing, a dinette table to the left sat coated in dust. To the right, a consignment-store couch nestled against a separating wall. On the other side of the wall, a lukewarm refrigerator, another cheap table set, and a stove built during the dark ages filled the kitchen.

Many of the items in the apartment decorated the den of the home he had once lived in on the other side of town. Those days were gone, though. The memories of what-once-was disintegrated, much like the furniture in this place.

Beyond those two rooms, the single interior door inside the apartment cut into a wall. It led to his mother's cave, a dark abyss reeking of ash and phlegm.

Knock. He rapped his knuckles against the cold, dense wood.

The gap beneath the door shined in flickering colors.

Knock. Knock. Silence within except for the television's low murmur. He waited a few seconds and then twisted the knob.

Though the room was black, Richie knew his mother was lying on the bed covered in a tattered quilt. It had squares sewn in a checkerboard pattern. A Frezza family photo was transposed in every other square.

A trip to an amusement park.

A rare beach day when his parents were sober and smiling.

Richie's fifth grade yearbook photo.

Memories of a life that felt ancient, really. The images, tarnished and aged much like the quilt's owner, reeked of a semi-happier time. On her makeshift nightstand, an old fruit box she'd found in the street months ago, stood a half-empty bottle of gin and an ashtray still supporting a lit cigarette.

"Mom, you awake?" Richie entered the room.

"Why aren't you at work?" She reached for the smoke. The ruddy tip of the lung dart glowed.

"I'm not working there anymore."

"Did you get fired?" The slurred words poured from her mouth.

"Nah, I found something else. Something better."

He sat on the edge of the bed and glanced at the television. Some corny TV judge rambled on about choices and consequences. The defendant, chewing gum and snickering, lethargically agreed.

Ironic and relevant, he thought, glancing toward her. *Some of us make choices because we have to, huh.*

She rolled toward the fruit box and flipped the switch above the headboard. The skeletal remnants of his mother appeared in the glow.

The dim light highlighted years of ravaged drug use. Her flushed and thin face, now outlined by graying hair, morphed into a less familiar person with each passing day. Small broken blood vessels traveled across her cheeks like spider webs. Open sores and bruises traversed both her fragile arms, turning once tan skin into a minefield of scabs and yellowing patches.

Without hesitation, her hand grasped the plastic bottle of gin, and her arm upended the bottle.

A rancid odor of sweat slapped Richie, sending the bile in his gut swirling.

Gulp. Gulp. Cough. Gulp.

"Think you should be drinking so much?"

"Think I give a shit what you think?" She flung the plastic carcass across the room.

"Maybe, I'm worried about you, ma."

"What a sweet thing to say. Ha! You care about yourself. Just like your asshole father." She dragged on the cigarette again, burning the remnants to its filter, and then smashed it in the ash tray.

"Well, I can surprise you."

"Why aren't you at work?" She brought her eyes to the television screen. The melodramatic score of the show stabbed from the speakers.

"I told you, I found something else. It's going to be better."

"Not that boxing shit again. It's a pipe dream. A fantasy."

"Look, ma." Richie resisted the urge to flee. He remained at the side of the bed, patting his mother's bony leg. "I just wanted to make sure you're all right."

"I'm fine. How long until you'll have money for rent? I can't pay for everything around here. The deal was you handle the rent. I already take care of the lights, cable, groceries—"

"And the gin and cigarettes, too."

Her eyes cut upward, and she shook her head with the familiar disapproving, commonplace expression. Not anger or disappointment. The face said, *I know you're right, but I'll never admit it.*

"My show's on."

"Yeah. I know." With a frown, he back-stepped toward the door.

She turned to the television and lit a new cigarette.

Without another word, he left the room.

He used a melting bag of frozen peas to ice his hobbled hand.

Richie browsed through the mail toppled over like buildings struggling in the wake of an earthquake. He separated junk from bills and sat at the kitchen table. The true goal was to find his mother's disability check in the rubble, but it was one piece of mail she coveted. That envelope was worth getting out of bed for. Each month it bought booze and Pall Malls. Sometimes the remainder covered the light payment.

Richie clutched the cash from Benny and sifted through the various sealed letters marked *past due* and frowned.

"Two-thousand isn't even close to enough."

CHAPTER FOURTEEN

A quarter-full, dust-laden bottle of whisky nestled between the back leg of Joe Gallant's desk and the wall.

Over the years, he'd glanced at it for a moment or two, but on most days, it didn't register in his brain. This early Saturday morning, though, his eyes canvassed every intricate line in the label and each speck of minute dust on the cap.

A grating noise, the iron security gate plunging open out front, snapped the thought.

He meandered from the back office, through the darkened hallway, and unlocked the deadbolt.

"How we doing, kid?"

"Morning, Joe." Richie avoided eye contact, and his voice fell flat.

"Get some rest last night? We hit hard yesterday, huh?" Joe opened the door wider, allowing him to slide by.

"I'm okay. Sore but ready."

Joe closed the door with a thud. "Gotta visit from one of your chums yesterday."

"They're not my friends. It all happened so fast." He

knelt on the rubber flooring and unzipped the bag, shuffling through its contents. "I'm not sure what the hell is going on."

"I do. These guys need another kid to get slaughtered in the ring. You'll do for now, and then they'll cash their checks and move on to the next payday."

"I'm not gonna pretend to know why they picked me." Richie found the hand tape hiding beneath a roll of athletic bandaging. "But something tells me that's not the plan."

Joe ignored the asinine comment and limped in the direction of the office, flipping light switches as he passed them. He returned with a coffee mug etched with the words *I'm a Ray of Fucking Sunshine* and a newspaper tucked beneath his armpit.

Richie fiddled with the tape, awkwardly trying to attach it.

"Come here." Joe took the roll and stuck some strips in place. "What happened to the hand?"

"There was a misunderstanding. It's okay."

"The eye, too." Joe lifted Richie's chin and examined the fresh cut beneath his brow. "A misunderstanding?" *Or a beat-down? Don't lie to people who trust you, kid.*

"I reacted. Wasn't thinking yesterday."

"Ha. You're not thinking now if you really plan on going through with this."

Richie's head drooped and his stare fell to the floor. "I'm doing what I think is right."

Sensing the kid's apprehension, Joe shifted his approach. "Look, if you're dead set on it, the training is different now. There's gonna be someone on the other side who wants to hurt you. Punching speed bags and sparring a few guys is different from stepping in the ring. If we're moving forward, we've gotta get to work."

"So, you're not mad?" Richie's head rose, revealing furrowed brows. "You'll train me?"

"Of course." Joe set the coffee mug on the edge of the ring and plopped the newspaper to the canvas. "But take a look at this."

Richie obeyed and perused the front page. "Budget cuts for the school district?"

"Page 6 C, kid."

Richie flipped to it and read the article's title.

"Amateur boxer stabbed in hospital"—Richie peered up from the paper—"wounded but alive."

"That's the one."

"Police investigators have suspects in mind. The victim, a young middleweight boxer named Timothy *Thunderstorm* Vietta, refuses to cooperate or press charges." Richie's voice lowered to a near whisper by the last word.

"Ring any bells?"

"What's this have to do with me?" The bravado returned, though Richie's feigned ignorance irritated the old man.

He can make the connection. This little . . .

"There are other towns, other trainers"—the echo of each word bounced off the empty gym walls—"other places to do this, Richie."

"Why do you think I walked in here in the first place? All I got in the world are these." Richie raised his half-taped hands. "*This* is my out."

"The road to dreams is full of nightmares, kid." Joe stabbed the article with his finger. "See what you're getting into? If you rub elbows with dangerous people, crazy shit happens. I know this town. Smells like *him*, but who is going to say anything? Nobody has the balls to stand up."

"I know who and what he is, but I don't have a choice."

"Jesus Christ. You can't think this will end well. What happens if you lose?"

"I don't plan on losing. Besides, you just said you'll train me."

Joe frowned and scratched at his chin. "We haven't started yet. There's still time—"

"To run? Hightail it out of Ridgemont Cove? How could I do that, Joe? Tell me. What would I do with my mom?"

"Vietta had a choice, and he made it. You can still make yours." He patted his shirt pocket in search of a soft pack of smokes. Anxiety within scalded his senses and the bottle hiding in his office beckoned. *I've done this before. You gotta listen.*

"I've already decided. If you want to back out, that's a choice you have to make. Let's be real. What did you say the other day? 'Am I really going to stiff Salvador Purelli?' Can I really say no?"

"You know, I've been here for thirty years." Joe lit the cigarette. The inhalation burned down his throat. "Before that, I served overseas. Saw shit so sinister, it would turn the toughest guy to goo. But none of it compares to Purelli. I'm too old to say no, kid. You still can, but either way, I'm not letting you do this alone."

"Then we do it together."

Joe grabbed the article and retraced the words again. "Fine. We gotta be smart. But promise me something."

"What?" Richie rotated the injured hand to tighten the wrist strap.

"If it gets too crazy, we leave together. I've got relatives in Wisconsin. You can come with me. You and your momma."

A car horn bellowed outside, and both men brought

their eyes to the door's window. Joe tucked the paper beneath his arm.

"It won't come to that." Richie released a combination of hooks, uppercuts, and jabs. The velocity spurred a gust of wind inches from Joe's face. "This is the game I've got. Only one I want."

Joe thought about the bottle in his office. He'd reverted to liquid medication when the lights blotted out. When times were darkest, *they* were to blame. And now *they* were back.

"I got two thousand to start." Richie's eyes enlarged, pushing small wrinkles to his forehead. "That's my rent for a few months. One fight. Do you know how much bait I'd have to pack to make two grand at the dock? And it's just the beginning."

"Real jobs don't pay shit, but they're honest."

It fell silent then. Richie didn't hurl a comeback and Joe didn't want to argue the inevitable.

A humming filled the gym now. The air conditioner, brought back to life after Joe cut a five-hundred-dollar repair check, drummed its incessant beat.

Richie dropped to a knee and straightened the laces of the athletic boots splitting at the heel.

The old man propped his shoulder against the ring's corner post and brought a stare to the water stains covering the ceiling tiles. They'd grown in the last few months, and he'd contemplated climbing into the attic to search for mold on several occasions. The thought always ceded to common sense: *what I don't know, can't hurt, right?*

"I can't do this without you." Richie popped up from his crouch and patted the old man's shoulder. "If you teach me, I won't lose. You have my word."

Joe extended his calloused hand, a truce for the moment, and Richie reciprocated with a thin smile.

"Looks swollen. You gonna fight like this?" Joe turned his fighter's hand and investigated.

"I said I'll handle it. You've got to trust me."

"I do, kid. I just don't trust them."

CHAPTER FIFTEEN

Benny Bianchi parked his Cadillac here for ten years to lift some cash from Joe "The Giant Killer" Gallant. This Tuesday, the car nestled in the same spot, but the motive was different.

They welcomed Richie Frezza into their little slice of the criminal enterprise, so micro-managing and monitoring came with the territory. The instructions from the boss were to monitor the kid's progress, but in no way should he distract the flow of training. Purelli's orders, a less comforting sound than a serpent's hiss in the pitch of night, rang in Benny's ears again.

Make sure they are training. Keep Richie's hand iced, Benjamin. When it is ready, you let me know.

So, Benny Bianchi sat outside of Knuckles Up, glaring through the small square window etched in the door, with a bagel in his mouth and a coffee in hand.

Richie lifted a cylinder block in the air, tensed his stomach with his feet a few inches from the ground and Joe dropped a medicine ball on his abdomen. This continued for three minutes, and each passing second saw Richie's feet dangle closer to the canvas of the ring. On a couple of occasions when toes grazed the floor, Joe's cane cracked Richie's extended legs.

That old codger ain't playing around, Benny thought. He glanced back to Sonny.

His driver, now sporting a new pair of shades, sat stoic in the Cadillac, hands locked onto the steering wheel. The cackle of an early morning sports radio call-in show seeped from the open passenger side window and reached Benny's ear.

"They talk about the Oregon game yet?"

Sonny shook his head. The volume ceased from within the car. "Huh, boss?"

"They give a spread for the Oregon game? We gotta fill out player cards and drop them off with Myles later."

Sonny held a scratch pad and pen above the car's roof. "I'm on it."

Pleased, but unwilling to show Sonny any form of appreciation, Benny turned to the gym.

The scene reminded him of the film *Raging Bull*.

Richie, now sweating rivers with droves of water popping from his skin, skipped over a twirling rope increasing in momentum. Joe sat on a stool near him with a stopwatch in hand. His teeth gripped a metal whistle.

Benny sipped from the Styrofoam cup. His phone buzzed.

"Hello." He pinned the device between his ear and shoulder and then shifted the coffee from his left to right. "Wait a minute." His eyes followed a blonde jogger clad in pink yoga pants and a neon top. "Ain't you cold, honey?"

The woman giggled uneasily and shook her head. "Working up a sweat."

"You sure are. Keep it up. It's paying off." His head

swung to the left as she passed as if her ass and his eyes shared magnetic properties.

"Benny," the voice on the line said. "We gotta problem."

"Why is it you never call with solutions, Donnie? What's the deal?"

"Sorry. I'm in a bind here."

"What's the issue?"

Benny glanced through the window. The kid's face flushed a dark red as he outpaced the jump rope.

"Clemons is out. Dumb shit got locked up last night."

"Can't trust anybody these days, eh? Who was he fighting?"

"Martinez."

"Nobody can fill in?" Benny finished the coffee and crumpled the cup into a misshapen ball.

"Not this soon."

"I gotta talk to the boss, but he'll probably say to scrap it. What's it matter? There's eight fights, right?"

"Benny," Donnie's voice now lowered several octaves, "there's a lot of dough on it. Clemons is the favorite. We drop the fight; it scratches the odds of the slate. We have to put on a show."

"Well, what the fuck do you want me to do? I can't make a fighter appear—"

Benny tossed the smashed cup across the sidewalk and looked through the window again.

Now, Richie wrestled protective headgear in place and bounced on his toes. A sparring partner, an unfamiliar man about Richie's build and age, tapped his gloves together in the opposite corner of the ring. Joe barked some instructions, though Benny couldn't make out the words. Then, the two fighters shot out from the corners.

Richie circled and attacked. He feigned to his left, waited for his opponent to swing, and then ducked under an errant punch to deliver a cracking shot to the man's unprotected ribs.

The sparring partner fell into the ropes of the ring, covered his head with his gloves, and endured a flurry of punches. Richie stalked. Strikes flashed in fury, popping the sparring partner's head like a leaf struggling to defeat a fierce wind.

Joe limped forward and jabbed his cane between them.

"Hold up, Donnie." Benny used his coat to wipe at debris clinging to the window. "I may have something for you. Stay near the phone."

The show continued. Richie's power and speed took over. The sparring partner feigned and ducked without success, absorbing quick combinations to the body and head. Richie's footwork and precise jabs stunned the man, ripping the left cheek with three unanswered shots.

Benny skirted the three steps and stopped in front of the Cadillac.

"Any word on Oregon?"

"Nah, boss."

"All right. Keep an eye on the kid. I gotta make a call. There's a phone on the corner near the diner."

"Your phone dead or something?"

"No, dipshit." Benny formed a gun with his thumb and pointer and shot himself. "A call to the boss."

"Oh, right. I can watch the snot-nosed punk." Sonny stepped out from the Cadillac.

Benny sauntered down the sidewalk.

In the alley between Knuckles Up and a vacant building once home to a consignment shop, two haggard men huddled around a steel barrel. Flames from inside licked the rim and emitted crackles. Benny strolled past and heard them break into whispers.

Continuing east toward the payphone, he searched for spare change in his pocket. He never had a use for it except for times like these. The boss insisted all calls to him be made on public phones, and never should the same phone be used in one day.

He approached the phone. A woman sweeping the steps of the diner peeked up from her broom. He ignored her and pulled a few quarters and a dab of lint from his trousers. Benny yanked the receiver off its hook and slid a coin into the slot.

He felt a stare on him, and given the secrecy Purelli championed, he turned to find the woman glaring. A momentary eye staring contest ensued, but the dial tone in Benny's ears snapped his innate tough-guy routine. He turned to the booth and dialed The Tango.

After three rings, a cheerful voice said, "The Tango, Ridgemont Cove's premier Italian Ristorante. How may I help you?"

"Yeah. I'll take the house special with three extra sides of marinara."

"Oh," the voice blurted, its glee evaporating. "Right away, sir."

Benny craned his neck a bit and glimpsed the woman's stare from his peripheral.

"One moment while I transfer you," the girl from before said.

"Hurry it up. Ain't got all day, toots."

The line clicked over, sat silent for a moment, and then a raspy, accented voice rung. "Yes."

"It's me."

"How can I help you?" Purelli's words crackled over the receiver.

"Donnie called. The house has a problem."

"Is that so?"

"Down a man for Friday's slate. No fill-ins available." Benny turned into the booth, blocking a gust of wind traveling over the street.

"No way to drop the match?"

"May piss a few people off. Donnie says it'd be better to find a solution."

"Your proposal?"

Benny smirked. The guy rarely said anything anyway, but over a public phone—impossible to trace without cause and a signed warrant—the term "pulling teeth" was an understatement. "The kid."

"A wise decision?"

"From the looks of it, I'd say the hand is okay. Ready for a debut."

"I trust your judgement."

The call ended, and then the shrill dial tone burst into Benny's ears. He laughed to himself again. Even if a cop was tapped in, listening in some inconspicuous white van like in the movies, they'd gather nothing from this ten-second chat.

He reminded himself that even though boxing wasn't illegal, the gambling empire and extracurricular activities the family built and siphoned from, indeed were.

Maybe let the boss call the shots.

He racked the phone and pulled out his cell.

Why waste the quarters? I'll need more at some point today.

He draped an arm over the roof of the booth and plugged in the number.

"Promotion Boxing." Music and muffled voices crept through the earpiece. "This is Donnie."

"I'm a man of solutions."

"Who's your fighter?" Another heavy breeze passed over and static crunched in the line.

"A new kid." Benny cupped the speaker with his thick palm. "Big dollars. Set the bets."

"On who? The newbie?"

"Do as you're told. Set the fucking bets."

A moment of hesitation followed by a sigh. "Bring him in today. Need his measurements and signature on a few pieces of paper. Then we can send final numbers to the others."

"You let me worry about the others. Get everything ready. I'm on my way." Benny closed the flip phone and dropped it into his coat pocket.

He turned to rush back toward the gym, but the woman's stare was like a tattoo, fixed and unwavering.

"Lady, you gotta problem?"

"No, sir," the woman replied. "I was just wondering what a fancy dresser like you was doing talking on a payphone. Then you pull out a cell right after. Peculiar, huh?"

"What's it to you? Mind your business."

"Actually, it is my business. This here is my diner." She pointed behind her and draped her other arm over the broom handle.

Benny stomped toward the woman, his jacket flailing wild with each stride.

"It's a public phone."

"Says right on the top, for customers of Ms. May's Diner. I'm Ms. May, and you aren't no customer."

Benny's fists clenched. He wanted to knock the arrogant woman's head off and considered it for a moment but relented. Purelli wouldn't want any disturbances. The fight, and bets for that matter, were lost if Benny woke up in a cell. He pulled a wad of bills fastened by a gold clip inscribed BEB.

"Well, we'll call it even." He flung a twenty at her shoes.

Ms. May shrugged. "I s'pose we will."

Benny turned again. The patter of the woman's feet stopped his ascent.

"I know what you're up to."

"Now you're sniffing around in my business, lady."

"Sure enough, mister, but I want you to know there are good people here, so treat 'em as such. Besides, we don't need your kind here, stinkin' up the place?"

Benny reddened, and small pops of sweat poured from his greasy forehead. He swiped at the drips.

Who the hell does this broad think she is? Fuckin' Mother Teresa?

A slight wind lifted the twenty-dollar bill sending it fleeing across the sidewalk, and Ms. May flattened it with the bristles of the broom.

"Pick up your blood money." She swept it toward Benny. "I make my living right."

Benny scooped the cash from the sidewalk and headed away from the diner. He shot a glance to the alley, curious if the vagrants were still talking shop. The barrel poured smoke, but the men had abandoned the area.

Ahead, Sonny sat on the hood of the Cadillac with his veiny arms crossed over his chest. A toothpick jutted from his mouth, hopping to each corner.

Benny approached with a huff, garnering Sonny's attention.

"Everything good?"

"Yeah. Start the car. Be gone for a minute."

Benny straightened his suit, raked his hair back, and strode toward the gym.

Through the window, he saw Richie jerking on the lifeless body of the sparring partner. Benny tugged the door open. The warmth and stench of sweat slapped him in the face, drawing water from his pores.

"Good morning, gents." He wiped at his damp brow. Showing no interest in the man prodded and slapped like a drunken fool on a park bench in Rose Wood Park, Benny draped his arms over the bottom rope of the ring. "What do we have here?"

"Wait." Richie tapped the man's lifeless face and removed the headgear.

A trickle of blood fell from the guy's mouth. A hoarse cough, like that of a smoker before a morning cigarette, exploded from his throat.

"He's coming around." Richie awkwardly fished the man's mouthpiece out with his gloved hand, sending it tumbling to the ring's floor. "Hey Victor, you awake?"

Victor's legs twitched and brought life to his torso. He lifted his head from the canvas.

A line of blood streaked down his chin and onto his chest, losing its brilliance as it mixed with sweat.

Joe charged out of the shower room in a frenzy, limping toward the ring. He held wet towels that dripped splotches to the floor. He tossed them to Richie. "Put them behind his head and around his shoulders."

"Damn, kid." Benny's lips clawed backward in a snarl. "Take it easy on the help."

Richie glanced across the ring, said nothing, and did as Joe instructed.

Joe tottered into the sparring ring with an ice chest and poured water on Victor.

"What the hell, Joe?" Victor rose and stumbled backward, slapping the liquid from his face and neck.

"Shut up." Joe flung the chest out of the ring. It clanked to the ground and spun toward a weight bench. "If you had kept your left up like I'd been telling ya the last ten minutes, that hook wouldn't have put you on your ass."

Richie, who had been studying Victor, turned to Benny.

"Let's talk outside, kid." *Time to pop the cherry and see what you're made of.* He shot him a smile and jabbed his pointer finger to the door.

"Give me a sec'." Richie helped Victor to a stool in the ring.

"I'm okay," the woozy fighter said. Water droplets beaded through his buzz cut and jumped from his forehead.

"Joe, I need to go." Richie nodded to the door. "We still on for tomorrow?"

"Yeah." The man's cane shook in the air along with his voice. "We'll talk in the morning."

"Vic, you okay?" Richie tapped the battered man's shoulder.

"Go fuck yourself." The dazed boxer blew blood-tinged snot from his nose. "You got lucky."

"How many times I gotta tell ya, Vic?" Joe wound up for a sermon. "Keep your left up."

"We gotta go, kid." Benny thumbed toward the exit.

"Go." Joe waved Richie off.

The kid took the stairs two at a time, hit the sidewalk with a feather light step, and stopped at the back door with a final look toward the gym.

Sonny sat in the driver seat with a cell glued to his ear. He looked in Benny's direction, at Richie for a moment, and then laughed into the phone.

"So, what's up?" Richie bit at the tape on his right hand. It wouldn't budge.

"Come here." Benny grabbed his wrist. "We need to take a ride." He used the nails of his fingers to scratch at the tape. A few passes and the right glove loosened.

"Where to?"

"Got ya a fight." He worked on the left glove. "Need to come with me and weigh-in for the Friday night line-up."

"Already? That's soon. Can I even make weight?"

"What is this, a date? What's up with the fucking questions?"

"Sorry." Richie shook the gloves off. They fell to the sidewalk with a thud. "Just started training for real a few days ago. Figured you'd give me time is all."

"You've had *time*. How's the hand?"

"It's all right." Richie held it up for inquest, scooped the gloves off the sidewalk, and then followed Benny's stride toward the Caddy.

Sonny got out and propped the driver side open. "Hey, shit for brains."

Richie shot Sonny a sideways glance then returned his gaze to Benny. "And if I'm not ready?"

"Boss says you're ready. I say you're ready. So, you're ready."

"What about Joe? What does he think?"

"Again, with the fucking inquisition." He tapped the roof of the Cadillac. *Going to have to whip this little snot into shape.* "To be honest, kid, I don't give a shit. Purelli says it's a go. Do I need to repeat myself?" Benny plopped into the front seat and pointed to the back door. "Ass. Seat. Now."

Richie paused and glanced at the fading Knuckles Up sign affixed to the roof of the building.

"You waiting on an invitation?" Benny tapped the side panel and Richie climbed in without another word.

CHAPTER SIXTEEN

"That was easy." Richie dropped the ballpoint pen in the cup near the register.

"That's it." Donnie blew on the fresh ink sprawled across the contract. "See ya Friday, champ."

Richie left Promotion Boxing and marched to the idling Cadillac.

Benny, seated in front with a lit cigarette, greeted him with a sneer. Smoke poured from his pursed lips and twirled out of the small opening in the window.

Sonny glanced up as Richie tugged the handle and forced the door open. "What took so long?"

Richie slid into the backseat, ignoring Benny's lackey, who was fiddling with the radio.

The man's bald head was perspiring a bit, an unusual occurrence in the gnawing winter. Traffic passed by in the reflection of Sonny's sunglasses, and Richie knew the eyes behind the dark lenses zeroed in on the backseat and not the road ahead.

"Everything straightened out, kid?" Benny rolled the window down further, and frigid air hiked through the car.

"Said I'm signed up." Richie adjusted the rear air-conditioning vent, hoping the heat in the car was at optimal performance. "Fighting some guy named Martinez."

"Good. Sonny, let's go. We gotta lot on the menu today."

"The thing with Lou?"

Benny's eyes furrowed, and his lower jaw shifted toward his driver. Richie caught it all in the rearview and glanced away. He didn't want to overstep, and he damn sure didn't need another beatdown session to transmit information through blood and sweat.

The car pulled from the curb and merged onto the road.

Sonny traipsed through side streets. An odd left turn here or an unnecessary right there. Richie assumed it was a diversion tactic, but there never seemed to be anybody following them.

Maybe these guys knew more about the prowess of police. Maybe they were just careful. Maybe I should shut up and mind my own business.

A buzz cut the silence and Benny reached into his pocket.

"Yeah. Huh?" The cigarette bobbed up and down between his lips. "No worries. Boss has me running errands." He exhaled a cloud of smoke. "Naw . . . Go handle the thing we talked about yesterday."

Benny flicked ash out the window, and a few remnants of the dead tobacco missed their target, landing on Richie's pants.

If you were anyone else, I'd clock you. He swiped the gray clusters from his sweats.

"Yeah. I'm bringing the kid home. Okay." Benny hung up and glanced to the rearview mirror. "Donnie say anything else?"

"Nope. Just said to be there Friday. I'm fighting Martinez."

"You did good."

"So, this is legit?"

"Boxing ain't illegal, kid." A short laugh followed a dry cough and the cigarette butt escaped through the window.

"Well, why is Donnie so freaked? Dude looks like he's scared to death."

"Too much coffee." Benny turned to Sonny and chuckled. "Good old Donnie. He pissed his pants the first time he met Purelli and that's not an exaggeration."

Sonny's grip on the steering wheel tightened, turning his knuckles ghostly white. The Cadillac slowed for a pedestrian jaywalking.

Benny huffed and shook his head in disbelief.

"The guy literally soaked his Dockers." He tapped Sonny's shoulder. "My Grandma, GiGi, could run faster. God rest her soul."

Richie, not sure what to make of the situation, sank into the backseat. "So, the boxing matches aren't illegal—you know, underground?"

"Naw. Don't sweat it, kid." Benny's phone buzzed once more. He hit a button on the side and killed the vibration. "It's all regulated by the Boxing Commission and considered semi-professional level. But the rules and standards are far more lenient."

"Figured with such short notice, it'd be an issue."

"We can place anybody into the ring." Benny turned and faced the backseat. "There are no issues, my young friend."

Richie leaned toward the front seat to match Benny's eye-level. "You just take care of them, huh?"

A slight smirk crossed Benny's acne-scarred face and

then he nudged Sonny's mammoth shoulder. "Problems are no good for business, but shit happens. Right?"

"Like a port-o-potty, boss."

Benny's smile widened, revealing a gold capped tooth in the bottom. Richie hadn't noticed it before.

"Anyway." Benny dropped back into the seat and clicked his seatbelt in. "Donnie, like most of the people in Ridgemont Cove are too smart, or maybe too scared to say no. Either way, it works in our favor."

Joe came to mind, and guilt surged. The same guys who'd been extorting his little piece of the pie were lining Richie's pockets now. "So, you guys clean up every time?"

"Wouldn't say that." Benny's thin grin flattened in the reflection of the rear view. "It's called gambling, not winning. But, more often than not, the house wins. And in this city, we're the house, bank, and collection agency. You're on the right side, kid."

"Who's gonna bet on me? Nobody knows who I am."

"Even better. Low expectations equal big-time scratch. The only thing you need to worry about is fighting in three days. Leave the numbers to the professionals."

CHAPTER SEVENTEEN

Benny's eyes locked onto the kid's reflection in the rearview.

"What do you know about this Martinez guy?" Richie rubbed his neck then stretched.

"Not much." A wet, loose cough broke free and rattled in Benny's chest. "We'll find out, though." He grabbed a cigarette and lit the crunched end.

Richie glanced away then shook his head.

Benny answered Richie's questions in vague, stock responses. The kid knew little about the process, and worse, knew nothing about his opponent. Something to rectify and soon when given the all clear.

"Those things will kill ya?" The words flowed with a familiar ease from Sonny.

"What, you a doctor now?" Benny smacked his driver's chest with a weighted backhand.

"Easy, boss. I'm driving. We'll all die sooner than planned."

"Eyes on the road, mouth shut then." Benny blew a cloud. It fogged the front end of the car.

Sonny said nothing but lowered his window.

The Cadillac meandered through a few tight alleys and then merged onto Center Street.

A fruit vendor, and his customers braving the cold for a fresh slice of watermelon or kiwi, watched the sleek car's approach.

Half a block north, a scantily dressed redhead—a professional in her own right—kicked out her hip and jutted a manicured thumb.

Benny lowered the window and whistled at the woman.

"Hey, baby." She spun around, squeezed her breasts together, and pursed her lips.

"How much you think she wants, Sonny?"

"Whatever it is, she ain't worth it. Catch gonorrhea from broads like her, boss."

"Gono-what?"

"You never heard of gonorrhea. Nasty stuff. Makes your dick smell like a port-o-potty."

Benny drew back with a half-laugh and half-scowl. Sonny joined, the wrinkles of his face bulging and pink. "I'm going to look it up. Anyway, kid, we'll have a full jacket on Martinez tomorrow. Measurements, training information, medical records, and family members."

"What for?" Richie scratched the stubble on his head. "Why do his parents or siblings matter? They don't fight."

Shrill horns and brakes scratching gravel roared.

"What the—" Benny's eyes jumped from Richie's reflection to the road.

A group of young skateboarders cut across the median.

The driver of a produce van, tires still smoking and sizzling, leaned halfway out the window. "What the fuck?" His voice rose over the clamor. "Get the hell out of the street."

"Blow it out your ass, old man." The shortest boy in the group shot the bird, and his friends joined in unison.

Sonny slowed the Cadillac to a crawl when they neared, but the troublemakers sliced a few yards up the street and disappeared behind a building.

"Dipshits." Sonny accelerated and checked the rearview. "Got shit for brains. Younger versions of our friend back there, boss." He jabbed a thumb toward Richie and then changed lanes.

"Leave the kid alone. He's going to be an earner."

The Trails entrance appeared in the driver-side window. Mildew covered the white lettering of the neighborhood sign. Black spray paint scrawled the community motto of "A Scenic Trail Fit for Families". Empty beer cans and fresh graffiti painted the uneven sidewalks lining both sides of the main entrance. Moss and stringy weeds extended from the numerous cracks, tinting the pathways a slick green.

On the eastern side, a trio of women strutted in high heels. Each wore a different neon pair matching the sequined skirt fit tight around their hips like plastic wrap. Men tilting over the balconies whistled. Their bodies swayed and liquid sloshed out of the opened cans in their hands.

"Hey, babe." A bloody-eyed man from the nearest balcony tossed his arms in the air. Droplets of beer rained on the sidewalk. "I got somethin' for ya."

The woman in bright orange stilettos jumped out of the line of streaming alcohol. "You wanna play"—she shook her breasts and hiked the skirt higher than it was already—"you gotta pay."

Her two friends followed suit, and the men tapped their cups in blubbering laughter.

"I'll pay," the same man said. He dug into his pockets and flashed a wad of green. "But I play rough."

The guy's friend muttered something. The ladies giggled but then staggered forward to a vacant porch and trifled through their purses.

"Jesus this place is a shithole." Benny's eyes were now on the side mirror. "First thing I'd do with the dough is move my mom outta here. Wouldn't wanna catch—what was it called, Sonny? Gono—"

"Gonorrhea, boss."

"Right. Kid, if you got the means, take care of the family. If you don't, figure it out anyway. Nothing more important. Guess your dad didn't get the memo, huh?"

"I wouldn't know. Haven't seen him in a while. Goin' on six years now."

"Life's a bitch, kid. We all got problems. You're on the right track. Stick with me."

"How much do I make on my first fight?"

"You already got the advance. Depending on bets, you'll clear thirty percent of the purse. Bout like this"—Benny unfolded a stick of gum from its wrapper—"another three." He popped the piece in his mouth and tossed the wrapper out of the window. "Anyway, plenty of dough for a kid to move his momma outta' the gutter."

"It's a start."

"Remember, though. You don't make any money. In this circuit, amateur boxing is unpaid. We're tossing a little your way because we're stand-up guys. Anyone asks, though, you *didn't make money. Capisce?*"

"Yeah."

"All right, good then." Benny peered into the backseat. "So, a few rules to go over."

Richie glanced from the window to the rearview.

"What rules?"

"You gotta girl? A piece of ass you wine and dine?"

"Nope."

"Good. Rule one is simple. While you train, no getting your dick wet. Pussy complicates things. We don't need you chasing tail and getting distracted. Good on that?"

"Yeah."

"Here's the rub, though. You win your first fight, and I'll give you a tasty treat on the house."

"What kind of treat?"

"Her name's Candi. A sweet little dish from Moonlighters. Set of tits you could get lost in and an ass tighter than a snare drum. You'll love her, kid."

"Moonlighters, huh?" A light chuckle passed Richie's lips.

"What's so funny?"

"Me and an old buddy from high school tried to drop in there once."

"And?"

"A fat bouncer with a nightstick sent us on our way down Lilac Road."

"Kid. It's all about who you know."

"So, the girl, she's a hooker?"

"Get a load of the fresh fish, Sonny." Benny nudged his driver's arm and heaved forward. His belly ebbed with the chuckles. "You gotta problem with hookers, young fella?"

"Nah, just never needed one, I guess."

Benny's smirk filled the rearview. "You never *need* a hooker. They're a luxury, not a necessity, kid." He cackled again. "It's a business. Some say the oldest in the world. Prostitutes have been sucking dick since the cavemen times."

"How'd they pay? Twigs and berries?" Sonny cracked a smile from the driver's seat.

"Maybe." Benny's laugh shook the car. "Fuck, Sonny. For a man of few words, the shit that escapes your mouth shines like gold."

Richie giggled then slapped a hand over his mouth. "What's rule two?"

"Just as important. No booze and no drugs. Non-negotiable. You represent us now. Got it?"

Richie offered a shrug but grinned.

"Bold, reputable men must act with a certain decorum." Benny did a partial wink "But it's okay to pay for a service—a blowjob."

"Well, there's a lot to learn, huh?" Richie unlatched his seatbelt and tightened a loose lace on his shoe.

The car pulled up to the apartment, and the normal hoodlums and low-life garbage traversed the sidewalks and balconies. Down the street, in a collage of bright colors and skin, the three women from earlier advanced.

"Look," Benny said with the same serious tone as before, "keep your head in the game."

CHAPTER EIGHTEEN

"I'm all in, sir." Richie stepped out and stood on the sidewalk by the curb.

"Good to hear, kid. Get your mind right. Friday is only three days from now." The Cadillac window hiked up and sped off. It pulled a U-turn, crept by the same three women, and the brake lights flashed.

One more look, eh?

Scaling the porch steps, he shot the customary mind-your-surroundings glance over his shoulder. *Clear*. He reached for the knob and found the door ajar an inch, emitting a soft yellow stripe into the gray outside.

A quick swivel of the head in each direction revealed nothing. Silence.

Mom's already drunk and acting stupid?

She often frequented the rundown cluster of buildings in the rear of the complex. Squatters Row, as the neighborhood called it. A place you could score heroin and contract syphilis in a matter of minutes. *Or gonorrhea?*

It was a quad of four, incomplete two-story buildings. A fire ravaged them during the initial stages of construction, and when the flames ceased, the inspection department levied an inquiry into a possible arson case.

Three years later, the RCPD's investigation crawled like an ant stuck in peanut butter. A case involving the darkest bruise of the city didn't rank high on Ridgemont Cove's to-do list.

Richie's only experience in Squatters Row was more a horror comic than a memory.

A neighbor, now since moved and for a good reason, awakened him at two in the morning. Still foggy-eyed and dreaming, a younger Richie dragged himself to the complex.

"She's in here." The neighbor nudged a door clinging to the hinges with most of the screws missing.

An odor fled the entranceway. Garbage stacked and leaning against bare yellowing walls dispensed staggering odors of rotten meat and waste.

Faint drops of blood splattered the foyer walls and cracked tile flooring. A hallway led to three openings where doors once hung.

Some woman, more a zombie than a human, reached out and stroked his arm. "Quick suck for a buck."

"Don't touch me." Richie shoved her through the first doorway.

She crashed into a huddled group of junkies nodding in and out of consciousness, the drugs taking hold and winning.

The far opening, partially obscured by a mattress standing on end, emanated slight groans.

Young Richie followed the noises, keeping his footsteps as soft as possible. Cockroaches crackled beneath his feet.

He pulled the mattress back. A shirtless man covered in sweat gyrated his hips and howled, forcing himself into the limp body of Richie's mother.

She lay open-mouthed with a syringe jabbed into her

arm. A thin line of blood dripped from the skin and down to the floor.

Horrified, thirteen-year-old Richie thought not of revenge but his mother's safety. Afraid to move though, he cowered outside of the room with a hand over his mouth to muffle the cries. For what seemed like forever, he waited until the man's grunts faded.

Rising, the guy stood to full height. "She's a nice piece of ass, youngin'. Want a turn?"

Richie, grasping the doorknob of his mother's apartment, deleted the memory as best he could. *Move forward not backward.* He pushed inside.

The hallway light flickered in its plastic fixture—strange given his mother's incessant tactics to save money.

You always needed some coin down at Squatters Row, ya know.

A jagged shadow leapt across the living room wall. Richie caught its tail end. A current of adrenaline surged, much like in the alleyway days ago.

Then, the unmistakable click of a cocking gun rebounded in the empty apartment. From behind the separating wall of the kitchen, a masked man with a silver pistol stepped forward. "You alone?"

Richie's hands shot up. "What? Yeah."

"On the ground. Facedown." He jabbed cold steel against Richie's ribs. "Your buddies. They gone?"

"Yeah." He cooperated, kneeled on all fours, and then lowered his frame to the tile.

With the gun pointed toward Richie's head, the masked thug huffed in air with a wheeze like two-pack-a-day smokers often do.

He disappeared from Richie's peripheral. Moments

later, blinds peeled back and scraped the window near the front door.

"All alone," the gunman said. "We're good to go."

The bedroom door hinges yelped. From inside, another disguised figure emerged. He wore all black and held a pistol close to his thigh, a gloved finger tapping its barrel.

"Where's the money?" The second stranger walked the length of the kitchen and stopped a few feet beyond the separating wall. "Lock the door, Harold."

"What money?" Richie craned his head. "Where's my mother?"

"Who's got the fucking gun?" Harold shoved his pistol into Richie's face. "Me or you?" It pressed below the eye socket. "Now, where's the money, tough guy?"

The metallic scent of the firearm wafted, garnering Richie's full attention.

"We know you have cash. Saw you counting it." A stinging odor of nicotine and whiskey filled Richie's nostrils.

You already got the advance.

These were the men perched atop the second-floor balcony five days ago. They'd eyed Richie the afternoon Benny dropped him off.

"Tell me where my mom is." Richie hunched in a push up, as he did so, a boot connected with his ribs, and he toppled over.

"Where's the cash?" The other man sniffled and blew the contents of his left nostril to the tile. Blood stained mucus splatted to the floor near Richie's head.

Harold delivered another kick. Pain streaked through Richie's abdomen and stole the wind from his lungs.

"We know you got it." The second man, the leader, or brains of the operation from what he could tell, circled the living room. "Give it up, and we'll get outta here."

"You're making a big mistake." Richie huffed in air. Another blow forced him to the fetal position, cradling his sides. He languished for a moment, fighting to breathe. *Is she even here?* At last his head perked up from the tile. "Where's my mother?"

"Oh, a tough guy, Harold." The leader kneeled next to Richie then cackled. "Go get her."

The subordinate obeyed, drifting toward the bedroom in a sloppy waddle. From inside the room, garbled shrieks filled his ears like the screech of a squeegee on dry glass. The door slammed shut then shouts gained definitiveness and grew louder. Weight of a body crashed on top of Richie.

"There she is."

Richie rotated his hips and embraced her. Her skeletal figure vibrated. "Are you okay?"

The leader dragged her from Richie's grasp by the hair.

"No," she squealed, drawing it out, and then said something else, but choking tears and a swollen lip impeded the words.

"Where's the money?" The leader asked again, yanking her head to the side and jabbing the barrel of his weapon beneath her chin.

"Let me up, and I'll show you."

"Think we're stupid?" Harold snarled, driving another kick into Richie's exposed ribs.

This strike had no effect. The adrenaline, amplified by absolute anger, traveled in his blood like a live virus. "I think you're very stupid."

"Enough of this shit," the other said, "cough up the money, or mom and I are going to have a little more fun in the bedroom. I've always needed two pumps."

"I could go for seconds." Harold released a shrill giggle.

"Just tell them," she whimpered, crossing her arms as if

to fend off the disgust looming within the room. She fell to her knees.

"Shut up, bitch." The man jerked her hair harder and her chin flung upward, revealing a red circle imprint on her pale throat from the gun's barrel.

Without thinking, Richie launched toward the armed man. The asshole was going to pay. He strained to tackle the leader. Another blow from Harold landed to his side.

Rising again with lungs near collapse, he lunged forward.

Harold drove his shoulder into Richie's chin then slammed the butt of his gun to his forehead. Blinking spots smothered his vision, and he staggered backward and fell to the tile.

"You try that shit one more time," the leader said, "and I'll tie you up and force you to watch. Last chance. Where's the fucking money?"

"I'm going to kill you." Richie allowed his shoulders to hit the floor. He laid flat, staring at the popcorn-textured ceiling of the cheap apartment. Sticky warmth slid down his cheek, tickling the stubble on his face. No pain accompanied the mess.

"Tough talk from a guy on the floor. Doesn't need to be like this." The leader shoved Richie's mother across the room. She landed in the corner of the foyer. Her impact caused something on the other side of the wall to tumble to the floor. It crashed with a thud.

"Give it up, and we'll be gone." Harold now stood beside his partner. "No harm, no foul."

The mouth opening of his mask spread over thin lips. A few blackened teeth poked from the gums, and in the dim light, a shiny gold plate on the bicuspid winked with a dull sheen.

"Tell them, Richie." His mother, wearing a purple blouse he'd bought for her birthday last year, cowered with legs crossed. The shirt, now torn at the shoulder, exposed a red bruise peeping from the fraying strands of fabric.

"Okay. Okay. Top cupboard. Above the fridge. There's a false backing in the cabinet."

The leader stood. "Keep an eye on him." The man cut into the kitchen and disappeared from Richie's view.

Dishes rattled and other objects smacked to the kitchen floor, the echoes reaching the foyer.

Harold, with a gun still pointed at Richie, swayed back and forth like he was on a boat. Pale blue surrounded by stark red blotches peeped out from the eye openings of his mask.

Richie rolled to his stomach, fighting the incessant thumping in his ribs.

"Stay right there." The gun shook in Harold's hand. "I'm warning—"

"Got it," the leader shouted from the kitchen.

Harold's head turned for a slight instant, and Richie sprang into even footing. Staying low and shooting from his stance like a deployed missile, he covered the gap between him and the gunmen in a second.

Harold squeezed the trigger, but no gunfire erupted. He raised the pistol and swung. The clumsy strike bounced off Richie's shoulder, dislodging the weapon and breaking the man's balance.

The gun clipped to the floor.

Richie ripped Harold's mask off, intent on seeing the face of the coward, and continued the assault with a bevy of punches. The strikes split deep rivets above the intruder's eyebrows. He alternated fists now, each blow bouncing Harold's head on the tile with sickening thuds.

His knuckles reddened and grew slick. Blood splattered the sleeves of his hoodie.

An ethereal grunt filled the apartment, and then Harold's body flattened against the floor with a low hiss.

One down, one to go.

Richie searched for the gun. It had landed near the front door, and he crawled to it, leaving bloody handprints across the tile. The gun slipped from his grasp at first, and after Richie dragged his hands down the front of his hoodie, he tried again and snagged the pistol with a firm grip.

Remembering years back, when he and his father had a relationship and actually behaved in that manner, his twelfth birthday came to mind: an outdoor shooting range and gun tutorial.

What was the first step?

He turned the gun in his hands and flipped the safety slide down.

What luck. If this little tab had been pointed the other way, I'd be dead right now.

With caution, Richie gripped the pistol in both hands. The barrel pointed toward the kitchen wall, and his right finger glided into the trigger guard. "Harold's down. Come on out."

Is it loaded?

He pulled the slide, but it wouldn't budge. Fumbling through the process, he tried to remember how these things worked.

What am I missing?

He inspected the firearm, and through sheer luck, grazed the slide stop.

It took three attempts for him to rack the slide, but after jostling for a moment, a bullet flung from the chamber. It dinged to the tile and bounced a few feet closer to his mother.

With an exerted effort, he extended for the bullet and captured it as it spun on its side.

How do I load it?

He examined the weapon again and pressed the magazine release. It slipped out and landed with a bang. Richie scooped it and turned it right-side up. Another bullet, shining bronze, sat ready. He pushed the magazine into the pistol's grip and racked the slide again. Once, this time, is all he needed.

Richie's mother whimpered in the corner of the foyer. Black mascara cascaded down her face like scribbled streets on a map. She clutched her stomach and shivered. He considered moving into the kitchen to pummel the other man, or if necessary, practice his aim. Make him pay for it, all of it. But he had to protect the fallen, the injured—the raped woman who breathed life into him.

"Don't leave me." She moaned like a dying soldier. Her eyesight fell to the gun, and she shuddered, her shoulders shaking like the onset of flu symptoms.

"Are you okay?"

She dove into his opened arms. Her emaciated body trembled against him. "Just don't leave me."

Tears formed channels of water over her cheeks. The mascara roads faded to gray smudges, and she resembled an amateur attempt of Hollywood black-face motion pictures of the early thirties.

"Stay right here. The other one is still in the house." Richie released her, and she shrunk into the corner with a whimper.

He leaned against the wall separating the living room and kitchen. After an internal three-second countdown, he kneeled and rounded into the open space with the gun drawn, scanning left and right.

Clear. Quiet.

Now he eyed the closed bedroom door.

"Last chance, asshole." Richie examined the gun.

Safety off. Magazine clicked. Bullet in chamber. Finger ready.

He turned the knob, heard nothing, and barreled through with the firearm extended straight out.

Clear. Quiet.

"We're okay, ma." His tired arms fell to their respective sides.

Harold's blood dripped from Richie's knuckles, creating dark oval blemishes on the fading carpet of his mother's room.

A square ray of light cut the darkness, illuminating the family quilt lying flat on the bed in a tinted haze.

From the open window, the neighborhood's daily dance of debauchery played like a stereo—drunken exchanges, the whistling of perverts, and the stench of drug abuse. And somewhere within the melee, inaudible but vivid in his mind, the footsteps of a rapist clutching two-thousand dollars faded in the distance.

CHAPTER NINETEEN

The Greyhound's wheels squealed to a stop, and the door opened.

"Last stop. Belleview." Al, the lanky driver with an over-sized nametag, stood. "It's six o'clock and quitting time."

Timothy, the only passenger left, rose. Arms overhead, he stretched, working the kinks from his tired bones and aching muscles.

An overhead compartment stood eye level.

"Need some help?" Al bounced beside Timothy, clicked open the hatch, and grabbed the carry on.

"Thanks." He slipped the backpack over a shoulder and limped from the bus and made a beeline across the street for Milt's BBQ.

The Mom-and-Pop joint smelled like heaven.

"What can I get for ya?" A teen girl, more interested in her phone than the register she manned, smacked a wad of pink bubble gum.

Behind her hung a chalkboard with the weekly specials itemized in blue and pink scrawls. Tuesday offered pulled pork and coleslaw. "Daily deal with extra sauce." Timothy grabbed a chilled drink from the bin marked 'free soda with dinner purchase'.

"One pulled pig and slaw. Wet." She keyed the order in with one hand and scrolled her phone with the other. "For here?"

"Nah." Timothy pulled a ten from his back pocket with the bandaged hand.

"To go," she shouted over her shoulder. "That'll be $4.99." A pink bubble emerged between her pursed lips, grew to a five-inch diameter, and then deflated.

Tired of bland hospital food and room temperature water, his stomach welcomed the change. His mouth drenched in anticipation.

A five-minute wait heightened the excitement. When Little Miss iPhone slid the Styrofoam to-go box across the bar, Timothy took a quick bite, setting his taste buds on a better than sex frenzy.

He bagged the box himself and left, headed toward his parents' house.

The sun began its inevitable droop behind the row of elm trees, and he trekked the dirt path toward *Vietta Corner*, the local moniker for the family pepper farm. Their property sat on seven fenced acres. In the summer, leafy vines ran the length of the land, striping the brown soil in rows of green and yellow. In November, clumped dirt and caving holes pocked the square lot.

He marched up the driveway. Not far from the house, a line of sprinklers moved in unison and bathed the front yard. The tick of their water spray matched the chirps of early-rising crickets.

He climbed the porch steps of the farmhouse. "Anyone home?"

"We're in here." His father's voice traveled through the screen door. It was time for their evening sweet tea siesta.

"This from Mom's private stash?" The garden his mother took such pride in, produced many fine spices and herbs, some of which renowned chefs would envy.

He entered and poured some from the pitcher and swished the liquid, sending the leaves swirling in a tall, chilled glass. Mint tea, a favorite of his mother's since he could remember, provided a sliver of comfort with each sip.

"How does it feel?" His father pointed to his hand.

"I got lucky, pop. It hurts, but it could have been much worse." Timothy extended an arm out to his mom whose cheeks captured slight tears. "Really, ma. I'm fine."

"How long you here for?" His father drained the glass.

"For a bit. If that's okay."

"Of course, it is." His mother gave him a quick squeeze.

"Where is Annabelle?" He held his father's gaze.

"Over with the Bransons for supper. They have a little girl her age." His dad stood and arched his back, a popping of tendons palpable. "We'll set your room up."

The next morning, Timothy sat cross-legged on the porch, twirling a piece of straw in the uninjured hand. His eyes diverted from the strand of hay to the aging oak in the front yard.

Annabelle, his sweet baby girl, swung from the tire Timothy's father installed many years ago. She swayed back and forth with a smile pasted on her face, yellow pigtails bouncing in rhythm. The tire swing appeared from the shadows, caught the vibrant sun's glow, and then receded back into the cloak of the tree's shade.

She looks like her. The same button nose and wide eyes. The chin slight and delicate.

"Daddy, watch this." Annabelle squealed and rotated

herself in the tire. It spun in a circle, and she roared in delight.

"I see you, Bella." The front door creaked open, and Timothy's neck craned.

His father emerged from the doorway with two beers in hand. He sat on the landing beside Tim and extended a cold bottle.

"Little early, huh?" Timothy took the beer and popped the cap. "Thanks."

"She's getting big. How long's it been since you've seen her?" He tilted the bottle back and took a swig. His sun-reddened face, both wrinkled and sad, revealed an older man than he remembered. Beneath his ball cap, graying hair peeked out from under the brim.

"Too long." Timothy matched his father's gulp. It burned, and he couldn't recall the last time he'd enjoyed an ice-cold brew in the sun.

"She's blood. Always welcome."

"She's lucky to have you guys."

His father took a swig of the beer and drew a glance toward the tree. "Be better if she had a stable set of parents. Have you seen Ruby?"

"Nope." The mere mention of *her* name shot tingles through his chest. "Not for a long time. I want to check in on her, though."

"I talk with her every once in a while. She seems to be doing better. You can hear it in her voice." His gaze drifted to his vacant planting field. "I sent her some pictures of Bella a few weeks back."

"Thanks, pop. I appreciate you keeping her involved. I'm sure it means a lot to her." He took a swift swig from the bottle. "Mom playing nice?"

"She is a stubborn woman. Things take time, son.

Things got ugly. She's trying to protect you—you and the little one. That's it."

Annabelle squealed in the tire. She evaporated behind a thick carpet of shade for a second and then swooshed down with a giggle.

"So, what's the plan, Tim?" His father chugged for a moment and belched. The faint circles of light purple beneath his eyes bulged. "You got any clue?"

"Not sure. I need to get back in the gym." Timothy sipped his beer and caught his daughter's next descent from the shadows.

Her giggles carried on the slight breeze, providing a pleasant undertone to the now uncomfortable conversation he knew would transpire but was not ready to participate in.

"The gym? You serious? Look at your hand." He pointed at Timothy's bandaged appendage with both brows creased in disbelief.

"Gotta start rehabbing. I can't let them win, dad."

"What? You think you stand a chance? I'm not pretending to know it all. You've done a good job of hiding the last few years." He drained the rest of the beer and burped again. "But take the hint."

"Huh?"

"Next time they'll kill you. That"—he pointed to Timothy's hand—"was a warning. You do understand that?"

Timothy rubbed at his forehead, scraping the stubble of his shaved head. "I should have never come back here."

"Then why did you?"

Timothy cast a solemn look to Annabelle. "Just wanted to see her."

"You can have her, son. It's over. Come home."

"I can't. I'm sorry you don't understand that."

"You were always tough. Not sure it's a good thing." Looking away, he twirled the empty beer bottle by its neck.

"Learned it from my dad." Timothy forced a smile and sipped again.

"Well, this is different." He now held Timothy's gaze. "You're talking about Salvador Purelli. Tough doesn't matter if they don't play by the rules."

"I gotta try." The staples in his head itched and ached. *Percocet needs to do a better job.*

"I'm worried about you." He gripped Timothy's knee and squeezed. "You're my blood. I love you more than you'll ever know."

"I love you too, dad." Timothy's voice softened amid a stifled sob fighting to rise from within. "You gotta trust me on this."

"So, you're going to fight the mob? Jesus Christ, Tim." The old man's hands shot up, palms visible and vibrating. "How much do you need to lose before you quit boxing?"

"It's the only thing I've ever been good at." Timothy tilted the bottle and emptied the backwash to the dirt at the foot of the staircase. He then pointed to Annabelle. "I do it for her, you know?"

"My point is you don't have to, son. I'm not getting any younger. Move back here, take over the farm, and be a father to your little girl. She needs you."

"I spent every summer plowing, planting, and plodding. Every winter, chopping wood. It's not me. I don't want to be a fifty-seven-year-old man digging in the dirt."

"Rather be twenty-four and dead, huh?" His father's eyes became razors, an expression followed by a stiff smack to the jaw in other circumstances.

"You know what I mean."

"I'm afraid I don't. Digging in the dirt has served me

well. I've provided for my family, and now for yours. I've created wealth. And equally important, I *am* a respected member of the community. I don't look over my shoulder every day hoping I'll live until five o'clock."

Timothy's chin dropped to his chest. He clipped the bridge of his nose between the pointer and thumb of the undamaged hand. Embarrassment washed through him. He had no right to challenge his father's livelihood but raising Annabelle on a pepper farm had never been an option. The plans were different a few years back. Benny's claims of outrageous money were intoxicating, and the reward outweighed the risk.

"You've been playing a dirty game for a while. Your mother doesn't sleep, son. I don't care how fast you can prance around a ring and punch other men. It's meaningless. You can't outrun a bullet. You're a farmer, Timothy Daniel. It's part of your blood."

"It's what *you* want, pop. It's always been what you wanted. Gramps taught you, and it worked. You passed on the knowledge to me, and it didn't. Aren't I allowed to make my own choices?"

"You've made a few bad ones." Timothy's father rose. The wooden steps groaned, and a second later, the hinges of the screen door protested in a high pitch. "See there. Always something needs fixing. I could really use another set of hands around here."

Timothy, still facing Bella's oak tree, swiveled his neck and dropped his chin to his shoulder. "I've got to do this. I'm sorry."

"And while you're fighting and chasing mobsters, how do I explain to your daughter daddy's gone again? Farming may not be in your future, but being a father is. There's no getting around it, son."

Irritated by the tone of the conversation and gaining less acceptance from his father with each passing sentence, he stood. "I've got to get going. My Jeep still here?"

"I imagine it's in the garage." He jabbed a thumb in the direction of the detached building sleeping beneath the shade of more oaks. "No mobster limousine coming to pick you up this time, huh?"

"Those days are over, dad. Do you have the keys?" Timothy extended his hand.

"So, that's it? Gone again?"

"When I'm back next time, it's for good."

CHAPTER TWENTY

"Ma, it's okay. I'll be fine." Richie drew his mother to his chest like a parent cradling a crying child. "You gotta go. It's not safe here."

The ghost face she wore, pale and blank, revealed vulnerability. "We could call the police. Tell them about the men who—"

"No." He held her at arm's length, resisting the urge to shake sense into her for fear he would bruise her twig arms, brittle from osteoporosis. "We're gonna handle it. No five-oh."

"But they"—she pulled the ripped blouse over her body and tears welled in her eyes— "what they did."

A booming knock echoed in the room.

"Hey, kid?" Benny's gruff voice carried. "It's me."

"Yeah. One sec'." Richie grasped his mother's shoulders. "Ma, go to Cynthia's and stay away from the Row."

Richie opened the door, and she slid by without saying anything else.

"Start from the beginning." Benny stepped in with

Sonny at his heels. He pointed to the cut on Richie's head. "Wait a minute. What happened?"

"I'm fine."

"It's a problem if they don't let you fight."

"I don't care about that." Richie's outburst surprised even him. He waited for a verbal assault from Benny or even a smack from Sonny. Neither happened. "This is all that matters." Richie shuffled from the foyer into the small dining room and the two gangsters followed.

The trio formed a semi-circle around the bound intruder.

Harold, a colorful mummy, tied to a dining room chair with bungee cords and neckties and hosiery, sat wide-eyed. A thick welt protruded from his forehead, and a large gash seeped liquid beneath it.

Richie pointed to the beaten man using the silver gun. For some reason, he liked the power it possessed. Its weight and smooth grip felt natural, almost innate. "Here's the asshole."

"Where the hell did you get the piece?" Benny asked, his eyes on the pistol in Richie's hand. "Is that thing loaded?"

"It's his. And no, I took the magazine out." He flipped the gun upside down to reveal the empty grip then tapped his pocket with the free hand. "Got it here."

"Don't mean there's not one in the chamber." Sonny tried to swipe it.

"All right." Benny spread his hands out toward both men as if separating two fighters in a clinch. "Been enough bullshit already. Now, what's the deal with this blubbering mess?"

"They came in here last night, in my home. This guy, Harold, and his buddy."

"You're just calling me now?"

"I didn't know what to do."

"Um." Sonny nudged Richie's arm. "Kidnapping isn't a smart thing to do. What was your plan here, shit-for-brains?"

"I don't know. I thought I could figure this out. Been up all night and realized I needed your help."

"Help with what?" Benny asked.

"They stole my dough."

"The two g's?"

"Yeah. My advance."

"Wait a minute. You called me over here because this punk stole two grand?" Benny eased the muzzle of Richie's pistol down. "Watch where you're pointin' that thing."

"I told you. It's empty."

"A gun is never empty, kid." Sonny motioned with two fingers to holster the weapon. "Don't aim unless you plan on firing."

Benny cleared his throat and nodded toward Harold. "On the phone this morning, you made it sound like you were dying. What do you want me to do about this?"

"I want you to protect your investment." The words dripped like venom, and Richie recoiled, aware his tone was out of line.

"Come again?"

"People in this town need to know who I am. I'm with you guys now." The next words, purposefully cautious, floated in the air, and hung. "Protect your investment."

Benny's eyes widened, and he yanked Richie's arm, spinning him toward the kitchen and away from Harold.

"Let's get something clear here, kid. This ain't a business partnership. You work *for* us."

"You put your stamp on me, right? I'm representing the Solanos. People gotta know."

"He's right, boss." Sonny leaned in to join the whispered huddle.

"Oh, you want to chime in, too? I forgot this was a fucking democracy. I'm in charge here, not you two cocksuckers."

Sonny stepped back with his hands up, and Richie shot him a glance. A nemesis before, but now an ally. Even though he held a grudge after Sonny popped him in the barn, the two had made amends.

It's just business, kid. Sonny said later. *Get used to it.*

Benny glared at the bleeding drunk tied in the chair.

The guy was half-conscious. His head bounced from his chin to the air, like a toddler fighting to stay awake.

"Damn." Benny let out a long breath that whistled more than a kettle over a flame. "I think he pissed himself."

"He's going to do a lot more." Richie drove the butt of the gun into Harold's cheek. It welted in seconds.

The man groaned and rolled his shoulder over the balloon forming beneath his skin.

"Okay, okay." Benny grabbed Richie's wrist, but the grip on the gun was glue. "This isn't the movies. How's the guy gonna talk if he's dead?"

It's just business.

"He should be dead." Richie leaned against the foyer wall; the gun still secured.

"What about the other guy? The one with the cash. Did you get a look at him?"

"They were both wearing these." Richie lifted a black mesh mask smelling of rum and sweat.

"What can you tell me?" Benny laced his fingers

through Harold's hair and yanked, jolting the man's head back in the process.

Harold's lids opened then slid shut. Both nostrils leaked blood to the floor. Red circles splattered on the cheap tile. The bridge had cracked beneath the skin, and a jagged cut, now growing in volume, sprang toward his left eye.

"He's just some guy I met in lockup last week." A low whistle accentuated Harold's words from the air passing through his broken nose. "He said he knew where we could get some quick cash. Gave me the mask and gun, and we came here. I swear, I don't know nothing else."

"You got my smokes, Sonny?"

Sonny tiptoed around the crimson puddles on the floor and handed over a Marlboro then sparked a flame for the boss.

"Harold, right?" Benny exhaled. A whirl of smoke escaped his lips.

"Yeah." Harold's half-open eyes followed Benny's voice. Each one blackened and swelling larger with each passing moment.

"I'm afraid you're gonna have to do better."

"What do you want from me? That's all I know."

Benny jabbed the cigarette to Harold's neck.

"Fuck." The low-life struggled against the restraints. "I got nothing, man."

CHAPTER TWENTY-ONE

The foul odor of burnt hair dangled in the air.

"I can do this all day." Benny twirled the shaft of the cigarette between his fingers. "If you don't give me more"—he took a drag—"my friend here is going to bash your puny brains in. And I'm not going to be inclined to stop him."

"Nothing else to give." The shrieks morphed into pathetic blubbering. "I'm telling the truth."

The fresh burns on Harold's neck festered and reddened like a high-speed sunburn on a July beach day.

The bleeding man shrugged his shoulders to his neck with a whimper. Sweat dripped from his bangs, the liquid transforming the bruises on his face into the color of plums.

"That's your story, eh?" Benny flicked the cigarette to Harold's face. He glanced to Sonny. "Hey, is my drill in the car?"

Sonny pressed forward and fished the car keys from his pocket. "Yeah, boss."

"Drill?" The bound man squirmed, lifting the chair a few inches from the floor in a pathetic attempt to escape confinement.

"Yeah," Benny mused, grabbing the keys. "You want to play tough? I'll start drilling holes through your chest."

"No. Wait!" Harold's pleas reached a high pitch. "I'll talk."

"You better start." Benny tracked toward the front door. "Because I'm feeling like Bob fuckin' Vila right now."

"Okay. Okay." Harold's head drooped and a flush of red poured from his nostrils and splashed to his lap. "What do you want?"

"Let's start with his name, dickhead."

"Greg? Georgie, maybe. Hell, I don't know. He said, '*easy cash*,' and I was thinking about powder. We weren't best friends or nothing. It was supposed to be quick. Please, I—"

Richie jumped from the wall and slammed the silver pistol into Harold's face. "You drug addict piece of shit. That's what this is about?"

Benny cut between Richie and Harold. "If I gotta tell you one more time, it'll be the last. We clear, tough guy?"

Richie retreated to the wall with a sly smile. A gash above Harold's right eye dripped dark sludge. The cut widened from the weight of the blood and trickled to junkie's mouth as it gained momentum.

"Get this guy off me." Harold bounced in the chair, but the neckties and cords refused to give.

Benny grabbed him by the collar, unleashed a backhand that echoed in the hallway and then sat him upright. "You said you met in lock up, right?"

"We were released Tuesday night." Tears and blood clogged Harold's nose and throat, meddling his words.

"If I get a picture, could you point him out?"

"Yeah. No more, man. I'm . . ." His head dipped forward and then fell limp.

Benny turned to Richie. "Come here."

Sonny followed into the kitchen.

"I got a few people I trust on the RCPD payroll. I'll get a list of names and pictures of people released from jail Tuesday night. Sonny and I will head over there. In the meantime, kid, you stay here." Benny clutched Richie's shoulder. "And for Christ's sake, don't kill the poor bastard."

"They raped my ma." Richie's eyes widened. Small drops surfaced in the lower lids. "Either way, he dies."

"What do you mean they raped your mom?" Benny's grip on Richie softened and his shoulders hunched. "You serious?"

"They were laughing about it. Sick pricks. I want them dead." The last sentence boomed, eliciting a shriek from Harold.

"Check the emotion for a second." Benny's thoughts wandered to his own mother, an illiterate immigrant who struggled through three menial jobs to keep shoes on his feet and food in his belly. "I feel for you, but you're not in charge. Understand?"

"If it was your mom, what would you do?"

Cut him into a million pieces and feed him to the gulls at Punch's Point, that's what.

"It ain't me, kid. There's a difference between you and me."

"What's that?"

"I've been in this life for long enough to earn that right. You want revenge? Vindication? You play by the fucking rules."

"What am I supposed to do then?"

"For starters, not call me. But now, you got me involved, so we play it my way, or we hang up the cleats and call it a night." He patted Richie's face and drew him in, keenly aware of the kid's slight tremble, the kind that accompanied tears unwilling to pour. "There's a code in this business. Chain of command. You understand?"

"Yeah." Richie broke free from Benny's embrace and returned to the foyer with the gun still gripped in his palm.

Sonny followed his exit and wrapped an arm around him. "It's okay, kid. We'll set it right."

Richie's gaze stayed locked on Harold and he didn't respond.

"Sonny"—Benny slapped his partner's back—"you stay here. Richie comes with me."

CHAPTER TWENTY-TWO

Rage with a side of vulnerability proved hard to swallow. Outside on the porch steps, Richie choked on the raw emotions.

"Park it." Benny dialed a number into his cell phone and brought the device to his ear. "Take a breather." His eyes ping-ponged from the buildings across the road to the sidewalk.

Richie didn't obey. Instead he tapped the gun beneath his shirt and drew a glance toward the half-burned buildings in the distance. The late afternoon sun tinted the sky, and the battered apartments bathed in its orange hue.

Benny didn't seem to mind or notice his disobedience and huffed into the phone. "Hey, it's me." He stepped a few feet from the porch and stared at the onlookers across the street.

Richie caught his gaze and followed its direction.

A pair of men on the third-floor balcony smoked cigars. Their heads bounced in rhythm to the beat of music blaring from a stereo.

Down the street at the mouth of Squatters Row, a trio of standing skeletons huddled, their eyes darting across the complex. Two of them exchanged items in a slick handshake.

Richie peered beyond them and saw a couple seated near the entrance of one of the buildings. A horde of people exited, and the pair moved from the step to avoid being trampled.

Thoughts of his mother, defenseless and broken, resurfaced. He'd told her to leave. Be safe. *Stay away from the Row.*

In his heart, though, he knew mom skipped past Cynthia's apartment and joined the fray of addled drug users. By now, she was on a flea-infested mattress with a needle pricking her arm.

He'd find her after. *One problem at a time.*

Covering the mouthpiece of the cell phone, Benny glanced over his shoulder. "You still got the piece?"

"Yeah." Richie lifted his shirt. The gun's handle laid flat against his taut abs and jabbed out from the waistband. Deadly metal grazing skin, the power intoxicating.

"Hand it over."

"Not until he's dead." His hand cinched onto the grip as if losing it meant certain death.

"Listen, you little prick." Benny covered the cell phone with one hand. "Once I get my friend in the PD to give us photos, we're gonna take care of it. But killing two guys over a couple grand brings heat. Staying off the radar is more important than your pride or revenge. Enough of the tough-guy shit. Give me the gun."

"So, what, we get the cash back and send them on their merry way? They violated my mom, Benny. They know where she lives. What's to stop them from coming back?"

"What's to stop me from cracking your fucking head open? Don't say another word."

Richie huffed and dropped his shoulders.

The cigar smokers leaned over the railing of their balcony, intrigued by the show unfolding. Loud obscenities in quick succession poured through the radio's speaker.

Benny glared at the men, who, after a short stand-off, receded from view, and the volume of the rapper's voice dulled to low a murmur.

"It needs to be approved. Chain of command, kid."

Richie relented, though an urge for vengeance consumed him. However, compromising the relationship with Benny, and Purelli too, meant violence would tread on this doorsill sooner than later.

The revelation stung.

A brutal beating of the mummy tied to his mother's garage-sale chair quelled some of the hatred, but it left the two men alive. *Do they deserve that?*

His life would become jittery glances through the window when headlights flashed the pane. Locking doors and then checking again.

"This isn't a request." Benny held his hand out. "Give it here."

Richie obeyed, but the grip of the weapon stuck for a moment in his hand.

"Okay, thanks," Benny said into the phone. "Drop them in the usual spot." Benny killed the call, stuck the gun in his waistband, and then pointed to the Cadillac.

"Your guy gonna help us?" Richie opened the door.

"I'm getting photos." Benny double-timed around the car. "We'll have them in an hour or two."

"Where we going now?"

Benny ignored the question. "Get in the car."

Richie slid in.

A blur of houses and trees manifested and evaporated through the tinted window. He said nothing as they departed The Trails. Not a single word uttered when the interstate exit ramp appeared in the shoulder of the highway, and when Benny blabbered on about making smart choices and not taking stuff personal, Richie seethed but remained silent.

The vision of the masked man on top of his mother replayed like a smut film where the reel cuts distorted the picture. Unable to shake the thought, he embraced it. Wanted to *feel* it. So later, he'd possess justification for the degradation inflicted upon those responsible.

He pictured their bodies contorted, his mother frozen in fear, the animals forcing themselves into her.

The memory see-sawed from today's events and the horror show of six years ago in the Row. Cowering and unable to help, thirteen-year-old Richie froze in fear. His mother flat and unmoving, enduring a brutal rape that may as well have seemed like a dream. He didn't know if in her drug-induced stupor she recalled that night.

She remembered today's assault. The clear eyes and tears proved it. *And if he'd been there this time?* No cowering. No uncertainty.

The movie replayed for thirty minutes, each version more vivid and graphic. Every time it reran, the anger and rage bubbled within him. Guilt crept in as well, needling through the emotions. It all started with the envelope of cash.

Just a little taste, kid.

With hands cramping from gripping into each other, the blood found no solace between his fingers. His mind drifted from the past to the present, and when Benny smacked his arm and said, “Hey, I’m talking to you,” Richie thought only *they’re going to die.*

CHAPTER TWENTY-THREE

The Cadillac parked in front of the same secluded barn. Hidden from the roadway and two miles from the nearest house, it provided privacy for numerous crimes over the years and would serve its purpose again.

Benny clicked the ignition off. "You ready?"

"What are we doing here?"

"Protecting our investment. C'mon."

Richie followed his lead and trudged behind.

Benny unlocked the crossing bar on the door and slid it up. An earthy wind sliced through the creaking boards lifting a robust and musty odor from its planks.

He curved right and fiddled with the shiny padlock on the rusted doorknob of the storage room then jammed a thin key into the lock. It clicked open.

"You ever kill anyone?" Benny's brow rose in an exaggerated arc.

Of course not, you little prick. That changes today, though. One way or the other.

"No," Richie whispered under his breath.

Benny squared his shoulders and lifted his palms upward. "These hands have. It's not something you forget."

The memories of his various victims played through his mind like a VHS tape on fast-forward.

Eleven.

The tape stopped, and the corpse of Joey "Bombers" centered in his mind's eye.

A propensity for explosives gave the moniker life. After falling out of favor with Freddy Solano, who at the time was still healthy and free, a fresh-faced and thinner Benny Bianchi accepted the contract.

Benny stalked the target's movements, most of which revolved around Joey's nightclub The Vista, a dumping ground of scum and sinners pounding liquor and snorting coke. "Bombers" lived a life of routine which included sticking his cock in pretty blondes who couldn't vote yet.

The Vista closed at three in the morning. "Bombers" spent the next half hour dropping cash in a safe and settling bar tabs with some of the regulars. Then, almost every night, an underage and giddy barmaid snuck over to his parked silver coupe. After casing the joint for a week, Benny planned the attack.

On a warm and clear June morning, Joey's head was cocked back on the headrest of the driver's seat, enjoying a young mouth engulfing his prick. Benny blasted three shots through the windshield.

"I don't understand." Richie's head shook.

"Of course not." Benny popped the padlock from its stem. "You have no fucking clue and can't understand because you've never opened the vault."

"The vault?"

"Yeah. When you kill someone, it opens." Benny

unhooked the lock and dropped it into his coat pocket. "The ghosts can't get out. They're in there forever."

"Ghosts?"

"Hell ya. Scratching, reminding you they're dead, and it's your fault." He nudged the storage door open with his toe. An acidic, lurching odor cut the air. Heat expelled from the opening carrying the stale stench of urine, feces and sweat.

Richie fell back a few feet, as if the room produced hurricane gusts of wind. "Jesus Christ." He hunched over coughing. A few seconds later, he straightened and tapped his chest. "What's that smell?"

"Someone dying. Another ghost for the vault."

"What are you talking about?"

"The fucking vault." The mobster tapped his temple vigorously. "Where the ghosts reside. Inside your mind. There forever."

"How many do you have?"

"You wearing a wire? You trying to get the jump on me?"

"What? No."

"Prove it. Lose the jacket."

"Are you serious?"

Benny jerked Harold's pistol from his waistband and pointed it toward the kid. *Someone dies today. I hope it's not you.* "Take it off."

"All right." Richie shrugged out of his hoodie then pulled the white tee over his head. He turned in a circle. "There, you happy."

"Can't be too careful. Nothing personal." He lowered the gun and lodged it into his pants. "Now, what did you ask me?"

"How many people have you killed?" Richie slid the hoodie back on.

"Eleven and counting." Benny's stomach turned over on itself, like an ice cream dispensary in an old malt shop, where the cream churned in a plastic window for the customer to see. "Not something I'm proud of."

"It happens to everybody?"

"What, the vault? As far as I know. Doesn't matter if you're a sociopath, an average Joe, or an army vet." Benny grabbed Richie's elbow and guided him to the door's threshold. "The vault is built with the first death you're responsible for. I don't care how sick or sane you are. Even Charlie Manson has a vault. I guaran-fucking-tee he's got one."

"What are you getting at, man?"

"You ready to open yours?" Benny crept into the room. "Come on."

Vomit bubbled upward, and he swallowed hard. No matter how many depraved and disgusting things he involved himself in, the smell of the abducted and neglected never got easier to endure.

The thin rope brushed his cheek. With a yank, the room glowed in a soft yellow.

A stained brown wall with hung tools sat opposite a built-in shelving area holding cattle feed.

A moan wafted into the damp, musty air and echoed.

In a crumpled mess, Roger Cranswell lay bound at the wrists and ankles, clothed in rags and soiled in excrement. Brown stains of hardened blood caked the dirt floor like morbid sponge paintings.

"Jesus Christ. Who is this?" Richie, a few feet behind Benny, gagged and coughed again. He swallowed hard enough for Benny to hear, as if forcing rising bile down his throat.

"His name is Roger Cranswell." Benny pinched the bridge of his nose.

A bloodied, gaunt face with hollow eyes tilted toward Benny's voice. The skeletal expression of the doomed man. Dry skin covered his lips, forming flaky yellow patches. Old blood had matted most of the man's frizzled hair.

Richie shot Benny a confused look. "This the guy on the news?"

"One and the same. A poor investment." Benny retrieved Harold's gun again and extended the firearm. The grip jutted toward Richie. "Take it, kid."

Richie's mouth gaped open, but his hand reached for the silver pistol.

"This ain't the movies. There's no coming back from murder." He released his hold on the weapon. "If you squeeze the trigger and someone dies, your vault opens."

Richie palmed Harold's gun. "I'm sorry. I didn't mean to disrespect you. I know it's not easy."

"There's the problem. You don't know shit. You think you do, but you don't. This guy has been here for a while." Benny leaned over Roger Cranswell and studied his face. Thin and ascetic like the survivors liberated in Auschwitz. "I got orders this morning, but my vault's getting crowded."

"What did he do?"

"It doesn't matter." Benny broke his examination of the condemned and shifted his focus to Richie, who now stood motionless with wide and blank eyes. "Orders are orders."

Roger Cranswell twitched and whimpered.

"Put a bullet in his head."

"What?"

"No, wait." Cranswell shimmied toward the open doorway, gaining less than an inch with each exhaustive shrug through the dirt.

"I've got no beef with this guy." Richie slid over some mud-infused hay and lost his footing. His forearm scraped the shelf and a few coffee cans tumbled to their sides, vomiting various nuts and bolts to the dirt floor.

"Kinda like I don't care about those assholes in your apartment." Benny tapped the gold watch on his wrist. "Time's ticking, kid."

"This is wrong." Richie shook his head, bringing a sensitive glance to the bound man.

"Murder is never right. Doesn't matter if it's this guy or dear old Harold at your mom's house. Either way it's wrong." Benny nudged forward, standing inches from Richie's face. "But we do what is necessary. It's business. Never personal."

"No, this is different." Richie's hand shivered, and the gun clicked against his jeans.

"See, that's what you're not getting. It's the same. Any life is life." Benny pointed to Cranswell, who by now had only four feet to reach the door, though those inches may as well have been miles. "You say we should protect our investment. I gotta make sure this is long-term. You understand? We can handle those perverts who hurt your mother, but nothing gets done until I know you're serious about this business."

"So, what are you saying?"

"It's time to open your vault."

"I can't." Richie dropped the pistol to the floor. It bounced off Cranswell's foot and fell to the dirt with a thud.

"You've gotta choice, kid." Benny gripped Cranswell's feet and pulled him into the room. He then walked to the door with palms raised. "What's it gonna be?"

Cranswell rolled over, tears gushing, a yellowed hand raised and trembling. "You don't have to do this. Please."

Richie looked to the doorway and then to the man. "I have to. I'm sorry."

"No, you're not." Benny's voice rose above Cranswell's cries. "It ain't personal, so you ain't sorry."

"I have a wife. Kids. Please. I just want to go home." The man's pleas echoed, and for a moment, Benny felt a tinge of guilt.

It passed.

Richie leaned against the wall then drooped down. He crawled to the gun.

A guttural, exhausted shriek ripped loose from the condemned businessman's throat.

Richie knelt to one knee and trained the barrel to the Cranswell's forehead. "You don't"—he wiggled in a pathetic, slow-motion heave like a pupa in a caterpillar chrysalis—"You don't. Please."

The kid wiped sweat, or maybe tears, or both from his face and stood. The tough-guy shit evaporated. Now, his eyes screamed *help me,* but his hands held firm to the pistol.

That's it, kid.

Cranswell continued the desperate lurch to salvation. A final physical plea to safety. But in the warm embrace of the barn, one of two things happened: rebirth or death.

Richie gripped the handle and aimed, steadying the weapon amid watery eyes.

You're one of us now or you're not, Benny thought. "Bombers" popped back into his head, a reminder everyone had to start somewhere.

As if on cue, Richie pulled the trigger.

CHAPTER TWENTY-FOUR

When Richie opened his eyes, finger still squeezing the trigger, he saw the damage—a hole the width of a dime above Cranswell's hollow, closed right eye.

A jagged line of red dripped over the bridge of his nose and into his gaped mouth. The entrance wound, a slice of charred black skin, widened. Blood escaped his body one final time.

"Give me the piece." Benny pulled a handkerchief from his pocket and flattened it over both of his hands. "Right here."

Richie obeyed without response. His stomach pitched, and his mind reeled under construction. *A new vault coming to a town near you.*

Benny wiped the grip, slide and barrel then gave the trigger extra attention. He dropped it next to Cranswell's corpse. "Let's go."

Back in the Cadillac, Benny clicked the engine on and tossed the handkerchief into the center console. He adjusted the heat. "The first one is the worst. It'll pass."

Richie heard Benny's words of encouragement and

attempted to reply, but his throat bubbled. He propped the door open and spewed his half-eaten lunch onto the dirt driveway. Returning to his seat, a weak apology ejected from his mouth.

"Proud of you," Benny continued, shifting the car in to reverse. "You've earned a stripe in my book."

The car backed down the path.

"What happens now?" Richie wiped droplets of blood from his hands. The liquid smeared and faded but stuck to his skin. "With—"

"—not your concern." Benny plucked the handkerchief from his breast pocket and tossed it into Richie's lap. "Clean yourself up."

What would become of Cranswell's body? Richie couldn't help but wonder. Benny said it didn't matter. *So, what,* he thought, *I leave it at that?*

"What about fingerprints? DNA? Shit, man."

"The gun ain't registered to you. DNA? You never touched him. Besides, once he's gone, he's gone. Lotta undisturbed holes in the ground."

A surging flare of guilt swept through him. *Once he's gone.* "I just killed him, Benny."

"Never say that again."

"What?"

Benny's head turned, and the blasting fire of his eyes told Richie to use common sense, for once.

Little dabs of Roger Cranswell had misted his face and now stained the white, pristine cloth he held.

"You'll learn to live with it, kid. Welcome to the big leagues." Benny snatched the handkerchief and shoved it into his shirt pocket.

"So, now what?" Swelling fear thumped his chest. A

sickening feeling resonating and piercing his side muddled his voice. "Harold?"

"I'll take care of it. Get your mind right. You go get a bite to eat. Show those pearly whites in public. Sonny's got Harold and I'm working on his partner. You called us for help, so let us help."

Though the Cadillac cruised in the fast lane at ninety, the drive back to Ridgemont Cove played in slow motion. Each car they passed or sign that whizzed by reminded Richie the real world still engrossed them. Life, as it was, marched on. *Well, for some.*

Silence languished between them in the front seat, weighing on Richie's shoulders. He snapped from the coma as the car skidded toward Center Street.

"Look." Benny flicked the turn signal with his thumb and checked the rear view. "Go in the diner and order something." The Cadillac slowed.

"I'm not hungry." Cranswell's face emerged from the cloud of thoughts swirling within. The wound in his brow seeped black and smoke twirled in the opening. "I want—"

"I don't give a shit about what you want. This is your stop." Benny pulled next to the payphone in front of the diner. His pudgy finger pointed toward it. "Use that phone to call me in two hours. You remember my number?"

"Yeah." He pushed through the door without another word and climbed the steps.

After a brief greeting, Ms. May poured him a slew of Arabian medium roast. Ten minutes later, he sat propped on the barstool emotionless, his vision focused on the cup of coffee sitting cold and bitter on the counter.

An old couple in the rear booth stared at his reflection in the mirror. He was sure of it.

We know what you did, young man. It's written all over your face.

"Them some dangerous people you runnin' with." Ms. May jolted Richie from the ridiculous paranoia.

He lifted his head. "Uh-huh."

In a studio apartment down the street, a bound man at the mercy of Sonny Denardo slipped in and out of consciousness. In a Cadillac, Benny Bianchi trolled through the neighborhood in search of information. Intel that would crack another life in half. Somehow *dangerous* didn't quite describe them accurately.

"Ms. May knows a thing or two, boy," she continued, spraying the bar with blue fluid and wiping the drops in swooping circles. "They dangerous."

"You have no idea."

"Sure enough, I do. Them fellas walk around town like they're movie stars or something. Tell ya one thing, boy, this ain't Hollywood."

Richie peered out the window. A white Impala pulled to the curb, its tint masking the driver in darkness. Beyond the vehicle, a couple jaywalked and jumped the median.

Ms. May rounded the bar, offered a mechanical smile to the elderly folks in the booth, and then sat on the stool next to him.

"I've never seen ya in here so late. Almost early bird time."

"Training hard." He lied. "I gotta win."

"Or what?"

"I need the cash. If I win, I get more money." The fact she thought he'd been training all morning and not committing a murder made Richie feel shameful. "Move my ma and me to a different area, safer." If she'd known the truth, it would break her heart and end one of the few meaningful relationships he had.

"We all need money. How's you go about getting it is up to you, ain't it? My momma always said, 'Black folk better get used to making green, cuz without it, we in trouble.' I was never afraid to put in a hard day's work, but never did I get mixed with them types of men."

"Well, my mom doesn't say much, Ms. May." Richie envisioned Roger Cranswell's mother, bloodshot eyes bulging from crying.

Once he's gone, he's gone. The vault doors, brilliant with resplendent gold hinges, parted and wrenched open.

Cranswell's bony face, a pale white illumination in a stark black backdrop, appeared with a snarking smile. The bullet hole prevalent and dark. His death real and overpowering.

"Well, I say a lot, Richie. And I'm telling ya, stay away from them. They're bad eggs—rotten to the core."

Richie huffed—*if it were only so easy. If I could pry the bullet from his head, load it into the pistol, and stick the steel barrel in my throat maybe then, I'd be able to stay away from them. Stay away from it all.*

Now, he knew better. Turned out to be far much more information than he'd ever dreamt of.

It's just business.

"Hopefully, I win a few fights, and I'm able to get outta here."

"Men like them won't let you leave, boy. Once you walk in the kitchen, they'll expect you to cook."

The bell above the door chimed, and a man stepped through the entrance. He offered a slight smile, and with caution, grimaced with each strut. With a swollen cheek and bandaged hand, he fell into a booth nestled behind the old folks.

Ms. May offered a cheery smile and waddled over. "Welcome to Ms. May's. Just you this evening?" She held a mug at eye level. "Coffee?"

"Yeah. And tonight's special."

"Comin' right up." She scribbled his order on a guest-check booklet.

Richie sipped his coffee, now frigid and tasteless, and used the mirror to watch the stranger.

The face and frame jogged a memory, but Richie struggled to attach a name to the body. Beat to shit, but broad in the shoulders and chest, he resembled an athlete. A fighter, maybe.

"Know him, boy?" Ms. May refreshed his coffee, adding some much-needed warmth.

"Maybe." He responded without breaking the gaze in the mirror. His hand gripped the mug and forced it to his mouth, though at this moment, caffeine held little interest to him.

"I think I saw him before, too."

The man's bandaged hand scratched at his forehead beneath the brim of a flat-billed hat.

Thunderstorm.

Richie leaned over the countertop to enhance his view.

The swivel door flung open, and Ruby decked out in her pink uniform and white lace, offered a short smile.

"Hey, darling." Richie fell back to the stool, pushing the memory of Timothy Vietta from his mind. "Happy to see you."

"Hi. How's it going?" Ruby clutched at something in her apron pocket. She looked up, her eyes drawn to the computer monitor near the register, and tapped at it with her delicate finger.

"It's going. Been—"

"Tim?" She sloped forward to look beyond Richie. "Is that you?"

Giggling and skipping like a schoolgirl playing hopscotch, she made her way to the booth *Thunderstorm* occupied.

He smirked and stood to greet Ruby, wincing when he propped himself up with the wrapped hand.

The embrace displayed full-fledged passion, not platonic. Sensual, not friendly. The mirror's reflection offered a poignant view of once-lovers finding each other.

She stood back and removed Vietta's hat. On his crown, a line of clean thread intertwined in his skin like a shoelace. "So, it's true. My God, are you okay?"

"I'm fine. Nothing some Percocet can't fix." He smiled and returned the hat snug to his ears.

"I can't believe you're here."

"It's been too long," Thunderstorm said, his voice now heightened and clear.

"I saw you in the newspaper." Ruby caressed his arm and then grabbed hold of him again.

"Which time?" He returned the embrace and lifted her feet off the floor. "I've been popular."

"Don't act like that. You look beat up." She pointed to the wrapped hand and frowned.

"I'll live." He slid into the booth. "Can you chat?"

Ruby snuggled in beside him. She clasped his bandaged hand. "It's not serious, Tim?"

"I've been through worse."

Richie's eyes darted back and forth between the two of them. Images of their lives together as lovers formed. In this make-believe loop, they kissed hard and wet. He was inside of her. Sweat and saliva traveled their skin.

Richie downed the coffee and considered turning around. About to do just that, the question from Ms. May startled him.

"Boy, don't your momma live in The Trails?" She wiped the counter for a second time from behind the bar then slung the towel over a shoulder.

"Huh?" Richie's eyes broke from the mirror. "Yeah. So?"

"Check it out." She dropped bottle of cleaner to the shelf below and then bit into the remains of a ham and cheese on rye. "Looks like your neck of the woods."

A small television hung above the mirror displayed a half-distorted picture, and a live news feed blended in the broken pixels.

"Turn it up." Richie envisioned Sonny alone with Harold.

Had he killed him? Had Harold broken free? Did someone see what happened and report it? No, it wasn't possible. This was just another Squatters Row episode. Nothing more.

A woman in a blue blazer and pantsuit stood at the entrance sign Richie had avoided for many years. She wore a flesh mask of serious but rehearsed emotions—her face thin and blushed to perfection.

She spoke into a wireless microphone, but the television speakers offered only distorted levels of static.

"You can't turn it up? Don't you have rabbit ears on that thing?"

"No. Connects to an antenna." She sighed and wiped her hands on the dingy towel draped over her shoulder. "The pigeons roost on it. Maybe after your first win you can buy poor ole' Ms. May a new TV?"

The broadcast cut to a different scene with the same reporter. Buildings behind the woman on the air were the familiar patched, stained yellow. Small exterior windows, some reinforced with cardboard, acted as a stage to the play unfolding.

Below the reporter, ran a moving graphic banner presenting "Woman Discovered in Abandoned House in The Trails."

CHAPTER TWENTY-FIVE

Utensils clanked on cheap plastic plates, their drumming a melodic undertone to some God-awful music belching from a set of speakers perched on shelves in the back corners of the diner.

"Got any quarters?" Timothy's wrapped hand slid across the table and a single finger pointed to the jukebox. "Think that thing has any White Zombie?"

"Doubt Ms. May stocks the juke with heavy metal." Ruby's chin dropped and her eyebrows hiked, unveiling those emerald eyes in a more vivid window.

"Maybe it's time you start throwing your weight around here." He let his undamaged hand fall under the table and graze the skin beneath her laced skirt.

She returned the gesture with a wink.

At the bar, the young guy grabbed the corded phone from the woman behind the bar. "Come on. Somebody pick up." His right leg shook in vibrations.

"I've got to get over there," the man screamed, loud enough to be heard over the crisp music. He bolted through the door in a rush. The woman behind the counter followed his exit with her eyes and then brought her attention to the small television propped in the corner.

"What was that about?" Timothy nudged Ruby, who seemed oblivious to all happenings outside of the little booth.

She shrugged. "No clue. Richie is pretty intense."

"Richie, huh? You know him?" Timothy shifted in the booth to face her.

Ruby's dimpled cheeks, pale and fair, simmered in a slight red. "It's not like that."

His hands rose. "None of my business."

"Do you want the truth?" She gripped his unhindered hand and placed it on her chest. "I've spent a long time trying to climb out of the hole, and finally, I'm on track. Sobriety is about learning to love yourself. I haven't had time to do much else."

"I'm happy for you. You look great."

"But I swear, I haven't—"

He squeezed her hand, the warmth and silken touch a reminder of what they'd been through and left behind. "Like I said, you don't owe me an explanation."

She released the embrace and cast a sad peek to the kitchen swivel doors. "So," she said, the warmth of her voice gone and replaced with a rigid business-like tone, "what did you order?"

"House special. Saw it on the sign out front. Is it any good?"

"I'll go check on it for you." She shimmied out of the booth, straightened her apron, and charged toward the bar area, each stride accentuating her taut calf muscles.

"Ruby, wait."

She ignored him and pushed through the swivel doors.

A few minutes later she returned with the House Special in hand.

"Refill on the coffee?" The voice remained stout with an edge, stiffer than the clank of the plate on the tabletop.

"What did I say? Why are you so upset?" He scooted further into the booth and tapped the empty seat next to him. "Come on."

"Because, Tim." She swiped an emergent tear with her shoulder. "It's been over a year since I've seen her. Seen you. And you come in here and act like nothing I've done or tried to do matters."

"Wait." His head shook, and a smirk formed. "You're angry that I'm not mad you've seen other people."

"No." Her voice rose, and she stepped forward. A few patrons at a high-top across the room peeked up from their plates. In a lighter tone, she said, "I'm mad that you can't see I want you. You're the only one."

He patted the seat next to him again. "We've got a lot to work out, but it can't be fixed in one day."

"Why are you here then, Tim?" She snuck a glance toward Ms. May, but the woman's eyes were still trained on the television.

"Let's start small. I came here because my dad said this is where you worked. I wanted to see you, even after everything, because you're what I want, too."

The blush in her cheeks returned, though this time a few tears drummed down them and came to a stop at her pink, glossed lips. "You mean it?"

Timothy dug a fork into the mashed potatoes resting near a piece of singed meat he couldn't quite identify. "Yeah." He dropped the utensil to the plate. "Maybe we can get something to eat?"

She laughed, the chortle garnering the attention of the

customers at the high top. "We're known for coffee and pie. Not the—" She used his fork to lift the meat from its plate and tilted her chin to exaggerate a pensive look—"flank steak."

Timothy pulled the Visa from his wallet and tossed it to the table. "You off soon?"

She rotated her wrist and checked the time. "Half an hour."

CHAPTER TWENTY-SIX

Richie sprinted to The Trails, huffing swoops of frigid air. His muscles contracted, and shards of cramps attacked his stomach, but he pushed forward until the blue and red lights flashed in monotonous blips scarring the face of Squatters Row.

Be someone else. Anybody.

He repeated the phrase over and over, but each time the four words crossed his brain, he felt it less likely. The pit in his stomach gained momentum. *Be someone else. Anybody.*

The yellow tape shined in the police cars' light show. He approached, heaving in air, and forced himself through the perimeter. A few Row lifers stood in a huddled blob, each sniffling and hacking phlegm. In front of them, guarding the caution tape, a red-eyed police officer sweating the stench of body odor and cheap coffee intercepted Richie.

"Step back, sir." He recited the tired, robotic phrase. "Police business."

"Who is it?" Blood rushed to his head and throbbed in

his ears. "Gotta name? Linette Frezza? Fifty-three. She's wearing a purple shirt and jeans. Please. Is it my mother?"

"Sir, we're processing the scene. At this point I can't tell you anything. If you'd wait over there." The fat-fuck in a flat tone akin to a professor in his thirtieth year on the job pointed to the eastern curb of the Row. "We'll talk with you in a minute."

"Wait, please."

The curly-headed pudge-factory gave him a dismissive nod and turned to a trio of onlookers overstepping his precious yellow tape.

A gurney came through the door then. Two gloved men brought it down the steps. The white sheet covering the deceased flapped over. For a moment, and Richie was certain, a thin jeaned leg thrust out from beneath the cover.

For the second time that day, Richie Frezza fell to his knees and hurled. Though this time, only coffee spurt from his mouth. A man wearing a thick coat over a dress shirt and tie knelt beside him moments later—a dull badge clipped to his belt read RCPD.

"Sir." He patted Richie's back. "Are you okay?"

"Purple sweater and blue jeans?"

The cop nodded. "Yes. But it may not be who you think."

"It is. I know it." Richie struggled to stand, but his knees felt like concrete.

"Take it easy." The man rubbed between his shoulder blades.

"Drugs, right? That's what it was?"

"Not sure. Call was for an unresponsive, white female. No ID. Not much to go on right now."

"I told her to stay away from the Row. Swallows people up."

The officer dropped to his haunches and extended a handkerchief. "This neighborhood has a stigma, ya know?"

"Yeah. I live down the block." He wiped at his mouth with the rag. "Don't need to tell me." Tears dripped from Richie's eyes. He stood and glanced at the gurney loaded into the ambulance. The doors, propped open and slicing the night, reminded him of the vault. "It's my mother. I feel it."

The cop exhaled and stood. Snakes of fog hovered above him. He cupped his hands and breathed into them. "Any identifying marks you can give me? Tattoo, scar, something?"

"Left ankle. Nasty scar from a car accident when I was two." Richie's stare extended to the onlookers. Grub and scum with heartbeats. "Rose tattoo on her left shoulder."

"Hey, Mike." The officer shuffled toward the ambulance. "Hold up a minute."

A short conversation followed with a few peeks from Mike in Richie's direction. He lifted the bottom of the sheet, and the cop peeled the sock of the left foot down.

The men climbed into the ambulance and the doors shut.

A rose. It's right there on her shoulder.

The doors opened, and the man made his way back. His face, unemotional and tight, seemed used to death and delivering bad news. "I'm very sorry for your loss."

Richie's legs gave in and he hit the asphalt with a thud. Now, tears streamed. The officer's confirmation opened the ducts and nothing could stop the flow of salt and liquid.

"My name is Detective Barto. I know the last thing you want to do right now is deal with the paperwork."

Richie's sobs masked the final words. He heard just a jumble of disconnected sounds.

"Sooner than later." Barto extended his hand. "We'll need an official identification, and then you can begin making arrangements. I can drive you, if you'd like."

Richie took the man's hand and stood. "You said unresponsive, right? No pain?"

"No trauma, at least not what I can see. The medical examiner will give a cause of death. If it's suspicious, they'll order an autopsy."

"Suspicious?" Richie's hand climbed his nose and then the pointer and ring fingers swept tears from beneath his eyes.

"Yeah. But I think you're probably right. We get calls out here once a month for drug overdoses. Most people live. Some don't. I'm sorry to be blunt, but I've learned sugar coating moments like this help nobody." The officer nudged Richie's elbow and pointed to his cruiser.

Richie staggered toward the car, his legs still weak and uncooperative. Barto held the door for him and closed it after he slid in the front seat.

The ambulance cranked on and crept toward the back exit of The Trails, using a small side street cutting through the Row. Barto followed.

Ten minutes later, the cruiser parked in front of the county morgue. "It may be a few minutes. They still need to process the body—I mean, deceased. Just head in and give your name. And again, I'm sorry."

"Thanks." Riche clicked the handle. A rush of frosted air swooshed into the car. He stepped out and ambled toward the building.

Sorry? What a funny word for such a fucked-up situation.

Fatigue set in as he sat in the waiting area. It dragged Richie's eyelids.

Each moment of the day surfaced within his mind. Fighting Harold and losing the cash. His mother's assault and the expression on her face. Murdering a stranger. Roger Cranswell's gaped mouth and pale face. A vault built to capture the dead. And now the dagger—a lethal drug overdose.

Maybe it was more? Suicide? No, that's crazy. Is it?

"Sir," a woman's voice carried through the room, "we're ready for you."

Richie stood at the counter partitioned with stained glass.

A sliding window opened, and she slid a clipboard holding a stack of papers across the threshold.

"I'll need your ID. While I complete things on my end, you can fill out the forms. Then we'll release the post-mortem picture, and you can make the identification."

Richie presented his license and flipped through the documents on the clipboard, flicking his signature across the pages.

A few minutes later, the woman opened the other side of the partition to reveal a computer monitor. "Are you ready, Mr. Frezza?"

"Yes." Richie dropped the pen in his hand and gripped the countertop. The monitor flashed white and gained focus. Linette Frezza's face appeared on the screen.

"It's her," he said in a whisper. "That's my mother."

"I'm sorry for your loss," she said, her tone unflinching.

Richie then thought if he'd ever be able to speak Cranswell's name with such a flat voice.

"Do you have funeral arrangements?" The woman tapped the counter.

"I've got nothing." Richie wiped a tear rolling down his

cheek. He glanced at the woman's name tag. *Annie*. "I need help, Annie."

She reached into a cabinet beneath the desk. After fiddling with a few hanging folders, she glided a card across the threshold. "We'll release the body to them. Cheap and quick. Call them in the morning."

"Thanks."

"Can I get you a cab?"

"No. I'm good."

Outside, the drop in temperature cut through his loose-fitting hoodie. He began the six-mile slog to The Trails in anger.

Then rage allowed pontification to peek in.

People who matter to others have extravagant funerals. Expensive flowers to hug a decorative bronze casket, the final resting place of the departed. Printed and laminated prayer cards fill the hands of teary-eyed guests.

Droves of grievers clad in black huddle into a church. Each elbow their way in to view the dearly departed and console one another. Exaggerated gasps and sobs fill the ears of all in attendance, as if the world's collective heart burst right then.

A gaudy reception in honor of the dead, but it's more for the ego of the living.

People eat and drink. They share stories deemed unimportant not long ago, but now offer priceless conversational fodder to combat grief.

But, disposable people in the slums of Ridgemont Cove don't matter, so funeral processions and reception banquets aren't on the itinerary.

When a drug-addicted piece of trash overdoses in a half-charred apartment building inside the most despised neighborhood of Ridgemont Cove, people don't care.

I'll change that. They'll care now.
Harold was going to die. No other way around it.
Open the vault, Roger. I found you a roommate.

CHAPTER TWENTY-SEVEN

"Harold Remnick and Georgie Silva? Sound like a couple of goombahs." Benny puffed a cigarette on the outside patio of The Tango. The sun's final glimmer of red fell victim to the night. Wind bit at his skin and smoked the cigarette for him.

"Yeah. I ran the names." Her voice cracked through the receiver. "I dropped the photos in the PO Box."

"Aren't you a doll? You sure about this, Deb?" Benny switched the phone to the other ear and pulled a pen from his shirt pocket. It snagged on the white handkerchief from earlier. Specks of Cranswell's blood dotted the cloth.

Gotta toss this thing. "All right, spell 'em for me." He jotted the names on a cocktail napkin.

"They were both released on the same day. I see this guard once in a while. He was on shift. Said those two were tight during their stay."

Benny tried to ignore she was involved with other guys. They weren't married or anything, but he didn't like the idea of sloppy seconds.

Who was he kidding, though? He had three ladies in

Belleview. A few dancers at Moonlighters. Hell, the waitress in section four had gobbled his junk an hour before her shift started this afternoon.

Still, something about this broad made him tingle. He liked her.

"Where can I find Georgie?" He flipped the collar of his coat up around his neck.

"He gave us an address in Sharpton. Hold on a sec." Static blared through the earpiece, and Benny assumed she was shuffling through papers. "2917 Walker's Height."

"Okay." Benny added the address to the cocktail napkin and stood. "This is great. Nice work."

"Now the business stuff is out of the way, am I going to see you soon? When are we going to have some fun?"

"Work first, play later. I've gotta handle this." Benny crossed the parking lot and stuck his key into the Cadillac's door.

"But I need handling. Been saving PTO. We could take a vacation. I hear it never gets cold in the Bahamas. I've got a few new skimpy things for you."

"I'm busy." *Hmm. Guess the other guy isn't up to snuff.*

"Don't be like that. I need you."

"In time. Daddy's busy."

"Fine." Her tone fell flat. A hint of irritation hung in the air, but Benny chuckled and ended the call.

Just a broad. A sexy wild, broad in uniform.

CHAPTER TWENTY-EIGHT

It neared seven o'clock when Richie reached the mouth of The Trails. Steam poured from his face and exposed legs.

He jogged toward his mother's apartment in silence, ignoring the hooting from various balconies. *Ya'll can get it too. Just not today.*

To Richie's surprise, the Cadillac sat nestled to the curb. Its exhaust pipe released gray smoke into the air, and Richie peered through the tinted window. He could see the shadowed silhouettes of two men and considered knocking on the door. Thinking better of it, he turned toward the apartment stoop and climbed the steps.

The locked door thwarted his plan of rushing in and killing the man. By the time he'd popped the key in and opened the door, Benny and Sonny were waiting. Harold still sat bound and bleeding.

"Take a seat, kid." Benny pointed to the kitchen table. "I've got news."

"I thought you were in the car. What's going on?"

"Sit down." Benny circled Richie and shoved him toward the kitchen.

"I want him dead." Richie eyed the mummy in colorful binds.

"Hey, what did I say about you barking orders? Chain of command, kid."

"Fuck the chain. My mother's dead and it's his fault." Richie teared again and felt slight embarrassment. Looking weak in front of these men would do him no favors, but the water rushed in free channels as his mind struggled to control his body.

Harold's head perked up. The swelling from the beating transformed the thug's face into red lumps and purple streaks.

"Slow down. What are you talking about?" Benny gripped Richie's arm.

"She's gone, man. My mother. It's their fault."

"How? What the fuck are you saying?"

"I just identified her body, Benny. Doesn't matter how, does it? Both of them are going to die. I held up my end. Now it's your turn."

"Whoa. Slow down, kid." Sonny's head jerked back. "What happened?"

"No cause of death yet. But they don't need to tell me. She was my mother. A junkie, but my mother. She—" He wiped at his face. A rash of heat bursting across his forehead. "She overdosed. I know it. And it's their fault." The last sentence shook in his throat.

"I'm sorry." Benny gripped his shoulder.

"You're the second person to tell me that today. I don't want apologies. I want blood."

"We'll take care of it." Benny shot a glance in Sonny's direction. "Right now, I need you to sit and relax. No sense bringing emotion into this. That's how mistakes are made."

A slight whimper from Harold emanated, and the three men moved back to the foyer.

"This your partner?" Benny plopped a mugshot in Harold's lap.

The man winced and surveyed the photo.

"Answer me." Benny grabbed him by the neck, squeezing until the whites of his knuckles matched the pallor of the punk's face.

Harold coughed and gagged, forcing a head shake amid the stranglehold. "Yes."

Benny released the grip and motioned to Sonny with an extended thumb. "Get Lorenzo."

A moment later, the front door banged open. Richie recognized the brooding Italian as a participant in the alley brawl. He held a bleeding stranger by the neck and flung him to the floor.

"We got the right guy?" Lorenzo faced Benny. "If so, the prick here has been lying through his teeth."

"It's him." Benny loomed over the bloody man. "Thanks. Take a step outside."

"You need me?" Sonny asked, leaning against the door frame.

"Yeah. Close the door."

Lorenzo slipped through the entrance and Sonny shut it.

Benny clawed onto the back of Georgie's neck and lifted him from the ground. "Kid, grab me a chair."

Richie pulled one from the table and then eyed the rapist—his anger smoldering. An internal inferno flowered blue and ferocious. It blanketed the guilt and shame, burning the pitiful emotions to ash. All was black, and streaks of blackened smudge darkened the silver vault doors within his mind. *Who's next?*

"Sonny, tie him up and grab me a knife from the drawer," Benny said with a nod to the kitchen. He shifted his focus to Richie. "Put a sheet down. Grab something for the mess."

"Wait. What are you going to do?" Harold glanced to Georgie. The bruising on his brows impeded the circles of his eyes, but pure terror sparked in his pupils. "What did you tell them, man?"

"Shut the fuck up. I'll let you know when it's time to speak."

A moment later, Benny held a six-inch boning knife in his hand, Georgie's restraints mimicked Harold's, and both of the bruised and swollen assholes sat in chairs resting on the quilt from Linette Frezza's bed.

"You want to use that?" Benny asked Richie with a finger pointed at the quilt.

"No use for it now," Richie returned, casting an unblinking stare at the men seated in his mother's kitchen furniture.

They squirmed in their bindings, but Georgie's attempt held more ferocity. A few hooking punches to the gut from Sonny stole the vigor from his plight.

"Now or never." Benny pointed the faux pearl-handled knife to Georgie's pinky. "The money or your finger. It's simple."

"What money?"

Benny struck Georgie's jaw with a backhanded slap. It cracked like lightning on a still night. "Don't make me out to be an idiot. You stole money from this apartment. Where is it?"

"I don't know anything about the money."

"So be it." In a flash, he sliced Georgie's pinky off to the bottom knuckle. Blood spurted from the severed appendage, and for three seconds, it didn't seem to register in the guy's brain.

Then, a coarse scream bellowed in the little apartment, and Sonny stuffed a dishtowel in Georgie's gaping mouth.

Harold squirmed and sobbed.

Richie reveled in the destruction. The man's pain stoked the fire further. No longer would he be weak-hearted. Some people deserved what they got.

Just like Georgie. Harold. Shit, even Cranswell.

"Okay, okay." Georgie mumbled through the rag stuffed in his throat.

"You scream again, I'm taking another one. You got that?" Benny pulled the rag from Georgie's mouth and grabbed the bleeding hand with it. Richie noticed he squeezed, paying particular attention to the mangled digit, and then pushed his other forearm into the whimpering man's throat.

"The money is in my truck." The words struggled to escape his lips with a cough sprinkled between each vowel. "I'll take you there."

"There was no truck at your house when we scooped you up. You lying to me?" Benny released his grip.

"No." Blood slewed from Georgie's finger, painting the quilt on the floor red. A dark splatter desecrated the Frezza family beach photo. The sawed-off pinky rested between his feet, right-side up. "I swear. It's at a bar near my place."

Benny shoved the soaked rag into Georgie's mouth. "Let me clean up, Sonny." He wiped at the residue staining his palm. "Wash this and drop it in a baggie," he then said, holding the blood-streaked knife out.

"What can I do?" Richie pressed forward, itching to be more than a spectator.

"Flush the finger and untie these pricks. Then tell

Lorenzo to call a cab. We need the Cadillac for our little field trip."

CHAPTER TWENTY-NINE

"We clear?" Benny stood inside the apartment and spoke through the sliver of air the opened door created.

"Yeah." Richie pushed through and started to close it, but a hand stopped it from latching.

"All quiet. I've got a blanket down in the trunk. The guy still bleeding?" Lorenzo asked.

"Sonny's handling it. If we're good to go, load 'em up." Benny jabbed his thumb over his shoulder.

Lorenzo clutched Harold's neck and dragged him from the apartment by the head. The squeals and pleas now mere whispered whimpers. As Lorenzo did this, Sonny wrapped Georgie's hand using a roll of athletic wrap from Richie's gym bag.

The sliced digit bled into the cloth, but each time Sonny rolled a new layer over the wound, the protruding dark spot shrank. The ending result was a club hand, like football players sometimes sported to protect broken bones.

"You feel that sting in your back?" Sonny asked Georgie.

"Yeah."

"That's my gun, and if you do anything other than climb in the trunk, I'm putting four slugs through you."

Georgie stiffened and then started for the door, the bald brute matching him step for step.

Benny followed, bounced down the stairs with a few careful glances each way, and then hurried to the Cadillac.

Harold, crammed in and whimpering, cradled his stomach. Sonny gave Georgie an extra shove, and the man fell into the trunk head first.

"We'll talk in the morning, Lorenzo." Benny slammed the hatch down, and it echoed like a gunshot. He turned to his driver and young protégé. "Let's go, fellas."

Inside the car, none of the men spoke, no need to. Dead silence communicated all.

A light mist fell, coating the street. Sonny swung the car out of The Trails and toward the interstate.

The Cracker Jack, a slum bar near Georgie's house, had a few cars in its parking lot. Sonny circled to the south end, and sitting askew off the concrete, a half painted pickup truck's bumper impaled a bush line. Richie's envelope hid beneath some receipts and a few empty beer cans covering the passenger side floorboard.

Excellent for the kid but doesn't make a rat's ass difference for the cokehead rapists.

Now, Richie gripped the envelope in the backseat of the Cadillac, crinkled and ripped in its corners, and counted the remnants.

"All there, kid?" Benny spoke to the rearview and gnawed an unlit cigarette. Faint cries from the trunk trickled through the backseat.

Benny turned the volume dial a quarter inch. A baseball game's broadcast muffled the men's desperate pleas.

Little late for the apology game boys. Which one of you has the balls, I wonder?

"Missing some." In the reflection of the mirror, Richie flicked through the bills, half-counting. He closed the envelope and tossed it to the empty seat beside him.

"It's better than nothing, right?"

"I don't care about the cash, man."

"Oh, no? Pretty sure that's why you called me."

"That was before—"

"Look." Benny lit the smoke and pressed the window button. "Right now, that sack of cash is the most important thing you got. Hate to sound insensitive, kid, but funerals ain't cheap."

"Gonna have her cremated. Supposed to call in the morning."

Sonny reversed out of the bar parking lot then eased across two lanes, stopping at a yellow light. Grunts and pleas emanated from the trunk.

"What are we gonna do with *them*?" Richie asked.

"We're going to handle it." Benny turned in the seat to face Sonny, his weight shifting the Cadillac's balance. "Head to the farm."

Ten minutes later, the car nosed toward a tree line, where a dirt road knifed through the green and led to an awning of elms. At the other end of those elms, tucked into a natural wilderness cul-de-sac, the barn sat still and quiet—waiting for another victim.

When the Cadillac parked in the dirt driveway, dust climbed the haze of the headlights, masking the barn in a brown glow. Benny turned in his seat and rested his elbow on the center console to face the mixed up youngin'.

"You've had a long fucking day. And trust me, things

will get worse before they get better. Losing a loved one isn't easy. Why don't you sit this one out?"

Richie swiped the envelope of cash on the seat and held it up. "This is why we're here. Those two assholes wanted *this*. But what they took was much worse. I want to watch it happen."

Benny sunk into the seat and blinked, leaving his lids closed for a few seconds. *I was a shit-for-brain kid once, too.* His second kill came to mind.

His reward for whacking Joey "Bombers"? Another contract. The Clemente brothers came next. The degenerate gamblers and pimps racked up debt and could no longer pay the interest consistently. Solano issued three warnings, and when the cash failed to materialize, a contract was ordered.

Benny tore Vincente in half with a close range shot from a borrowed Remington Premiere. The guy fell backward through the front door with eyes glazed and mouth gaped like a fish out of water. Pink, stringy matter seeped from his gut and Benny could smell the sizzling intestines.

Purelli, still a soldier at the time, phoned Alfredo with the news and issued an ultimatum: dig deep and find some dough or die. As was expected, Alfredo ignored the proposal and vowed vengeance. Two days later, outside of a motel wrought full of ill hookers and drug infested hoards, Benny snuck up on the elder Clemente sleeping in an idling Mercedes. A syringe jabbed in the vein of his toothpick arm. The vendetta had lasted less than forty-eight hours. A single shot from a silenced pistol through the heart sufficed.

"You sure, kid?" Benny forced the Clemente brothers from his psyche and focused on the rearview. Richie's reflection in the rear view presented an unflinching gaze. "All right. Let's do it."

Sonny hurled Georgie over his shoulder like a lumberjack carrying a fresh log. The man's squirms were now light, almost untraceable to the eye.

Richie yanked Harold from the trunk and tossed him to the dirt. He then hooked his arms beneath the man's armpits and dragged him toward the barn door.

The captive mumbled through choked sobs and kicked his feet, scarring the dirt path in deep divots. Benny walked behind, placing his steps in the grooves dug in from Harold's heels.

Inside the barn, the two men sat in the same chairs Richie and Purelli had used. They winced and moaned; Georgie's exaltations livelier. Shaking and sniffling, the two previously masked men now wore shell husks of their former human selves. Depleted, they peered at Benny and the rest of their captors with the eyes of zombies.

"Give him the knife, Sonny." Benny cocked his pistol and jammed it into Harold's forehead. A red circle spanned on the outside of the barrel against the pale face.

Sonny pulled the same boning knife used for Georgie's impromptu surgery from his pocket—he'd secured it in a plastic grocery bag—flipped the bag inside out and dropped the knife into Harold's lap.

"Stick it through his heart," Benny said. "Do it. Or I give him the same option."

"I can't, mister." Harold looked at the knife. Urine soaked the fly of his pants then ran to the soles of his shoes.

"Stand him up." Benny pointed the pistol to Georgie.

Sonny hoisted him from the chair. He landed off-balance and swayed into Richie.

"Watch your step, you piece of shit." Richie's piercing left jab sent Georgie to the barn floor. He tried to gain traction and rise, but the injured hand failed him.

"The boss said get up." Sonny clawed into the man's back, flinging him to the center of the barn.

Georgie got to his knees, and with caution, steadied himself and stood.

"Same offer." Benny placed the barrel to Georgie's temple.

Without a word, Georgie's healthy hand grasped the knife and shoved it through his partner's chest.

Harold's eyes gaped open.

"You son-of-a-bitch," he said. A thin stream of blood jumped from his mouth with the words. "You really did it." In a second of sickening slow-motion, he collapsed to the floor of the barn. Wet coughs spewed darkening saliva and black chunks.

"Don't let him suffer, you insensitive prick." Benny pointed the gun to Georgie's chest. "Finish him."

Georgie fell to his knees and crawled a foot to the twitching body. He muttered something to the writhing man, pulled the blade from Harold's chest and then jammed the knife through his neck.

"Most sensible thing you've done today. On your feet." The gun in Benny's hand ticked upward.

Georgie obeyed and rose. Streaks of Harold's blood climbed his cheeks. "I killed him." His head drooped and scanned the dirt floor. "You letting me go?"

"Never said we would." Benny glanced to the kid, who at that moment glared at the corpse and growing puddle of blood beneath it. "What do you think, kid? Should we let him go?"

"Please man," Georgie said to Richie. "I'll get the rest of the money. I don't want to die."

"And my mother"—Richie grabbed him by the collar—"I'm sure she didn't want to die, either."

"I didn't kill her, man."

"You're the reason she's dead." Richie forced Georgie into the wall draped with gardening tools.

"No, man. No." Georgie's hand lifted above his head. Blood from the pinky stump bled through the crude bandage Sonny had concocted, and trickles of red slid down his arm. "I'm sorry."

"You're gonna be sorry, when we're done." Richie released him with a shove then spat at him, spraying droplets across his face.

"Please. I just wanted the money. It wasn't personal. I've gotta family."

"Family?" Richie turned to Benny with an incredulous smile. "You believe this guy?"

"What do you want from me? You have half the money. I'll get you the rest, plus interest. Hell, I killed him for you." Georgie sobbed, pointing at Harold's limp body with the wrapped hand.

"Your wallet and keys." Benny pulled him from the wall.

"Huh? What keys, man?"

"The keys to your truck, asshole."

Georgie used the uninjured hand to pull a keyring from his blood-stained jeans. He tossed them to Benny. The wallet came next.

"The truck is payment for the remainder of your debt." Benny sifted the license from the wallet. He handed the card to Richie and then pocketed the keys. "This is a reminder. If you ever step foot in The Trails again, we're coming for you." He jabbed a finger into the man's chest. "You mention this farm or night to anyone, and that knife with your fingerprints gets mailed to my friends in the RCPD."

"So, you'll let me live?"

"My friend here," Benny gestured to Richie, "wants to kill you, but I believe in leverage. And now, we have that. So, today you live. But nothing's guaranteed, Georgie Silva. Don't fuck up."

"What about him?" Richie asked. He pointed to Harold's still body.

"First things first. Sonny, you got the bag?"

Sonny pulled the grocery bag from before out of his pocket.

"Take the knife out and drop it in here," Benny ordered Georgie, shaking the flimsy plastic. "Try anything stupid, and I'll bury you."

Georgie knelt and pulled the knife from Harold. It released with a wet whoosh. Spurts of dark liquid sprang from the gash, covering Harold's blank face in smears of red.

Benny held out the opened bag and Georgie dropped the blade in. He shoved his pistol in his waistband then tied the plastic bag shut. "Now get him the fuck out of here, Sonny."

The driver muscled the lucky-to-be-alive prick out of the barn.

"What do we do with this guy?" Richie stared at the limp body draining pints of blood on the dirt floor.

"Let him bleed out for a minute. Then we drop him somewhere public, so the pigs find him and start investigating. Hopefully, they show it on TV and Georgie sees that we own him now. Once we do that, a little lime on the blood in here and maybe some pig shit, nobody'll know a thing."

"The cops come here?"

"Been using this place for years. And if they ever did, it ain't connected to any of us. On paper, Marshall Taylor owns it."

"Who is that?"

"Don't concern yourself with stuff that doesn't concern you." Benny fished a pack of cigarettes from his coat pocket. He snagged one from the flip-top box and lit it. "But what you need to do at your place is a little more involved."

"What do you mean?"

"When you get home tonight, bleach everything. You got a mop bucket and Clorox?"

"Yeah." Richie shrugged. "We put the quilt down, though."

"You ever heard of Luminol?" Benny exhaled a cloud of smoke. He wheezed a bit and massaged his throat.

"Nah."

"It can find blood that you and I can't see. It's this magic fuckin' potion the cops use."

"You serious?" Richie's face contorted. The brows inverted, and he sighed.

"This guy." Benny kicked loose dirt toward Harold. "And our friend out there, left blood all over the place. Trust me when I tell you, the blanket wasn't enough. Now, if you don't clean every inch of that apartment with bleach, and these savvy forensic assholes spray Luminol, they're going to know blood was on your tile at some point."

"Everybody bleeds." Richie's hands raised as if to silently call Benny an idiot.

"Once they know blood is there, then they can run DNA, smart guy." Benny puffed the cigarette again and flicked a snake of ash to the floor. "But, if they can't detect blood, they can't test it. You with me? So, let's say Georgie grows a pair and runs to the cops. He brings them to your doorstep. They spray Luminol and you have traces of Harold's blood all over your fucking apartment. Do you see how that could be a problem for you?"

Richie nodded, and Benny watched the 'holy shit, I'm in too deep' expression cross the kid's face.

"Enough chit-chat." Benny dropped the cigarette to the ground and raised the bagged knife and shook it. "We've got more important shit to do right now. Go grab that weed-blocker and rope from the storage room. Don't need this bastard bleeding all over my trunk."

Richie obeyed and sauntered to the interior door. He returned moments later with a thick roll of black tarp slung over his shoulder and rope in his hand.

"Drop it here." Benny tapped dirt in front of Harold's body with his foot.

Richie did so.

"Now run it the length of his body. Roll him onto it. It doesn't matter of his legs are sticking out, but get his chest and throat covered."

"This is crazy." Richie grabbed the lax end of the tarp. He held it firm and kicked the roll. It spun forward, unraveling across the dirt.

Benny bent down and grabbed Harold's shoes. He swung the lower half of the corpse on the tarp.

"You want to be one of us or pretend? Can't rule the world if you're locked up."

Richie followed Benny's lead and moved the upper half with a grunt. "I want to be a boxer. That's all I ever wanted."

"Well, looks like you're going to have to pull double duty now, kid. Tonight is something that changes the dynamic of our relationship."

"What now?"

"Roll him up and tie it. Like a burrito, eh?" Benny smirked and flicked his cigarette.

Richie knelt and ran the rope over the tarp, rolling it the

length of Harold's body. Little by little, the man disappeared beneath the rigid black fabric, until just a pair of shoes stuck out.

Benny gripped the guy's high-tops. "Grab your end. Let's get him to the car."

Outside, Sonny sat on the trunk of the Cadillac. He jabbed his thick fingers at the screen of his phone.

"Pop it." Benny said, struggling to maintain a grip on the dead weight. "This fucker is slipping."

Sonny jumped from the car and clicked the handle. The hydraulic openers of the trunk depressed and whistled. Georgie, chewing on a rag and twisting his bound wrists, lay in the fetal position.

Richie and Benny heaved the corpse on top of him and Benny clicked the trunk shut.

Back in the car, Sonny fired the ignition. "What's the plan, boss?"

"We take the prick home after Richie's had time to clean."

"And Harold." The driver backed the Cadillac down the dirt path. "Taking him home, too?"

"Dropping him somewhere with a lot of foot traffic. I want it on the news, so our friend Georgie shits his pants for the next few days." Benny checked Richie's reflection in the mirror. "You good with that, kid?"

"You're the boss."

CHAPTER THIRTY

Richie sat on a bench running through the center and extending the length of the Waller Complex locker room. Black metal cubbies lined each side. On the eastern wall, an entranceway cut into the steel arrangement and led to a shower room. Above, fluorescent tube lights flickered in their yellowing plastic cases.

The pungent stench of commercial-grade bleach from the two-day clean-up wafted from his skin and he hoped Joe's aged nostrils didn't track the scent.

Guess it's better than fish guts.

Joe swung a final loop of tape around Richie's glove trim and stuck it down. "Tight enough?"

"Yeah. I'm good."

The vault opened. Harold appeared, gaunt and scared, the boning knife's red-streaked handle jabbing from his throat. The ghost's mouth widened, and silver from the blade cut the black in a glimmer.

Ready? Harold asked. *This is what you've always wanted, hotshot.*

Bleach returned to Richie's nose. The vault sealed with a sucking pop.

"Bend forward. I need to put some more jelly on that cut. Can't believe you walked into an awning, kid. We're lucky they didn't disqualify you."

Can't believe you bought that bullshit story.

"It's just meant to be, I guess." Richie tilted his head down and the cooling petroleum jelly swiped over the cut created by the pistol-whipping.

"Let's win a few fights and make some cash, so we can hire a cut man. That's all I'm saying." Joe finished and lifted his chin. The men's eyes locked. "Keep your right up. Any boxer worth his salt would notice that gash and aim for it. You ready?"

Richie punched his cheeks and stood.

He followed Joe out of the locker room and into a hallway then deviated through a corridor marked employees only. This pathway led to a maple colored curtain where two men in yellow security shirts stood cross armed. On the other side of the cloth partition, a buzz of voices hissed.

"Ladies and gentleman"—the static announcement hushed the crowd—"we welcome you to this evening's first match. It is a middleweight bout and is scheduled for six rounds. Introducing first—"

"This is it, kid."

The security guards peeled their respective ends of the curtain back. Vibrating noises amplified. Multi-colored lights flashed the ceiling, darting throughout the arena like enormous, vibrant bubbles.

Richie tapped the gloves taped to his trembling hands and bounced through the entryway. Slick sweat rolled the length of his arms and misted in a violent splash when the gloves connected. He scanned the crowd. A sparse collection of onlookers dotted seats of near-empty aisles.

Seemed louder, he thought, focusing his eyes on the ring now. *Not too many people give a shit about the first fight, I guess.*

Not too many people give a shit about you, Harold hissed, reappearing for a slight moment of time.

You're one and done, Cranswell chimed in. A black vapor poured from the bullet hole in his forehead and snaked down to his nostril. He inhaled the gust of darkness and spat it out of his mouth. *Done.*

Richie's eyes scrunched, willing the vault to close. When they reopened, he was halfway down the aisle leading to the steps of the ring. He gazed upward. "Friday Night Fight" banners hung from the low rafters. They swayed like flags at half-mast.

The loudspeaker, crackling through the crowd's drunken screams, said, "In his debut, fighting out of the blue corner and weighing in at one-hundred and fifty-eight pounds, Richie Frezza."

The voice, though masked by static in the speaker, had a familiarity to it.

"Hey, is that Donnie?" Richie climbed the steps.

"Focus on your Goddamn opponent." Joe forced the top rope down. Richie straddled it and then bounced in. "And watch that cut, kid."

Inside the ring, the squirrelly, mustachioed redhead shot him a wink and rotated the index cards in his hands.

Richie bobbed and shadow boxed, absorbing the crowd's guile acceptance. He sprung around the ring for a moment and then sat in the stool propped in the corner post covered in blue matting.

"And now introducing his opponent." Donnie raised the

mic to his mouth and pointed toward the entry curtain. "Making his third appearance in the RCAB, with a record of zero wins, two losses and one no-contest. Fighting out of the red corner, and weighing in at one hundred and fifty-nine pounds, Ragin' Roberto Martinez."

Richie eyed the man's approach and sized him up. He'd seen a few reels of tape on the guy's previous matches, but those images of research had been deleted for new memories, fresher and more violent.

He's the first to fall. More to come.

Martinez rolled his shoulders and waddled forward, entering the ring with his eyes locked on Richie. Short and nearing the thirty-year-old mark, Martinez was more father-of-three than middleweight powerhouse.

"He's got the reach." Joe's arms slung over the top rope like limp noodles. "Get inside and work that dough stomach."

"Or just knock him out? How about that?"

"Don't get cocky. He's been here before, kid."

"But I was born for this." Richie tapped Joe's hands with his gloves. "I won't let you down."

Martinez shot Richie a sneer and drew his thumb beneath his neck. He backed into the red corner and raised his hands. A few spectators cheered. A couple others booed.

With the entrance over, jitters subsiding, and an opponent on the other side, the crowd of about three-hundred evaporated.

Just me and you now.

"Fighters, approach the center. The official for this evening is Chance Carmac." Donnie stood to the side and then hooked his arm under the referee, jutting the mic to his mouth.

"Gentleman," Carmac said, "rules and instructions

were read to you in the locker room. No low blows and wait for my signal after a clinch. Questions?"

Both fighters shook their heads.

"Good. Tap gloves and return to your corner."

Richie popped his gloves on top of his opponent's and smiled, backing away with his eyes cemented in place. The last few weeks faded. Pain and anguish. Sadness and hopelessness. It all disintegrated. Everything he felt and regretted vanished. One objective remained.

Knock this chump out. Period.

Joe slipped Richie's mouth guard in. "Go get him, kid."

The bell for round one chimed. Its echo reverberating within Richie's head. The vault appeared; its striking silver doors open. Cranswell and Harold sat on the familiar chairs from the barn. Motionless, except for black eyes rotating within their sockets. Both ghosts' lips peeled back, revealing skeleton grins, wide enough to deform their faces. Fear dribbled down Richie's spine.

"Look out," Joe's voice broke through the trance.

Martinez had come out in a rush, stalking, and changing his stance. An errant hook fell off target, but its velocity created a fierce whooshing wind.

Richie ducked a jab, bounced off the ropes, and took command of the ring's center.

Martinez advanced. He shot three jabs and two landed. The punches, quick in succession and heavier than expected, stung Richie's left eye.

Another jab flew at him, but Richie parried the blow and countered with two crisp body punches. Martinez winced and threw a wobbly hook. It connected with Richie's cheek, but slid from the skin before causing damage.

The two circled, feigning punches and shifting stances.

Martinez broke the stand-off and charged in with an uppercut combination.

One punch tagged Richie's chin, popping his head back. The crowd roared, the volume like that of Madison Square Garden and not this rinky-dink arena.

The vault door slammed shut.

Business first.

He weaved past another jab and landed a cocked hook, rocking Martinez's jaw. Blood spurt from his mouth and splattered across Richie's glove. He fell back into the ropes with both gloves protecting his face.

Richie unleashed body punches in combinations of three and four. The strikes tagged the man's ribs, each landed blow causing a stiff grunt from Martinez.

"That's it," Joe screamed. "Soften him up."

Martinez absorbed the beating, but kept the top covered, presumably unwilling to present his jaw. Richie swayed left and rattled off three digging right hooks to the fighter's stomach.

With a reddened torso, Martinez dropped a glove to protect his left.

As if a target had been painted on the schmuck's face, Richie stepped into a punch, delivering a demonic right hook. Its crack echoed in the arena, and its force stung Richie's knuckles through the glove.

The thundering pop elated the crowd, and the Waller Complex vibrated like Moonlighters on a Saturday night.

His opponent shuffled forward like a drunken sailor, swung at air, and collapsed.

"Back to your corner." The ref waved his hands and separated Richie from the fallen fighter. He turned to Martinez and crouched with a hand outstretched. "One. Two. Three."

Each spoken number accompanied by a digit on his hand springing up.

"Four. Five."

Martinez's head lifted from the canvas at a slight angle and then bounded down again.

The ref waved his hands without finishing the count. "It's over. Medic!"

Joe pushed through the ropes. "Holy shit, kid." He wrapped his arms around him and held on, bear hug style.

The crowd's cheers grew louder.

"That's the best you got?" Richie scaled the blue turnbuckle and saluted them, sweat jumping from his raised arms. The volume of praise increased. And for a moment, he was in The Garden, where thousands of fans screamed his name.

In the opposite corner of the ring, a doctor tended to Martinez, but the man didn't budge. He was open-mouthed and still—his eyes fading marbles.

He looks like Harold.

Back in the locker room, lights flickered black and yellow like that of an aging dance club, hanging onto strobes and techno music.

"You okay?" Joe ran his wrinkled hand over Richie's forehead.

"How's the cut?" Lingering thoughts tugged at him, threatening to suck him into memories of that night.

"Good, kid." Joe sat on the stool in front of Richie. "That hook was a thing of beauty." He scraped at the tape of the left glove, found an end, and then pulled it like a loose thread on a sweater.

Unable to find his words, Richie nodded.

"You're less excited than I figured you'd be." Joe balled the tape and tossed it to his feet.

"He was a punk. Not too much to be proud of."

"You kidding? First round knock-out in your debut fight? Tell you what, you got the gift. I'm sorry I didn't embrace this sooner. I may have held you back."

"You've been good to me, Joe." The words came out thin and labored.

The ride home from the barn invaded his mind, splitting his attention. The vault doors crept open.

Keep it together. Don't crumble now.

"Kid?" Joe prodded, slapping Richie's face. "What's wrong?"

"Nothing. Nothing at all."

"Well, get excited. This is a big deal. Only thing left now is a nickname."

"Huh?" Richie bit into the tape of his other hand, freeing an end from his skin. "Like a ring name?"

"Yeah. What about 'Ferocious' Richie Frezza? Has a ring to it. What do you think?"

"Not bad." Richie rubbed the irritated skin where the tape had been. "I've gotta better one."

"Oh, yeah? Please indulge me, Shakespeare."

"Ghost." Richie's eyes flickered like the strobe lights of the locker room. It was the perfect alter-ego.

"What the hell are you talking about?"

"That's my name. Richie 'The Ghost' Frezza."

CHAPTER THIRTY-ONE

Timothy's Jeep trekked toward the marquee in the foreground. The headlights cast a white sheen over the sign. The letters behind the glass case presented:

> *Ridgemont Cove Community Center Welcomes*
>
> *Boys and Girls Club – 4:30*
>
> *Senior Pilates – 5:45*
>
> *Miracles are Life – 7:15*

Timothy glanced to the digital clock. "You're late. It's seven-twenty."

"No biggie." Ruby unbuckled her seat belt and flipped the visor mirror down. She brushed at a piece of stray hair, errantly flung askew from the open window's assault of wind. "Coffee and doughnuts take up the first ten minutes anyway."

"You come here every Friday?" Timothy flicked his turn signal and slowed. "Takes discipline, huh?"

"That's one thing I've lacked for a long time. These meetings keep me grounded and remind me of what the past felt like. And," she closed the visor after another quick glance, "it's good to have structure. Gives you meaning, ya know?"

"I do, my dear." His mind tracked memories of just a month ago. Training until every muscle screamed for reprieve. Sweating breakfast from his pores in the sparring ring. Neon lights hung in the rafters of the Waller Complex flashed the amped crowd in multi-colored glows. The pain of a punch and relief of a victory. *Meaning.*

He turned right. The headlights of his Jeep now illuminated the front entrance to the community center.

"I used to play basketball here." He nodded to the building. Black and gold graffiti slashed the beige paint. "It was nicer back then."

"It's getting ugly around here."

"Maybe it always has been, and we were just too naïve to notice." He slid the Jeep into a slanted parking spot to the left of the front door.

She grasped his forearm resting on the center console. "Are you sure you don't want to come in? We're allowed to bring guests."

Timothy shifted the car to park and turned to her. "Maybe next time."

A frown, faint but discernible, crept across her face, adding a wrinkle to her chin. "Okay. I'm glad you drove me. Start small, right?"

"Yep. I'm happy to do it. We can make it a standing date. Seven-fifteen at Miracles of Life."

Her hand squeezed his arm a bit harder, and she leaned in. "Its Miracles *are* Life."

"Cut me some slack." He tilted his chin and met her waiting lips with his own. "I'm still new at this."

Their tongues locked, slow and deliberate, and Timothy

felt the urge to pull her in close and kiss until their mouths bled. She must have felt it, too, and she backed away. "I've got to go, Tim. Don't get me started."

"Sorry." He wiped saliva from the bottom of his lip. "How long do these things take?"

"An hour or so." She rifled through her purse and pulled a pack of gum from the side pocket. "You waiting on me?"

"Always."

She got out and climbed the steps of the building. A haggard and disheveled woman his mom's age greeted her. The two exchanged a few words and then disappeared through the door.

He scanned the parking lot, found nothing of interest, and rotated the volume dial of his radio.

"And welcome back to 106.9, The Cellar, your home for Friday Night Fights. I'm Jackie Pernell and my co-host, Bobby Slayton, is here with you as well to bring you all the action and commentary. You can stick with us all the way through tonight's main event."

"And what a fight it should be, Jackie. Bryce O'Leary, the undefeated Irishman takes on the savvy veteran Miguel Tapia. Both looking for a win and getting one step closer to an amateur title shot against Royce Burrow."

Timothy turned the dial a tick then reclined his seat. "Royce Burrow's a steroid ingesting cheat. I was on my way to meet him."

Was.

The radio broadcast cut into the thought. "It should be something, Bobby. A lot of firepower in the main event. And speaking of power, let's talk about that first fight."

"A doozy, Jackie. What a finish from the youngster."

"For those of you just joining us, the youngster my

esteemed colleague is referring to is nineteen-year-old Richie Frezza, and man oh man, what a knockout of Roberto Martinez."

Frezza? Never heard of you.

CHAPTER THIRTY-TWO

Interrupted by Benny's paw clanking against the front door this morning, Richie's much-needed slumber called to him. Now, he sat in a plush leather chair focused on a two-dimensional wave on the far wall of Purelli's office fighting his eyelids to cooperate.

Sunlight from the early morning coated the oil painting in a light haze, dragging the definitiveness of the colors into shadowed versions of themselves.

Look at you, Cranswell said in a hissing tremor, *made it to the boss's office. What did it cost? Oh, not much, just your little black soul.*

Salvador Purelli rapped his fingers on the cedar. The click-clack returned Richie's focus to the present.

Purelli's jewelry reflected in the sheen of the desk's wax coating. The methodical pitter-patter and Benny's heavy breathing drummed together in a light orchestra echoing in the expansive hideaway.

Seated in the second-floor of Purelli's restaurant The Tango, Richie remained apathetic, shooting nonchalant glances around the room.

Play it cool. Ignore those guys in your head. Why? Because they're in your fucking head, man.

So much had transpired between the meeting in the barn and now this early Saturday appointment. Eagerness to move forward with these men climbed within his veins. But the realization that doing so meant that more voices may invade his head, stifled the urgency to fully understand why he'd been summoned.

"Impressive." Purelli perused the newspaper in front of him.

Richie scratched at the stubble forming a square patch at the point of his chin. He couldn't remember the last time he'd gone three days without a shave. "Thank you, sir."

"First-round knockout." The boss looked up from the paper, his black diamond eyes flickered behind the gold-rimmed glasses. "Large profit."

Richie's gaze centered on the painting again.

An enormous oil canvas, melded in blues, grays, and greens. The frothy wave roared through the sea on a dreary day. It captured the anger and beauty of the ocean in a compact collage of paint strokes.

Behind Richie, from where he and Benny had entered, a small leather couch and marble table nestled in the corner. On the opposite side, against a wall-length window, a matching marble bar and rack combination held wine bottles and crystal stemware.

"Kid did well, eh?" Benny called from the couch.

"Acceptable in some respects." Purelli took a cigarette from a silver case on the desk and rested in his chair. With a swift strike of a match, he ignited the tip.

Richie squirmed in his seat and the involuntary shake in his legs began.

Purelli adjusted his tie clip and then smoothed the

fabric. Smirking, he laid the burning cigarette into a crease of the geode ashtray. He flattened the newspaper stretched across the desk and gazed out the window.

Unsure of how to proceed, Richie turned to get a glimpse of Purelli's window view.

Below, within a cross-section of streets, the weary and degraded Ridgemont Cove prisoners traversed sidewalks and empty alleys, searching for meaning or plotting devastation. They yearned for more, and Richie, now firmly within the grasp of *more*, pitied their futile dreams.

More is less sometimes.

His mother's face, a younger version akin to his elementary school days, appeared within his mind. Unblemished and clear eyed, she laughed. And he *felt* himself smiling.

Then, as quickly as she appeared, Harold's lean and pale face superimposed the image, turning the angelic face into a red-eyed demon.

He controls it all, the ghost said. *The streets and empty alleys run through his city. You're either guests or trespassers, but one way or the other, he'll turn your pockets out and strike you down.*

Salvador's rash voice cut the air. "This business with the two men has put undue pressure on me."

Richie's eyes traced the mobster's stare for a moment and then reverted to the wave painting again.

"I'm a careful man," Purelli continued, picking up the dying cigarette and puffing a drag. "I cannot be an accomplice to your problems. We helped you—my investment. But the favor must be repaid."

Purelli then stood, exhaling a cloud of smoke that blanketed the office. Richie tracked him through the window's reflection and lost the image as it ran from his peripheral.

What remained was a concrete sky dotted with black clouds hung high.

"He was in a tight spot, boss." Benny plopped in the chair next to Richie and motioned to the silver monogrammed case leaning against the ashtray. "May I?"

Purelli returned to the desk with a pitcher and three crystal glasses. He poured water into his cup and then returned to his seat. "Have as many as you would like, Benjamin."

With the care one would handle fragile china, Benny opened the container and helped himself to a cigarette.

The match burned and sulfur filled Richie's nostrils, and unusual relief to the bleach still clinging to Richie's skin after two showers. In the jumping flames, Richie imagined Harold's ghost waking again. He shuttered, bringing his eyes to the floor.

Get it together, man. It's all in your head.

Purelli clicked his ring against the desk. "You seem distracted, young man. Is everything okay?

"Yes," Richie lied, meeting the man's eyes in full for the first time since he'd entered the room. "Just tired, is all."

"Ah. I know the feeling." He looked to Benny. "But my fatigue is different. You see, I am tiring of unnecessary risks."

Benny tapped his cigarette into the ashtray and hunched over, shrinking in the chair.

"How many boxers do you think have sat in that chair?" Purelli's slender finger pointed toward Richie's seat.

"I'm not sure. I really—"

"Zero." His hand formed a circle. "And do you know why?"

Richie peeked to Benny. The big guy stared forward

and the cigarette in his hand vibrated a touch. Richie returned his eyes to Purelli's unwavering stare. "No."

"Because fighters, fight. Nothing else." The volume increased with each word until Richie drew back and dropped his hands to his lap.

"Boss." Benny's head perked up. "Don't blame the kid on this."

"I blame myself, Benjamin. But what is done is done. We have lent our young friend a favor, and now I suppose reciprocation is in order."

"I don't understand." Richie lurched forward and rested his elbows to his knees.

"We have assisted you in a personal matter, and now the debt must be repaid. I cannot divulge too much. Never know who may be listening." Purelli nodded to the ceiling and tapped his ear. "Let us say that you have a better understanding of the organization. Would you agree?"

"Yes."

"And since your privy to this new information, it is in my best interest to protect the integrity of my business. There must be trust on both sides. Do you understand?"

"Yes."

"Good." He snapped his fingers and eyed Benny, who stood from the chair.

The big guy fetched an envelope from within his vest and tossed it into Richie's lap. "Twenty-two."

He hurried to rip it open, certain he'd misheard the amount. His fingers slipped beneath the fold and started tearing the flap when Benny's hand gripped his chin and pulled it up.

Purelli's demonic glare slowed his greed. "Half now."

Richie drew back, though his fingers still grazed the thick envelope. "This is only half?"

"You've earned it, kid." Benny slapped his back then mimicked a few jabs that hit the air in front of him.

Shocked to have made this sum at all, Richie thumbed the top of the unveiled bills.

Purelli's hands clasped together like a tent, and he rested his chin at the steeple. "The night went well. Not too many thought you had a chance. Our investment has paid dividends already. I hope to see this partnership flourish."

"I do too, sir. What do you need from me?"

"In this business, trust is earned." The boss leaned forward and his three chunky gold bracelets scraped the wax of the desk. He jabbed his finger at Richie, its sincerity sparking revulsion through the fighter's bones. "It is time to repay the favor."

CHAPTER THIRTY-THREE

Timothy woke in a stupor, overjoyed from the needed release but aware of the previous night's cost.

Love me. Fuck me. Oh, now you hate me again.

He caressed her head. A soft tingling wave ran through his injured hand. Her shampoo, a coconut blend, clung to his fingers and rose to the air with each gentle turn of her hair.

The Monday morning news show, Wake Up Ridgemont Cove, filled the screen of the television hanging on the far wall. The anchor, Susan Teagan, ended a story about a rehabilitation center closing under scrutiny of insurance fraud and then jumped into a story about a man's body found wrapped in a commercial-grade weed blocking tarp.

"What's wrong with this town?" He asked aloud but didn't expect a response.

Ruby nestled closer and pulled the covers to her shoulders. "Just more reason to sleep another Monday away. Go back to bed."

He ignored the order. The coconut scent grew stronger,

and he relished the fragrance, sucking in the vapors like an addict.

Daylight, a soft gold veil, peeped through a small crevice unbridled by the window shade, illuminating her uncovered bare feet.

"Can't sleep, hon. I've got to find a trainer."

"What's the rush? Thought you said to start small."

"I meant us. Not boxing. The longer I wait, the less relevant I become." Timothy traced the nape of her neck. Her skin smooth beneath his fingertips.

Ruby shifted in the bed, bringing a watchful glance upward. "Maybe it's time to prioritize. Try new things."

Uninterested in opening wounds still fresh from the argument with his father on the subject, he searched for a topic more pliable and pleasant. "You never talked much about the meeting the other night. Is it a hush-hush kind of thing?"

"If you'd come in, I wouldn't have to tell you anything."

"Next week. I promise." He rolled his chest toward her, careful of the wrapped hand pinned beneath her shoulder. "So, what was it about?"

"The usual. A few people got their silver chip."

"What's that mean?"

"Six months clean."

"When will you have that?" Timothy's uninjured hand fell to her face, cupping her cheek.

"Seventy days and counting." She kissed the base of his pinky.

"Hopefully, I'm there for that one. I'm proud of you."

She wiped sleep from her eyes. "I'm not going back to the life, if that's what you're thinking."

"I wasn't." He kissed the top of her head then traveled to her lips.

"Down, boy. I haven't brushed my teeth."

"All right." He laid flat again, his eyes back to the television. "Tell you what. You get that silver medal, and Annabelle and I will take you to dinner after."

"Are you allowed to make decisions like that? Thought your dad was in charge. He sent me a picture a month or so ago. She's gotten so big, Tim. Those pigtails are out of control." A giggle escaped her lips and Ruby locked her legs around his beneath the covers. "We chat from time to time. Haven't heard from your mom, though."

"She is stuck in her ways, babe."

Babe. It had been so long since he'd used the endearing moniker and never thought when the time came to say the loving nickname again, *she* would be in bed with him.

"Do you think—" Choking her voice back, Ruby used the comforter to wipe at a scoundrel tear falling.

"I promise. Let me soften them up. If you hit six months and they say no, I'll overrule them."

"I'm doing better. I feel better. I just—"

"Right now, they're in charge, but time can do wonders." He flung the covers from his naked body.

"Sorry about it all, Tim." She sniffled. "I was so messed up."

"I didn't handle it well, either. I'm just glad you're okay and Bella is happy."

"Swear on my life. I think about her every day. I don't want her to forget who I am."

"She hasn't forgotten. One day, this will all work out. It feels different this time. I want it to."

"Me too." She rose on her elbows, and the blanket dropped beneath her breasts.

"It's amazing." He rolled from the bed. The movement

just a week ago would have sent jagged streams of pain through his head and hand.

"What is?" Her pink lips pursed, and she shook her shoulders, letting the pear-shaped breasts gyrate. A sly smile lifted her cheeks and the dimples formed.

"Don't be a tease." Timothy laughed and bent to find the clothing she'd peeled from his body near the nightstand.

"Excuse me? When have I ever refused you?"

"The Down Under Dance ring a bell?" A vivid memory etched in his mind. "You had the blue sequined dress and your hair curled. Kissing all over me. We get back to my parents' house—"

"You're forgetting that we snuck some of your dad's rum. I didn't refuse. I just passed out."

"Fair enough. Hey, do you remember," he blurted, unsure of why the thought had risen at this particular time, "when your dad tried to kill me?"

"Oh, God." She half snorted and buried her head under the covers.

"For real, I thought I was dead to rights." Timothy stepped into his boxer shorts and chuckled. "He came around that corner, shotgun in hand—"

"He wouldn't have pulled the trigger." She rose from the shield of fabric, the pale cheeks now flush. "Daddy liked you."

"Didn't seem like it."

"What was he supposed to do? You were fucking his daughter on a school night."

"Fine. I don't blame him, I guess." Timothy shrugged the jeans he'd been wearing for three days now on one leg at a time. "Froze my nuts off, though. I had to walk ten blocks in my underwear."

"I'm sure it wasn't loaded." A devilish grin danced across her lips.

"Good times, huh?"

"The best, babe."

I loved her once. Maybe I still do.

Timothy stretched the neck hole of his shirt and eased his head through the opening. Her smile wavered and drips of liquid slid down her cheeks.

"He was a good man, Ruby." The shirt clung bunched to his neck like a boa. "I didn't mean to bring it up."

"It's okay. It's good to talk about the pain. Work through it. That's what the meetings are all about."

He reached for her, but she turned over, enveloped in the covers like a cocoon.

Timothy drew back, as if he'd touched a raging flame. He hesitated for a moment then circled the foot of the bed. With a cautious grip, he pulled the covers down, revealing Ruby's tear-filled eyes. The white pillowcase beneath her head turned gray in spots from the wet splotches.

"I loved your dad." He kneeled to meet her eyeline. "Your mom, too. Every time I drive through that intersection and see the tulip wreath hung in their honor, it brings a bubble to my throat."

"I can't go by there." She sniffled and used her palm to wipe beneath her nose. "I drive ten minutes out of my way to avoid those flowers."

"Why?"

"It hurts, Tim. Serious pain. And it's not just that they're gone. It's a reminder of what I became afterward. How I was a coward and left Bella without a mother. Left you."

"It's not your—"

"No." She raised a hand to his lips. "I'm to blame for this. It's something I struggle with every day."

"Stop." He threw his head back and sighed. "You didn't get drunk and drive a pickup into your parent's car."

"My world stopped that day, and I didn't try to fix it." A howling cry filled the room, and her body shook beneath the covers. "I ran away and numbed the pain. Did despicable things, things, that if you knew about, you wouldn't be standing here right now."

"It's in the past." His eyes blinked a single tear. She was right. That day changed everything.

The car crash filled Ridgemont Cove's newspaper headlines. A drunken idiot in an aging truck t-boned their Mercedes idling in wait of green. The Dodge skipped over the sidewalk, executed a charming chocolate kiosk, and climbed the Millers' Mercedes.

Claire, Ruby's mother, died on impact, her neck snapped beneath the weight of the two-ton truck.

Douglas lingered. In the hospital the outlook was positive, but a surgery on his leg to repair ligament damage yielded an infection. MRSA took his life three months later, nearly to the day of his murderer's sentencing. Twelve years. Out in nine to live his life free if he was a good boy.

"I didn't help the situation." Timothy used his thumbs to swipe the tears from beneath her eyelids. A drop fell in the crease of the bandaged hand and snaked down to his wrist. "I could have been better to you and Bella. Bought into my own hype. I got wrapped up in the life."

"And I was slowly ending mine." Her cries softened to breathy whimpers, and she grasped Timothy's hands still cupping her face. "And poor Bella."

The innocent child had been along for the ride, and an exchange of harsh words on a frozen night in December two years ago drove the wedge through the foundation, splitting the two. Reconciliations marred with attempts at sobriety from her and paternal absenteeism from him ensured the wedge's strength sustained. The last fight woke half the street and blue and white cruisers knocked on the door. Not long after, he returned the diamond.

"But we've learned from it." Timothy's lips caressed her forehead and then dropped to her ear. "I love you. Always have." He stood and popped his arms through the sleeve of his shirt.

"Don't leave. Not yet."

"I need to train. We can't pick up the pieces without money." He picked at the fraying bandage of his hand. "Still have plenty left in the tank."

"In two years, you won't have to box."

"Why two?"

"On my twenty-fifth birthday, the family trust is under my control. No more allowances from the attorney making thousands a month for nothing."

"I'm not pilfering your inheritance—your parents' money. I've never taken a handout and won't start now. Besides, I have a debt to clear."

"With who?"

"The less you know, the better. I promise you, everything I'm doing is for us—Bella, you, and me. But I've gotta get my shit together. A few wrongs need to be righted."

"How are you going to train?" She pointed to his hand, the bandaging ruffled and frayed at the ends.

"I'll figure it out."

"Just come back to me." She turned away and hugged the pillow.

"Always."

He closed the bedroom door behind him and found his

keys on the kitchen island. Daylight broke through the circle window, shimmering off the blue specks in the granite.

Outside, Ridgemont Cove shrugged its blanket off with the birth of a new sunrise. A light rain fell, slicking the street in a ghostly haze.

The tires of the Jeep screeched through the mist. He flipped the radio dial, searching for a rock song. *Nothing better than fast drums and loud guitars,* his dad often said.

Timothy agreed.

He drove three blocks west, purposefully seeking the tulip wreath hung on the streetlight of Montero Blvd. Something within told him he needed to see it.

Reaching the intersection two minutes later, he located the flower arrangement hung on the post, its colors amplified by the rain.

On the sidewalk, a wave of late-night crawlers, red-eyed and staggering, returned from parties in search of beds or a final fix. One of the men leered in his direction and said something. Timothy upped the volume of his radio and turned down Wilcox Street.

A few dealers made headway to their stomping grounds to meet the early morning rush. The fellas took residence on the corner ahead, known gang territory of the Ninety-Nines. A few blocks further up, a blur of loud color and caramel skin, power-walked to the bus stop in six-inch heels.

As Tim's Jeep tiptoed by, the Ridgemont Cove regulars slanted quizzical glares.

In this part of town, the unfamiliar were ostracized. This vehicle had not traveled these roads in a while, and the watchers of the underworld took notice.

Timothy aimed for Knuckles Up Gym, a small brick building near Ms. May's diner. He'd made a mental note of it Friday when he scooped Ruby up and chauffeured her to the NA meeting.

Her guttural cry from earlier rang in his ears, but when he nestled the Jeep's right tires to the curb, a few spots down from the gym's entrance, it vanished, and a storm of tingles surged through his stomach.

Round two, Thunderstorm.

CHAPTER THIRTY-FOUR

Across town, the early sun blinked through a soft rain. Richie sat shotgun in the Cadillac for the first time. He and Benny drove beneath the overpass of I-7 on Ventura Avenue. Road signs for downtown appeared in the distance. Further still, the various buildings sketched the gray skyline in whites, pinks, and yellows.

"We gotta fix a problem." Benny adjusted himself in the seat and pulled slack in his lap belt. "Purelli thinks it's a good way to get your feet wet."

"And earn my keep? What kinda problem we talking about?" Richie stifled a yawn.

He wasn't sure why he felt so lethargic. Yesterday—a Sunday of ice packs, takeout and NFL—zapped the mongrels of his mind for the most part.

"This little errand ain't an initiation rite, kid. Whole lot more goes into gaining *our* trust."

"How much more? Cranswell wasn't enough."

"More than two weeks. And, no, Cranswell was payment for Harold. Far as the boss is concerned, we're still at ground zero." Benny wheezed then coughed. Phlegm dribbled from his mustache. "Hand me a napkin or something. Think I'm coming down with a cold."

Richie flipped the door of the glove box and found a pack of tissues. He tossed them to the big guy. "Are you sure it's not the two packs a day?"

"Jesus Christ, you my wife?" He dabbed at his lip and flicked the crinkled tissue out the window.

A billboard advertising eatery goods and a pair of motels flanked the exit ramp. Taking the turn, the Cadillac merged onto Mallory Street—the main artery of downtown. The road, lined with weeping willows on either side, hid beneath the branches above, shading the asphalt like a canopy. A quarter mile ahead, a cluster of buildings outlined in brick walkways and palm trees bathed in the early morning haze of sunlight and misting precipitation.

"So, here's the rub. We gotta guy who needs a spanking. Nothing too vicious but drive the point home. Our patience is running thin."

"So, just rough him up?"

"Yeah. Kinda." Benny turned left off Mallory and nosed into a parking spot in the lot of RC Commerce Center.

A minute later, the two men crossed the reception area stride for stride. A secretary reading a book didn't seem to mind (or care) that neither of them signed in to the clipboard hanging from a chain on her desk.

At the elevator, Benny waddled in first. "Hit the button, kid."

"Floor?"

"Three."

The elevator chugged upward—the ride a silent fifteen seconds, save for an instrumental version of Jon Secada's *Just Another Day* spurting from the thin speakers in the ceiling.

Richie considered mentioning a story involving the song and a girl he'd once dated, but as his mouth opened, the realization of his purpose in the elevator strangled the thought dead.

Business.

The elevator bell dinged and the opened doors presented a hallway. At the end of the corridor, a frosted glass Citron Trucking Incorporated door cut into the wall. The light was on.

"Follow my lead." Benny opened the door and marched past the circular welcome desk. "Donald? Where are you, buddy?"

Richie fell in step behind the boss, following him to a wooden door with Donald Glover—CFO etched in a bronze name plate.

Without a knock, Benny popped it open.

Seated, with eyes trained on a computer screen, a round-faced man with bushy hair on the sides of his head and a few stragglers atop clicked at a keyboard.

"Hey." The man stood and ambled around the desk with an extended hand. "Benny? What are you doing here?"

"Put your hand down, ya lying sack of shit. You gonna get your boys in line?" Benny tossed a chair on its side and saddled up to the man, nose to nose.

Richie flanked to the CFO's right with a puffed chest and stiff posture. He glared at him with a tight-lipped scowl, though Donald seemed to be more concerned with Benny's presence.

We gotta a guy who needs a spanking.

"The drivers are supposed to park their cargo and walk." The man's hands rose, and he backed away, bumping the front of his desk. "I told them to do it. They don't want to listen to an old man like me. What am I supposed to do?"

Richie stalked the man's retreat, close enough to whiff coffee remnants on his breath.

"What the hell does it matter to them?" Benny's head cocked back, and he snarled. "They don't pay a fucking dime. It's an insurance scam, Donald. Insurance pays the premium. Everything was perfect for three months. Our warehouses were full, and you were getting your cut. But now, you don't return calls. Deliveries are missing. That's bad business."

"They're not listening. Adjusters are on everybody's ass. My guys are scared."

"Well boo-fucking-hoo, Mr. CFO. Either they listen to you or else."

A smirk lifted one side of Richie's mouth. "You're worried about the insurance companies? You think we're a bunch of straight-laced, briefcase holding wimps?"

"I can't force them." Donald's eyes glanced toward Richie for a moment then returned to Benny, who now stepped forward and broke any escape Donald had. "Besides, it's starting to look suspicious. We need to cool down. We had twelve trucks reported stolen. The companies are catching on."

Benny jabbed a finger into the executive's chest. "I tell you when we cool down, capisce?"

With his hands higher, Donald sat on the edge of his desk. "Take it easy. I'm just saying we could use a little break and then pick things back up after the first of the year."

"Oh, I see. You think you have a say. You're calling the shots now?" Benny's voice boomed within the office. "We do as we're told. Don't we?" Benny shot a glance at Richie.

"Yes, sir, we do." Richie nodded in agreement.

"And right now, I'm told to get you in line." Benny's left hand shot out like a cannon ball and gripped Donald's throat. "You need to get the boys in line. If it doesn't happen, well—" His face aped the expression of a doctor who treated a terminal patient.

"What can I tell you?" The words, weak and rasped, seeped from the man's reddening throat.

This old bastard has some balls. I'll give him that. Not too bright, though.

"Fix this." The grip intensified, flushing the white from the man's face. "The trucks need to keep coming."

"I-I, ca—"

"You can't what? Breathe?" Richie swiped a letter opener from the desk and jabbed the tip into the man's neck, piercing the skin.

Benny released the hold. Donald bent over and hacked, wheezing for a few seconds until he straightened. "My job is on the line here. One or two trucks every quarter is doable, but what you're asking is greedy."

"You do realize you've just insulted Mr. Purelli. Not a wise decision."

"I meant no disrespect." He dabbed at his neck and inspected the hand. A trickle of blood smeared his palm. "I'm just saying there are other ways. If—"

"Richie, grab him." Exasperated, Benny stood the chair he'd knocked down earlier back on its legs and sat. A grimace crossed his face.

Donald tried a block, but Richie's hands were through his defense and squeezing his collar in seconds. He flung him over the desk and an array of files, loose papers, and office supplies followed him to the floor.

"You gonna beat up an old man?" Donald's voice came

out in a strained falsetto.

"You sound like those little doo-wop teenagers. Annoying shit." Richie hurdled the desk, pulled the man up with ease, and slammed his shoulders to the wall.

Benny reached for a People magazine on the side table near the window and flipped through the aqua colored print and half-ass celebrity gossip. "I'm not going to do anything. My friend here, though, he's having a rough week. He's itching to break something. Trucks coming tomorrow or what?"

"I can't promise you."

Benny nodded to Richie, who drove his elbow into Donald's face. The man's glasses cracked and sunk to the faded blue carpet.

"It's up to you, Donald. Guarantee delivery?" Benny flipped the page of the magazine.

"I can't." Donald covered his nose. Red seeped between his fingers.

"Another spanking, kid."

Richie cocked his shoulder back, lifted the elbow level with Donald's face, and swung it with the momentum of a two-ton pendulum freefalling. Its impact sent threads of tingling pain through Richie's arm.

"This could get very painful. Once we're done with you, we can pull your son in here too." Benny winked at Richie. "Same fat face and ridiculous mustache like his father."

"Please." Donald said, the word preceded by whistling as air sifted over fractured bone. "I'll do my best."

"I don't want your best. I want your guarantee." He tossed the magazine to the desk and leaned back in the chair.

Another elbow drove into Donald. This one caught just

below the eye. A gash opened, revealing a thin strip of raw flesh.

"All right. Stop. The trucks will be there."

Blood droplets canvassed the plaques of customer service excellence on the wall behind Donald's desk. Richie released him and stepped toward the window.

People now traversed the sidewalks clutching paper coffee cups. All meandering their separate ways. Always somewhere to go. Always in a rush. Always oblivious to the undercurrent and what lurked below.

Is that me now?

Richie frowned. A thick line of blood dripped to his knuckles. Its slide down his skin sent revulsion quaking through his body.

"Don't make me come down here again." Benny stood and straightened his hair, still askew from the short choking session of the CFO. "We have an arrangement. Understand?"

"Yes. I—" Donald sneezed, sending an explosion of black blood from his nose. He collapsed, cradling his face with both hands.

"One more reminder, kid."

Richie's shoulders drooped. *More?* He stepped forward and drove a piercing kick into the man's ribs. Flames shot through his ankle. Sensational, tingling pain.

A grunt, followed by a moan, passed Donald's lips, and he fell sideways onto the carpet. Blood seeped from his nose and dripped backward toward his blank eyes.

Standing over him, Richie did a half bow at the waist. "If we have to come back, your son gets round two."

"Nice touch." Benny clasped Richie's shoulder. "You did good, kid." He guided him to the exit. "Let's get back to Joe's. Get you ready for a real fight."

CHAPTER THIRTY-FIVE

Timothy stared at the walkway leading to Knuckles Up Gym.

His dashboard read fifteen till eight. *Any minute now.*

A man in a ragged hooded sweatshirt and blue jeans entered his view. Walking with a noticeable limp, he pulled keys from the sweater's pocket and struggled with the door handle.

Timothy waited for the inner lights to blink before treading toward the stoop of the building. It sat on a cracked sidewalk lined in weeded bushes and graffiti-stained newspaper dispensers.

Once inside, the scent of sweat and metal, an acidic but comforting odor, enveloped the clean air pushed in from the outside. The tarnished low steel beams of the gym's roof matched the weight benches and dumbbell racks lining a mirror wall reflecting a yellow haze of grime from years of fighters' sweat and grit.

A whirring air conditioner pinged in defiance of the winter chill.

In the middle, a small sparring ring, accompanied by

heavy bags and weightlifting equipment, completed the layout of every crumby boxing gym blueprint.

"Can I help you?" A gruff voice uttered from a darkened hallway in the rear of the building. The hunched walker from before, now relying on a mahogany cane, emerged from a blackened corridor.

"I'm looking to train." Timothy strolled toward the ring and wrapped an arm over the bottom rope.

"Looks like you need a doctor." Joe passed the cane to the other side of his body, and his knee buckled a bit. A small wince creased his dull, blue eyes.

"Already spent too much time with them. I'm looking to get back."

"Define back?"

"Guess you could say I'm in between promoters. I'm ready to fight again."

Joe scoffed. "I've heard those words pour from the mouths of many young men. Come in all smiles and grit. Leave bloodied and broken." His hand raised to his mouth, and he coughed, chucking the mucus into his palm. "Everybody wants to be Muhammad Ali."

"I don't float like a butterfly or sting like a bee, sir. I knock people out." Timothy inched forward, raising his uninjured hand in a fist.

"You look familiar." Joe limped closer and wiped his hand on his sweater. "Let me get a good look at ya. Whatcha go by?"

"Name is Tim. Timothy Vietta."

"Ah." Joe nodded. "Didn't recognize the new hairdo."

Timothy extended his hand, but Joe stood expressionless.

"Why here?" Joe's hands rose shoulder level and

expanded, his body forming a defiant cross. "A contender like you could do better, I'd think."

"I can't go back to my last guy."

Timothy eyed the sparring ring. The worn canvas floor yellowed from years of scuffing. Rope posts, large tarnished steel toothpicks, squeezed to death by the four lines of tattered ropes stretching to each side.

"What, you don't want to be followed around by the fat grease ball and his slick boss?"

Startled, Timothy brought his eyes to Joe. "You know about them?"

"I know about *you*, Thunderstorm." The old man shrugged the hood of his sweater on. "I'm afraid I can't help."

"Why not?" Timothy grunted, his shoulders raising in insolence.

"I just prefer not to, I guess."

"I'm not mixed up with them anymore."

"Exactly." Joe limped toward his office, the silhouette disappearing in the blank dark.

"What's that supposed to mean?" He yelled with a heavy voice that bounced off the walls.

"I'm already training one of their fighters." Joe's voice broke in volume. "Don't need two. Besides, you're damaged goods."

"Wait a minute. You afraid of them?"

"Boy, you best be goin' on your way." He limped out of the hallway and into the rising daylight struggling to dominate through the windows of the gym. He pointed his finger like a teacher scolding an obnoxious student.

"I have nowhere else to go—to rebuild."

"If *they* know you're training here, it puts him in danger."

"Your fighter's going to end up hurt." Timothy raised the bandaged hand. "Nobody wins with Salvador Purelli."

"See that door." Joe used the cane to motion toward the entrance. "You can see yourself out."

"I remember you now. You're Joe Gallant. The 'Giant Killer' of Ridgemont Cove."

"What I was, and who I am now, are two different things." The cane trembled in his hand but still served as a reminder of Thunderstorm's exit. "There are plenty of trainers. Go find someone else."

The front door groaned open.

A young man carrying a mesh gym bag walked through. Timothy could see the rough outline of his traps and shoulders beneath the long-sleeved Knuckles Up shirt.

So, this is the fighter.

"Morning, Joe." The new arrival dropped his headphones around his neck. Muffled music filled the dead morning.

"Right on time, Mr. Gallant?" Timothy shot the old man a sneer, whose expression had tightened a bit. "This must be your guy."

The fighter's head swiveled to Timothy, the eyes wide and mouth creased. "What's going on, Joe?"

"He was just leaving."

"We haven't met." Timothy extended the unwrapped hand.

"I know who you are." The new arrival pushed past the greeting and started toward the door labeled Locker Room.

"Who are you?"

"Richie Frezza." He spoke over his shoulder with a huff, annoyance even. "The one cleaning up your mess."

Well, I'll be damned. The hotshot knockout artist from Friday night.

"Never heard of you," Timothy lied.

Richie turned with a sneer and stalked forward. "Well, I've heard of you, *Thunderstorm*. Gotta say, not impressed."

The replacement. Purelli's quick fix to the Vietta problem. This just gets better and better.

He withdrew his hand and matched Richie's forward step. Though only twenty-four, Timothy had worked the ring and circuit like a professional. Cockiness on Frezza's part revealed immaturity.

Let's ruffle those feathers.

"And how far up the ranks have you climbed, tough guy?"

"One rung at a time, asshole." Richie pushed forward again and rolled the sleeves of his shirt to the biceps. A bruise on the right elbow streaked like a purple comet and died on the guy's forearm.

Timothy offered a solemn nod. "You'll get pushed off soon enough."

"Enough with the dick measuring contest, boys." Joe slid between them like an aggravated referee being ignored. "Too early for this nonsense."

Timothy heard the order but stood still with an intensifying stare. "This is bigger than you. You'll see what I—"

"There's the ring, has-been"—fire sparked in his eyes and Richie's voice morphed into something sinister and familiar—"you still got what it takes?"

"One win in the preliminary against a nobody, and you're ready to take on the world?"

"So, you *have* heard of me?"

"Pipe down." Joe lifted the handle of his cane and nudged his fighter's shoulder. The other hand pushed into Timothy's chest, knocking him back a pinch.

"You're lucky I respect this man, *Thunderstorm*."

Richie's voice returned to its earlier version and patted Joe's shoulder.

"How about a raincheck?" Timothy shot a few ghost jabs and straights. "I just think you and your trainer here need to understand."

"And what's that?" Joe's eyes flicked below scruffy silver brows.

"You're not just a boxer to them."

"Enough." The old man's cane now pressed in his back, forcing him toward the door. "This conversation is over."

"I can take care of myself." Richie formed fists and tapped them together.

"I said the same thing." Timothy raised his bandaged hand to the gash in his scalp and swiveled his neck to reveal the wounded eye. "Congrats on the big win."

Richie crossed his arms. His pectorals jut out like granite. "I'm not you. We've got it handled. This town is ours."

"Wrong." Timothy marched to the door and flung it open. "This town is *theirs,* and it's dying."

CHAPTER THIRTY-SIX

The door closed behind Vietta and Richie slung the gym bag over his shoulder. He caught a glimpse of the hardened blood embedded in his thumb's nail. "What does he mean by that?"

"Hell if I know." Joe leaned on his cane and started toward the hallway. "Come with me."

"Should we say something to Benny?" Richie flanked to Joe's right, concealing the hand marked with Donald Glover's blood. Inside the office, he scraped at the dry red with his other thumb while the old man tended to the coffee maker.

"Naw. The guy's mixed up." Joe placed a fresh mug under the nozzle. "Why we startin' late today?"

"Thought I'd let you get some beauty sleep, buddy." Richie flicked the remaining bits of Donald Glover from his skin to the office floor.

"The Guido was okay with that?"

"Careful, man." Richie unzipped his bag without looking up. "You and I can shoot the shit, but don't let them hear you say things like that."

"He's already got his claws in ya, huh? Didn't take long."

Richie ignored the comment outwardly, but shame filled his blood and seemed to pulse with each beat of his heart, shaking the vault doors.

"Any word on your next fight?"

"Benny is picking me up at three. We're supposed to sign the papers."

"Who you fightin'?"

"No idea. Doesn't matter. With you in my corner, we're good to go."

"Don't get too cocky, kid. Thunderstorm is right. You beat one schlep on the wrong side of thirty. It'll get harder each time. The higher you climb, the tougher you face. Humility is a weapon, too. You haven't gotten the memo yet. All that 'this town is ours' bullshit."

Richie ignored the slight insult and sat in the chair opposite the rickety desk. "What did Vietta want anyway?"

"Wanted me to train him. Says he's getting back in the ring." Joe snatched a soft pack of Winstons and propped one in between his thin, paling lips. The coffee dispenser beeped, and black sludge began its crawl through the nozzle.

"And?"

"What do you think I said?"

"Why you, I wonder?" Richie propped the gym bag on the desk. Navigating through a swarm of clothing and athletic tape, he scraped the bottom and dragged out an envelope.

"I don't know. Doesn't matter." Joe poured some powdered creamer into the coffee mug and took a gulp. "What's that?"

"My paycheck. I was hoping you could hold it here.

The Trails is too risky." Richie dropped the thick cream-colored envelope on the desk. It thwacked with authority.

"What do you mean?"

"I wasn't going to say anything, but my house got robbed the other night." He regretted saying it as the last letter slipped from his lips. And he sure as hell wouldn't bring up his mother. Not yet at least.

"Jesus Christ, kid. Everything okay?"

"Yeah. But to be safe, I'm hoping you can hold my cash until I set up a bank account and all that."

"I'll put it in the safe. Only thing in there now is the deed to the building. Expensive box to secure a worthless piece of paper." Joe grabbed the envelope and pushed it into his sweater pocket. "The damn thing will serve a purpose today."

"There's more coming, too."

Joe frowned. "I hope you know what you're doing, kid. I'm starting to get déjà vu."

"By watching me?"

"I was young once. And stupid. Just be careful."

"I got it covered," Richie offered, aware his head was dipping below the water line and no life raft was in sight. "Besides, what am I supposed to do? Wait tables? Answer phones? Wear a stupid tie?" He slid his long-sleeve shirt off and tossed it into the bag. "I barely graduated from high school, man. All I can do is fight. And the way I see it, it's better to be on Purelli's side than not."

"We don't need to rehash the same conversation. I'm just saying to keep your eyes peeled." Joe clutched the envelope in his pocket and then pointed to the mark on Richie's elbow. "That's a nasty bruise. What happened there?"

Richie rotated his arm and feigned ignorance. "Hell if I know."

CHAPTER THIRTY-SEVEN

James Benussi, Sonny Denardo to the city's underbelly, sat on a bench of Punch Point's boardwalk facing east. A few yards below, a white beach challenged incoming ocean water.

Locals named it Punch Point, an homage to fabled 17th century pirate Torrent Punch. Legends abound of his conquests and hidden booty astonished tourists in the summer and kept children sweating in their beds during Halloween.

To the north, a cove spit water into a mangrove line. Stilted on thick stems, the lush blanket of leaves dug into pearl sand and curved like a question mark, its arc jutting out to sea. Coconut palms peeked above and cast large diagonal shade atop the mangrove leaves.

On the southern side, a wooden planked boardwalk ran the length of the shoreline and then curled out toward the ocean. Kiosks offering ice cream and apparel rested vacant—the tourists a memory of months past. Kayak and paddleboard rentals for *just* 99.00 bucks. On the top edge of the boardwalk, nearest to the ocean and above a cluster of jagged rocks poking from the water like a pimple, a fish and tackle shop offered lessons for a small fee—bait included.

An old man drifting in a rowboat flung a fishing line to the water. A glass beer bottle sweat beside his tackle box. Benussi's eyes tracked from him to a trio of sweater clad teens traveling into the mangrove line. At some point, he assumed, a salty gust of wind would carry the stench of marijuana to his nose.

The last snot-nosed punk disappeared from his view, and then he glared down the uneven planks of the boardwalk. Spray from the ocean drifted on the breeze, sending a radiating shiver down his spine. *Hurry up and wait.* He'd heard the words in his younger, less experienced days. And now, he loathed them.

The second hand of his watch made laps, and he passed the time pressing the imprint of his boot into the softening wood.

It was Monday evening, and he'd parked his ass on this bench, waiting for Mark Lasker. *It could be worse, though.* At least the weekly meet-ups happened here, a scenic view far removed from the chaos smothering his personal and professional life.

The man in the rowboat paddled toward the cove, and for a moment, Benussi's mind wandered toward a simpler time. Bait fishing with Jake, the sun red and pleasant. The thought faded when he checked the time again.

God forbid anyone inconvenience the high and mighty Mark Lasker.

Twelve minutes after six, a full twelve minutes late, Lasker shuffled up the boardwalk.

A thin-faced and gangling man, the suit he wore bagged at his shoulders, and the shirt protruding from his waist fluffed. He sat beside Benussi on the bench and crossed his legs.

Lasker's pale eyes, a contrast to stark facial hair planted on his jaw, swept the cove.

Benussi's eyes mimicked, not in search of something new in the landscape, but rather as an instinct.

The fisherman in the cove pulled his rod hard and fell into the belly of the boat. A faint yelp carried over the cove and the line limped from the water, a snag of seaweed the catch.

"James, how you doing?" Lasker finished his sweep of Punch Point and turned to face him.

"Same as always." James Benussi replied in a flat tone, fatigue drawing the words from his mouth.

"So, what have you got for me?" Lasker shifted in the seat, propping an elbow on the top slat of the bench. "I have to tell you, Captain Taggert's on my ass about this one."

"Some things never change, huh? I'm out here risking my life, and you guys hold your hands out and say 'more'."

"We've all got a job to do." The thin, pompous dweeb snorted and cracked a thin smile. "You're our eyes and ears on the street, but there's a lot more to Operation Firecracker."

Oh, you don't say? I didn't realize what a monumental undertaking rested on my shoulders. It's not like I volunteered to throw my life into the blender. In fact, I resisted the assignment until you assholes threw an ultimatum into my face. Do you remember, Mr. Lasker? You recall my urging to find someone else because of Joanne's MS diagnosis, ya fucking prick?

"Still just surveillance." Benussi said, aware he'd drifted off in thought and Lasker had no intention of sympathizing with his silence. "Nothing solid, yet."

"I need something, James, or you'll be summoned to the fifteenth floor, and I won't be able to help you."

"Let Campini bitch and moan." His eyes wandered back toward the mangrove line in search of a gray swirl of illegal smoke. *Just send me back to busting dope fiends and wife beaters.* "He can find someone else for all I care."

"You and I know that isn't possible." Lasker's pointed shoulders shrugged beneath the oversized suit. "So, any new intel? The quicker we press charges, the faster you're home, James."

"There's a new kid. Richie Frezza. I sent his details over the wire yesterday." Benussi pulled a cigarette from his front pocket and lit it.

"You smoke?"

"Just started."

Lasker held his hand out, as if expecting a cigarette. Benussi slid another from the pack.

Fucking prick.

Lasker lit it and dragged deep. "I'm not interested in some newbie. From what I'm hearing from Campini, Captain Taggert doesn't have time to justify the spending or man hours anymore. If we shut it down today, what would we have?"

"Benny Bianchi's head on a silver platter." Benussi's eyes drew to a young couple. The mother swaddled a newborn, and the father snapped photos with a disposable camera.

I remember those days. Miss them.

"It's a start." Smoke spilled from the corners of Lasker's mouth and swirled like the tongue of a serpent. "Murder?"

"Plus, aggravated assault, extortion, and a few hundred misdemeanors." Benussi huffed on his cigarette then picked up the accordion folder at his feet. He slapped it into

Lasker's lap. "Case notes, logs, and surveillance cassettes. You know, I can mail this stuff. We don't need to waste each other's—"

"What, you don't like chatting? Thought we were friends, detective." Lasker's playful tone pierced Benussi's ears like a sharpened sword.

He said nothing.

"You know the brass." Lasker rummaged through the file. The cigarette dangled from his lips and ash fell to the folder. "Can't trust the postal service with such sensitive material."

Lasker placed the small cassettes near his thigh and flipped through the notes.

"It's all there." Benussi leaned back on the bench, allowing the salt air to fill his lungs. He flicked the cigarette. "Time-stamped, organized in chronological order, and ready to brief the powers-that-be about the target's activity along with observations."

"I'm not seeing much of *his* name in here."

"Can't get close enough to him. It's all hear-say. They're careful."

"All right. I'll have a look." He crushed the half-smoked cigarette beneath his heel, demolishing the filter to a stump, etched in the boardwalk forever. "Look, James, I know you're doing your best. Keep it up. Something will break."

Taken by a rare occurrence of positivity, Benussi nodded and watched the fisherman re-bait his hook. A new beer propped on the cooler reflected the dying sun's rays and flashed glimmers of light across the water as the boat rocked in the waves.

"Next week?"

"Next week." Lasker returned the cassettes to the folder and stood. "Be careful, detective." He started down the boardwalk. Through the gathering wind, Benussi heard the planks squealing.

In his coat pocket, the bulky flip phone Benny provided vibrated in a low murmur. *I'm off duty, you thug.*

He pulled the silver cell phone from his pants pocket, a present from his wife Joanne. A new model, he still struggled to understand how a mini-computer acted like a telephone. Its silver casing mirrored the fisherman's beer and reflected the withering shine of today's sun. The small bulb at the bottom blinked incessantly indicating a new message. He pressed a button, and the voicemail began.

Hey, hon. I miss you. I hope this isn't catching you at a bad time. His wife's voice supplied a grounding beacon that made him long for home. *Jake made the varsity tennis team. Coach Grambling said he's the first freshman to do it since he's been coaching. Growing up fast. He misses you. I do, too.*

She paused with a sniffle, and he wondered if she had a cold, or if she—he couldn't bring himself to say it. The thought of tears clouding those eyes made his heart ache.

Her voice beamed over the line once more. *Any idea if you'll be able to come for Thanksgiving? Mom is making her famous sweet potato pie. The one you love with the roasted pecans and marshmallows. Anyway, give me a call when you get a chance. Stay safe, hon. It's almost over. It must be. Two years is enough, right? I hope so. I love you.*

Benussi ended the message with a striking jab to the phone's screen—*right back at ya, babe*—he closed his eyes.

At this time of day, she was probably on the green couch in the den. The faint glow of a multi-colored Tiffany lamp from her late aunt's Belleview estate illuminating a crime novel in her cramped hands. Crutches soon to be a wheelchair leaned against the antique fireplace. She spent most of her free time there. But worrisome phone calls also lived in the room.

When her father's heart attack six years ago fractured the family, she'd received all the "so sorry for your loss" calls on the same green couch, then brighter and less worn to the nub.

Soft pitter-pattering steps tore through the image. Benussi's eyes opened. The three teens from earlier had cut up the mangrove line and high-tailed it past him. And, as he'd suspected, an earthy stench trailed their getaway.

Night dripped in the dwindling sunlight and insects chirped awake ready to feed on human flesh. The couple down the boardwalk bundled close to each other, clasping hands and cooing at the baby.

He played the voice message again. Her voice comforting, but painful to hear.

It had been six weeks. No embraces. No kisses. No heated games of Scrabble supported by rum and soda.

Just the job. The thankless, dangerous, and trying job.

CHAPTER THIRTY-EIGHT

The lunch crowd of Ms. May's Diner clanked silverware on plates and gulped coffee and iced tea. Elvis Presley's *Suspicious Minds* poured from the speakers bolted in the rear of the restaurant. A tune Timothy didn't mind, considering the other drivel available in the jukebox.

He perched on the barstool across from the kitchen swivel doors sipping a coffee and slurping oatmeal-flavored water.

"How is it?" Ruby asked. She filled the napkin dispenser near him.

"About as good as the House Special from a few days back." He dropped the spoon into the mush and gripped the handle of his coffee mug.

"Someone's a Debby Downer. The search didn't go well?"

"Define well." He pushed the bowl forward and traced the jagged scabbing scar on his hand with his finger—the bandaging no longer required according to Dr. I'll Charge Whatever I Want and You'll Pay.

"Did you find a trainer?" An order check on a binder

clip flew across the line from the kitchen and someone yelled 'Order up'. She pulled the ticket and matched its contents to the food waiting beneath the heat lamp. "Suzy, table six is ready."

"Donnie wanted no part of me," Timothy said to her back. "Snubbed me quick."

"Why?" She turned and bussed the bar area beside him, scooping dishes and silverware into a gray bin. She dropped the two-dollar tip in her apron. A waitress, presumably Suzy, shuffled behind the counter and balanced the three steaming plates in her hands. She offered a slight smile to Timothy and then rounded the corner of the bar.

"I'm untouchable, I guess." He slugged more coffee. "John Norris from The Pit even said no. Those guys haven't had a contender in years. Thought I was a shoo-in."

"What about that place near Sharpton? Fink's, I think." She asked, but he could tell her mind was somewhere else. Before he could reply, she strut through the swivel doors with the bin clutched in her hands.

No, they don't want me either.

She returned a few moments later with a commercial dish rack, the cups pegged through the individual squares steamed and sweating. "So, no Finks?" She pulled the glasses and stacked them in fours before placing them beneath the bar out of his view.

"Said they were full, not interested."

"How?" She completed the job and dropped the dishrack at her feet. "Weren't you twenty and oh?"

"Twenty and one, now."

"Still. I followed your career, believe it or not. Don't these guys know you're a winner?"

He considered sharing a few particulars, such as Purelli's grip on the circuit, but relented. *She'll just worry.* "I'll get it handled. A few more places to try."

Suzy stepped into the bar again. "I'm in the weeds. Need a coffee for table three. Good-looking guy in the suit. Can you pick it up for me?"

"Yeah." Ruby peeked at the new customer then filled a mug. "You ready?" She asked with the pot in hand, nodding to Timothy's coffee.

"Let er' rip." He brought a glance to the mirror on the wall behind the bar and caught a glimpse of Ruby's new customer. Cobalt blue suit and pink tie. Clean face and blonde hair. A scar above the brow, noticeable.

This guy didn't take the hint in the hospital?

Seated in a corner booth of Ms. May's diner, Reese Campini stared out the window.

Timothy tilted cream over his mug and watched the white morph the black to beige. "I know him."

He looked up, but Ruby now appeared in the reflection of the mirror, scribbling the cop's order on her pad.

A moment later, she attached Campini's order to the line and swung it toward the kitchen through a square cut in the mirror. The ticket window, she called it.

"What about Knuckles Up down the street? Did you try there?" She asked with her eyes on two new patrons strolling through the door. "That's where Richie trains."

"I'm aware," he said, refusing to allow the cocky asshole into his mind any further. "Hey, did that guy say anything?" He jabbed a thumb toward Campini.

"Just wanted a cheeseburger and fries. Medium well." Ruby dropped her elbows to the counter and leaned in for a kiss. "You jealous?"

He pecked her, uncomfortable for some reason, and

shot a glance around the diner like a middle schooler afraid to suck face and get nabbed by the principal. "I know him."

"How?"

"He's the guy that interviewed me after this." Timothy raised his hand.

"And?" Ruby pushed up from the counter and swiped another ticket flying across the line.

"Nothing. It's nothing."

Timothy finished his coffee and watched Campini though the reflection, glancing away here and there to avoid his attention. But for the most part, the cop held a stoic stare out the window in the direction of Knuckles Up. Timothy's covert operation continued for five minutes or so until a new guest check flung through the ticket window and Ruby matched it to an order. *Cheeseburger and fries. Medium well.*

She returned a moment later and began to say something when Campini pulled his stare from the window to the mirror. His eyes met Timothy's.

"Afternoon." Campini's crooked smile accompanied the snide pleasantry. A few other customers' heads swiveled at the loud greeting and Timothy hunched down in a vain attempt to turn invisible.

"Thunderstorm? That's you right?"

Timothy rose with coffee in hand and slid into the opposite booth. "Afternoon, detective." He flicked salt and pepper shakers toward their carrier. "What brings you to this dump?"

"Just having a bite." The cop flicked a few fallen strands of his golden hair behind his ear. "Never seen you in here before."

"I could say the same thing."

"Chance meeting, I suppose. Fate is an interesting thing, Thunderstorm."

"I've eaten here a few times now. The food is shit. What are you really here for, detective?" Timothy tilted his coffee mug up but kept his eyes glued to Campini's.

"You know the gym down the street? Knuckles Up." He pointed toward the painted sign affixed to the roof eave of Joe's building. "They got a new fighter in there. He's all mixed up with your old friends."

"Friends?" Timothy sat back in the booth; the cold vinyl iced the dwindling scab on his crown. *Richie Frezza.*

"Yeah." Campini's lips pulled back and displayed a childish smile. "Your gangster buddies. The ones who stabbed you. Looks like they've moved on to fresh meat. We've got our eye on him."

"Like I said, I don't know what—"

Campini's manicured hand rose from the table.

"Enough of the bullshit. You've made your choice. I don't agree with it, but what can I do? The world keeps spinning." His index finger rotated in a sloppy circle. "I can't let one bump in my investigation bring the damned thing to a halt. A lot of bad guys out there to shackle and send to Sharpton Correctional." He dipped a fry into a slop of ketchup and popped it into his mouth.

Timothy flattened his palms on the table and leaned forward. "So, this isn't about me?"

"Aren't you vain?" Reese unraveled the silverware set from its napkin shell and grasped the flat knife. "Shit, just the other day, a guy turns up with a chunk of his chest missing. Deader than heat this time of year. Blade used to kill him was big, too. A lot sharper than this." He flipped the knife in the air and caught it by the handle then tapped its serrated edge an inch from Timothy's scabbed hand. "Say, how big was Purelli's knife when he stabbed you? It may be connected."

Timothy's eyes rolled at the staged and obvious ploy. He glanced to Ruby, unsure of how much she knew or if she was in earshot of this delicate conversation. Heat swept through him and pushed dribbles of sweat down his shaved head.

Reese chuckled with another tap of the knife. "Like I said, I'm not here for you."

"What are you here for then? You scoping out the gym?"

"Mr. Vietta, it's a police matter. Not your concern."

"Don't you need a warrant or something?"

"A warrant to sit in a diner and have a burger? You watch too much television, Thunderstorm." He gulped the remnants of coffee from the mug and motioned to Ruby for a refill.

"Don't call me that."

Ruby sidestepped a few guests waddling through the aisle and lifted a steaming pot. She tilted the black into Campini's mug.

"Thank you, miss." He shot her a tooth-filled smile.

"More?" She glanced at Timothy's cup.

"Nah. I'm good." He cupped her arm, relishing the warmth of her flesh. "I'm heading out."

"So soon?" The cop cut his burger in half and took a bite. With his mouth full, he mumbled, "We've just gotten started."

"If there's nothing else?" Ruby pivoted away from the booth.

The sway of her uniform dress swept across the back of her thighs, revealing a crescent-shaped scar from her youth.

"We have nothing to discuss, detective."

Campini chewed and drowned the remnants of the burger with a swig of coffee. "There you go again, being prideful."

"You know what?" Timothy slid his empty mug to the wall at the end of the booth. "This whole tough-guy cop routine works better when you're using it on an actual suspect. I've got nothing to hide, man."

"I see. Cute story." The cop clasped his hands together on the table. "I'm not a lot older than you, but I am older. Wiser. I've been locking up scum in this town for a while now." His upper body lurched forward, an odd mixture of ketchup and coffee drifting from his mouth. "I'm going after the top dogs now. The big fish, you could say. And when I lock 'em up, you're going to wish you'd fallen in line because I'm a man that tends to hold grudges. And trust me, Mr. Vietta." Campini's eyes widened, revealing needled pupils amid dark blue seas. "You don't want a man that chases evil for a living to hold a grudge against you."

Timothy maintained the stare, an old tactic from ring introductions. *First to flinch loses.* "Well, you're making one hell of a bold assumption there, detective."

"Am I?" The jovial expression returned, and the eyes shrank. "Enlighten me."

"You are assuming good will defeat evil." Timothy rose from the booth. He pulled a few bills from the pocket of his jeans and tossed them near his half-eaten oatmeal. "I'll call you later." He offered a short smile to Ruby and shoved through the door.

While he had no reason to help Richie or Joe, if he was ever going to train again, especially after today's unsatisfying debacle, letting them on to Campini's stakeout may prove valuable.

He followed an alleyway feeding into a main street south of the diner and shadowed the fenced-in walkway, careful to stay beyond the nosy detective's view. An iced wind tore through the tunnel, and the injured hand throbbed.

Ahead, at the rear door of Knuckles Up, a familiar Cadillac parked askew absorbed the light mist of frozen rain.

Benny the Beans.

Timothy approached the vehicle's rear, which protruded from the alley's mouth.

The back door of the gym tore open and a heaving chuckle bounced between the concrete walls.

Surprised, Timothy backtracked and ducked into the adjacent side street, which stood as a buffer to Knuckles Up and a vacant building. He peeked his head around the corner, but his exhalations spat smoke like a smoldering campfire, forcing him back into the alley and out of view.

"Thought you were picking me up at three," a familiar voice said. Cocky as it was direct.

Richie Frezza in the flesh. Looks like Joe's golden boy's gonna get his hands dirty.

"Change of plans. I can't believe the little prick came here. We gotta find him."

Timothy recognized the deep, phlegm-filled wheezing voice of Benny Bianchi. He turned the bridge of his nose onto the corner of the building gaining the use of one eye to confirm the supposition.

"I've seen him at Ms. May's. We can check there." Benny stood opposite his driver, Sonny; his arms draped over the hood. "We'll swing by before we hit Donnie's."

Nick of time. Counting them lucky stars today.

"If he comes back, want me to get him?" Richie Frezza,

bundled in a hoodie with only his profile visible, opened the back door.

"Let me handle it." Benny tapped the roof of the car as if to say get in, and the three men slid into their seats.

The doors, almost in unison, clanked shut, reverberating throughout the alley. The brake lights flashed red in the gray air, like a demon's eyes in smoke. The eyes grew brighter as the Cadillac reversed.

Oh shit. Is this the only way out? Timothy backed into the alley, unsure if he crouched in the car's destination.

Make a turn, any turn. His shoulders now pressed to the brick, and his eyes closed. *Run to the other end? What if there is an alley ahead and I pop into open view? What if they're coming here? Think, Vietta. Think.*

The engine of the vehicle groaned, and though he couldn't see it, he felt the car nearing. He glanced down the alley, a thirty-yard sprint, maybe. Timothy lifted himself from the wall and dug his shoes into the minced asphalt.

Tires spun on loose stone, the noise a frightful alarm within him. *Go. Run for it.* He started, though as he did, the Cadillac's engine seemed to cough and not scream. Exhaust from the car floated into the opening where he hid. *They turned. There is an alley ahead, and they turned. Right?*

He peeked from the corner. The Cadillac was gone.

CHAPTER THIRTY-NINE

"I want to help you handle him. I shoulda knocked him out yesterday." Richie sat behind Sonny and arched over the center console.

"Nah." Benny buckled his belt and reclined the seat. "You did the right thing. Chain of command, remember?"

"I just don't like the guy."

"Hey, you do the right thing, and you're rewarded."

A phone fell into Richie's lap. "What's this?" He examined the cell and flipped the earpiece.

"What's it look like, kid? Got you a phone. Now you don't need to run home and listen to the answering machine. Jesus Christ, who still has house phones these days?"

"Thanks." Richie searched through the contact list. Only BB appeared on the screen. "This you?"

"Yep. And that's not all." Benny adjusted the mirror visor and Richie caught his eyebrows dancing up and down. "I'm gonna give Candi a call."

"Candi?"

"The tasty treat from Moonlighters. Your reward."

"Oh. I forgot about her." Richie slid the phone into his pocket.

Benny's roar shook the car. "Trust me, after she's through with you, you'll never forget her. Just do it right, though."

"What do you mean?" Richie caught Sonny's stare in the rearview, an odd sense of bewilderment ripped through him. The guy never said a lot, but today he'd been mute.

"She's a stripper, sure. But, if you want to get her tasty mouth around your prick, ya still gotta pony up the dough. Wine and dine, my young friend. The better the date, the farther she'll go. And like I said, I'll give you the scratch. My treat."

"Thanks." *Murder a dude, beat down a pretender in the ring, and what do you have to show for it? Some hooker's mouth.*

The Cadillac navigated through a few side streets and then merged onto Worthington Avenue.

Benny now had his cell phone to his ear. "Hey, yeah. Looking for Donnie."

Richie fell back into the plush seat. Today's session, a heavy dose of cardio and high-interval-training shocked his muscles. He'd struggled to stand upright in the shower afterward. The rhythm of the tires over asphalt created a melody like a lullaby, and Richie's eyes closed.

The last few weeks had been a whirlwind. He was escaping it, if only for a few moments. He wanted to sleep for days and wake up to find it had all evaporated away. The vault deconstructed. Mom still in the room, high but alive. Joe puffing cigarettes and critiquing his punching style. Benny an acquaintance on Thursdays, and Purelli a mere myth. He didn't know Roger Cranswell, Harold, or

Georgie. Ruby was still playing the game and Timothy was a joke in the headlines.

"Donnie, I don't give a shit if the line-ups are set." Benny's voice reverberated in the car. A fine mist of spittle sprayed the interior windshield and coated the keys of the cell phone. "I got Richie Frezza on the way to you. Find him a fight now."

Richie's eyes opened.

Still real. The vault shined, harboring the black souls of his dead. *Roger and Harold are dead and I'm to blame.* The vault closed, but an image of Joe in the ring with punching pads locked on both hands sprung to mind. *Joe's hating me more and more each day.* The picture of the old man faded, but now Ruby's smile surfaced. *Timothy fucking Vietta stole my girl.* A new memory crept in. Linette Frezza, face full and eyes sparkling. Years before the Row. *And mom.*

"Kid." Benny leaned across the arm rest and patted his knee. "We need you to win a few more. Then we won't have to worry about getting you booked. They'll come to you."

"Huh?"

"Hold up, Donnie." Benny brought the phone to his chest. "Hey, you awake back there? Get a load of this little twerp, Sonny." He smacked the big guy's shoulder, but the driver said nothing. Hands gripped to the wheel; posture stiff. "Like I was saying, kid. We need to up your clout."

"I thought Mr. Purelli owned the whole thing? Why do we have to go through Donnie?"

"He owns the—" Benny bit at his lip and shook his head. "Put it this way, aligning yourself to a legitimate business requires trust."

A phone rang. The dull vibration shook inside a cup holder between the two front seats. Sonny scooped it up.

Grunts interspersed with pauses and sighs. This went

on for a few moments and then Sonny killed the call and dropped the phone back to its resting place.

Benny, never missing a beat during Sonny's silent call, screamed into his phone at Donnie. "I'm almost there. Find me a fight, you prick."

Outside the car, through a frosted window view of the frozen city, buildings bloomed into more eclectic and modern structures—a departing view of the slums.

"Who was that, Sonny?" Benny pocketed his phone.

"The wife." His blue eyes darted from the street to the rearview mirror.

"Short and sweet with the broad, too?"

"Gotta be."

"When you gonna bring her around? Shit, I've known you a while now. Not one invite for dinner."

Sonny shrugged his shoulders and turned the Cadillac into the parking lot of a standalone building draped in tinsel and Christmas lights. A pair of mechanical elves stood at each side of the door waving candy canes.

"Not even December yet and Donnie's got it looking like Santa took a shit." Benny motioned for Richie to go ahead. "Gimme a minute."

Richie opened the door, and a gust of frigid air smacked his face. He climbed the steps and gripped the handle of the door with Promotion Boxing etched in the glass. As he touched the knob, the vault opened.

Not again. Leave me alone.

That's not part of the deal, Harold said.

We're part of you now, Cranswell added.

CHAPTER FORTY

"Need a favor from you, Sonny." Benny inspected the closing door of Promotion Boxing, like a scientist examining a specimen. He waited for it to shut, as if Richie's ears could pick up the conversation.

"What's up, boss?"

"This Vietta situation could be a problem." Benny's arms crossed like a toddler scolded for spoiling dinner.

"How so? Why snoop around?"

"Fuck if I know. He's making the rounds though. Stopped by to ask if Joe would train him. I got calls from other clubs he's visited."

"He's got some balls. Purelli shoulda' killed him when he had the chance." Sonny turned the key in the ignition. The slow purr of the Cadillac faded along with the heat inside.

"What have we talked about?" Benny's lips slanted down; the thin mustache arched like a black parabola. "We don't use his name. Never know who is listening. Cops been known to plant a bug or two in a Cadillac."

"We swept it this morning."

"Don't matter, Sonny." Benny's finger jabbed toward his driver's temple. "Can never be too careful."

Sonny's thick arms rose and formed a V. "Should we step outside to talk then?"

"Don't be a smart ass. It's the principle of the thing. Anyway, the hospital was a message."

"Doesn't sound like Vietta got the hint."

"That's where you come in." Benny leaned back in the chair, smiling. He eyed a petite blond outside of Cash & Loans. "Find the prick."

"How serious a statement are we making?" Sonny removed his shades and swiped at a red mark forming at the bridge of his nose.

"Just locate him. When you do, give me a ring. Okay?"

"What about you?"

"I can drive myself. Besides, I got the kid if I need a little muscle. After this thing here," Benny nodded to the door Richie just walked through, "take one of the Lincolns in the garage and find him. When you do, call me. The kid can't find out either."

"Purelli gonna waste him?"

"Are you brain dead?" Benny smacked Sonny's shoulder, hard enough a strike to sting his knuckles and shake the gold rings on his fingers. "What's the matter with you?"

"Sorry, boss." Sonny rubbed at the area Benny struck. "I'm under the weather. Not thinking right."

"Well, get right and do as you're told."

"All right. Why can't Richie know?"

"He's a natural, but some things need to be close to the vest." Benny's eyes caressed the young woman again who now dug for something in her purse.

A sexier version of Deb, tighter in the right places.

"Where do I start? Ridgemont Cove is a big place."

"Keep an eye on Ms. May's." Benny cracked the door open and whistled at the blonde. "Check his parent's house in Belleview, too. Hit The Pit and Fink's while you're at it. Joe said he was looking for a trainer. Like I said, once you find him, keep it quiet and let me know." He shoved the door wide and stepped out.

"Hey there, beautiful. Too chilly to be dressed so sexy."

CHAPTER FORTY-ONE

When Timothy reached the back entrance of Knuckles Up and tugged on the handle, the steel door shook in its trim but didn't budge. He crept toward the sidewalk, aware Campini's eyes were on the front door.

How long can I sit here?

On the street, parallel parked in front of the payphone, three cars hugged the curb. The one nearest Timothy, a white Impala, had cop written all over it.

So, what? Wait until this guy climbs in his awfully disguised undercover cruiser? It's thirty degrees.

The bitter cold mist sprayed harder now. It molested his lungs and pricked the scab of his scar, icing the staples still in place that would supposedly be absorbed by the skin.

Not if they're frozen.

He looked to the gym's entrance and then back toward the Impala. *What now?*

His leg vibrated, and in the midst of solving this quandary, he faintly heard the monotone ring. He scooped the healthy hand into his jeans and pulled his cell out.

"Hello." With the phone a foot from his mouth, he investigated the number on the screen display.

"Hey." Her voice responded, angelic and soft.

"Ruby?" It hit him. She solved the maze without knowing it. "Listen—"

"No, you listen." Her voice hardened, morphing into annoyance. "You underpaid your bill, Tim. That comes out of my end."

"Sorry. I left in a hurry."

"I know. Why?" The clanging of dishes and buzz of conversations throughout the diner muffled the question.

"Look. I can explain. Do me a favor, though."

"Why should I?"

"Jesus Christ, hon." Timothy breathed in. Chilled air scraped the lining of his throat. *This woman.* "I'll pay double when I get back there. Just listen. Is the cop still there?"

"Yeah."

"Where exactly?"

"In the booth, where else?"

"Okay." He poked his head out in the open street and glimpsed the reflection of the sun on the windows of the diner. "Go talk to him. Keep his eyes away from the window."

"Are you okay? How many Percocet did you take?"

"Just do it, hon. Please."

"Whatever you're up to, I don't want to know."

"Are you going to go talk to him?"

"Yes. I'll do it." The line clicked dead.

Timothy counted to ten and slid onto the sidewalk, shimmied with his back on the face of the building, and jumped the three steps leading to the entrance.

Joe sat on a stool wrapping a young fighter's hands with

athletic tape. The boy, not more than twelve, wore a face of grit and anger, unmistakable rage. He gave Timothy the once-over. "What happened to you?"

Timothy remembered his face and stitched head. "Went to battle. Lost."

Joe smirked at the comment then brought his eyes to the boy. "Mikey, hold still, I'm mucking the wrap up."

"Sorry." The young fighter kept a scowl toward Timothy, but his hand straightened and stopped moving.

"I need to talk to you," Timothy said.

"I'm working." The old man passed the tape over Mikey's knuckles, pressing within each groove and doubling the wrap again. "Besides, we got nothing to talk about."

"I need ten minutes." He glanced from Joe to the kid. "Hey, buddy."—Timothy nodded to the boy—"why don't you do some stretching while we talk?"

"I'll give you five." Joe rose from the stool, knees popping.

The boy wandered over to the dumbbells and struggled to curl weight far beyond his physique.

"On the mat." Joe shook his cane in the air. "Stretches then pushups."

A frown crossed the boy's lips.

"How old is he? Shouldn't he be in school?" Timothy eyed the young fighter.

"You want to waste time talking about my customers or do you want to get to the point?" Joe crossed his arms and cast a listless glance toward Mikey. Metal on metal clanked with each attempt to set the weight down.

Words swirled in Timothy's head in and out of order. *Inform, don't intimidate.* "I think the cops are watching you, Joe."

"This is Ridgemont Cove." The trainer clapped his

hands with an aped expression of awe. Thick echoes danced in the rafters. "They watch everybody. What's your point?"

"Some bigwig cop from the Organized Crime Division. Doesn't concern you?"

"I've got nothing to hide." Joe rubbed his knee and watched the boy perform a push-up. "That it? I've got a paying customer to get back to."

"No." Timothy hoped the news would shake Joe a bit and give him a little leverage, but the old codger's stubbornness proved hard to crack. "I heard them talking. Benny and Richie. They're gunning for me. I'm not sure for what, but your boy is right in the thick of it, man. He's freefalling off the cliff."

"I'm not stupid and neither is he." Joe gimped toward the hallway. His left leg buckled with each stride. "You're wasting my time."

Timothy followed the old man's path. Stale nicotine poured from the open office door.

Inside, Joe sat at his desk. A tattered poster of a much younger and stronger Joe Gallant caught Timothy's attention.

When he was just six, Timothy's father had ordered the mega-fight on pay-per-view. Sitting cross-legged on the floor, a young Thunderstorm mimicked the *oohs and ahhs* of the adults in the Belleview farmhouse. It was the only time his dad and he had ever shared an affinity for two guys slugging each other's brains out.

Joe Gallant pranced around the ring. Jabbing and evading. Jabbing and evading. And then the unthinkable happened. Right in the small Belleview farmhouse, on a twenty-inch Panasonic television, Ridgemont Cove's Joe Gallant fell to the canvas.

The blurred picture on the screen showed the referee reaching the ten count. Could it be?

"He barely touched him," Timothy's father had protested.

"It's a fix," Pat Barnes screamed from the porch.

And then, the farmhouse went mute and the clicking wings of the crickets outside filled the silence.

Later, Timothy learned the weak punch knocked Joe Gallant out of boxing forever.

The newspapers ate up the scandal of the preposterous notion that Joe Gallant had thrown the fight. Accusations of a gambling addiction spewed from the pages. Some reports alleged he'd lost on purpose, so his debtors could rake in dough against the ridiculous odds slated by the casinos.

Freddie Solano, the undisputed boss of the Solano crime syndicate at the time, warded off press inquiries regarding his involvement.

"Of course, he's involved," Pat Barnes had told Timothy's dad over a beer.

Timothy played with GI Joe action figures on the deck, absorbing every word of the conversation. The highlight of the day? Solano owns everything.

Timothy never wanted to believe it. But the following days proved not all men are righteous and good.

After the fight, the Boxing Commission ousted Joe and issued a lifetime casino ban. He disappeared, slipped out of the limelight. Joe "The Giant Killer" Gallant faded like the static of the little twenty-inch Panasonic television in the small farmhouse in Belleview.

Now, standing in Joe's office and speeding up his chances of lung cancer, an inkling of doubt permeated somewhere deep in his mind, growing.

Timothy pushed the memory aside and sat in a chair

opposite the desk. "It's not just boxing. These guys are stalking me. I know it. Eventually, they'll find a reason to come after you."

"*Richie* has an arrangement with them. I train the kid." Joe cradled his fingers atop the mound of straw gray hair and pushed back in the chair.

"You can't possibly be so naïve." Adrenaline swept through him. He wanted to grab the old man by the shoulders and shake until he admitted Timothy's words made sense.

Joe's lips tightened. The pale eyes sunken in the wrinkled sockets widened. "You have two minutes left." He pulled a bent cigarette from the crumpled pack on the desk.

"Help me. I know your story. No parents. You bounced around orphanages until you were ten. Started fighting. Vietnam. Undefeated as an amateur. Got your shot in the big time. It's what I need, Mr. Gallant. I need *my* shot."

"You had your shot and blew it." He lit the cigarette, dragging hard. A spiral of smoke escaped his mouth and then shot up his nostril.

"Shouldn't I get another? Don't we deserve a fresh start? You can sympathize, can't you?" He looked at the poster again and then back to the older, wrinkly version. "Look, I need to stay off the radar. Let things cool down. Once I get back in the ring, make some money and square up with Purelli, it all goes away. It's my best option."

Joe flashed a nicotine-colored smile. "You ever heard about death and taxes?"

Timothy now grinned, remembering the six-pack he and his father shared on his eighteenth birthday. "There the only two things in life that are guaranteed."

"That's right. You're not as stupid as you look. But you're forgetting one. There's a third." Joe exhaled another cloud and ashed the cig into an ashtray perched on the desk. "You don't cross Purelli. If you do, it's lights out for good."

A dull ache at the base of Timothy's throat surfaced. Fear.

"What are you saying?"

"At some point," Joe said, the gravel voice now softer, "he's gonna kill you. That's why I can't help. We shouldn't even be talking. I hope today is the last time you walk through my door. Nothing personal, Thunderstorm. It's survival."

"All the more reason to get out of here. Help me leave." Timothy sat forward, draping his arms across the edge of the desk. "I'm sure you had the same conversation with Richie."

"I did." Joe's eyes tracked the poster now. "I tried to get it through his head. Some people gotta learn the hard way. Just like you did. What do you owe them?" Joe, elbows on the desk, leaned in. "Be honest."

"I was a ten to one favorite. My guess? He lost around a hundred or so."

"A hundred thousand? You're as good as dead."

"He could have killed me at Ridgemont Memorial. He didn't for a reason." Timothy rubbed his thumb in a circular pattern against the index and middle digits of his sliced hand. "A dead man's debt is no good."

"Huh?" Joe leaned back in the chair, and its spine squeaked beneath the weight.

"It's what Benny used to say." A summer night from a year ago appeared in his memory. Bianchi flipped through a stack of hundreds, grinning in delight as the victim of their beating panted and protested. *It's always about money.* "Purelli wants his cash. I'm no good to him dead."

"And where the hell are you going to get a hundred grand?"

Timothy's unscathed hand rose from the desk and balled into a fist. "The only way I know how."

"Well, you sure as shit can't train *here*."

"Point me in the right direction. Someone safe." Relief coursed through Timothy's body. The old man's defiant demeanor softened.

"I'm not making any promises."

"Understood." Timothy's feet tapped the floor of the office, excitement renewed.

Joe dug into the desk drawer and yanked out a writing pad. It plopped on the desk with a thud. He snagged a pen from an aging coffee mug and began scribbling.

"His name is Marty. He's in Sharpton. Tell him I sent you. And remember, this didn't happen." Joe ripped the paper from its pad and extended it across the desk.

Timothy took the page. *Thunderstorm is back.*

CHAPTER FORTY-TWO

The kid pushed through the doors right after the snotty blonde turned away with a sneer.

"What'd he tell you, kid?"

"Some guy named O'Leary." Richie blew warm air into his cupped hands.

"This week or next?"

"Next Friday."

"That so?" Benny toyed with the notion of pulling Donnie's throat through his ass, but climbed back into the Cadillac instead.

Richie hopped in the back and scooted to the center seat. "Is that okay?"

The Cadillac pulled away from the curb and swung into the nearest lane.

"Bryce O'Leary is a veteran. Tough guy. He's undefeated. Seventeen wins with fourteen knockouts. We tried to get him on board. Irish boys beat us to the punch. I hate those grimy Guinness drinking bastards." Benny turned to Sonny and awaited acknowledgement or confirmation from the big guy. Neither materialized.

"So, we know all about him, right?" Richie asked.

"Yeah, kid. We've done our homework. The guy is a plodder, slow but powerful. My question is why your second fight is against him? Donnie is pissing me off. Sonny," Benny rapped on the man's chest, "stop the car. I'm going in to—"

"I can take him."

"Yeah, boss." Sonny glanced to the rearview mirror. "Can't change it now. Makes the kid look weak."

"Oh, you have an opinion, too?"

"I can take him," Richie repeated.

"You don't lack confidence. I guess that's something."

Benny huffed and sat in the seat. Annoyed with the interruptions of two underlings but conscious of the rationale, he drew the window down.

Frigid wind sliced into the Cadillac.

"Where to, boss?"

"Take the kid home."

Sonny reversed from the parking lot, cut an elderly, honking driver off and merged into traffic. The car inched forward in a sea of taillights.

"I can take him." Richie sprawled in the back, his eyes two glowing orbs of confidence.

"All right. But you need to get your head on for this one. The Irish prick is a whole different animal. Martinez couldn't hold his jockstrap. We gotta get you—" Benny halted. A buzzing complemented the whistle of the frozen gusts outside.

"You gonna answer it, kid?" Benny shot Richie a glance through the rearview.

"Not mine."

Sonny reached for the black cell phone in the cup

holder. It laid dull and silent. "It's me." His hand lurched into the left pocket of his slacks.

"When did you get a second cell?" Benny's hand shot two digits to the air.

"Always had one." Sonny switched the new phone, a silver flat screen, into his driving hand. He grabbed the wheel with his left and turned the car onto Port Avenue.

"I've never seen it. Why do you need two?" Benny grabbed the black phone in the cupholder and flipped it open. "Hiding from the wifey?"

Sonny smirked. A light rain pattered the windshield. Drops died and exploded on the glass.

"Well, are you gonna answer the fucking thing? I'm trying to have a conversation here." Benny pointed to the pulsating phone in Sonny's hand.

"Don't recognize the number. Probably some asshole trying to sell me aluminum siding."

"What the hell are you doing? What's going on?"

"Nothing, boss. Just a wrong number. Not worth your time."

"Stop the car." Benny's voice rose an octave, and the kid squirmed in the rearview mirror's reflection. "I said stop the fucking car." He tossed the black cell to Sonny's lap. The driver pocketed it, but clutched the other phone tight, his knuckles whitening.

"Okay. Okay." Sonny nosed the Cadillac to a curb; the wheels clipped the raised concrete, and the car jostled. He turned the ignition.

Sonny's jaw pulsed, but the eyes hid beneath the shade of his sunglasses. Benny continued the stare like a poker player ascertaining the validity of an opponent's bet.

The silent thug treaded dangerous waters. Insubordination at your nine-to-five may warrant a meaningless write-up, but in this world, such actions resulted in a write-off. Right off the fucking planet.

"Who was it, Sonny? You lying to me?"

Benny's nostrils flared and a faint sweat surfaced on his forehead.

Sonny, blue eyes fierce and unflinching, said nothing.

"Who called?"

Thick silence warmed the car. Sweat dampened Benny's palms, an inkling of treachery causing his body to tense.

The two stared at each other, neither willing to break. The poker game continued, but Benny held the aces. *C'mon, ya prick. Say the right thing.*

Sonny flinched first, letting out an exaggerated breath. "My wife knows both numbers. We're going through some shit. Not a big deal. I'll straighten it out."

"Your family comes second to *this* family. What does she need that's so important, she can't stop calling you at your place of *business*?"

"I'll straighten her out. It won't be a problem again." The silver phone in Sonny's hand started vibrating again.

"Why don't ya answer your phone and do it now?"

"I'll talk with her later, boss. It's nothing important." Sonny poked at the screen and the buzzing ceased.

Benny's eyes peeked at the screen display and then jumped to the rearview.

Richie connected with him for a short second then forced a blank stare to the rain spattering the glass of the windshield.

"Let's get Richie home. He needs to rest. Sound good, kid?"

"Yeah."

Without a word, Sonny turned the key. The Cadillac awoke and headed to The Trails.

CHAPTER FORTY-THREE

For the better part of two weeks, Ms. May noticed the black Cadillac drive into her view at odd times, day or night. She had seen it more frequently in the last couple days. It would circle around, sit idle for a few moments, and then the bulky bald man would get out. The fat guy from the payphone would exit from the front passenger door. And on occasion, Richie would emerge from the back. Sometimes he crossed the street and got *in*.

Regardless, Ms. May was far too familiar with the damn Cadillac.

It spelled trouble for Richie—a message the mixed-up boy had no intention of capturing. Try as she might, he was stubborn.

"Here you go, Ms. Thomas." Ms. May placed a steaming plate of turkey breast to the table. "Extra stuffin', as always, dear." A dish from the other hand went to Mr. Thomas. "And the meatloaf special here. Anything else ya'll need?"

"We're fine. Thanks," Mr. Thomas replied, unraveling silverware from the napkin.

"If you need me, just holler. I'm alone for a couple minutes until my girl Ruby gets back from the Quick Stop."

"Why is she there?" Ms. Thomas asked with a mouthful of stuffing.

"Getting change." Ms. May shrugged, somewhat embarrassed her drawer needed tending to.

She returned to the bucket of suds. A worn sponge swam in its bubbles. She scrubbed a booth near the window. Headlights pierced the glass like lighting striking in the pitch of night. Then, a shadow crossed into her peripheral.

Damn Caddy.

To her surprise, a white sedan trolled past instead. It crept forward and parked on the opposite side of the road.

Ms. May finished wiping the booth and turned her attention to the four high top tables lined near the front entrance. The Friday night dinner rush yielded messes since kids ate for free. Broken crayons and children's menus scrawled in nonsensical lines of color scattered the floor.

She bent to snatch the papers, the old hip creaking and stinging. She rose, carefully, with a ball of crumpled paper. Through the window, she saw two men exiting the now parked white sedan. They threw cautious glances to each side of the street as they crossed over.

She shuffled to the kitchen to throw the paper menus in the trash and empty a sludge bucket of grime and leftover meatloaf.

Freddy, wearing a stained apron reeking of tonight's dinner rush, dumped it for her. "Slow out there now?" He yanked the sink's faucet nozzle and sprayed the inside of the container down.

"Just the one table."

"Mind if I grab a smoke then?" He poured blue soap

from a plastic bottle at the leg of the dishwasher and turned the nozzle to full blast. The water bubbled frothy white and climbed the bucket's sides.

"Go ahead, now. I'll take care of this."

She returned to the bar intent on cleaning the high-tops, but stopped and placed the bucket down.

The two men stood at the bar's edge.

"Evening, ma'am," the bigger of the two said. The words hung in the air and sounded like "evenin' mime".

"Welcome to Ms. May's." She placed two clean menus in front of him. "Coffee or something stronger tonight?"

"Coffee'll do. Two." Pasty white and sporting a short-trimmed beard, the man's eyes, green bullets sunken into white flesh, matched the ink of a neck tattoo creeping from the brim of his collar. A snake's tongue flicked up to his ear.

Ms. May reached for two mugs beneath the counter. She slid one to each man and pulled the coffee pot from the warmer. "Cream and sugar?"

"No." The slighter of the two said. A younger version of his friend, he wore a button cap. Dark red hair flipped from under it. An orange goatee outlined his thin chin. He too had brilliant green eyes, though thicker and spread apart. He swiped the menus in a rough grasp and flung them back toward her.

"We're looking for the owner." The tattooed man with the snake desecrating his neck pulled a coffee stir straw from the silver cup on the bar and chewed it between jagged teeth.

"Well, you found her. I'm not buying whatever you're selling. I can fix you dinner if you'd like, though."

"We're not here to sell you something."

"Or eat, huh?" A shiver ran the length of her spine, and

she didn't know why. Something didn't smell right in the air, and it wasn't the leftover ground meat from the kitchen. "Just coffee? Fine by me. That'll be three, plus tip."

Neither man moved for a wallet or stopped the trance-like stare. "Are you acquainted with a Richard Frezza? Young guy. Boxer type," Snake asked.

"Now what's that got to do with anything? If you're not eating and not trying to sell me something, that's one thing." Ms. May shuffled the sugar packets in a carrier, her eyes lifting to the men in a peek. "But I'm not entertaining questions about the folks I know."

"So, you *do* know him?" Snake sipped from the mug, an exaggerated 'ah' followed.

"I know lots of folk. What about it?" She lined the length of the bar with fresh placemats. Next came the silverware. "Been here a long time."

With the setup complete, she leaned on the mirror lining the wall and looked around the diner careful to avoid eye contact. The Thomas' table sat vacant; food untouched.

"Now, what in Jesus' name happened there."

The talker draped his gorging arms across the bar, revealing more tattoos painted on the white flesh. A Celtic cross ran up his forearm. A gold tooth gleamed in his mouth. "We asked them to leave."

"You did what?"

"Looking for a bit of privacy." His mouth widened, and the gold cap blinked amid the nicotine stained whites. "It's just us now."

A tingle of fear choked her throat. Her eyes scanned the restaurant, surveying the empty tables, the eerie silence of dead air. A headlight beam from outside struck the window, and she followed its trot to the front door. The deadbolt was locked.

Now she hoped Freddy could hear this conversation. Maybe he'd forgotten to take the smoke break.

What am I thinking? That lazy hack has a Pall Mall burning right now. Ruby might walk in, though. Breaking change for the register don't take more than ten minutes.

"Ma'am, there's no need to be nervous," Snake said.

The kitchen swivel door stood a mere foot away. A short burst of energy and balance could lead to safety.

Mr. Button cap thwarted the ruse when he rounded the end of the bar poking out in front of the kitchen entrance. A fragrance, not cologne but not unpleasant, wafted toward Ms. May.

"What is it ya'll want? I gotta good mind to call the police." Her usual dominant voice shattered in her throat like glass.

"Hear that, Sean?" Snake laughed with a sneer toward his partner. "She's going to call the cops." His neck jutted forward, and he reached into the waistband hidden by his shirt, pulling a snub pistol. It laid on the bar top, gripped by his tattooed fingers, its barrel scowling in Ms. May's direction.

Where's that lazy cook? Where's Ruby? Anybody!

"Let's make this simple," Sean said, producing a similar weapon from his jacket. "Mouth shut and ears open, lady."

Cornered and now sweating, Ms. May felt the tremble in her feet sliding the length of her body and ending at her chipped fingernails. "What do you want?"

Snake climbed a stool and plucked a new straw from the silver canister. He spat the old one to the floor. "A message delivered."

"What do you want me to do?"

"I think she's starting to get with the program, Sean. Nothing like a pointed gun to get the blood curdling, aye."

Sean stepped closer, his shoulders wide and muscular. The scent emanating from him now decipherable. *Daphne.*

Ms. May recognized the flower. She tended to a garden in her backyard during her free time. Daphne, among few others, bloomed during the winter months.

"Richie is going to be in a fight a week from today." Snake swigged from the coffee mug. "A win would be bad business for our employer."

"You want him to throw the fight?"

That's what this is about? Boxing? What the hell do I know about boxing?

"No." Sean now stood inches from her. "Richie will not fight at all. Do you understand?"

"No, not one bit." Ms. May's voice broke and tears formed in the corners of her eyes.

"Well, start to." Sean gripped her throat, banging her head to the mirrored wall. "I'm done playing nice."

"Relax, Sean." Snake's tone reminiscent of a parent, uninterested in disciplining a toddler.

"Go to hell. We've got a job to do. Enough pussy-footin'." His grip tightened, the thumb and index finger now jabbed beneath her jowls. "You understand yet, bitch?"

She couldn't speak, but mustered a slight nod. He released his clutch forcefully, her head banged into the mirror again. She grasped at her neck, massaging under her jaw. "Okay, I'll tell him. Please, just go."

"He is *not* to fight next Friday." Sean reached into his coat pocket and plucked a bundle of daphne flowers. He smelled them, grinning. "And, Gertrude May of 111 Hammock Street, if he does fight, we'll put you in a wheel-chair. Be hard to garden then, won't it?"

"What if he don't listen?" Ms. May's shoulders

slumped, the soiled apron ruffling at her gut. Her legs begged to flatten and ease the weight of her frame.

He crushed the flowers into a misshapen ball and threw them to the floor. "Then we'll be back."

CHAPTER FORTY-FOUR

Richie's eyes traveled Candi's bare skin. Her crossed legs, the color of cream, poked from tight jean shorts. Sitting in the passenger side of a rented Beamer—*thanks for the scratch, Benny*—expressive hand gestures complemented Candi's words, widening the shirt opening over her full breasts.

He half-listened, more interesting in when this date would transform into something a bit sexier, a bit naughtier.

"Did you like the Thai restaurant?" Richie brought his eyes to the windshield. The heater cycled the intoxicating scent of the coconut drifting from Candi's skin.

"I did. Never been there before."

Sure. Let's pretend this date doesn't mirror all your other ones. "So, Punch Point then?"

"Yeah. I know Dizzy's Dips still opens on Saturday nights." Her legs unfolded, and the jean shorts rode higher, closer to the jackpot. She winked. "Get a little dessert, maybe?"

"Kinda what I was thinking."

The Beamer pulled into the parking lot a few minutes

later. They strolled the boardwalk like tourists, eating frozen cream in forty-degree weather. He finished a mint-chocolate chip triple dip and her birthday batter cone disappeared.

They reached the northern end. Sand ramped up in a break of the walk's railing, allowing for a clean trail to the dense mangroves. She led the charge and Richie dragged behind, ogling the apple shaped ass bouncing in dark denim.

"You're not cold?"

"Warm blooded, baby." Candi tugged his arm harder and lowered beneath a thick limb. "C'mon, it's down here."

A dirt path zig-zagged through the brown stalks. Hermit crabs, braving the chilled sand, picked at the ground and disappeared as the couple's proximity neared. The ocean burped salty air and mist sprayed their faces.

Candi peeked over her shoulder with a teasing smile. "Almost there."

Richie couldn't help but contemplate how many others had been led to this exact spot. Johns tugged along for the delicious reward. Though skanky and on the wrong side of thirty, Candi's taut body and tight curves kept the bulge growing beneath his zipper.

Deeper in the mangroves now, she stopped and whipped around with a swift semi-circle turn. Without a word or Richie's objection, she started. *A pro indeed.*

The younger girls play with it. Kiss it. Not Candi.

She swallowed it, her head bobbing like the buoys of the ocean hiding behind the mangrove line.

The world stopped then. Salt air evaporated. Ghosts brewing in the vault withered like petals of a doomed rose. He thought dreamily, enjoying the moist mouth that cost more than the light bill due this month. And from nowhere, as if implanted in his brain by a sick magician, he thought of 7^{h} grade.

Johnnie Baxter's parents sat cross-legged on the couch. Ms. Baxter, a shrew of a bitch, had caught Richie and her precious Johnnie fighting. Well, fighting wasn't the right word. Beat-down for the ages sounded more appropriate. Johnnie squeezed between them; a worthless bag of ice stuck to a large mound of skin protruding from his forehead.

"Why'd you do it, Richie?" The shrew rested her elbows on her knees and jabbed a finger to her chin.

"He stole my bike." Richie massaged the red bumps lifting on his knuckles. "I didn't want to."

"That's not what he says." Mr. Baxter puffed his worm-like chest in an attempt to establish dominance. Thirteen-year-old Richie's eyes rolled.

"We met at the park. He asks if he can take my bike around for a spin. Next thing I know, he's hauling ass down the street laughing."

"It was a joke, Rich. I was coming back." The pipsqueak moaned, moving the ice from his forehead to his bruised left eye.

"But you didn't. I found you at Carver's Grocery showing the bike off to Nellie and Angela."

"But, Rich—"

Mr. Baxter crossed his arm over Johnnie, hushing him. "We'll have to call your parents. Is your mom home?"

"Probably not."

"What about your dad?"

"He's across town. Haven't seen him in a while. You can try."

Richie provided the number and Johnnie's dad stood with a huff.

The shrew stared beady-eyed with pursed lips, the look of "how dare you touch my son" written on her bony face.

A louder than needed one-sided conversation ensued in the kitchen and Mr. Baxter's head needled into the open kitchen doorway after a pause of gruff shouts. "He's on the phone."

Richie stood with his eyes on the carpet. Slowly, unsure if he should just bolt out of the house, he moved toward Mr. Baxter's floating head and took the phone.

"Dad?"

"What's going on, Richie? This man tells me you've been in a fight."

"It wasn't my fault. I—"

"Un-fucking believable. I got your mom slashing my tires and you smashing the fucking windshield. When are you going to grow up? You like hitting people? Think you're a big man, huh? Jesus Christ. Jeeeesssuuusss Chriiiiiiisssssttttt."

Tears fell to Richie's cheeks. The man he'd once aspired to be, unflinchingly devoted to, tore his heart out again. It hadn't been enough to skip town with a younger version of his mom. Now, as he stood arms-length away from this larva with glasses and the muffled cries of a sissy who couldn't take a punch, his father reiterated the fact Richie nor his mother wanted to accept. Dad moved out and on. Gone.

"Why'd you do it? Make you feel tough?"

"Yeah, dad. And you know what? I'm going to keep doing it. Maybe to you next time."

The line clicked dead.

He stared at the phone for a moment, relief sweeping through him.

It felt powerful to express his true emotion. Standing in the Baxter's kitchen that day, Richie Frezza learned life's path began as an etching and the artist bore the responsibility of stroking paint.

He felt good. No, he felt great. Goddamn it's great. It's amazing. "I'm gonna—"

With an arched back, his hips thrust forward, unloading weeks of hatred and anger into her mouth. A carnal grunt escaped his throat, wakening him from the dream. Staggering back, thick branches halted the fall.

"That's a good boy." Candi swallowed and dabbed the mascara running over her cheeks with the shoulder of her shirt.

Light-headed, Richie exhaled. "Jesus. I've never—"

"You like a little Candi, don't you, baby?" She scooped dribble from her chin with a gaped and empty mouth. "It's okay, darling. There's more coming. Take me back to a warm bed and this will look like a PG flick."

Richie bent and lifted the crumpled jeans at his feet. "Benny wasn't kidding. My God, you're good."

"C'mon, baby. It's Candi's turn." She grasped his hand and led the charge back toward the boardwalk. They broke through the cover of the mangrove line a minute later, holding hands again, her apple ass bouncing with each stride.

CHAPTER FORTY-FIVE

Lasker reviewed a briefing file supplied by Reese Campini. Operation Firecracker, priority one by a long shot, had been compromised. James Benussi, a man punctual and obedient in most meetings, today ran late to the rendezvous point.

With the danger involving the operative, any misstep in communication warranted fear from the department.

His thin, manicured fingers flipped to the page he'd read nine times since arriving to Punch Point.

OPERATION FIRECRACKER
Briefing: *Week 103*
Operative: *James Benussi*
Alias: *Sonny Denardo*
Date: *November 12th, 2003*

- No change in daily activities. Operation Benussi has witnessed additional instances of extortion perpetrated by Benny "Beans" Bianchi and Richie Frezza.

- Their target, Citron Trucking, headed by Donald Glover, has been forcibly (through intimidation and threats) extorted to participate in insurance scam regarding stolen trucking shipments. Full breakdown attached.

- Stolen goods are sold through RC 1st Pawn, licensed and operated under Lorenzo Cantu, a known Solano soldier. Further examination of the business license through RC Fraud Division, shows business to be legitimate—licenses up to date, taxes paid in full, etc. Salvador Purelli (Target 1) has no documented affiliation with RC 1st Pawn or its sister company, RC 2nd Pawn, in Belleview.

Notes:
Sonny Denardo might be compromised.
I need to speak with you. Now.

His eyes jumped from the file to the southern tip of the boardwalk. Benussi, huddled in a leather jacket and beanie, sauntered forward. Red cold spots covered his cheeks and nose. Lasker fought the increasing wind, cupped his hands around his shivering lips, and lit two cigarettes. Each ember glowed like reptilian eyes stalking the dusk.

"Evening. I don't have long. Saturday nights are like the mob's nine-to-five." Benussi took the cigarette and sat.

"Okay. No small talk. You've been compromised?" He slapped the file onto the operative's lap.

"Maybe." Benussi's eyes bounced from the file and then to the cove.

Lasker cast a solemn glance in the same direction.

Winter frost blanketed the water's brackish hue, lightening the color. A couple, imperceptible shadows from this distance, emerged from the mangrove line holding hands.

"What happened?" Lasker dragged at the cigarette. A dense cloud of smoke poured from his mouth, though a large portion was hot breath cooling from the chill in the air.

"Bianchi's acting weird." Benussi's chin pointed toward the sky and his eyes scrunched. "I fucked up. I knew I shouldn't have carried both phones."

"Both?"

"Yeah. I've got Sonny's and my personal. I never carry both. Never."

"So—" Lasker now turned to the undercover, resting his right leg on the bench.

"So, I got a voicemail from my wife. Shit, man. I haven't seen her going on seven weeks. Anyway, I listen to the voicemails she leaves. Kinda comforting, ya know?"

"I can imagine." Lasker took care to emit a tone of annoyance and not sympathy. He flicked the butt of the cigarette.

The couple from before reached the western portion of mangroves and trekked across a sand trail rising up the end of the boardwalk. The woman was dressed oddly for the weather. A simple blouse and no jacket. Jean shorts.

"Benny calls, like every morning, with the plan for the day. Before I leave, I listen to my wife's voicemail. Except that day, I'm having a rough go of it. For whatever reason, I don't know why, I slide the phone in my pocket." Benussi paused and tapped his forehead with a balled fist. "At the time, I didn't realize I'd done it."

"And someone calls the second phone in front of the targets." Lasker finished the thought with ease. "It's not the end of the world. How'd you explain it?"

"Spun some bullshit about having family problems and two phones, one for business and one for personal matters."

"Did they buy it?" Lasker shifted on the bench, planting both feet to the wooden planks. He rested his arms on his knees and scanned the view, as if mobsters may be lurking in the mangrove line listening to the conversation. Only the approaching couple moved in the landscape.

"I don't know." Benussi cradled his head in his hands, gripping the knit beanie. "I don't know. Maybe."

"Wouldn't they just kill you on the spot, if that were the case?"

"Probably." The operative's words muffled beneath a gust of wind. "You gotta let me wear a live wire."

"That's not possible. The transmission feed only goes so far. We'd have to deploy a surveillance team to follow you around." Lasker shook his head and rubbed his hands together. *Next time we're meeting in a bar. A heated bar.* "That's too risky and expensive. So, keep the recorder in your waistband and be careful."

The couple climbed the small hill leading to the boardwalk. A blonde of the prostitute variety and a young, athletic guy.

Lasker turned, expecting an argument, but Benussi's eyes now tracked the couple. He squinted through the dying daylight directly at them. "Oh shit." He pulled the beanie further down his head.

"What?" Lasker looked back at the presumed hooker and her customer. They reached the wooden planks of the boardwalk. She turned and kissed on the young man's neck. "Everything all right?"

"No." Benussi kept his eyes on the couple. His squinted stare broke, and he ducked his head. "He saw me."

"Who, James? What are you talking about?"

“I’ve gotta go.” Benussi stood, shielded his face from the northern side of the cove and power walked down the boardwalk.

“We still have to discuss—” Lasker cut the sentence short, aware his words were futile with Benussi’s distance and the howling wind circling the cove.

The couple approached and Lasker examined their faces. A slut and a newborn, basically. *What the hell just happened?*

CHAPTER FORTY-SIX

They'd made love twice. An animalistic hour of dancing skin and sweat to the melody of 92.7 *The Wave* first. Later, with stomachs full of pasta, a slow and rigid Round Two ended prematurely with both spent and lazy.

Now, with her green toenails wiggling in his lap, they drank Chianti from crystal stemware and took in Sunday Night Football.

"Long time coming," Deb said. "You know I need you more than once a week."

"Be happy with what you get." Benny caressed the arches of her feet in slow circles with a dead-eyed pontificating expression. "I'm normally jammed up on Christ's day."

"How nice of you to fit me in." She chuckled and sipped from the cup. "I'll get called in any minute. Never an easy night around here."

"We're both making sacrifices then, eh?" He squeezed her thighs, and she jolted with a laugh.

"Stop, I'm going to spill my wine."

He slid his hands toward her feet again and locked onto the game. "All right. Wouldn't want that, would we?"

"Not at sixty dollars a bottle." She sipped again.

"You're worth it, good looking. I take care of the people I trust." He tilted his glass back and gulped. "Not many people I can say that about these days."

"Something wrong?"

"I need a favor." His response was quick and jagged, as if her sensitive inquiry unlocked the words trapped in his throat.

"Anything, my love." She closed the robe across her chest and fed the cloth strap through the loops.

"Need you to look into somebody." He stared at the seven-yard running play on the screen but his mind traveled to last Tuesday, unable to shake the suspicion of Sonny's two phones. "Something's been eating at me."

"Who?" She pulled her legs from his lap and swung them to the carpet. I gave you all I knew about Richie."

"Somebody else. I've got a feeling."

"About?"

"Sonny."

"Oh, Benny. You just said you trust me." She put her glass on the coffee table then lowered the football game's volume. "He's clean. We did our due-diligence."

"You did a civilian background, right? I need more."

"Went back to his childhood. I remember the rap sheet. Nobody with his record could get a job in the PD." Her lips bunched together like she was kissing the air. "You think he's a cop?"

"Can't they doctor those things? Make up shit to throw off people like you and I digging?"

"Baby, this is Ridgemont Cove. Not a lot of honor to go around."

"Maybe I'm paranoid." Benny wiped at his face and pinched the bridge of his nose. "I vouched for him. If he ain't right, that falls on me."

"Why'd you think this?"

He relayed the phone debacle and Sonny's weak excuse. She listened with eyes glued to his.

"I think you're grasping at straws. His story makes more sense than yours."

"I don't know." Benny appreciated her input, but he *lived* the life. She walked the fringe. "Something ain't right." He emptied the Chianti from the glass in a swig.

"If he's UC, and that's a *big* if, files will be hard to come by. Intel like this is above my paygrade and expensive. Lot of pockets need to be filled."

"I've got money. Do you have contacts?" His words sprang like venom, and for the first time since he'd walked into this house, he felt like the Solano underboss.

"I can make a few calls."

"Well, I need something. Anything."

"I'll ask around—"

"Hold the thought." Benny's pocket buzzed, and he reached into grab the cell. He flipped it open. "Here's the son-of-bitch now."

CHAPTER FORTY-SEVEN

"Ms. May, why didn't you tell me sooner?"

She sat on one of the barstools staring at her reflection in the mirror—an expression of an injured animal awaiting a larger predator to finish the job.

"Couldn't get a hold of you. Didn't know you had a fancy cell phone now."

"You could have walked down to my house." He scanned the diner aware of his voice. Suzy, a waitress he'd bedded a few months back, filled the condiment caddy in a booth. "I'll call Benny." Richie pat her shoulder. "He'll straighten this out."

"So, what? He's going to save the day." She spoke with eyes transfixed on her reflection. The jovial tenor he'd become accustomed to now replaced with a grave, solemn tone.

Violent rain pounded the roof. The drumming of drops produced a continuous rattling louder than the jukebox selection of the Beatles' *Penny Lane*.

"He's our best shot to fix it. Before I call, though, you need to tell me exactly what happened."

"They don't want you to fight, boy. That's it. Said if you do, they're coming back here."

"Any idea who *they* were?" Richie shrugged off his damp sweater and hung it from a purse hook beneath the bar.

Suzy rounded the bar corner and Richie offered a smile. She ignored it. "I'm all set. Can I clock out?"

"Go ahead, child. The rain's gonna drive the stragglers away."

Richie waited for the scorn waitress to disappear behind the swivel doors. "All right. No clue who they were?"

"Nope. Came in Friday night. Said you not allowed to fight next week."

Richie plopped down on the adjacent barstool. "You got names?"

"Sean." Ms. May's head drooped. "He was a mean son-of-a-gun. Threatened me somethin' terrible."

"And the other?"

"Bigger. Tattoos all over. Had one of them Celtic crosses on his arm. A snake on his neck." She traced her finger from her throat to her left ear.

"Celtic cross? Were they Irish?" The jukebox volume carried steady beneath the question.

"That mean something?"

"My next opponent is Irish, so yeah."

Penny Lane is in my ears and in my eyes

For a fish and finger pie.

"Red hair." She turned to him, connecting eyes for the first time since he'd entered the diner. "Accents, too. I'd bet my last dollar they're Irish. And—"

"What?" Richie gripped her thick hand laying on the bar top. "What?"

"They're serious." She used the free hand to wipe a forming tear, but held tight to his clutch.

"It's okay." Richie squeezed the woman's hand harder. He'd never witnessed Ms. May cry. An ache ran through his chest and he blinked hard, forcing his own tears to evaporate. *Be strong. For her.*

Above the mirror, the small television displayed the evening news broadcast. A reporter draped in a dripping rain coat stood outside Sienna Oaks Shopping Plaza.

"It's here," the man shouted above slashing gusts of wind, "that the body of Harold Remnick was discovered wrapped in weed blocker. Initially a John Doe case, police were able to use fingerprint analysis to positively identify the deceased man."

The camera panned to the parking lot. "The case is alarming given the brutality of the murder and obvious disregard for concealing the crime. It's almost as if the murderer wanted to pose the body on purpose."

The screen then displayed a phone number and the same reporter urged for people to call with any information they possessed.

The vault doors hurled open, revealing a black corridor with a single spotlight. In a yellow orb, Harold's mangled corpse sat on a barstool like the one Richie sat on now.

Lookie there, he said. *I'm on TV. How you feeling, Richie?* The ghost gripped the knife in his throat and yanked it. Red covered his gaunt face, and he licked the blade with a black, pulsing tongue. *I'm just fine.*

Ms. May's hand wiggled from Richie's and he shook the apparition. "See this town, boy? It's poison. And I've done my best to avoid it, but now the evil is stepping through my door." Her finger motioned to the front entrance.

"We're not going to let anything happen to the diner."

"So, you're one of them now?"

The question attacked like a snake bite. Six simple words affirmed what Richie tried to avoid.

"I don't know what I am, Ms. May." He took both her hands in his. "But I promise you, nothing is going to happen to you or your business."

"Richie." She pulled away, her eyes back on the television. "You remember when I first met ya."

"Yes." He tried to reach the memory, but the vault kept appearing and opening. *Close it. Focus on something else.* His ears picked up the song on the jukebox.

We see the banker sitting waiting for a trim

And then the fireman rushes in from the pouring rain

Very strange

"You was a little boy crying on my steps," she continued. "Musta been six years ago at least."

"I remember."

The mirror's reflection clear and vibrant beneath the glow of the hi-hats and stark black night outside revealed tears dripping from Ms. May's eyes. "What was you crying about that day? You remember?"

Richie wiped at his forehead. "My dad. Mom drank herself into a rage. For some reason, I knew it was the last time I'd see him. I don't know how, but I knew it was the beginning of the end."

"Remember what we talked about?" She reached over the counter and dug beneath. She popped back up with the remote in her hand and killed the television. "What I tell you?"

Richie navigated through the ghosts. The vault open and welcoming. *Come on in boys*, Cranswell sneered. *We've got plenty of room.* Behind him, Harold cackled in the trunk of the Cadillac—the knife now in place, jutting from his throat like a maniacal ornament.

He trekked further within his memory, attempting to locate the bleak speck of time.

"You said 'Hatred is a tool of the devil. To live this life, you need love'."

Ms. May cupped his face with her dark and calloused hands. "Richie, don't let hatred ruin you."

"I'm okay." The words traveled over a sob pleading to be released.

"Child, there's hate in your heart."

"I'm okay." Richie rose from the bar with his back to Ms. May. He pulled the cell from his pants pocket then dialed Benny's number. The ringing began. "We're okay."

CHAPTER FORTY-EIGHT

"I don't like it one bit." Benny sat on the leather couch in the upper level of The Tango. Outside, through the expansive window in Purelli's top office, lightning cracked the sky, fracturing the dark gray with glowing white slivers. Benny rattled the ice in his bourbon then took a sip. "Something is off about this guy, boss."

"What is on your mind, Benjamin?" Purelli asked.

"I'm not sure. It just seemed fake. If he's acting weird about a call, he must be hiding something. What it is, I don't know."

"Law enforcement?"

"That may be a stretch, but who knows. *Non sopporto, I ratti.*" Benny pinched his nose.

"How can we know for sure?" Purelli breathed hot air onto the lenses of his gold-rimmed glasses and wiped the fog with a tissue. "Accusations such as these cannot be acted upon without cause." He slid the glasses back on.

"I've got a little birdie checking on it. Just wanted to let you know."

"Good thinking, Benjamin," Purelli said, his voice akin to a proud parent at graduation.

Benny heard, *Good job, buddy. You're next in line. Keep up the hard work and this will all be yours soon.* "I'll keep you up to date."

"Please do. And for the time being, give him unimportant tasks. I do not want to jump to any conclusions. He has been reliable to this point, so make sure before we act." Purelli stripped his tie from the collar and unbuttoned the top button of his shirt. "And where do we stand with our other friend?"

Benny hesitated. Even though a few guys on the take came in once a week with devices resembling metal detectors and canvassed the room searching for radio frequency waves, the pigs came up with new and inventive techniques every day it seemed.

"Everything good in here, ya think?" Benny tapped his ear and swept the other hand across his body.

"I should hope so. We have been speaking deliberately." Purelli opened the silver cigarette case on his desk. "Should I be concerned with our security?"

"No, of course not. Just being thorough, boss."

Purelli offered a thin smile. "Be thorough before you open your mouth. If you speak freely in my presence—" Purelli looked to the ceiling, the unlit cigarette stuck in his mouth like a lollipop stem. "—be sure you have ensured our safety."

"It's fine." Benny felt drips of sweat freefall from his armpits. "Sorry I brought it up. We're good."

"Excellent. So, our other friend?"

"We're still fishing, but we'll get a bite sooner than later. Problem is, Sonny is on the trail."

"That is fine." Purelli struck a match and lit the cigarette. "Let him hunt the little weasel while we chase his background down."

"I gotta ask. Why—" Benny reeled in the thought like a fisherman pulling a marlin from the deep blue. He stood from the couch with a look to the ceiling and another tap of the ear and waddled toward the desk.

Purelli's eyes, onyx diamonds behind the sheath of glass, stared at his approach with no emotion.

Benny grabbed a pen from the desk and turned a blank envelope over. He scribbled *Should we kill Vietta?* and placed the message in front of Purelli.

The boss looked down at the scrawled note and took a puff from the cigarette. He then ignited a new match, laying the envelope and it in the geode ashtray on the corner of his desk. The paper flamed brilliant then died, caving into itself like a dying spider and turning to ash.

"A mere conversation is what I seek. That is all for now."

"We'll find him." Benny swiveled from the desk and left.

In the hallway, he opened the door leading to creaking wooden steps. The stair case dived into a dry storage room for the restaurant. From there, he entered the kitchen. A few cooks stopped their preparations as he passed through.

"Hey," one bold little prick offered.

"Hey, yourself, pal. Back to work."

The man grimaced and turned to the stovetop. His friend jabbed his arm with a pair of tongs, his eyes on the simmering meat.

As Benny entered the dining room, his phone buzzed in his pocket.

Jesus Christ, Sonny. I'll call you when I'm good and Goddamn ready. He pulled the cell out and flipped the cover open.

RF surfaced in the black pixels of the screen display.

CHAPTER FORTY-NINE

"Thanks for coming." Richie shook Benny's wet hand. "This is crazy."

"Red goatees telling ya to lay off? Sounds just like Beckett." He coughed, the wheeze as raspy and wet as the thunderstorm raging outside. His dark hair fell flat and damp from the rain. The drenched silk shirt he wore revealed bulbs of flesh in chunky detail in the mirror's reflection when he hopped on a bar stool.

"Beckett? Runs the auto shop on 3rd, right?" Richie parked in a booth near the bar. The kitchen swivel door swung in slightly. Ms. May shuffled away in protest of the discussion unfolding in her diner.

You've got to trust me.

"It's a front." Benny pulled a comb from his pocket. Using the mirror, he stroked the rogue strands of hair back in place. "They haven't fixed a car in ten years. They run their whole operation from there. Guns, drugs, women. Those Irish pricks own the west side."

"Why do they care about me boxing?"

"Same reason we care about you boxing. Money, kid."

Benny helped himself to a mug from the counter and poured a cup of coffee from the silver Bunn brewer.

"But I'm a nobody to them. Didn't you say this O'Leary guy is a contender? What are they worried about?"

"Protecting their investment, I suppose. Maybe little ole' Richie Frezza got 'em scared." Benny sipped the mug. "Jesus, this coffee tastes like shit."

Richie thought about reminding him it was nearing eleven and the sludge had probably been in there since the morning, but he relented.

"So, what do we do?"

"Chain of command." Benny rotated in his seat to face Richie. "Tell you one thing though, we ain't backing out. Not now."

"I don't want Ms. May mixed up in this." Richie rose from the booth.

A crack of thunder shook the windows. Streaks of water gyrated and jumped from the glass. Dropping on a stool next to Benny, he stared at the reflection in the mirror. A foreign version of what once lived with this body stared back. Pale skin. Thickening beard and frazzled hair. Deep, dark and tired eye sockets.

"Listen, we're not letting those bastards get away with this. I know you care about her. I'm not a cold-hearted guy."

"So, what do we do?" He brought his eyes to Benny who was sipping the sludge again.

"We go talk to them, I guess. Like I said, we'll follow the chain. I'll make a few calls and then schedule a sit down." Benny pulled a pack of cigarettes from his front pocket. It dripped with the residue of rain. He grabbed a napkin from the dispenser and swiped at the droplets. "It'll all work out. My guess is they're flexing their muscles. Just reminding us they're around still."

"I say we hit 'em. Gotta keep Ms. May safe."

The ghosts' ears perked at the admission and Richie regretted the utterance.

Is that so? Cranswell appeared, smoke seeping from the hole in his head. *You can't get enough, can you?*

Richie scrunched his eyes for a second then opened them to see Benny's reflection in the mirror.

The man's chin dropped and an exaggerated sigh followed. "I get it. You're pissed, insulted, and want to protect your friend, but nothing happens without the boss." His pudgy thumb jabbed like a hitchhiker's. "I need a smoke. Take a walk with me."

"It's a hurricane out there."

"Go get an umbrella then, daisy. What's the matter, you scared of a little rain? Get up." Benny started toward the door without looking back.

Outside, beneath the failing green awning in front of the Cadillac, he puffed the cigarette. A street lamp a yard ahead, lit the lower half of his face.

Heat lightning blinked. It brightened and evaporated, staining the sky orange for intervals of a few seconds. A cluster of stars, visible but not bright, peeked through the sheets of rain.

"Where's Sonny?" Richie peered into the car parked snug to the curb.

"Giving him a couple of days off."

"Ah. It makes sense now." Rain dripped from the awning and Richie cupped the falling water in his hand.

"What makes sense?"

"He's always with you, so I thought it was kinda strange when I saw him yesterday." Another wave of lightning illuminated the black sky. Thunder grumbled.

"You saw him? Where?"

"Candi and I went to Punch Point last night. Man, I gotta tell you, that chick can—"

"Back to Sonny. What happened?" Benny's words tightened like a noose.

"Nothing." Richie's hands rose. The awning's spray-off bathed them. "I was there with Candi. We walked the boardwalk and Sonny was with a guy on one of the benches."

"What guy?"

"I don't know. Some dude."

"What'd he look like, kid?"

"Thin." The part of that night his brain had saved had nothing to with the toothpick talking to Sonny. "Gray suit. I don't know, just an average looking guy."

"You hear what they said?"

"Nah. Candi and I were walking toward them." Richie paused, now unsure of what he saw. "I thought it was Sonny, anyway—"

"Was it Sonny or not?" Benny gripped Richie's shoulders. "Think carefully."

"Yeah." Certain his eyes hadn't failed him, Richie nodded. "We walked toward them, and he got up and scooted down the boardwalk."

"Didn't say anything to you?"

"He left in a hurry. Looking back now, I figured he knew Candi and didn't want to spook her. Maybe?"

"Maybe." Benny flicked the cigarette. Its glow died in the rain-swept street. "Go back inside, kid. We'll hook up tomorrow."

Benny flung the Cadillac's door open. The engine revved, and the tires spun under the asphalt. It tore through the puddles of Center St. without the head lights on.

CHAPTER FIFTY

"I've had it!" The bald sheen of his head, a usual beige pallor, burnt red. Detective James Benussi slammed a thick fist on the desk.

Reese Campini's new coffee mug gyrated and expelled a bit. The overflow dripped down the cup and swam to a paper on the desk. He hated cleaning up messes—like the enormous clusterfuck in front of him yelling and screaming. "I understand, detective."

"You don't understand shit. I've been in too long. I need to get pulled. Now Richie may have seen me with Lasker, and they're already suspicious. Pull me now." Benussi slammed the table again. He shook the hand with a grimace.

The coffee cup quaked, and Campini lunged to halt it from toppling.

"We aren't finished yet." He shook coffee drips from his hand and wiped the remainder with a tissue from the box on the desk.

"I *am* finished." Benussi leered at an enormous pile of stacked paper on the desk and pointed. "Look at what I've done for you."

"You've done a commendable job, but I'm afraid it isn't enough."

"Enough? I've seen them murder, run gambling, and a whole list of other illegal shit. It's all in those pages." The undercover pointed to the mound of papers with a grunt. "We can fry them all. The sooner the better."

"Yes." Campini sipped from the wet coffee mug. "But it doesn't implicate Purelli. He's the target. If Benny Bianchi was the goal, I'd pull you out right now. The mission has not been completed. We want Purelli."

Benussi's head cocked back. A hoarse laugh filled the office. "I've been twisting and turning in this life for two years."

Campini clicked the keyboard in front of him. The monitor woke and displayed the calendar for the day. *Already behind.* "I understand your frustration, detective. I get it."

"Oh, do you?" He planted both palms on the desk and shoved forward. "Is your wife near the end of walking and soon to be wheelchair bound? You missed your son's last two birthdays?" The imposing bull of a man huffed, scattering a few stray papers to the floor. "I'm getting nowhere. Nothing to show for the blood, or the time, or the nightmares."

Campini directed the mouse of the computer to his email. *Twenty-seven unread.*

"You hearing me?" Benussi leaned forward again.

Campini reclined in the chair, unsure if words would turn to punches. "Nightmares? You still seeing the department psychiatrist? It is a requirement."

"Oh yeah. Plenty of time for her while I'm in the shit. Sneaking out to meet Lasker is hard enough, which by the way, needs to stop." Benussi's shoulders rolled, and he backed away from the desk. "If Richie did see me with him, how do I explain that?"

"You're the pro, detective. Say it was a long-lost relative. Your attorney, maybe? I don't know, just make it work."

"What will be enough for you people?"

"Just take a seat, please." Campini bent forward and smoothed his tie. "You know how this works. We need concrete evidence. Putting Bianchi away accomplishes nothing. Purelli simply promotes from within and doesn't skip a beat. We have to cut the head off of the snake." He leafed through a thick manila folder with eyebrows rising and falling then looked to his operative.

Benussi peered out the window.

From the fifteenth floor, Downtown Ridgemont Cove laid out like a painting, the edge of the Navajo Reservation in the distance. East, Belleview surfaced as a vague patch of color.

An enviable view for anyone, but especially him I suppose.

"I can't get close to him." Benussi said, with his eyes still on the landscape. "I've been telling you for six months. You do read my case notes, right? The guy's a ghost." The man's fingers flittered. "Different crews for each arm of the family. I'm with Benny and the kid. We handle boxing, gambling and muscle. A different squad sells drugs. Rackets and scams belong to Lorenzo Cantu's crew. I got a ton on that sick prick, too."

"He's not—"

"I know, I know. Not target one." Benussi fell into the chair, his hands shaking, mocking.

"We need to stay put. If we pull the plug, then everything you've done over the last twenty-two months has been for nothing."

"What I've done." Benussi's head rolled back, and he spoke to the air. "I've done too much."

"I know it's been rough lately. Based on your reports, at least."

"Rough? You mean tying a guy up and leaving him for dead in a barn? Or maybe you're talking about shoving a dead body into a trunk and dropping it in the middle of a parking lot? I'm just as responsible as they are." The last line came out weak and fractured. Benussi's face flushed.

"We knew going in this would be a difficult task. I can sympathize with you, detective. But you must understand, we need more than we have. Three more months. Six tops."

"I may be dead in six months."

"I spoke with Lasker." Campini flipped a file folder open and sifted through a few documents. He located the most recent report prepared. "I think you played the phone incident off well. Just keep your eyes peeled."

"Easy for you to say, sitting up here watching the world go by."

"Watch it, Mr. Benussi. I'm still your superior." The phone hummed on the desk. "Campini here."

"Meeting started three minutes ago." Captain Taggert's scratchy voice poured through the receiver.

"I'm in a debrief with Detective Benussi now, sir. Your office in five?"

The line clicked then went mute. Campini dropped the phone back to its dock.

"More good news?" Benussi dabbed the small tears in the corner of his eyes.

"I need to cut this short. Captain needs me. Let's go through the quick version." He rifled through a few more logs in the file. "The corpse we found at Sienna Oaks is one of the guys from the barn? Harold Remnick, right? Purelli's order?"

"No. That deal was all Benny."

"Really? Bianchi didn't get approval?" Campini jotted a note in the file folder and dated it. "What else?"

"It's in my case logs." Benussi's head grew redder, and his steel eyes flared. "I'm not repeating myself over and over. We're both busy men."

"Okay. Okay." Campini's hand rose from the file and waved. "For now, we can shelve the investigation? Don't need other officers stepping into Firecracker."

"Yeah. Hope you don't have a bunch of newbies chasing their tales."

"I believe Shaw is on it. I'm sure she's tracking leads. I'll make a call to her superior. Anyway, tell me more about this Richie Frezza. You've mentioned him quite a bit in the logs."

"Mixed-up kid." Benussi's head drooped and shoulders hunched. "Getting caught up in the life."

"Could he be an asset moving forward?"

"I don't know." The operative stood in a flash, raking the legs of the chair across the office floor. "Maybe he'll replace me. Or maybe they'll kill him." His hand formed a fist, and it shook. "These guys preach loyalty, but I'm not sure any of them believe it. It's a what-have-you-done-for-me-lately organization. Kinda like this?" His arms extended outward and panned the room.

"Have you been in regular contact still?" Campini ignored the slight, aware that poking this bull in his current state would yield little results.

"Not really. I called to check in yesterday. He never answered."

Campini's elbows rested on the desk; his hands clasped together. "Odd, right?"

"Yeah. And what's worse, for me, is the last time we spoke in person he gave me an assignment. One that could crack this wide open."

"What was it? I don't have record of it in the reports." Campini sifted through a different stack of folders and inadvertently bumped a pencil holder. Its contents raced across the desk.

Fucking messes.

"Find Timothy Vietta." Benussi ran a finger across his throat.

Campini nodded as if in on an inside joke. He collected the pencils and returned them to their cup. "They want to kill him?"

"Probably."

"Why?" Campini's mind wandered back to Ridgemont Cove Memorial. He and Marzetti shunned by the injured fighter. *I'll get the truth. I always do, Timothy.*

"I heard in passing, so I'm not sure." The operative's eyes crunched as if he were powering through an overload of sadistic data in his head. "The bookies had an over/under of round three. Word is Vietta was gonna take a dive, but he didn't make it out of the first round. Kinda fucked up Purelli's fifty thousand dollar bet on Mahomes after the third."

"Why would an undefeated fighter like Thunderstorm lose on purpose?" Campini shook his head, unable to connect the information presented.

"That's like asking why I've got nightmares after two years of this. Salvador Purelli is in charge." Benussi returned to the desk, planting his thick hands on the top. "Of everything."

Campini's head shake morphed into a slight nod. "I see. All the more reason to get a case that sticks. Still, I've been investigating Salvador Purelli for years. He runs the gambling operation even though we can't prove it. Why take the risk?"

"He didn't." Benussi cracked a smile, not one of pleasant memories Campini assumed, but one of admiration. "It was a Goddamn shoo-in bet. All the money went on Thunderstorm. Mahomes is a schlep, a phony, a punk. Vietta could beat the guy on one leg with a hand tied behind his back."

"But he didn't."

"Exactly. Purelli lost his ass on his own ruse. It's not about the money now. It's his ego that's hurt."

"And then the attack in the hospital."

"Right. Sent him a message. It's the 'How dare you fail me?' mentality. Now, Vietta is nosing around and trying to get back into the circuit. Purelli wants to bury him is my guess, but if he can recoup the cash someway, well, all the better."

"Why not just kill him in the hospital?"

"Surveillance cameras, right? He knows about them." Benussi sat back in the chair, it squeaked beneath the weight. His arms crossed and posture returned to a stiff statue. "Stab the kid, threaten him and walk out. Kill him, and the cameras don't lie."

"Why am I finding out about all of this now?"

"I just learned of it. I had suspicions, just like you, but Benny's orders confirm it."

"This could be good." Campini' rubbed his hands together and chuckled. "What if we used him as bait? Lure the bastard into a situation with Timothy and get him talking while you're recording. Maybe Purelli loses his cool and does something stupid. At the very least, we can hold him for a little bit and build the rest of the case."

"You're dreaming. I've never been with Purelli by myself. Now, with Richie seeing Lasker and I at the boardwalk and Benny's suspicions, there is no way in hell it happens."

Campini reclined in the chair and cradled his hands atop his gelled blonde hair. The short-lived excitement now replaced by the revelation that Benussi's words rang true. *Salvador Purelli is in charge. Of everything.* "Shit, you're right."

"And even if I could get that close, we still have one problem?"

"Such as?" Campini sat forward and checked the time on his computer. Captain Taggert expected him in five minutes, and five is what he'd get.

"Thunderstorm is in the wind. No eyes on him in the past week."

"Then get back to work, Sonny."

CHAPTER FIFTY-ONE

I'll train the kid, but I'm not shaking hands with you thugs. Joe had grown sick of these *Mafioso* types years ago. *Not again. Not this time.*

They were supposed to be fixtures in a past life—a fading landscape in the rearview. So, what the hell was this guy doing in the gym?

"Richie just left a few minutes ago. Figured he was with you."

Joe hung his cane on the lip of the ring platform, keeping it within arm's reach. He extracted the newspaper situated under his arm and opened the quarter-folded, turning to the sports section.

Similar to maggots on rotting flesh, he and his kind crept forward, spreading like a powerful plague. Benny the Beans. Salvador Purelli. *And now this guy.* Sonny whatever-the-hell-his-name-is who had strolled through the door, making himself comfortable.

"Not here for him, Mr. Gallant." The mammoth stalked forward, steel-eyed like a soldier conditioned to fear nothing.

"Don't have a lot of time to speak, but something tells me it doesn't matter." Joe, seated on the corner of the sparring ring, glanced up from the newspaper.

Morning light began its ascent through the windows, leaving half of the gym still shrouded in darkness.

"I'll be a minute or two."

"Then let's get it over with." Joe placed the Monday edition onto the floor of the ring. His hand traced a groove in the canvas.

Hundreds, even thousands, of men and women stomped the padding of this ring. Joe had coached and screamed, sobbed and grimaced. He'd met so many, and in his lifetime, changed so little.

"I've got a packed day." A pronounced indentation from Richie's sparring session this morning gashed the middle of the ring. "Got a group of young ones arriving any minute now."

Joe wondered if Richie had changed. *Or was he one of many who would disappear like the creases did?*

"My associate said Timothy Vietta was here." Sonny perched the black, square sunglasses he wore atop his shining head. "That true?"

"Yeah." Joe gripped his cane and stood from the ring with its aid.

"Any idea where he is now?"

"Nope." Joe smiled inwardly. *Like I'd tell you a thing or two, you wise-guy piece of shit.*

"I don't believe you." Sonny pressed forward and wedged his toe to the bottom of Joe's cane. "Try again."

"You want the truth, boy, or should I spin you a fairy tale?" Joe switched the cane to his other hand.

Of course, he did know *something* of interest. Thoughts

of his old war buddy, Marty, who he entrusted to train Thunderstorm a week or so ago, surfaced.

Joe met Marty in 1965, after President Johnson decided not enough Americans were dying in Vietnam. He and Marty, both eighteen and angry at the world, dropped in to South Vietnam with about three thousand other hard-nosed, shit-for-brains kids. When they weren't sleeping in a shroud of bugs, fighting incessant downpours, or firing their M1 Carbines into a noisy dark wilderness teeming with the enemy, they'd box.

"I can't tell you what I don't know." The rubber bottom of Joe's third leg, the cane, tapped the toe of Sonny's loafer.

"I imagine you know more than most." Light shined off the slick planes of the gangster's head.

"Nah. No one tells an old man anything these days."

"Okay. Any idea of where he might be?" Sonny's temples pulsed like bugs flittered beneath his skin. "It's important, Mr. Gallant?"

"I don't know the guy. Met him once." He pulled on the smoke and exhaled a cloud. It floated and broke in pieces, reaching the rafters above in a pale gray tint. "Are we done?"

"No, we're not." The reply, deafening to Joe's ears—much like a shell exploding near a platoon's barracks during a fiery night in Binh Gia—rung loud and clear. "I know you're keeping something from me. I got orders, Mr. Gallant. I need to know where he is now."

"I need a convertible and big-titty blonde, but that ain't happening. Guess we're both out of luck, bub."

"I'm not playing with you, old man." Sonny took a step. His nose an inch from Joe's. "Start talking."

"What do you want me to say? The kid came in and

asked for help. I told him about Richie and our arrangement with you. He walked out. All there is to tell."

"You're lying." Sonny grabbed Joe's forearm. "Do I need to call Benny down here?"

"What's the matter?" Joe felt the grip of the man tightening, the pressure burrowing to his bone. "Can't handle intimidating an old man by yourself?" He pulled from Sonny's grasp. *Wouldn't have lasted a night in The Shit with Marty and I, you half-ass gangster.*

"You don't know what you're doing. This is important." Sonny's hand rose and widened three inches from Joe's neck but stopped. He dropped it, slapping it to his thigh. "Ah. You're just a sad little man."

Joe, unimpressed with the insult and faux bravado, slogged toward the gym entrance.

"Mr. Gallant." Sonny's voice followed after him. "If I don't find Vietta, the cops will. And then everyone is in deep shit. He knows too much. Last chance."

"If I hear or see anything, I'll let you know." Joe nudged the front door open with his cane and nodded toward the early morning sun. Its glow strengthened, creating a welcoming crisp heat in the chill of late November.

Sonny huffed and ambled forward. A crisp vibration sprang in the dead air and he dug into his pockets, pulling a buzzing cell phone out.

"Looks like you're busy, Sonny." Joe smiled. "So am I."

CHAPTER FIFTY-TWO

Benny parked the Cadillac in a razor-wire fenced lot behind Beckett Auto & Tire.

Two Irish toughs stood near a closed steel door. Lanky, tattooed arms poked out from the taller man's sleeveless shirt. An inked snake traveled his neck then sprang toward his ear. The other man, bundled in a jacket and beanie, stared as Benny and Purelli approached, eyes zeroed in like green scopes.

"You're late," the tattooed one said. "It's nearly three." He gripped the metal handle of the door and slung it open.

"Sorry to keep you waiting, Ozzie Osbourne. Nice artwork there." Benny looked the guy up and down with a sneer.

"The name is Niles, my well-fed friend. This is Sean." He pointed to the bundled hoodlum with the scope eyes. "We'll be needing your hardware."

"You expect me to walk in there without my piece? You guys sniffing your own product?" Benny's finger tapped his nose then he snorted.

"You'll get it back." Sean stepped forward and lifted his

sweater to reveal a pale stomach. He spun a full circle. "Nobody's armed in there."

"If I give you my gun, then you'll be though."

"You." Niles jabbed a finger toward Benny's nose. "Requested this meeting. You will not see Mr. Beckett until we know it's safe. Do I need to pat you down?"

"That will not be necessary, gentleman." Purelli opened his coat. "I am unarmed already. Guns are bad for business."

"Then you." Sean said with a nod to Benny. "Hand it over."

Purelli's hand gripped Benny's wrist. "Business, Benjamin."

He reached into his coat and pulled the Luger out.

Sean took it and dropped it into an empty oil drum beside the door. It clanged against the steel interior, like a drummer's final heightened note. "Don't forget to grab it on your way out." Widened lips puffed Sean's pale cheeks. He and Niles entered the auto shop.

"Oh, I won't." Benny extended a hand to the open door and Purelli slid by without a word, but a faint snarl detectable.

Niles led the two into an office, an add-on building using a shared wall of the mechanic shop. The door closed, and the air from the chill of the open garage bays stifled. The office sat stale and hot, impervious to the dropping temperature outside.

Grease and stale nicotine swam in the warm air. Outside, through the one window of the room, the back end of his Cadillac and a host of junked, rusted cars came into view.

He and Purelli sat in front of a steel desk, its front a wide chrome slab used to build pickup truck tool boxes.

Years of grime and guck tarnished it. The grooves in the metal saturated in black residue.

"We might as well be target posters." Benny glanced around, unsure why they'd chosen *this* as the meet-up locale.

"Foolish thoughts." Purelli shifted in the chair and crossed his legs. "Beckett would not dare."

"We're on their turf, boss. Unarmed, to boot."

The western section of Ridgemont Cove, an irregular shaped chunk of forty square miles and home to three separate factions of Irish toughs, comprised a third of the city's land and accounted for fifty percent of the murder rate.

"We won the war, Benjamin. A truce is in effect." Purelli opened his jacket and glanced toward the window.

"When he gets in here, we going to remind him of that?" Benny turned his eyes from the vacant desk and met Purelli's stare.

"I'll handle it." The boss replied, pointing his thin finger to his chest. "We must tread lightly."

The door of the office swung open. Beckett, flanked by the assholes from earlier, stood at the threshold.

Benny and Purelli rose. "I appreciate you meeting us, Mr. Beckett."

The Irishman ignored the pleasantry and took a seat behind his desk. Sean stayed on his right and Niles curved in front of the desk, setting up shop on his left.

Purelli's eyes, still black coals, lay behind the sheath of gold-rimmed glasses. He dropped down to the chair and motioned for Benny to do the same.

"I was hoping to act like gentlemen," Purelli said, removing the glasses.

"Of course, anything for you." Beckett grinned and shot a glance to Niles.

The sarcasm lingered and Benny's nose lifted in disgust, its aftershock putrid like the remnants of a clam bake.

Beckett chuckled and reclined. The spine of the chair creaked, matching the volume of his squeaky snorting. Short, curly hair waved from his high forehead as he chortled. "So, what can I do for you?"

"I would like to know why you are threatening one of my associates." Purelli nibbled on the rubber of the glasses' left stem.

"Very serious accusation, my old friend."

"Mr. Beckett, we are both very busy men. Let us avoid the needless banter."

"As you wish, Mr. Purelli." Beckett scratched at the trimmed sideburns framing his ruddy, vein –streaked cheeks.

"Now, why did you send men into the diner?"

"Who's wasting time now?" Beckett unleashed a bellowing laugh. His two-henchman sneered in obedience. "You know why. We asked her to deliver a message."

"Message received. I am afraid I cannot let you bully my fighter. He *will* fight your man."

"That won't do." Beckett's artificial smile, now replaced with a thin-lipped frown, better representing the building tension. The two men flanking Beckett straightened, as if in anticipation of a brawl.

Benny adjusted himself in his seat, wiping a paw at the empty space where his gun typically resided. "What's the matter? You afraid you might lose?"

Purelli's head tilted with closed eyes. An expression Benny was used to. It meant *keep your mouth shut.*

"Nothing at all to do with it, my Italian friend." Beckett's grin returned in a wider version. "I've got my reasons.

And as a professional courtesy, I'd like you to pull your fighter."

"Well," Purelli said, taking the lead and shooting Benny a crooked expression, "with no specific reason, I am not inclined to cooperate. This is business. Let us negotiate as businessmen."

"Get a load of the *Goombah.*" Beckett turned to Sean. "A businessman?"

"Careful, Mr. Beckett."

"Heed your own advice. In this part of town, I'm the—" Beckett's eyes scrunched for a moment, presumably finding the right word. "—the *Don.*"

"I am not here to insult you. I am here to discuss business. As businessmen do, Mr. Beckett."

"Businessmen don't have slaughterhouses on farms, now do they? Oh yeah, I've heard about your tactics. You and I are nothing alike. Don't put me in your company."

"Bold statement there, Paddy." Benny shot forward, his chair crashing into the wall behind. Sean lunged forward, grasping his collar.

"Enough." Purelli slipped his slender frame between the two. "Act like men. This is not the schoolyard."

"All right." Benny straightened the chair and sat.

"Again." Purelli clenched his jaw, a pulse now noticeable. He dropped into the seat. "Let us negotiate, Mr. Beckett."

"Point blank, I'm telling ya to pull your fighter. Period."

"We are discussing a boxing match. I cannot understand your reasoning and I am—"

"The reason is simple," Beckett said with a snarl. The happy façade crumbling. "Everything you touch stinks like a dead dog on a hot day. I don't want your name near my promotion."

"You have been misinformed. My name is clean in boxing."

"Cut the horse shit, ya hear? Every time you're involved, something shady happens. I've worked too hard and spent too much money to get my man to where he is. In another fight or two, O'Leary turns pro. I can't have his integrity called into question because of the likes of you."

"Have you not thought about what a win over your man would mean for our fighter?" Purelli flicked a piece of lint from his pants and frowned. "It could further his career quickly. I say they settle it in the ring."

"You're not listening, are you? I don't want your stench near my man." Beckett wagged his index finger. "His name will not be blemished. Take your man out. Enough said on the matter."

Purelli rose and adjusted his jacket and tie. "I was hoping to come to a more peaceful resolution, Mr. Beckett."

"It can be peaceful, my Italian friend. You know what to do."

Purelli turned to the door and Benny followed. From behind, Beckett repeated, "You know what to do."

Back outside, with Niles and Sean at his heels, Benny retrieved the Luger from the oil drum. He and Purelli crossed the dirt lot and climbed into the car.

"I hate those pricks." Benny stuck the key in and the Caddy woke from its snooze.

"That is fine. You are welcome to feel that way." Purelli grabbed Benny's chin, forcing his neck to swivel. "But you never let them know it. If you want to be boss, you must learn to negotiate business without emotion." He released his grip. "Now, get me out of here. The stench of these men is too much to bear."

"With pleasure." Benny reversed the vehicle, spiraling

dust from the lot into the gray sky. He merged onto the street. The marks and bruises of Ridgemont Cove appeared and vanished through the tinted glass. A few silent minutes later, he glanced to the boss.

"So, what do we do then?"

"About what?" Purelli's eyes were still drawn to the changing landscape outside.

"These Irish pricks. We can't let them get away with this."

"They want to appear strong. It is a test."

"Testing us for what?" Benny merged into the interstate entry lane. A green sign on the ramp displayed *Ridgemont Cove East–10 miles*.

Purelli lit a cigarette and drew the window down. "He wants to corner the boxing market, is my guess." He exhaled a stream of smoke and it twirled out of the window. "He seems to think we will allow it. It's a test. How much can he do before we push back?"

"Lotta money elsewhere." Benny adjusted the rearview and glared, sure a car had followed them on to the highway. "Think they're tailing us?"

"Do not be paranoid. I suspect they were just as happy to see us leave as we were to go."

"Can't trust these guys, boss." Benny shifted his eyes to the side mirror, expecting the white sedan from before to putter behind him. It came up on his left and zoomed by. "Especially if they think we'll lay down."

"That we will not do." Purelli dragged hard, the cigarette ember sizzled and popped. "If we get a fighter who starts winning, we can use the income and all the expenses to clean our money. Beckett is a rude, vile Irish thug, but he is not stupid. In this line of business, dumb people do not last."

"But why get so greedy? There's plenty for everybody."

"The more income you can legitimize, the better your books. Keeps the Feds away. He wants the entire thing and so do I. We control the market for the most part, but we have no muscle over the fighters. Total ownership should be the goal."

"What about this O'Leary guy? We gonna let Richie fight?"

Purelli flicked the cigarette to the road and brought the window back up. Smoke leaked from his nostrils. "We need to send a message of our own."

"What do you have in mind?" Benny's excitement grew like the speed of the vehicle under his foot.

"Like I told *him*. I am a businessman. And what does the smart businessman do?"

"What?"

"Eliminate your competition." The boss's black eyes widened and he smirked. His thumb grazed under his neck and dragged from ear to ear. "Without O'Leary, they have no fighter. No market. No goods."

Benny's head shook, and he grimaced at the innuendo. Not enough for the boss to notice hopefully, but enough to prove to himself he wasn't a monster.

"It's simple economics," Purelli said.

CHAPTER FIFTY-THREE

Reese Campini jabbed the button labeled 22. The elevator lifted within the shaft and speakers crackled before spitting out an instrumental loop he'd heard for eight years.

Since his brief meeting with Captain Taggert yesterday, thoughts of a more formal sit-down consumed him. Then, this morning an email indicated an appointment request. A massive ass-chewing awaited. *At least he didn't take a bite yesterday in front of the council.*

Captain Taggert, a hard-nosed twenty-two-year veteran of the RCPD, gave less than two-shits about the wunderkind in charge of Operation Firecracker, but Campini reveled in his accomplishments.

He'd earned the right to head such an important operation, and regardless of the naysayers and whoa-is-me dickheads in the precinct, he would not fail.

I cannot fail.

When the elevator opened, Campini took a sharp right toward the glass double doors. He passed his ID keycard through the security scanner and awaited the green light. It blinked and a faint buzzing motor began. The doors propped open.

Taggert's secretary, an old woman wearing far too much make up, sat behind a navy marble counter and did not waste time with a false smile. Rather, the snide look of a teenager just picked last in gym class greeted him. A nasal voice offered, "You're late, Reese. He'll be with you in a moment."

The Captain pushed through a set of doors to the left of Ms. Sunshine a few minutes later.

"Let's go." He held the door open and motioned for Campini to rise and get a move on.

"Morning, sir."

Taggert said nothing and strutted back through the door.

The men traversed a long, maze-like hallway. Pictures of previous Captains on each side eyed with various admonishing glares. *My portrait will stare at schmucks one day. One day.*

They reached the office.

"Take a seat, Reese."

Campini obeyed and slid into a white leather chair with gold beads running the perimeter of its legs. *This is how the other side lives, I suppose.*

The captain rounded the edge of his u-shaped cherry finished desk and dropped into an identical seat, though his was wider and teal.

Taggert, dressed in a dark suit and vibrant red tie, ran his fingers through the mop of white hair atop his head. He clicked at his keyboard, the screen's reflection setting the left half of his face aglow in a light blue haze. "Just a minute. Too many fires to put out today."

"Take your time." Campini studied the framed photos

set on the shelves bookending a color map of Ridgemont Cove. Taggert and Mayor Selman holding putters on a sloped green at Whispering Trails Golf Club. Another presented him in a tux accepting an award from a woman who resembled a young Margaret Thatcher. The third, a wide-angle shot of the RC Baseball Club, where the captain's reputation as a slugger grew with each passing year.

"Reese." Taggert looked up from the screen. "We've got to talk about Operation Firecracker."

"I figured."

"It's November twenty-second. Just shy of two years, now. The taxpayers of this fine city have whipped out millions. I'm a bit uninspired."

How much have they shelled out for this office, my dear captain?

"We're getting close. Cases of this size take time."

"Close?" Taggert leaned back with a frown. He lifted his hand and hovered his index finger above the thumb. "Close won't cut it. After twenty-two months and sixteen million dollars, I'd hope for completion." The hand fanned and swiped the air like a tennis player calling a shot that grazed the line in.

"We've hit a few snags." The room grew warmer. His armpits dripped beneath the steel colored suit he'd picked especially for this meeting.

"I need results. The mayor is on my ass about this investigation. It comes up every month at administrative briefings. I've put it off as long as I can."

"Put what off, sir?"

"Shutting it down." Taggert's fist knocked the desk. "We can't rationalize the spending. The money and resources need to be directed to other issues." He swept his arm toward the floor-to-ceiling window of his suite. "The taxpayers out there care about drug dealers on the corner and the climbing murder rate. Safety is always number one at town meetings. Kids keep shooting up schools and teachers are feeling up little girls in the locker room. We've got a load to deal with and not too many give a rat's ass about Purelli."

"He's a huge part of it, Captain." Campini hunched forward, wide-eyed. *Is this guy serious?* "We get him, you can bet your ass forty percent of the drugs getting shipped into Ridgemont Cove don't make it into the city limits. His arrest and conviction will break the Solano controlled shipping and packaging unions. Murders will drop, too. We can attribute two murders a month on average to Purelli or his enemies. Taking this guy off the street should be the public's *only* concern."

"If all of this is true, why the hell haven't we closed the case?"

It was a fair question, and he had no answer to appease the higher-ups. Purelli had been too slippery up to this point. "We lack substantial evidence."

"Ah." Taggert reclined, setting his arms on the chair's rests. His fingers formed a tent that obscured his mouth. Another glance out to the city.

"We're close."

"What does that mean, Reese?" The finger tent collapsed into a ball. "Is there some magical break you're expecting? What will change in the next few months that keeps you so confident that we're *close*?"

"I've got my best man undercover. He has infiltrated the Solanos, become one of them. Never been done for this long or to this extent." He grabbed the sides of his chair, lifting it above the crisp blue carpet, and shuffled toward the desk.

Campini wiped at his damp face. *I hope to hell I'm not blushing.* "He's been through hell, and I'm confident his hard work will pay off. It's only a matter of time. Purelli will fall."

"I know he's a big-time player, but the public is concerned about what's in their face. Purelli is like a mythical figure they don't think about. He might as well be the fucking Easter Bunny."

"We've got some new leads we're working on. Sonny is making headway," Campini countered, cautious of sounding impotent. He opted not to mention Benussi neared the clutches of insanity and the Solano organization might know his true identity. *Those are details for a later time.*

"It's not enough. I'll shoot you straight. You deserve as much." Taggert folded his arms across the desk, his posture stiff, but speech endearing. "We're pulling about a third of your resources."

"What?" The utterance loud and spontaneous, Campini recoiled for stepping out of line. The Captain sat still. "Sir, I need every man and piece of equipment you can spare. I can't finish this case shorthanded."

"I understand this complicates—"

"Are you kidding?" *Whoa, fine line between brazen and insubordinate.* "I'm sorry for interrupting, but *complicates* isn't the right word. This handcuffs me. Captain—"

"Don't." Taggert's calming aura blustered. His voice sharp and eyes unflinching. "Don't act surprised. We're averaging twelve murders a month and now this killer is on the loose wreaking havoc."

"The blonde murderer? We're sure it's a serial killer." *Any chance you can recognize Purelli as a serial killer? Maybe then I'll get some fucking support.*

"Yeah. Forensics and FBI profilers confirm it. Public is getting antsy. Five blondes dead, three more missing."

"So, I'm getting shelved."

Taggert waved his hands as if insulted. "No, but I need to put money into the Homicide Department. We're sending six of your men and half of your surveillance equipment. My hands are tied."

"How can I do this when you take guys and gear?"

"Look, be happy we don't shut it all down. I need *something*." Taggert clicked the keyboard of his computer with a nonchalant stare to the screen. The changing lights of the monitor reflected on the photos positioned on the shelf. "Tell me, to this point, what do we have?"

"Enough to put Benny Bianchi to death. We could cripple about half of Purelli's crew."

"Great. There's your headline. What's the problem?"

"We didn't do this to appease the media, sir." He slumped in the chair like a kid who'd just failed the test. All the math solutions were correct, but no work had been shown on the paper. "As I said, we don't have anything substantial on Purelli."

"If we bring in Bianchi and the rest of the thugs, would it hurt him?"

"For a time, maybe. I'd hate to drop the hammer and miss the right nail."

"Would he relocate?" Taggert smiled. "Get out of our jurisdiction and become someone else's problem?"

"Doubt it. My guess? He lies low and rebuilds. In a year, we're back to square one."

Taggert opened a drawer in the desk and sifted through a few hanging files. He pulled a hefty a stack from one and dropped the papers on the desk. "You know what these are?"

"No, sir."

"Budget logs. This right here, detective." Taggert tapped the stack. "Are all that matter. We're civil servants paid *by the people*, Reese. *The people* want results. And if they don't come, resources are reallocated elsewhere."

"I need time. Don't shut me down."

Taggert flipped through the logs, a grimace creeping across his face. "You've got three months and then we move on and cut our losses."

"That's it? Nothing else?"

Taggert clicked the keyboard again and drew his eyes to the computer monitor. "Your most recent case notes have been uploaded. I'm curious, why not pull Bianchi in? Maybe flip the bastard?"

Insulted, Reese rubbed at his eyes and smiled. "We've kicked it around. Problem is, as soon as we do that, Purelli will catch wind of it. A murder contract will be signed for Bianchi. If we manage to get to him and secure him safely, then we're talking Witness Protection, fighting the highest-priced attorney Purelli hires, hoping Bianchi goes through with it, and bracing for his family, neighbors, and fucking dogs to get whacked."

"Well, it may be time to flip the coin." Taggert clicked a few more keys. "Be better to take down some rather than none."

"When it's said and done, even if Bianchi agreed and I'm almost certain he wouldn't, we have to deal with Freddy Solano." Campini's hand rose above his head to indicate hierarchy. "He'll replace Purelli and it all resets. To end the Solano family, we have to get Purelli. Hand in cookie jar, caught red-handed, whatever expression you want to use." Campini's breathing elevated, as if he'd rehearsed this speech a hundred times but forgot the lines." He's the key.

Arrest him with a stack of evidence piled as high as the Eiffel tower and threaten to fill the needle. If we get Purelli to talk, he gives us Freddy Solano and the entire organization crumbles."

"I may be old and out of touch, but isn't Solano in prison?"

"Yeah. Due out in eighteen months. If we flip Purelli, we take him off the street and lock up the entire crew while keeping Solano in prison for good." He leaned forward in the chair, resting his elbows on the desk. "Captain, I need more time. A *'he-said, she-said'* court case involving Benny Bianchi will accomplish nothing."

"It's your call, but at this point, you've got nothing. And the purse strings are tightening. I can't budge on it. You've put a lot of work into this case and the department recognizes it. But if you don't connect Purelli to something serious and soon, we'll have to go after Bianchi and hope for cooperation. Shit, Sammy the Bull flipped on Gotti, right?"

Campini winced at the weak analogy, now sure the Captain's loyalties aligned more with golf outings and cocktail parties than Johnny Public's safety. "Thanks for your support and belief, sir." He stood, careful to return the chair to its original position.

"Detective," the Captain said, his eyes back on the computer screen, "three months and it's done."

Outside of Taggert's office, he flipped open a department-issued cell and moped through the hallway. The former Captains' portraits cast glares now more quizzical and animated.

Buried under a phony app labeled *Calendar*, lived a covert text-message portal. A quick swipe revealed the one number programmed. *Benussi.* The message would be sent to another fake app in Benussi's phone. The agreement was to use the software engineered by RCPD's best to make contact and never for actual communication. With Taggert's unflinching stance on Firecracker, the rules needed to be amended. He typed:

We have to make a move soon.

The more witnesses the better.

Send me all you know about Frezza.

I'm making a house call.

CHAPTER FIFTY-FOUR

"What's with the get up?" Richie reclined in the bucket seat of a white Lincoln town car.

"The guy is clever." Lorenzo Cantu stuck a handgun in the waistband of his soiled slacks then covered his bare chest with a fraying sweater. "We've got one shot at this." He peered into the driver side window. "Gonna require a little acting and showmanship."

Lorenzo considered the target. He'd handled worse with more violence, but a hit like this would open doors and shock the city. *My kinda party.*

Middleweight boxers' weights ranged between one hundred fifty and one hundred and sixty-four pounds. Bryce O'Leary, a mammoth in the division, weighed one-hundred and sixty-three.

He stood six feet tall with long and bulging arms. At the end of those arms, fists of dynamite awaited a spark of their wick. Clean shaven with eyes of green—a jaw line sturdy and pronounced like Jefferson, or perhaps Lincoln, O'Leary reveled in the limelight and the media's obsessive attention.

News outlets named him Bryce *Bang-Bang* O'Leary.

The result was always the same. A trademark wicked uppercut followed by a left kidney shot. Opponents' heads cracked back with a pop and then they hunched forward and crumpled after the slicing body blow. *Bang-Bang.*

After two and a half days of reconnaissance at the behest of Mr. Purelli and waving a couple of bills at a pair of sleazies who catered to the Irish boys, Lorenzo's intel led him here.

"You sure he's coming?" Richie asked.

"While you've been training, I've been putting in real work." *Little kiddie thinks I'm an amateur.* Lorenzo ran his finger over the three-inch scab nestled beneath his hair line. Since the brawl in the alleyway, its size had diminished, but it served as a constant reminder that he didn't like the new guy. "He'll be here. Every morning that Irish jack-off jogs to Gina's Café in the Sienna Oaks Shopping Plaza." Lorenzo nodded over his shoulder to the triad of stand-alone buildings behind him. Trust me, I've done my homework."

"What time does he show up?" Richie glanced through the windshield and then back to Lorenzo.

"Soon. Head back to the spot we talked about." He tossed a newspaper clipping onto Richie's lap.

"What's this?"

"A picture of him. What? Were you just going to guess which guy to follow?"

Richie turned the paper over and studied it. "Okay. Good call."

"No shit, youngin'." Lorenzo snugged a beanie on over his ears. "All right, circle around. You good?"

Richie nodded and shifted the Lincoln to drive. It sped off and sliced through the morning fog, breaking the vapor into scattered blotches of gray.

Lorenzo glanced west. Motionless landscape. He'll show up. *Any minute now.*

The plaza entrance, bookended by concrete marquees with glass display inserts, revealed a half-empty parking lot. A cluster of sedans and SUVs sat in front of Gina's Café. The medley of breakfast sausage and eggs drifted across the lot and reached his nose.

He glanced west again.

Lorenzo clutched the grip of the Glock in his waistband and pulled it up. From his pocket, he pulled the silver silencer Vinny provided this morning.

A glimpse to the west. *Come on. Come on, big boy.* He screwed the silencer on the barrel and shoved the weapon snug in to place, the elongated barrel a little more uncomfortable than he'd anticipated.

He squatted with his back on the eastern marquee of the plaza near a trash can tagged with graffiti. With an extended hand, he plucked a Styrofoam cup wedged between the flap of the garbage can's lid and metal rim. *This'll do just fine.*

Lorenzo's phone buzzed in his pocket. He retrieved it and flipped the receiver open aware of how odd he seemed. *A homeless looking guy staring at a cell phone.* He glanced around the street, spending special attention at the apartment complex in front of him. A few windows, unbridled by blinds or drapes, blinked with internal lighting but no peering eyes watched the beggar and his cellular.

A simple text crossed the screen. "He's coming."

A shiver of anxiety ran to his fingertips. He'd always enjoyed this part. *The trap. The hunt. The destruction.* He glanced down the street again. Fog hovered above the street and a lanky silhouette moved within it. Behind, thin headlights poked through the gray.

O'Leary's strides grew longer, and with each step, the silhouette morphed more and more into a man. *An Irishman.*

He reached the street running perpendicular to Sienna Oaks Shopping Plaza, glanced both ways then slowed his pace. He crossed and Lorenzo dropped a handful of change into the cup. "Change?" Lorenzo shook the Styrofoam.

The Lincoln skulked by, emitting a curl of exhaust turning the fog into a charcoal hue. It hugged the shoulder of the right lane and bent into a U-turn.

"Sorry." O'Leary patted the pockets of his pants and offered a shrug.

"Just a coin or two will do." Lorenzo wobbled the cup. The coins rattled numbly.

The Irishman ignored him and took another step forward. Car brakes squealed from behind. The Lincoln parked askew and opened its passenger side window.

"Pardon me, buddy. I'm a bit lost." Richie now wore a blue cap and pair of black sunglasses. O'Leary bent toward the open window.

"Where you headed?" O'Leary crossed his arms over the vehicle's threshold. Lorenzo stood; tingles traveled the length of his arms in a boost of dopamine lightning.

"Trying to find Eighth Street. Gotta doctor's appointment." Richie tilted the cap and brushed a mound of bronze hair beneath the brim. He connected with Lorenzo for a second but his eyes jumped back to the target.

"Ain't you a fighter? I think I know you." O'Leary crouched on his haunches, his head now level with the door handle.

"I'll be damned, ain't you Bryce O'Leary?"

Lorenzo slipped the Glock from his waistband. Bryce didn't notice. *Why would he?* At eight-fifteen on a Thursday morning in pursuit of a delectable Café Hash Special, the whereabouts of a crusty vagrant don't necessitate extra attention.

"And you're Richie Frezza?" O'Leary rose and glanced toward the street. Lorenzo's feet stayed planted, but he swayed out of the Irishman's peripheral.

"In the flesh, my friend." Richie replied, his eyes darted from the boxer then to Lorenzo.

"We're not friends, Mr. Frezza. I'm going to have to hurt you. If we even fight."

"A fight's coming. Guys like you and I, we're magnets for violence. It just seems to follow us like shadows across the grass. Am I right?"

Lorenzo raised the Glock, gripping the handle with both hands, shoulders squared like a cop in training. One last look to both ends of the street. *All alone.*

"Maybe. I'm not some chubby Mexican pushing forty you can bob and—"

A slight pocket of air from the pistol grazed the base of O'Leary's head. *POP*.

The man's head jerked forward from the shot and smacked into the roof of the Lincoln. O'Leary fell forward. Brain matter and charred pieces of skin coated the front seat. His weight dragged backward as the remainder of his body fought gravity. The body collapsed, lodging the man's legs beneath his back in an inverted angle across the curb. An oval exit wound above the left eye still simmering from the destruction.

Lorenzo lodged the silenced pistol to the Irishman's chest and pulled the trigger. The muffled shot hissed like a trapped rodent and O'Leary's body vibrated from the impact.

Bang-Bang.

CHAPTER FIFTY-FIVE

Richie slept little. Interspersed between slight dozes the same dream invaded.

Lorenzo climbs in the car, scooping O'Leary's brain matter from the passenger seat. Blood, splattered like spaghetti sauce bubbling in a pot, covers the dashboard and roof. Three strands trickle down the windshield.

He and Lorenzo bring the old Lincoln to Tom's Salvage and Tow. They slide the keys into an envelope twice as big as Richie's best pay day.

"They'll never know a thing." Lorenzo says with a wink.

A hydraulic compactor squeezes the Lincoln, its top and bottom plates meeting in the middle until the car is a sliver of metal. Then they drive in Lorenzo's car to Belleview, scratch the gun, drop it in bleach, and bury it on the Navajo Reservation.

At eleven-thirty, right when he managed to sniff the REM phase of his sleep cycle, the ghosts cracked jokes to celebrate the new arrival. *Welcome to the fold, O'Leary.*

Their incessant clamoring shook Richie from the couch. He found the jubilation of the dead in his mind an annoyance. It wasn't a matter of shame. After a while, the terrible things you did lost their effect. There were only so many times you could truly regret something.

His mother's death was different. She escaped the vault and stood near the outskirt of his psyche, a frail and pathetic figure. He mourned her and loathed the others.

Sorrow festered within him like an open wound baking in three days of an unforgiving July sun, yet each monstrous action acted upon added a new layer of the hardened shell in his mind. *If you don't think about it, you'll learn to forget.*

Good luck with that, Cranswell screamed like a buffoon.

Coward, O'Leary said. He licked a strand of blood pulsing from the exit wound on his forehead.

Harold appeared from behind the other two, but Richie's buzzing cellphone on the living room table slammed the vault doors.

"I'm here." Tossing the covers to the base of the couch, he swung his feet to the beige carpet. Richie hunched over the glass of the table. His reflection stared back. Purple pouches grew beneath his eyelids and he wondered if he'd ever sleep again. "What time is it?"

"Little past midnight. Nothing over the phone." Benny's wheeze matched the crackle of a disturbance in the line. "When you hang up with me, toss that one. I got you a new burner."

"Okay." Richie picked at a cold bowl of macaroni and cheese with a plastic fork. It turned to dust in his mouth.

Tastes like death, huh? Harold burst from within the vault, his body fragile and emaciated. *Another helping, pal?*

A bitter laugh turned into a mocking howl and Richie's ears rang in a high pitch. "Shut the fuck up."

"Huh? What did you—"

"Sorry." Reality crept into his mind. He glanced around

his mother's apartment then brought the phone tight to his ear. "Not you, Benny."

"You okay, kid?" The gruff edge prominent in most of Benny's speech softened.

"Yeah."

"Get your head right. We need to meet. You know where?"

"Yeah." The call ended and Richie clicked the phone's top back in place and glared toward the closed door of his mother's room—unopened since the night Georgie carved Harold's throat in the barn.

Richie shrugged into a shirt, slid on socks and shoes, and charged from the apartment. Frosted air filled his lungs and frozen wind pricked at his face. He considered grabbing a coat, but such a venture required reentering the apartment.

Nope.

With iced hands and a chill traveling his lungs, he moved toward the back exit of the neighborhood. Center St. knifed into 3rd St., a perimeter road of The Trails and escape route of the zombies in Squatters Row.

A few men mumbled to each other and huddled around a makeshift fire in a steel drum, one of the many left-overs construction crews dumped after the fire.

"Hey there, buddy." The man nearest to him said. He sniffled and dragged his forearm across his nose. "Gotta few bucks?"

Richie ignored him and tossed the phone into the flames.

"Willing to trade," the other said. In the fire's glow, his deep-sockets cast shadows across his thin cheeks. A jagged tooth arched beyond his lips. "I got ladies willing to party."

"Not interested." Richie backed away with both eyes on them. Neither man blinked, and he turned toward the exit.

Another zombie sat cross-legged on the walkway of the first building. A tattered coat hung from her skeletal frame and glowed in the moonlight. Her head popped up when Richie approached, revealing an acne-scarred face that peeked from the collar. She dragged on a cigarette and coughed.

"Hey baby." She grinned, the remaining teeth in her mouth like miniature crumbling sand castles. "Need a little loving?"

"Another time, maybe." Richie cut through the alley between the buildings.

More vagrants and addicts. Crackling tinfoil emitted foul smells, and the orange glows revealed bleak, gaunt faces—suffering and pain abound. The bright-eyed teen within him desired to help. The hardened killer sought to maim.

Ignoring both impulses, Richie ducked beneath a half-linked fence and left Squatters Row.

The skyline bloomed purple and cast dark patches on the moonlit streets. The silhouette of Ms. May's Diner hooked out like the pronounced nose of the road's face. Parked a few yards north, just a black blob entombed in darker night, the Cadillac purred—its exhaust spewing choked smog. An orange flame near the car ignited a cigarette. Richie shuffled forward and a shadow behind the light grew clearer and larger.

"Sorry to make you walk in the cold, kid. But we can't be seen in or near The Trails."

"I don't mind. Fresh air ain't a bad thing." Richie rolled his shoulders then jammed his hands into the front pockets of the jeans.

"Fresh? It's freezing. My nuts are the size of peas right now." Benny chuckled and the heaving laughter rebounded from the still buildings like ping-pong balls. "Get rid of your phone?"

"Yeah. Tossed it in a fire."

"Good. Hey, who were you talking to earlier?" Benny dragged at the cigarette hard, his lips pursing like they'd bit into a lemon.

"Huh? Oh, the TV."

"Didn't take you for a casual viewer. Besides, what the fuck is on right now worth screaming about?"

"An infomercial. Stupid Sham-Wow guy and his beady eyes."

"Don't crack up on me, kid. This business is about tunnel vision. Move forward and on." Benny flicked the cigarette. The orange spark spilled to the ground and burst into a hundred miniature stones of dying ash. "Hop in."

He creaked the back door open and Richie obliged, happy to feel some heat. The mobster's entry in to the front shook the underbelly of the car. Benny continued, "We're expecting backlash from our Irish friends."

Richie nodded. The reaction had been discussed during the prepping stage.

"By now, they know their man is dead. So, we think it's best if someone is our eyes and ears out here, capisce?"

"Thought the plan was to strike again." Richie breathed into his hands and watched the smoke of his breath spiral around his fingers. "While they're organizing an attack."

"Well," Benny said, turning to the rear-view and locking eyes with Richie, "I do as I'm told."

Lot of that going around these days. Richie adjusted the back vent and the warm air blanketed his knees.

Benny turned in the seat. "We'll keep a look out. I want you to know, I got your interests in mind. We won't leave Ms. May unprotected."

"Thank you. I appreciate it."

Benny's words awoke the ghosts, and the car evaporated. The vault materialized.

Now you've done it, O'Leary squealed with a stoic expression. The eyes, dazzling green gems, floated in darkness. *My family will take revenge tenfold. You're all going to die. Every. Last. One. Of. You.*

Richie grimaced and shifted in the backseat. The voices relentless soundtracks of the misery he'd inflicted and now felt.

Another one bites the dust, Cranswell sang. *Hey, Harold, you know the tune, right?*

That band Queen? Ha. A bunch of sissies like our friend, Richie. A scared, twisted sissy. Ain't ya, Richie? Ain't ya?

Benny snapped the center console open.

The thud quelled the ghosts for a moment.

The big guy pulled out a thick white envelope. "You've earned it." He tossed it to Richie's lap.

"What's this for?" He flipped the top. A wide stack of bills and a new phone.

"It's the other half. We reward production. You've been earning. Our buddy Donald had three trucks reported stolen last week. I guess our pep talk worked."

Richie opened the phone and scrolled through the contact list. Like the other one, the lone number programmed was Benny's.

"Now, you need to lie low for a bit. Okay?"

"Understood."

"Good. And for your protection, we'll be moving Joe up to Belleview. You'll train in the barn for a little while."

"Huh?" Richie dropped the phone into the little package and leaned forward. "Why?"

"Just to be safe. What's the most obvious target of the Irish gonna be?"

Richie closed the envelope. Its contents brought a gripping fear replaced by the excitement of the previous weeks.

The next target? Angered by his unthinkable naiveté, he managed to utter, "I guess me."

"You guess right. We're on top of it, kid. We've warred before with the Micks. If they want round two, they can come get it." Benny's hand rose and his fingers flapped toward him. "But as a precaution, we need to hide you until it's straightened out."

A track of headlights glowed in the distance, covering the night in a yellow haze. They grew larger until their flash attacked the windshield of the Cadillac.

Richie's stomach ached. Sweat broke out in patchy rashes, dampening the area between his shoulder blades. The car passed and Richie exhaled a gust, realizing he'd forgotten to breathe.

"Joe understands." Benny closed the console. It clicked shut, the noise acting like an exclamation mark ending the comment.

"For how long?"

"Not sure. A week, maybe more. We're gonna schedule a sit down."

"They're gonna be cool and shake hands?"

"Nah. But they'll listen if they know what's good for 'em. O'Leary was a warning." Benny's index finger shot up. "They try to get tough, and full-scale war begins. They ain't got the resources or balls, kid."

Richie nodded, somewhat relieved. "How long until I fight?"

"Soon. We're not investing this kinda dough to have you on the sideline." Benny pointed to the closed envelope with a palm-up sweep. The scent of sour nicotine and Polo drifted to the back and meshed with the burning sting of the overworked heater.

Richie clutched the cash and turned the handle of the door.

"Meet Joe in the morning. And kid—" Benny's eyes pursued a car traveling toward the Cadillac, traipsing forward with its head lights golden eyes in the pitch. It turned at the cross street before Ms. May's. "Keep your eyes peeled."

They shook hands and Richie pushed into the night.

The buildings of Squatters Row emitted a cacophonous roar and Richie opted for an alternative route. He could handle a few of the sub-humans with no questions asked, but an envelope of cash may bring a swarm. He moved ahead of the Cadillac. Benny pressed the gas, and the car jumped forward. Its tires spun on the icy street, gained traction half-heartedly and then righted its course. Its shadow disappeared into the darkness.

He followed the Cadillac's route.

A block ahead lay a side street intersected by two vacant alleys. It led to the perimeter fence of The Trails. A casual walk down the chain link would rouse little suspicion and also evade the mongrels decaying in the Row.

He reached the side street Harmony Ave. and darted into the first empty alley. Ahead in the moonlight, the fence shined like a beacon. Below the glaring steel post atop the fence, a white Impala idled. Smoke from the exhaust climbed upward. *Who is driving that around here?*

The chain link fence had been visible during Richie's trek through Squatter's Row and the stark white car would have captured his attention.

It had *not* been there.

Richie clutched the envelope of his spoils and misdeeds, now angry the thick hoodie still hung dead over a stool in the apartment. He tucked the cash in his waistband beneath the cover of his shirt.

In a brisk trot, he aimed forward with shoulders cocked. The car seemed to stare down on him, holding a glare of contempt.

A cop? An Irish hit squad ready to cash in? A dealer awaiting customers who isn't afraid to pull the trigger? Move your ass, man.

Fifty feet from the chain link now.

As soon as the alley opens, hit the right turn and keep your head down. Don't say anything. Don't look. Just hustle.

The door of the car wedged open and Richie's heart beat tripled.

CHAPTER FIFTY-SIX

Reese Campini lurched out of his cruiser as the young boxer neared.

"Good evening, or should I say morning?" Campini stepped forward and tapped the gold badge clipped to his belt loop.

"Just passing through, no time to talk." The kid gripped at his abdomen and swiveled to the right.

"Wait a minute, now." He grabbed the young punk's shoulder and thwarted his attempt to push by. "I need to speak with you, Mr. Frezza."

"Do I know you?" Richie's eyes squinted, and even in the tinkling moonlight and fog, Campini recognized a flash of fear behind them.

"No, but I'm afraid I know you."

Richie pulled from his grasp and inched to the fence. "You got the wrong guy."

"I don't believe so. You're acquainted with a few fellas of interest, correct? You do know Benny Bianchi?"

"Nope."

"Benjamin Bianchi," Campini shouted with incredulousness and tracked the file cabinet in his brain. He plucked the folder labeled *Beans*. "Thirty-seven. No children. Known soldier of the Solano Crime Family and Salvador Purelli's right-hand man. A list of arrests dating back twenty-four years. Two stints in prison. Three years for burglary. One and a half for assault. Drives a black Cadillac Deville. License plate number N79-YQL." He stopped and awaited a reaction, a paralyzing fear, something. The kid's face remained emotionless.

"Who are you?"

"My name is Reese Campini." He unclipped the badge and held it toward the kid. "I'm a detective with OCD. Organized Crime Division. We have a lot to talk about."

"So, do I need a lawyer?" Richie pivoted and faced him.

"That's strange for you to say. Why would you need an attorney? I just want to chat."

"Am I under arrest or something?"

"Nope, you're not." Campini pointed to the car idling, puffing snakes of smoke into the black. "Want to get out of the cold?" He slid into the front seat without looking back. *Come on, tough guy. Run. Make it easier on me.*

The passenger side door creaked open and Richie slid in.

"We need to talk about your whereabouts this morning." Campini slid a card on the console.

"This morning?" Richie grabbed the card and traced his finger over the block script.

"Yes. This morning a man was killed in broad daylight right outside of the Sienna Oaks shopping plaza."

"I don't know anything about it." Richie flicked the corner of the card and brought a stare to the passenger window.

"Maybe you do and maybe you don't. I'm not here to interrogate you, Mr. Frezza. I'm here to help."

"Oh yeah? How you gonna do that?" Richie spoke to the glass. Campini watched his face, able to discern a faint silhouette in the window.

Ignoring the question, he continued. "The man was a boxer just like you." Campini considered how much to let on without overstepping the line of ethics. *Give him the nitty-gritty and watch him squirm or play it close? Fuck it. I'm out of time.*

"The first shot entered the bottom of the skull, or as medical examiners confirmed during the autopsy, the occipital bone. It carried on an upward trajectory of sheer destruction, fracturing the base of the head and sending bone chips scattering throughout the brain like missiles."

No comment. No reaction.

"Then another shot straight through the heart. Execution if I've ever seen one."

"Is that so?" Richie's eyebrows rose high in the window's reflection.

"Yep. Murdered at about eight-thirty on his way to breakfast. The café in the plaza said he was a regular. Ya see," Reese shifted in the seat drawing a long breath, "that tells me something."

"What's that, detective?"

"Somebody did their homework. They watched and stalked. This is a premeditated execution. So, the question then becomes, who has the motive?"

"Not sure." Riche turned to face him, the same bland and emotionless expression glued on like a mask.

"It'll be headline news tomorrow. Once the media gets a hold of this, damn. A public figure murdered in broad daylight. The brass is going to want this one solved fast." Campini gripped the steering wheel with one hand and wiped at the fog of the windshield with the other. "Have to clear it all up."

"Like I said, detective. I don't know anything about it."

"Let's start with your whereabouts this morning."

"Thought you said this wasn't an interrogation." Richie gripped the door handle. "Sounds like it to me."

"Nah." Campini's eyes drew to the windshield, smudges of light reflected from the street lamps through the glass. A trio of silhouettes trudged past the opening of the alley. *Heading to the sanctuary of bangers and addicts named the Row, for sure.* "Trying to connect the dots is all. Where were you this morning?"

"Training." The boxer's eyes tracked the floor mat.

"All morning?" Campini's radio transmitter crackled. He flipped the volume down. "Anyone able to back that up?"

"I was with my trainer until eleven. Home the rest of the day."

"That's your story?"

"That's the truth, detective." Richie met his stare and released his grip on the handle.

"I see." Campini pulled a square notepad from his pocket and retrieved the ballpoint pen resting in the cup holder. He scribbled on the page, the sheet out of Richie's view, and leveled his stare. "Well, if that checks out, I suppose I was wrong. Where do you train?"

This question acted like an electric shock, and the kid's body tensed. "Um. Knuckles Up."

"Ah. Right down the street here, correct?"

"Yeah." Richie's hands fell to his lap, the fingers fidgeting.

"You know, this murdered man was scheduled to fight

Friday." Campini tilted his wrist and surveyed the time. "Tonight. I just realized it is technically Friday."

"Really?"

"Yep." *Let's see what you're made of.* "Against you, in fact."

"O'Leary was killed?" The young man's jaw slacked, and an aped expression of startled mimicry grew in his eyes and cheeks. "I haven't heard."

"Yes. Coincidental too, don't you think?"

"I'm not following you."

"The man you're supposed to fight is murdered right before the bout. He's an Irish thug, running around with mobsters all over the western part of Ridgemont Cove. You're a known associate of the Solano crime family and protégé of Benny Bianchi. The two factions have warred before, Mr. Frezza, and for much less. It's coincidental, right?"

"It is shocking, but you've got some facts mixed up there, detective. I'm no protégé of Benny whoever-you-think."

"You didn't just exit his Cadillac with an envelope of money?" Campini pointed to the bulge beneath Richie's shirt.

"Have you been following me?"

"For a lot longer than tonight. Let's cut the bullshit." Campini leaned across the console and gripped the insolent kid's wrist. "You have my card. If I don't hear from you by Monday, and that would be unwise, Mr. Frezza, then I have to set an arrest warrant."

"Arrest for what?"

Reese side-stepped the question with a smirk and reached over to open the passenger side door. "Take the weekend to think it over." *Give me some time to check out your alibi and get Benussi to lay the trap, too.*

Ice air invaded the car and Richie hesitated. "I'm really not—"

"Stop. If by ten Monday morning you haven't called, I'm making my rounds and getting the paperwork filed."

Richie slammed the door behind him and ambled toward the chain link fence.

CHAPTER FIFTY-SEVEN

With every other stride he looked over his shoulder in hopes the cop's car had moved. When he neared the northern entrance of the neighborhood, the Impala lights blinked then shrank into the dark.

He stopped and pulled the new phone from the envelope. *What does this guy know?* He scrolled to the contacts icon, found Benny's new programmed number and pressed the button. *Pick up, man. Pick up.* The phone rang three times and connected.

"Gotta problem. Serious fucking problem, man." His voice felt foreign, as if a shrill woman's terror had been dubbed over his moving lips.

"Relax, kid." A droning whirl from an open car window muffled Benny's voice. "What happened?"

"Cops just stopped me." He glanced over his shoulder again, knowing the car wouldn't be there and still determined to prove it to himself.

"Don't say another thing about it. Where are you?"

"Heading home." Richie rounded a parked car and

strode down the sidewalk opposite the Row. "Supposed to meet him tomorrow to talk."

"Head to the farm with Joe in the morning. Camp out for a day or two. I'll get back with you."

The phone clicked off.

All right, boys. Come on out. He waited for the ghosts to attack and let him have it.

Nothing. Silence within.

That's even worse.

CHAPTER FIFTY-EIGHT

Moonlighters slept on Friday mornings, recuperating from Thursday's eighties themed night. Cheap well drinks attracted patrons of all ages. Those in their mid-twenties danced to songs popular during their crib days and older men snuck into the club below to unload a week's pay on blowjobs beneath the veil of VIP room tours.

Benny's eyes needed to adjust when he entered. Cold and blinding outside today, the windowless building with black lights attached to the walls played tricks on his vision.

He moved through the entrance lobby, still slick in mop water. A tattered curtain hung in a doorway etched beside a raised counter, where normally, a trio of muscle-headed goons checked IDs, distributed wristbands, and allowed patrons entry into the lair of the lascivious.

This morning, an aging B-team stripper named Precious manned the counter, and when Benny entered the lobby, she glanced up from her phone and offered a wink.

"Morning." He rested an elbow on the counter, his eyes on her cleavage spilling from a halter top struggling to contain the weight of her breasts and rolls lumbering at her waistline.

"Hey, Benny. Go ahead through, sweetie pie."

Beyond the curtain, stale sweat filled his nostrils. Glitter dashes sprinkled the floor in streaks, shining like rubies and emeralds scratched across the floor. A wide multi-colored trail split in three strands, two climbing the raised stages on each side of the aisle and one cutting through the pathway leading to a door marked No Entry.

Cody Parkins, a regular Moonlighter with an unpitying wallet, slumped over the bar and snored.

The scraggly haired bartender named Wes nodded and poured a glass of *Lavagulin* and slid it toward Benny. He topped the bottle and returned it to the cabinet that opened when the Solano underboss entered and never anytime else.

"*Salut.*" Benny tipped the glass and drank. He nudged Cody. "Long night, buddy?" The drunk muttered something inaudible and shifted in the stool, dropping his head between two thin arms crisscrossed on the bar.

"Yeah. Should kick his ass out." Wes tapped near the man's ear and shrugged. "The old man is tired of him."

"That a fact?" Benny's left eyebrow arched, and then he nudged the drunk with a fist.

"Yeah." Wes wiped the rims of two highball glasses and placed them in the dish rack. "It's bad for business."

"The old man answers to me." Benny finished the drink with a swig and wiped his sleeve across his chin. "If the money is green, keep on pouring. Another."

"You got it." The bartender lowered the dish rack beneath the bar and disappeared from view for a moment. He rose again, the same bottle of scotch from before in his hand. He filled Benny's glass to the rim.

Benny's head cranked back, and the liquid slid to his

stomach, burning the throat but aiding the suffering of an early morning headache. "Where's Candi?"

Cody peeked up with glass eyes and grinned. The stench of old tobacco and dry hops poured from his gaped mouth.

"In the back getting dressed." Wes sorted and dropped cherries and limes into the condiment caddy. "She was the star last night, I hear."

Benny stood straight up, his expression stone. "So, you gonna get her or keep fingering the fruit?"

"Oh, yeah." The dumbass drink-pourer wiped his hands on a rag and tossed it below the bar. "Sorry, Benny."

"Mr. Bianchi."

"Right. Sorry. I'll go get her, Mr. Bianchi."

Wes swung the length of the bar and walked between the two raised platforms pierced with chrome poles running ground to ceiling then through the door marked No Entry.

A few moments later, Candi strolled through the same door. She wore jeans and sneakers but had begun the transformation in the top half—strings over the nipples and green glittered arms. Cody stirred from his slumber and muttered something.

"Hey, baby." Candi strode the walkway between the elevated stages and turned toward the bar. Benny pecked her cheek.

"How's it going? Need a minute in private."

"Already? I'm not ready for you." She pointed a sneakered foot out and grinned.

"Not that kind of meeting, darling." Benny pushed from the bar and unclipped the chain barricading the VIP curtain. She took his hand, and the two pushed through.

"This place clean?" His mouth pursed, pushing the thin

mustache above his lip up. He swiped at a leather booth in one of the mirrored alcoves.

"Probably not." She slid into the booth. "What's on your mind?"

"You still got your regulars?" Benny sat on the opposite side. "Outcall business."

"A few. It's dangerous now. I've got a couple on the reg."

"Clayton O'Malley still?"

Candi blushed. Red cherries blossoming beneath cheap make-up. "Sometimes. Why?"

"How often do you see him?"

"Once a week." She crossed her glittered arms beneath her breasts. They plumped like cantaloupes in the skimpy top. "Why?"

"This week yet?"

"No. What's this all about?" Candi's voice lost its bite.

Questions like this meant danger to her, Benny thought. He could see fear written on her face. The eyes shifting in their sockets. The bottom lip chewed by the upper teeth.

"Relax." Benny knelt forward in the booth and held her shaking thigh. "I'd never ask you to do anything that may end badly. You know that, right?"

"Yeah." The response weak and fractured.

The small hometown girl with a dream of Hollywood's bright lights shone through the make-up and glitter.

When he'd found the waitress, she went by Samantha Fleming and read scripts during her allotted thirty-minute breaks—the allure of stardom an intoxicating fantasy.

A few bucks and introductions later, she'd followed the dream Benny sold. Now, the little slut perused scripts amongst neon strips glued to a stage where men's sweat, spit, and semen waxed the flooring.

But every so often, Samantha Fleming peeked through Candi's eyes. That caused concern for Benny.

Live the life in front of you and don't ask fucking questions. Recalling yesterday don't help tomorrow. Benny frowned and thought of Richie. *The kid could heed that same advice, too.* "I just need you to set up a date." He grazed her knee with three crisp hundreds. "Do your thing. I gotta feeling the Irish are planning something. I need to know when and where."

"We don't talk a whole lot, Benny." She eyed the cash, and her eyes told him the transformation back to Candi began. "It's business. I'm not—"

"Make him talk. Find out."

"This about the guy they found outside of the shopping plaza?"

"A war is coming." Benny used the money to draw circles on her thigh. "Who did what is irrelevant to you. Don't ask questions. Just take the money and say yes."

"Yes. I'll call you when I've got something." Candi gripped the bills and rose. "I need to get ready."

"Hold on there, darling." Benny held the cash tight in his fingertips and unzipped his fly. "Aren't you forgetting something?"

She snorted a laugh. "You're getting sweet on me."

"Do your job." Benny grasped behind her head and brought it toward his lap.

CHAPTER FIFTY-NINE

Timothy Vietta sat on the narrow bench in the locker room of Marty Kabot's gym. The place stunk of urine, and based on the last three days of training in this shithole, no cleaning lady worked here.

Joe put in a good word. Provided Timothy helped with some of the chores, Marty waived the training fee for a short time.

Timothy taped gauze over the troublesome hand. The pain was manageable, but the scab and stitching turned brown and crusted like a morbid pie from Ms. May's Diner.

A self-adhesive bandage covered the gauze and sent dull vibrations of pain throbbing through the wound. Next the boxing tape, and then eventually the glove, but he needed Marty for that. He stood and pushed through the door and out into the gym.

Much like Knuckles Up, Marty's place was a small warehouse structure. A few punching bags hung near the front door like plush skeletons strung out for Halloween. A sparring ring (in a bit better condition than Joe's) clogged the center, and a weightlifting area with two rusted racks of dumbbells and the corpses of lifting belts sat a few yards behind.

The racks lined a mirror wall, whose reflection gave an expansive view of the gym. Unlike Knuckles Up, the shower dripped water a degree above ice, the air conditioner kicked on when it felt like it, and the windows were cracked and tinted. In a few parts where the tint had peeled, daylight glimpsed through and left brightened circles on the dark gym floor. At four-thirty in the morning, though, the gym was a black pit.

"Coffee is in the office." Marty crossed the stretching mat in a grungy tweed sweater, the one garment Timothy ever saw. It covered sneakily beefy arms. Marty's slight belly flopped over worn gray sweatpants. He held a mug in his hand and flicked a switch on the wall upward with the other. A single naked lightbulb glowed above the sparring ring.

"Thanks, but I'm good for now." Timothy held out the half-wrapped hand. "Little help?"

"Suit yourself." Marty, a short and broad Polish man, placed his mug on the sparring ring's edge and grabbed hold of Timothy's wounded hand and applied thick, protective tape to the knuckles. "I need my fuel to start the day."

Timothy winced and struggled to keep the hand level. Marty had taken a look at it when they'd met, and before agreeing to train, asked for proof the guy's damaged body could take a beating.

"Still hurting bad?" Marty weaved the tape around each finger with a swift, experienced motion.

"I'm all right."

"Doubt it." Marty smirked, accentuating the puffy cheeks squeezing his crooked, L-shaped nose. "But you proved your metal when we met. I'll give you that."

"You went easy on me." Timothy forced a smile then recalled dropping Joe's name four days ago. Immediately afterward, he and Marty sparred. He shook off the rust and circled in large strides before landing a few shots. Every time a trademark *Thunderstorm* left connected, a rash of fire caused the limp arm to pull back. "I'm managing. Gets easier every day."

"I still think you should rest and eat painkillers like potato chips, but who am I to judge?" Marty pulled thin silver scissors from his pocket and cut the slack of the tape dangling from Timothy's hand. He pinched down.

Timothy expected it and stood still, allowing the darting slivers of shock to wreak havoc. "We're good." He extended his other hand and Marty started the process all over again.

Once finished with the tape, Marty slid gloves on.

"Need to see your jab improve." He strutted toward the heavy bags. "Jab, keep the right-hand flush against the cheek, and circle with each new punch."

Timothy obeyed. As an orthodox fighter, the left fired jabs, and each connection to the bag stung the hand.

This training lasted for twenty minutes, and by the end, his fingers burned beneath the cover of his glove and tape.

Light sparring came next, with both men donning protective headgear.

"Let's see the jab in real action, Timbo." Marty slipped his mouthpiece mid-sentence, garbling the last words.

Timothy threw a right straight and Marty deflected. The old man stepped beside the errant punch and tagged Timothy's chin with a soft jab.

"You keep protecting the hand." Marty spat; the words jumbled from the mouth guard. "And you'll never get better."

Timothy shot three jabs. The first missed, but the next pair hit pay dirt. Streams of pain snaked through his hand.

Marty's head snapped back, and he grinned wide revealing the red guard in his mouth. "Didn't think you had it in you." He looped a hook and Timothy backtracked, the gust of wind a force and he realized the old man put some power into it.

Marty spit his mouthpiece out and halted the action. "Teachable moment."

Timothy ignored the radiating pain in his head and endured the discourse.

"When I come with the counter, you're flat-footed. Put some bounce in those toes. Make me work for the punch."

"You're right," Timothy responded through his mouthpiece.

"Of course, I am. What the hell do you pay me for?"

Timothy spit his mouth guard out with a huff. "I don't pay you anything."

"In time, Timbo."

They sparred for another twenty minutes. Timothy bounced as he was instructed, evading more of the old codger's counters than before.

Slick in sweat, both men hunched over, their gloves resting on their knees.

"Ready for the weights?" Marty wheezed, showing a little fatigue for the first time this morning.

"Yeah. Same routine as yesterday?"

"If it ain't broke, right?"

Three days of an extensive weight training program had already begun the process of defining muscles in Timothy's shoulders and pectorals—though the sliced hand hindered the exercise's form.

At the conclusion of the weightlifting, the sun began to drop its circles of light through the tinted window.

"That's a good session, Timbo. Get showered and then meet me in the yard. Gotta a few things you can do for me." Marty unfastened the Velcro of his training gloves with a tug of his teeth.

"More weeds and trimming?" Timothy's hand throbbed beneath the glove. It wasn't enough to inflict debilitating pain, but it annoyed him.

"We'll get a few hours in the yard and then we'll come back for more. I've got a couple of—"

The familiar thump against the door indicated the newspaper's arrival.

Timothy pulled the wraps and tape on the trek toward the locker room. A stream of sweat poured from his shaved head and slid from the nape of his neck, rolling between his sore shoulder blades.

One day closer.

Reality jumped back into his mind. Annabelle in the chicken coop, giggling as Rambo and Penny pecked the ground and clucked. Ruby serving the same breakfast special, counting the seconds of her shift and the days of her sobriety. The cold eyes of Purelli. Demon black slits—a dark window into a soulless man.

"Timbo," Marty screeched from the entrance. "Getta load of this."

The *Sharpton Chronicle* waved in the air. A color photo of a sidewalk strung with yellow caution tape filled the top two-thirds. A detective stared into the camera, the lens capturing a solemn expression. The title read *Young Boxer Murdered in Downtown Ridgemont Cove.* Timothy swiped the paper and scanned the pages.

"The boy you were talking about?" Marty asked.

"Looking." *Richie Frezza dead already*? He traced a finger across the lines. "I'm not seeing a name."

"We should call Joe." Marty wandered toward the office and Timothy read the last few lines of the article.

No names were released, but the location of the corpse was near the Irish section of town. It could be possible the mob tired of Richie. It was a remote possibility, but a possibility, nonetheless. More likely, Timothy figured, Richie and his new friends had disposed of a threat. Purelli didn't shy away from playing dirty. If a murder lined the pockets of the Solano family or furthered the reputation of its acting boss, jump in the mud pit.

Marty came back from the office with a dated cell phone, an early nineties model with a large black antenna. He handed it to Timothy with an exasperated look. "I hate these damn things."

"I know who to call. You gotta phonebook?"

Marty stalked back to the office, mumbling about technology's intrusion of the world. He returned a few moments later with a tattered Yellow Book and tossed it on the sparring ring corner. Timothy flipped through the pages and found the restaurant section. He plugged the number for Ms. May's Diner into Marty's ridiculous cell phone.

After a short connection the phone died, and he redialed the number. This time, the ring reverberated in the enormous speaker of the mobile phone and then the voice of Ruby chimed in. "Thanks for calling Ms. May's, home of Ridgemont Cove's Original Apple Pie. This is Ruby. How can I help you?"

"Hey."

"Timmy? What are you doing? Where have you been?"

"Sorry, I had to leave town. Long story."

"Same old Timmy Vietta. Get yours and then you're out the door. This is Prom all over again."

It was a stinging remark, but he had no comeback. "Trust me, it's not. I'm kinda in trouble. I can't talk about it. I was hoping you'd help me out."

"Trouble? What's new?"

"I'll make it up to you."

"Whatever, Tim. What do you want?"

"Did the paper get delivered there yet? Did you hear about a murder a few days ago?"

"Hold on, I have a customer." Clanking dishes and muffled voices filled the earpiece and Marty's cell phone struggled to keep the volume clean. "Yeah, they're not saying the name or anything. Things are kinda weird here." The last words were whispered and muddled, like the mouthpiece was covered with her delicate, manicured hand.

"What do you mean?" Timothy eyed Marty's saunter across the gym. He'd lost interest and was onto the next challenge of the day. Weeds and mowing.

"Well, you know how I told you those mafia guys have been around here?"

"Yeah."

"Well, one of them, the guy that drives the Benny-guy and Richie—"

Frezza. "Yeah, what about him?"

"Well, he's been here since five this morning. Right when we opened. Plus, Ms. May's acting weird. She won't tell him to leave, and normally, nobody sits in here without ordering *something*. Ms. May doesn't play, you know? I'm not sure what's going on."

Timothy unscrambled this new information, searching for a connection.

Possibly a problem. Probably nothing.

The driver Ruby spoke of was Sonny. Part of Purelli's crew, but not a threat. They had spoken many times, but Timothy always felt the bald mammoth stuck out of place in the criminal underworld. He didn't possess the same sharp wit and congenial banter of Benny or Lorenzo or any other one of the soldiers under the *Don's* thumb.

Sonny never quite fit the mold. A serious and secretive man, beyond the grips of Purelli's influence it seemed.

"I doubt it's anything to worry about."

"There's something else, Tim." Her voice lowered to a whisper.

"What?"

"The guy keeps asking about you."

CHAPTER SIXTY

A tough son-of-a-bitch, Jeffrey Benussi laughed at little James's decision to join the police force.

"Let me get this straight," he had said with the casual frown he wore so well, "you want to risk your life to stop bad guys? Don't you know cops are criminals, too? If you want to put a dent in crime, join the service. You don't see me handing out parking tickets and worried about crackheads."

Benussi had responded with, "So it's okay to get shot at by a terrorist, but arresting a crackhead is no good?"

"A crackhead isn't hurting anybody. They just smoke crack and sleep. I'd rather fight the terrorist. Besides, those blue uniforms and mustaches, all those asshole cops have are just ridiculous. Look like a bunch of fairies in uniform."

"Protect and serve, right? I'll be helping people."

"Help yourself, little bro. If you're going to die, do it with dignity. Cops are getting cut down every day, and no one gives a shit."

Benussi ignored the riveting persuasion and enlisted in the Police Academy.

Now, a few decades later, he *wished* terrorists lurked from caves and slept in sand traps. At least he knew who *they* were.

Seated at the bar of Ms. May's Diner, the mirror's reflection presented a man aged beyond the birth certificate once a record of his life but now a paper slid into a classified folder. The investigation's progress crawled toward the realm of nothingness.

Benussi endured a recurring thought. He played the game Twister by himself. Right foot on *Destroy Your Marriage*. Left hand on *Get Close to Mobsters*. Right hand on *Make A Stupid Fucking Decision and It Will Cost You Your Life*. His left foot still awaited instructions, but none of the spots left on the board appealed to him. Could he scrap the board and walk out of the room? *If only*.

Ruby, who'd just whispered into the phone with cautious glances toward him every other word, stacked a few menus at the other end of the bar.

"So, who was that on the phone?" Benussi shook his empty coffee mug.

"A customer." She pulled the pot from the warmer and walked toward him, the soles of her shoes popping on the rubber floor mat running the length of the backbar. "Who else?"

"People call this early for apple pies?" Benussi toyed with the notion of revealing the gold badge. Intimidate and procure the info at any cost. Reveal nothing of your personal life. Preserve your identity. Double Life be damned. *Get me the fuck out!*

"It's what we're famous for." She stepped back and propped her elbows on the counter behind her. "You planning on eating?"

"Not really in the mood for pie." *Kinda like I'm not in*

the mood to babysit a fifties-themed diner. He poured sugar into the coffee and sipped. "Be nice if you had a little brandy in the back."

"Can't help you there." A pot clanked in the kitchen and then something spilled. The noise startled her, and she pushed through the swivel doors to investigate.

He scanned the diner through the mirror's reflection. Empty seats, vacant booths. "What the hell am I doing here?" He realized the words came out when his lips moved in the mirror, but he couldn't remember telling his brain to signal his voice box. Lost in thought, he sipped the coffee.

Benny's behavior. Protecting this diner. Trying to find Timothy.

In the last two years he woke up as Sonny Denardo. He had a purpose. Now, something crept into his psyche. An itch of regret tickled his mind without stopping. *They're testing my loyalty. Other than the cell phone debacle, what true reason do they have?*

The bureau did an excellent job with preparation and contingency plans for this exact situation. Complex background stories were created for undercover operatives. New printed identification. Personal past records deleted.

Still, leaks had a way of spilling the truth. Money could split those leaks into puddles, provided the right person listened. *Purelli swung the mallet and wedged this fucker into a geyser.*

Ruby backed through the swivel doors carrying a bucket of silverware.

"What do we have here?"

"Just some silverware to roll. Feel like helping?" She pulled a sleeve of napkins from beneath the bar and plopped it to the countertop.

"Sure." Benussi slid the coffee to his left and dug into the bucket. "Any tricks or tips?"

"Not really." She offered a thin smile then placed a fork on top of a knife. "Do this."

He mimicked her procedure, sliding the utensils together.

She put the pair of utensils diagonal across a square napkin and rolled the cocoon. "That's it. Riveting stuff."

Benussi tucked the silverware into the cheap cloth. "Like this?"

"You got it." She plopped a stack of napkins next to the pile of utensils in front of him. "Only five hundred or so to go."

He laughed. A real laugh. *Not some forced cackle from one of Benny's wise cracks.* "So, you really haven't seen him, huh?"

"You can keep asking, but the answer is the same." She completed a new roll and placed it next to the first one.

"Strange." Benussi wrapped his second set of utensils. "He always talked about you, Ruby."

She stopped mid-roll and looked up. "You know Tim?"

"Of course." *Here we go. Money and sex. One always gets 'em talking.* "I drove him around a while."

"He mentioned me?"

"Yeah." Benussi reached back in his brain. "You and his little girl. Ah, what's her—"

"Annabelle." Ruby's voice shook and the silverware in her hand vibrated on the countertop.

"Right. He always called her Bella. Cute little girl, at least from the pictures I saw." Benussi glanced to the mirror. The black night began its transformation to ashy dawn. "Lucky girl to have such loving parents."

She wiped at her cheek with the apron around her waist but said nothing.

"Did I say something wrong?"

"No." She finished another roll. "I know what you're doing."

"What's that? Just having a conversation."

"No." She scooped up the silverware in front of him and dropped them into the bucket. "Like I said, I haven't seen him." She slid the container down the bar and continued her task.

Shit.

He extracted a cigarette from the wrinkled soft pack on the counter and marched through the door, the chime of the bell an annoying gnat.

He lit the cigarette. The smoke burned orange and Benussi inhaled a thick drag. These people in the diner had answers. *No doubt.*

Vietta was somewhere in the area, but a public search would cause outright suspicion. Benny's orders were to guard the diner, and if Firecracker was ever to bear fruit, directives needed to be obeyed. The cigarette melted to ash in his hand. Its remnants crumbled and caught flight in a stiff breeze. Nothing remained but the filter. Just like Benussi. *Nothing.*

A white sedan hugging the curb approached from the east and parked in front of him. The passenger side window dropped down in its pocket. A man with a button cap nodded, a toothpick laying askew between his lips.

"Pardon me." He removed the pick and pointed toward the diner's door.

Benussi peered into the car, grasping the Browning BDM secured in its holster. A strange sedan with a friendly passenger at dusk outside the diner he was meant to protect warranted caution. "Can I help you fellas?"

"Is the diner open? Looking for breakfast." The driver now leaned over the console; a gold tooth nestled between yellowing teeth glinted in the dusk.

"That's what the sign says." Benussi nodded to the glowing neon flashing in the window. The driver hunched forward and traced the windows with a glare. The steel of Benussi's gun tingled beneath his fingertips.

A broad track of light appeared from the alleyway that split Ms. May's and an abandoned building. It grew whiter and danced across the street behind an identical sedan.

"Your friends are here, huh?" Benussi's internal radar woke, and the Browning jumped from its holster, but a barrel protruding from the passenger's window unleashed its destruction. The weapon's explosion screamed in the still morning, blasting flares of hatred and revenge. Benussi's hip absorbed the shot. It jerked him into a grotesque pirouette and then drove him to the bottom step of the front stoop. The Browning rose in a pathetic arc and fired. Three shots clanked against the sedan's body. A scream followed and gunfire exploded. Benussi heard the shriek come from the car.

Got one, he thought. *I got one of those sons-a-bitches.*

Then both sedans unloaded their passengers, and Benussi wasn't sure if the painful utterance had escaped from his own throat or not. *Couldn't be me. No pain at all. It wasn't me.*

But why, then, was he unable to get up?

Muzzle flashes lit up the gray morning.

His body contorted again, and a new wound gaped, unleashing a fountain of dark blood and raw flesh. Sheer adrenaline lifted his body, and he consciously watched himself run away, like a ghost hovering over the living.

The Browning woke in his hand. Nine shots, all high and off target. Glass rained amid the clouds of gun smoke.

A stinging pain ripped through his stomach, and a large chunk of his leg, a limb that powered the freestyle stroke in swimming competitions and aided his football team's ground game on Friday nights, vanished like invisible ink.

The Browning clicked harmlessly. The screeching of feet stepping on cracked glass shards filled Benussi's ears. The echoes neared, and the Browning took aim at the shadows.

Click. Click. Click. Click.

Ahead, gunfire popped, bullets shouted, and glass shattered. Four men stood shoulder to shoulder with rifles pointed at Ms. May's. Their shaded faces hidden in thin smog from gases expelled from the breech of the rifles. The building's windows and awnings popped open and convulsed like a patient shocked back to life by defibrillators. Pinging sounds darted from steel and then through the diner. Brick slices and shards of glass jumped in the air—a morose tango of explosions.

Benussi pressed the trigger of the Browning.

Click. Click. Click. Click.

"Hold."

He heard the distant voice. It seemed to levitate above the empty street. The shadows blackened and grew. In this moment, he remembered Benny's orders.

Failure. Shame swept through his body. *Boy oh boy, Purelli is going to be pissed.*

Sweat, or perhaps tears, dripped from his eyelids.

The stomach wound oozed, and Benussi's frozen hand clutched the gaped hole in a panicked frenzy. With dwindling energy and adrenaline, he dragged the weight of his limp body up the cracked sidewalk. One leg dragged across the cement lifelessly, while a bleeding hand dug into the stone, fighting for an inch.

"Finish him off." A new voice. Authoritative. Malicious.

Footsteps neared and Benussi pointed the Browning in the direction of screeching stone beneath his assailant's feet. As if wishing it was loaded could produce bullets, Benussi pulled the trigger.

Click. Click.

Vision worsened now. Hearing turned astute and calm. Wetness all over.

Blood.

"I think it's empty, my friend."

The Browning, a gun fired at a range in the safety of bulletproof booths and protective headgear, clanked to the stone. A victim of the ambush much like its owner, the hand fell flat and unresponsive.

Benussi stared through a salty blur of red and tried to wipe the sticky sludge away.

Do it, the brain said. *Fuck you*, the hand replied.

The arm lay limp, tired of the ordeal and unable to cooperate any longer. His shoulder, a melted pool of bone fragments and charred muscle, painted the concrete red and black.

"You have yourselves to blame." The shadow became a man kneeling close to Benussi's stomach.

"You just killed a cop." The words evaporated and trapped themselves in his throat.

Speak, the brain said. *Fuck you,* the mouth replied.

A lucid internal movie began.

He lay on a musty couch discussing *feelings* with some overpaid twerp with *Dr.* in front of his name. The man jotted notes on a clipboard as Benussi explained the turmoil squeezing his soul with the power of vice grips.

He tried to chuckle then. A vociferous anthology of cackles.

Laugh, the brain said. *Fuck you,* the lips replied.

"You still with us, buddy?" The driver of the sedan placed the rifle's barrel to Benussi's forehead—its metal a cold and demonic reminder. Benussi shivered. The barrel was real. This gritted sidewalk beneath was real. The blood was real. Death would be real, too. Then his brother's words echoed.

If you're going to die, do it with dignity.

Would this death matter? Did this mean anything?

Think, the brain said. *Fuck you,* the brain replied.

Benussi gurgled in protest and closed his eyes, a difficult feat considering the liquid infusion.

Definitely tears now.

CHAPTER SIXTY-ONE

"Does Richie know?" Salvador Purelli stood at the small marble bar wedged in the corner of his office, a grimace visible in the window's reflection.

"Not sure." Benny muscled his weight from the couch, his eyes on the back of Purelli's head. "He's been at the farm since Friday with Joe training."

It was nearing eight in the morning, and the bustling of The Tango's Saturday Brunch kitchen prep buzzed beneath their feet.

Purelli scratched at the stubble of a two-day beard. Subtle dark rings surfaced beneath the bottom lids of his eyes. He spoke to his reflection in the window, an oddity to Benny. When the boss spoke, his eyes held your attention and needled through you. *Something has him mixed up, for sure.*

"How long until the news broadcasts?"

"The noon cycle on every station is my guess, but the radio is talking now." Benny flipped the volume dial of the stereo sandwiched between two cd racks. A commercial for car insurance began its pitch.

"What did your friend have to say?" Purelli turned from his reflection and removed the gold-rimmed glasses. He pinched the bridge of his nose.

"A nine-one-one was called in about five-fifty. Shots fired near Center St. By six, all the pigs were sounding off and ambulance drivers were called."

"Casualties?"

"Not sure. Maybe Sonny got clipped. That'd make things easier for us. It sounds like the Irish got away. My girl said an all-out manhunt was called for two four-door white sedans."

"What about the hooker? She tipped you off, right?" Purelli ambled toward him, the eyes still unsheathed, fierce. "A man for a man, you said."

"She was right about the location." Benny felt his feet shuffle backward a pinch. "I don't think the guy she was sucking knew about the firepower they were bringing. Candi made it sound like a quick hit. But my contact in the PD says it was a slaughter."

"If they got Sonny, I will send them a bottle of champagne. One less rat in the cellar." Purelli grasped Benny's shoulders with both hands, his black eyes aimed and true.

"We're going to know by twelve." The boss's delicate touch turned his stomach like a sharp drop on a speeding rollercoaster. "Should I get the kid?"

"They can drive down later. The longer they are in the dark, the better. We need to gather all the facts."

"Well, the real reason I came over this morning was to talk about something else. All this shit happened, and we've been dealing with it, but we need to discuss a—"

"What else?" Purelli's hands hopped from Benny's shoulder like a child testing the burner of a lit stove.

"A cop stopped Richie."

"When? Why am I hearing of this now?" Purelli replaced the glasses on his face. His jaw tensed and the next words escaped between tight lips and a scowl. "What kind of questions?"

"You were off the grid yesterday. Couldn't get a hold of you." Benny shrugged and scanned the room, as if prying ears were opening at that moment. "They're asking about the boxer."

"Is he a suspect?"

"No. Well, not yet. He's supposed to call by Monday to set a meet." Benny slithered by Purelli, shedding the icky feeling. He glanced to the window.

"At the precinct?"

"Um, I don't think so. Why?"

"If they meet in a station, they will have the advantage. They can rattle him." Purelli pulled a cigarette from the silver case in his coat and lit one. "But a conversation at an off-site location could be them fishing or trying to turn him. Find out which it is."

"I'll talk him through it." Benny watched his reflection say the words.

Through the window, the light grays of morning trembled on the horizon. The sun bathed the buildings. An auto shop down the street advertised an oil-change special. Across the road, Fanny Aguirano set potted plants outside of her boutique. Another day in Ridgemont Cove, where mongrels fed on each other and wise guys stalked in the shadows.

"We need to be careful, Benjamin." Purelli's reflection appeared at Benny's right shoulder, and the scent of tobacco crept into Benny's nose. "Get up to the farm now."

Benny huffed and swiveled from the window. "Boss,

Richie is gonna lose his shit if Ms. May is one of those dead bodies."

"It would be tragic." Purelli dragged and flicked the tip of the smoke in a crystal ashtray sitting on a side table of the couch. "At this point, I am more concerned about the police. If the kid is a canary, we may have a serious issue."

"He won't talk. I'll coach him. *Lo Allenaro*."

"We do not know the extent of Sonny's surveillance. He spent a lot of time with you, Benjamin." Purelli backed toward his desk, the eyes black darts and steadfast.

"Let's hope he's in the morgue. Then we get an attorney to rip their case to shreds. The kid, though, is one of us. I'd stake my life on it."

"I trust your judgement. First things first. Get Richie and find out exactly what happened at the diner."

Purelli reached for the phone and pointed to the door.

CHAPTER SIXTY-TWO

Sweat poured from the curls of Richie's dampened hair. Cold whips of chilled air cut between the slats of the barn door, morphing the sweat into half-frozen drips. "More sparring?"

Joe shrugged. "Not a lot to do in this place." He extended his arms parallel to his shoulders. "I still don't understand why the hell I had to leave."

"Because it's not safe."

"Why the hell ain't it safe for me to be in my own gym?"

"It just needs to be this way." Richie's chin drooped. *How do I get this guy to understand?* "Benny thought it would be best for now."

"I'm done playing these games." The old man scoffed and shoved his hands into the coat's pockets. "I don't want no part of it anymore."

"There's no getting out."

"Sure, there is." Joe pointed to the door. "Out there is a pickup truck with a full tank. We can be in Wisconsin in a day or so."

"I can't leave." The detective from the other night

appeared in his mind. His image far more menacing than the ghosts.

Joe's face scrunched in contempt and he threw his hands up. "Keep me in the dark all you want. But I'm telling you right now, my loyalty to you only goes so far, kid."

"Don't say that, man."

"I just did." Joe limped forward and gripped Richie's shoulders. "I warned you about this. Now, I may be an old man, and I may be out of touch." Joe pointed to his head with his thin finger, it shook in a slight circle. "But I've still got a few marbles rolling around up here and I know if we're not allowed to train in the Cove, it's because we're in danger."

The vault opened. *At least one of you has some sense,* O'Leary snorted. He sat on a stool in an empty ring. No wounds to his head, his eyes full of color and alive. *Get out while you still can.*

"You hearing me?" Joe slapped at Richie's face.

Richie shook the thought. "Yeah. I understand what you're saying, but arguing right now isn't going to fix anything. We're here, so let's train."

Joe nodded, but Richie could tell his acceptance of this arrangement neared the snapping point. "On the mat, then."

Richie placed the mat in the spot where Harold died, covering the faint outline of blood still noticeable if your eyes searched for it.

Joe lifted the intensity without warning. His subtle smile, a prominent feature most days, replaced with a scornful frown—an annoyed expression one gets when batting away a nagging mosquito in a steamy summer evening.

During training, Harold's ghost slipped from the vault

and attacked. The ground of the barn split in two and misty fog erupted in large swooshes to drag him below. *Here we are. Just the two of us,* Harold said.

The apparition's arms formed from the fog and strangled him.

Joe caught him off guard with a light punch and Richie returned to reality, back in the barn, the ground solid, and the stain still below the mat.

Ninety minutes of sparring, coupled with another forty-five of cardio, sucked every drop of sweat from him.

"Get some water and meet me in the back. I need help hanging the bag." Joe limped away.

Richie trudged past the storage room. He didn't dare enter there and have to face Roger Cranswell.

The smug prick had gotten more boisterous in the last few days. A mocking or admonishing tone the norm now.

In the back corner of the barn, nestled behind the makeshift tomb, Joe screwed a colossal steel eyehook into the overhead beam.

"Why we back here?"

"Only place in here I can get room on the floor and a solid cross beam to hook into." Joe stood on an off-kilter step stool, its legs struggling to gain traction in the soft dirt.

Richie grabbed the bag leaning against the wall and extended its chain length as far as it could stretch. Together they lifted the bag and hooked it.

"What's the Goddamn point anyway?" Joe used Richie's shoulder to brace the drop from the stool.

"What do you mean?"

"I mean, why are we training?" Joe punched the bag. It swayed, and the chain creaked. "You don't even have a fight lined up."

"What are you talking about?" Richie's eyes darted to the open space in the room."

"I saw the paper. It's in the truck. You never said a word when you were reading it. A boxer dies and Benny's moving us to this shithole. There's more to the story here."

"They said things needed to cool down."

"Why? What the hell heated up in the first place? Did they do it?"

"No." Richie recoiled, hoping the grimace didn't reveal the guilt. *I did.*

"I know you think this is still about boxing, but it's not."

"Then what's it about?" Richie swatted at the bag, his punch altering its slight circular pattern.

"It's about them now. I doubt you ever fight again, and I really doubt they have much need for me anymore."

"You're paranoid, Joe. It's all going to work out. I'm not sure why they moved us, but it's temporary." Deceit came more natural in recent days, but fibs to Joe took extra effort.

Joe's piercing gaze said *don't lie to me, kid,* but his lips stayed tight. Quiet, then. Neither spoke.

A creaking door ended the standoff.

"Kid?" Benny's voice boomed.

"I'm not paranoid," Joe whispered. "Let's not forget, I've seen this movie before."

Scuffing footsteps neared them.

"Anyone home?" Benny rounded the corner and swept his black stringy hair back into place. "Need a word."

Joe shook his head and tapped the punching bag.

"I'll be back in a minute," Richie said, patting Joe's shoulder.

Outside, the black Cadillac idled. Benny plopped into the driver seat and Richie slithered into the front.

"You here about the cop?" The frigid AC clung to Richie's sweat, lifting a light steam from his skin.

"Yeah. We need to get you prepped."

"I'm supposed to call by Monday. We still have tomorrow." Richie glanced at the digital clock. It displayed 9:07 in blinking red dots.

"Call and set it up for today. Let's get ahead of this thing. But first, tell me what was said. Verbatim."

He obeyed and described the interaction with Detective Reese Campini.

Benny gripped the steering wheel but said nothing. When Richie fell silent, the car shifted into reverse. "I'm not sure what this guy is after. We need to be smart about this."

"All right." Richie fastened his seat belt then adjusted the heat vent. "You think I'll be okay?"

"I'll walk you through it, but you gotta make the call." Benny turned sharply and Richie lodged into the arm rest of his door. "If he says to meet at the station, you tell him no."

"Why?"

"Because I said so, okay? Are you not listening? We tread lightly and stack the chips in our corner."

"Okay." Richie adjusted himself in the seat. Slick sweat rolled from his shoulders to his arms, cooling the skin while the heater shot stagnant warmth toward his face.

The barn shrank in the distance as the Cadillac rolled down the dirt driveway.

"If he wants to meet in a neutral place, fine. Keep your answers short and vague. If the prick presses, say you're done and bolt."

"Understood." Richie said what Benny wanted to hear, but it didn't make much sense to him. *What does it matter where we meet? Lie through my teeth and then game-plan. Simple enough.* "Should I think about getting a lawyer?"

Benny winced, his eyes scrunching. The car angled toward a thin road running through the woods. In a half-mile, it turned to asphalt and merged toward the interstate. "Lawyer is last resort. We pay primo bucks for the best. I'm talking two-thousand an hour. At this point, they got nothing. Walk in. Shut up. Walk out. Capisce?"

"Yeah. What about Joe?"

"What about him? Less he knows, the better."

"He's my trainer. One of my only friends. Shouldn't he be in the loop?"

"The loop?" Benny laughed, and for the first time since this little interaction, Richie felt Benny's words and actions were genuine. "This is a straight line. I tell you what's what, you fall in."

The car turned onto the skinny exit road a minute later. Large oak trees stretched over the road and beyond. Beneath the awning of foliage, the temperature cooled. Specks of sunlight blotted Richie's sweat-soaked shirt.

"Something else." Benny offered a sympathetic frown. "Ms. May's got hit this morning."

"Hit?" Richie shot forward in the seat. His seatbelt blocked the force and threw him back. "What are you talking about?"

"It got shot up, kid. Goddamn Irish."

"Is Ms. May okay?" He unclicked the seatbelt and turned in the seat, draping his arm over the center console.

"We don't know yet. It's why I came to get you. Also, seeing this asshole cop now is more important than ever. We gotta keep up appearances, ya know?"

"Jesus Christ. Benny, I was just there this morning." Richie spoke into his lap. Tears began to form and dripped helplessly when Richie squeezed his eyes shut. "You sure about this?"

"Relax. Nothing to get upset over. We don't have all the facts. Anyway, my contact in the PD called me. She's gonna give me intel as soon as it comes to light. I'll find out more about this Campini prick, too."

Joe's words sounded off in Richie's head. Stark and unflinching. *This ain't about boxing anymore.*

The dirt road gave way to asphalt, and it forked into a tunnel of trees. The world darkened, and Richie drew the window down, now craving fresh air.

The vault opened and his ghosts stood in its doorway. Grinning skeletons. The breakfast protein shake from earlier slugged up his throat.

"Pull over a minute. I'm gonna be sick."

Benny unleashed a backhand. It landed with a resounding thwap. Stunned, Richie blinked the stars away. "Get your shit together. You're part of this. Conduct yourself accordingly. I vouched for you, kid. Don't crack up on me now."

The vomit receded. He felt a welt below the left eye surface beneath his skin, but Richie felt no pain. "You're right."

"I need your word, Richie." Benny's head swiveled slowly. His pupils climbed to the corner of his eye sockets. "Tell me you can handle this."

"I can handle this."

"Good." Benny shifted his gaze to the windshield.

Richie ran through possible victims of the diner. Ms. May. Ruby. And . . . "Where's Sonny? Is he okay?"

"Not sure. He's not answering the phone, but that could mean a lot of things. Either way, we worry about shit we can handle. Step one is meet the pigs. Then we'll figure out the next move."

The canopy of trees thinned and then broke. The sign for the interstate appeared as a small colorful block on the right. Richie's foot smacked against the floorboard and surging guilt coursed through his veins. Cranswell's head poked out from the vault door.

You're going to blow it. Too many mistakes. It's the needle for you.

Richie shook his head and squeezed the lids of his eyes together hard. O'Leary appeared next.

What did you expect? You could kill me and walk away scot-free? This isn't the movies, coward. You aren't Pacino. Ha.

Harold took center stage and the two others receded into the black depth. A spotlight hovered over him. Its rays reflected off the steel knife lodged in his throat.

If you'd just let it be. None of this needed to happen. He pulled the blade with a grunt. It squished like a watermelon being sliced. Harold licked the serrated edge. *I'm trapped in here. A hell you've created.*

"Kid!"

Richie snapped from the horror. "Huh?"

"I've been talking to you the last three minutes. Do you know where Lorenzo put the gun?"

"We stripped and buried it."

"Where?"

"The Rez, behind the barn."

"Okay. Good thinking. If the cops can't find the weapon, we'll be in good shape. All you have to do is put on a show for Campini, puff your chest out, and say as little as possible. You ready?"

"Yeah."

The interstate sign grew, the type clean and legible. Highway traffic morphed from blurs of color to defined vehicles.

"All right." Benny merged toward the ramp. "Make the call."

CHAPTER SIXTY-THREE

The stench of burnt gunpowder clung in Reese Campini's nose.

An outer perimeter of yellow tape stretched in a swooping semi-circle, canvassing the vacant building and flower shop to Ms. May's right and left, respectively.

The arc covered a fifty-foot section of the sidewalk and most of the oncoming traffic lane. Curious spectators eyed the police activity.

Four parked news vans lined the curb opposite the street. Representatives from RC 4, Channel 5, Greater Belleview News, and WXL 34 huddled in the media staging area. Large cameras hoisted on tripods scanned the carnage.

Going to have to address those vultures soon.

Closer to the diner, inside of the red tape outline, Campini scribbled in a notebook. He spoke to Patrolmen Hector Cortez, the first officer on the scene.

"Arrived at five-fifty-five." Cortez nodded to the corpse on the sidewalk, now covered in a white sheet. "Approached the male victim, administered a vitals check, ascertained he wasn't breathing."

"We can speak casually." Campini shuddered at newbies' incessant tendency to structure their sentences formally with words they never attempted in their social lives. "Just shoot me straight."

"Okay." Cortez's cheeks reddened, and he sighed. "After finding him," the patrolmen pointed to the corpse on the sidewalk, "I went into the diner with my gun drawn. The place was blown to hell, but I didn't see any victims."

"Good. Go on," Campini prodded, jotting a few times in the notebook.

"After securing the inside and radioing for back up, I went behind the bar. There I found the second victim. Checked her pulse, but she was dead."

"Other than the necks of these victims, did you touch anything else?" Campini looked up from the pad. "Anything at all?"

"No, sir." Cortez crossed his arms and rubbed at his triceps. "Moved to the kitchen area, but it was empty. The back door wide open." He pulled out his own notepad and flipped the front page over the cardboard backing. "Gertrude May and Freddie Alonso were seated near the dumpster."

"Thanks, officer." Campini eyed the growing number of spectators huddled near the florist shop. "Do me a favor and get those people out of here."

Cortez nodded and wandered toward the nosy citizens.

Crime scene technicians studied tire tracks with elongated, low beam flashlights. A car had backed over the sidewalk, run over the victim, and then gunned down the road. The techs photographed the marks and worked around the corpse.

Reese flipped to a blank page in the notebook and started a scene sketch.

Case: 10-927-83
Detective: Reese F. Campini
Assisted by: Deborah Shaw
Date: Saturday, November 26th
Crime: Homicide
Location: 1419 Center Street
Time: 09:51

Exterior Drawing

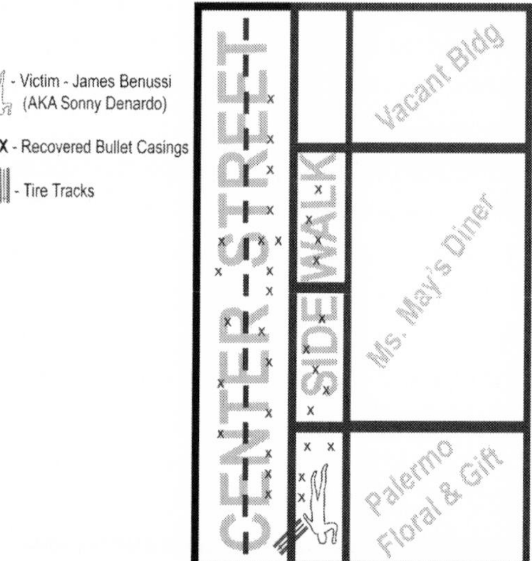

He labeled the diagram of the outside scene, and once it was finished, sauntered toward the dead man.

Jenny Kasper, a medical examiner nearing retirement, followed Campini. "It's kind of gruesome. Just letting you know."

"I'm sure it is." Campini knelt, and she pulled the white sheet from the body.

A shot had torn the top of his head off. Parts of his skull and brains lay a few feet from the body like stringy pink

Play-dough swimming in spaghetti sauce.

The bottom jawline of the dead man was preserved, and Campini wiped perspiration from his forehead.

Benussi.

A realization punched Campini in the mouth. The majority of the people who heard about this death would shrug it off as another mob killing. "Silent" Sonny maimed in front of a diner, another stitch in the hem of mafia lore.

Campini knew different but couldn't say anything yet. Purelli's incarceration was no closer to fruition than it had been two years ago when Operation Firecracker began. For now, the public needed to believe this was another murder in the dregs of Ridgemont Cove.

Benussi's body lay tangled twenty feet from Ms. May's Diner. The final resting position implied an attempted crawl from the gunfire. The Browning, Benussi's "drop" gun, lay lifeless a foot from his outstretched arm. Blood streaked the handle. The shattered windows of the diner had vomited jagged shards, blanketing the stoop and sidewalk in translucent glass pieces that emitted rainbow color variations when the sun's rays made direct contact.

"Identification?" Campini stood and watched Kasper stretch the sheet over Benussi's head.

"Wallets were bagged." She nodded to the diner's door. "Detective Shaw took them."

"Okay. Give me a brief rundown."

"Seventy-two casings identified, photographed, marked and bagged." Kasper held a clipboard in her gloved hands. She scanned the cursive lines of the preliminary report provided by Shaw. "Most of the shells were not from the Browning. A surveillance camera looking over the diner's street entrance is inoperable. Dead end there."

"Perfect." Campini started toward the diner, grimacing as another news van pulled into the line of the others.

Violent Crimes Forensic Unit congregated inside collecting evidence and snapping shots of the bloodshed.

"So far, nothing conclusive." The voice of a technician floated through the opening of the window.

Inside, Deborah Shaw, a lead homicide detective with forty solved homicide cases to her credit, spoke with the diner's owner, Gertrude May.

The woman sobbed, her hands flailing as she narrated the events of the morning. Shaw extended a sympathetic hand and cradled the woman, but she bounced from raging anger to loud, hawking sobs of grief.

Paramedics led Ms. May to the ambulance humming on the curb. Its lights blinked red and blue, the siren mute. Shaw descended the steps, speaking into a handheld recorder.

"Morning, detective." Campini offered a half-ass salute, unsure why he did so. "Gotta sketch?"

"Yeah." Shaw held a notebook up. "I'll get it digitized and sent over to you."

"This one too." Campini ripped the drawing he created from the spiral notepad and handed it to her.

"A terrible morning, huh?" Shaw took the sketch and folded it then slid it into her notepad. "This city won't give us a break."

"I've seen worse," he replied with a fake smile, sure that this morning ranked among the worst.

"Two deceased," Shaw said in her matter-of-fact-tone. "One male and one female. Gertrude May, the woman talking to the medics, is the owner. She can't provide much information. Heard a few pops, then the window went down and the diner was shredded."

"Any rhyme or reason for her diner being shot up?" Campini peered down the street. The small crowd of spectators gathered to the east now. Cortez shooed them away like flies.

"She needs to calm down first. I couldn't get much from her. She's hysterical." Shaw dropped the notebook in her jacket pocket. Reese gave her the once-over.

Tall and thin, nearing fifty, with a beige complexion and wrinkle free face. A face once very pretty before the badge, he imagined. Little specks of gray had begun their inevitable charge into her blonde hair.

She pointed at Benussi's corpse. "We know he's connected. Ms. May said as much, at least. Checked the wallet. Sonny Denardo. Mean anything to you?"

"I know the name." Campini considered how much to divulge. As a ranking officer in the OCD, Shaw would assume he knew about the mobster. Aware of the connection, he reveled in what those outside of the operation thought of "Silent" Sonny. The man was a renegade, but Goddamn, he put in the work. "What did she say?"

"He's been around before and drives a big mafia type around. My first thought is Bianchi. Think that's right?"

Campini nodded. "He's part of Purelli's crew. They call him 'Silent' Sonny." He cringed at the words. In their last meeting Benussi asked for reassignment. Family issues crippled his psyche. Too much violence and too little quality time. It just wasn't feasible then. Now, Reese prayed Benussi went off the grid for a few hours.

"Another one bites the dust. First the boxer and now this guy? Kinda coincidental, huh?"

"How do you mean?"

"O'Leary fought for the Irish Syndicate—a pawn for Beckett. Shot down in broad daylight. Two days later, an attack on this diner. Solano soldier killed. Sounds like a turf war to me."

Benussi considered Shaw's logic and ran different scenarios internally.

On the one hand, keeping Shaw in the dark about the operative Benussi would keep the investigation as tight as possible. Cops tended to talk, and with Operation Firecracker on life support already, involving outside parties carried risk. One reason Purelli had avoided capture for so long was because of the Solanos' grip on the city. Greasy tentacles had a way of reaching into public offices throughout Ridgemont Cove. Could Campini jeopardize the case by letting information slip to more ears?

At the same time, as the lead detective on the murder, Shaw deserved to be privy to all the information available. Effective cops are not created. They're born. Shaw had proven this with a stack of closed files and intuitive grit. She could be an asset moving forward in the case, for however long it may be. With resources being cut and surveillance teams' hours minimal, a new pair of eyes could be beneficial, if not necessary.

These alternative situations bounced from the corners of his mind until he said. "It's a stretch, but could be connected."

"Somebody wanted him dead. Tapped in the stomach, leg, shoulder and—"

"The head." The half-headed corpse of his operative singed in his brain forever.

"Point blank. Personal." Shaw nodded to Benussi's corpse. The white sheet vibrated from his body as the frigid wind intensified.

"What about the girl?"

"Ruby Miller. Employee. Shot twice. One in the hand

and one in the chest. Ms. May, who'd been in back when the shooting started, said Ms. Miller was behind the bar of the diner prepping the counter. Luckily, the place was empty, or this coulda been very ugly."

"Anything else?"

"The pattern of the other shots is a side-to-side sweep. Scene technicians say a lot of the bullets were fired high. In the ceiling, mostly. Not sure they intended on killing anyone else. We need to wait for an autopsy, but it wouldn't surprise me if Ms. Miller died from ricochets. He was the target," Shaw said with a nod to Benussi's corpse, "the rest was for show. A message."

"Wonder what the message was."

Campini mentally flipped through the most recent case notes Benussi had provided. Benny Bianchi's suspicions. The search for Vietta. *This could be an internal hit, but why shoot up the diner and risk killing the waitress?* It didn't fit.

Purelli proved too slick and intelligent to blast a block in half with rifle shells. Shaw's theory of the Irish ploy now seemed a far more believable scenario.

The ambulance doors closed with a loud smack. Ms. May stood on the curb. With her arms crossed, she looked at the remnants of the diner. Tears poured down her cheeks amid stifled sobs and whispered profanities.

"We need to bring her in." Shaw pointed to the woman.

"Can't make them go. You can only hope they change their mind. Anyway, I'm supposed to be meeting with someone today or tomorrow. It could clear some things up about this."

"I'm almost finished. I'll get you a typed report. Tomorrow okay? Another body's been called in. Shitty day."

"Shitty month." The words of Chief Taggert haunted him.

An investigation headed nowhere and now a dead operative. Resources slashed in half. Perhaps he should take advantage of another cop on the case? Shaw handled cases efficiently, and without paperwork snags that got caught up in court. "Before you go, we need to talk."

"About?"

"Operation Firecracker. Time to bring you into the fold."

Campini's phone buzzed in the jacket of his pocket.

CHAPTER SIXTY-FOUR

The early afternoon sun glimmered among storm clouds looming above. Each time it peeked through an empty sky, heat graced Timothy Vietta's back.

Pulling weeds outside the decaying gym for half an hour burned as many calories as jumping rope. That's what Marty said, anyway.

Lush stalks of stringy weeds and overgrowth lined the small brick walk and flower beds. All the plants drooped like upside down question marks, afraid to brave the cold.

Marty paced back and forth with a garbage bag. He'd bend down and pick up some leaf clippings here and there, but to the chagrin of Timothy, the bag was no heavier than when it was popped open.

A red paneled Chevy pickup pulled into the dirt path and parked. A cloud of loose dirt swarmed, dropping its residue on the walkway of the building. Joe stepped out, cane in hand, and limped toward Timothy, who had surrounded himself with piles of plants' corpses.

Marty met Joe halfway down the path and extended a hand. The two old friends greeted each other warmly, a mumbled conversation followed, and then they started toward the front door. Timothy rose and swiped at his black knees.

Back inside the dank of gym, the three men huddled near the sparring ring. Marty grabbed two glasses from his office and poured whiskey and Seven-Up into them. "Take a drink, Timbo. Training is over."

"How about me?" Joe lifted the hood then scratched at his head.

"Really?" Marty stopped mid-sip. "Thought you were on the wagon."

"Not today." Joe blinked a few times, and Timothy saw the glistening of tears forming in his eyes.

"Shit, man. Let's celebrate." Marty rushed back to the office then reappeared with a clean glass. He poured some whiskey and soda. "Bottoms up."

Joe took the glass and sipped.

"What changed?" Marty asked, planting himself on the ringside.

"Think I'm going to retire."

"Heading to Florida to play putt-putt?" Timothy smiled and sipped. It traveled down like molasses, burning all the way. He cleared his throat. "Think I'll stick to beer."

"I should have listened to you, Thunderstorm." Joe swigged again, showing no change in expression. "We're all in too deep now." His gruff, two-pack a day voice echoed.

The static-laden voices of the radio disc jockeys discussing the previous night's football game burped from the small silver radio in Marty's office. *Blaine McAllister threw for three-hundred yards and two touchdown passes.*

"What are you talking about?" Timothy sat next to Marty.

"I think they killed him." Joe finished the whiskey in a gulp.

"Who?" Marty shook his glass. The ice clinked against the fake crystal.

"O'Leary." Joe leaned on his cane for support and fished an article from his back pocket. "The dead Irish boxer. I think it was them." He extended the paper.

"Think it was who?" Timothy's mind reverted to the conversation and not the highlights of last night's game. He reached for the article. "How do you know it's the Irish boxer? The paper didn't give a name."

"I don't need the paper to tell me. I know it, Thunderstorm." Joe's tone dropped a sad volume. Shameful, even. "Purelli and Benny killed him. Maybe even Richie."

Marty stood from the ring, almost sensing Timothy's curiosity, and said, "You look troubled, old friend."

Joe took a swig from the cup. "I've got that feeling. Helpless."

"You mean, fear?" Marty circled, wrapping an arm around the shaken man.

"We've seen it before." Joe shrugged the sympathy hug. "Murder and mayhem."

Timothy sipped from the glass, realized he still hated whiskey, then put it down. "What are you all talking about?"

"Two kids stuck in the shit," Marty said. "Enemies hiding in shadows and fighting dirty. The piss-your-pants marches into Vietnam wilderness. Gunfights in down pouring rain. Hooting and hollering like madmen."

"But the final months of the 1969 campaign scarred us all," Joe admitted. "No use in pretending it didn't." The two veterans stared at the floor. Joe limped to the ringside and grabbed Timothy's glass. "We killed a whole village. Rotting corpses stacked on top of each other. Maggots feasting the villagers' bodies. Kids mummified in ash, half buried in charred huts. Death. Murder."

"It was a long time ago, Joe." Marty clinked his glass against Joe's. "We move forward. The past is back there."

"But it's *here* now."

"What?" Marty slugged Joe's arm. "You're talking crazy."

"People I care about. Close to the end."

"Who?" Timothy joined the pair, completing the huddle of whisky-infused conversation and wobbly stances.

"I don't know for sure, but things are starting to line up." Joe stepped back from the group, the glass of ice shaking. "Richie was supposed to fight O'Leary. The Irish guy gets murdered and we're moving to Belleview all of a sudden? Didn't make sense. But I still wasn't sure. So, I put the paper on the front seat as we drive up yesterday." Joe pointed to the article Timothy still held. "And Richie reads it all the way up. My father always said a guilty conscience speaks volumes. He didn't say a word, and it was strange. Then, the fat bastard picks him up and drives him out and not so much as says a word to me." He sucked in air and exhaled, as if surprised by the sheer bulk of words he'd spewed. "And you know what else, Tim?"

"What?"

"More people are going to die."

The gym fell silent from the statement.

All three men, half-buzzed from the whiskey and half sad from the news, stared in their own separate tunnels of vision unwilling to speak. The radio broadcast cut into Timothy's state of curiosity and disbelief.

Breaking news from Ridgemont Cove. An early . . . shooting off Center St. has claimed the lives of two people.

While details . . . gathered . . . tell you police . . . in some capacity . . . organized crime. An update . . . Stay tuned to 92.7, The Wave . . .

He looked up from his own trance and found Joe's open-mouthed expression.

"My gym is on Center St." The old man's eyes widened. "So is Ms. May's Diner."

CHAPTER SIXTY-FIVE

Richie sat on the curb for twenty minutes before Reese Campini's Impala veered into the parking lot of *Ben's BBQ* at three o'clock. A blonde woman sat upright in the passenger seat. Campini parked in the empty space to the left and rolled the window down.

"Hop in, Mr. Frezza."

Richie glanced ahead to a pair of teenagers climbing into a sports car with shining wheels. *That was me three years ago.* An urge to stand and lay out a sermon to the two surged through him.

Campini tapped the door with his knuckles. "You getting in?"

Richie rose, his leg muscles stretching and popping. The door unlocked, a loud and jagged sound. He slid into the backseat.

"This is Deborah Shaw, by the way. Homicide Division." Campini's eyes tracked Richie through the reflection of the rearview but his hand gestured toward the woman seated next to him.

She wore a light blush, accenting strong cheekbones. A gray pantsuit with a detective badge clipped to the left lapel of the blazer offset her cream-colored skin. A hint of flowers drifted to the backseat when she craned her neck and said, "Good morning, Mr. Frezza."

Richie said nothing and returned Campini's stare through the mirror.

The detective tapped a few buttons on the door arm rest and the window slid up. A succession of locks clicking sent a tremor of anxiety through Richie.

"Glad you came to your senses." Campini offered a sly grin. He appeared a bit haggard, a beard growing. A coat lay crumpled in the back seat and the pearl white necktie he wore hung askew and loose. "Right decision."

"Didn't have much of choice."

"We all have choices. You made the right one. You hungry? This place sells a badass pulled pork sandwich."

"No." Richie's hands clasped and sweat rose from the knuckles. "Let's just get this over with."

"Down to business. Excellent, Mr. Frezza." Campini opened the center console and pulled out a recorder. A true relic, its square body lined by a red REC dial and other gray buttons at the bottom. The top half was a speaker, and in the middle, a cassette tape labeled RF NOV 26 hid behind a plastic cover.

"Yo, what's with the recorder?" Richie eyed it like a stain on a brand-new shirt.

"We'll get to it. First, I need to know if you're willing to play ball."

"Play ball? What are you talking about, man?"

Shaw tugged file folders from the suitcase nestled between the console and seat. She handed it to Campini and shot a glance into the rear-view.

He opened it and spilled its contents, a stack of papers and photos bound in a rubber band.

"Telephone logs." Shaw tapped the documents. Dates and times penned next to highlighted conversation transcriptions. She then unwound the rubber band from the photos and laid one on the console. Her manicured index finger jabbed it. In this image, Sonny sported short brown hair, a thin mustache, and wore eyeglasses a bit small for his thick face. "Do you know this man?"

"Nope, never seen him." *Where is this going? How'd they get that pic?*

"Me either. Detective Campini told me about him today." Shaw unhooked her seatbelt and turned, bracing against the dashboard of the Impala.

Richie drew back and shoved the photos toward Shaw, an urge to flee beckoning.

Get out of the car. Run until you collapse, and when you do, get up and run some more.

"It's why we're here, Richie." Campini spoke to the windshield, though his eyes now livelier, glistening almost in the rearview. "You still have a chance to save yourself. We need you to play ball."

Richie glanced at the locked doors of the car. The two detectives, smug smiles crossing crooked faces, held the power. He fought the instinct to crack.

They'll have to do better than this.

"Like I said, I don't know the guy. Never met him. I'm in this car for one reason, detective. You threatened me with an arrest. So, I'm here. Let's get on with it."

"You think lying to an officer of the law is a good idea, Mr. Frezza?" Shaw's delicate voice transformed into sandpaper scuffing across wood. Rough and deliberate.

"I'm not lying." The vault crept open.

Not now. Not fucking now.

The doors slammed, a resounding thud rang his ears, and he shuddered

Did they hear it? Are you crazy? Get it together. You told Benny you could handle this, so handle it.

Shaw leafed through the photographs and dropped a color eight-by-eleven on the console. Richie traced over it and glanced at the bitch cop. She smiled wide revealing big teeth shimmering blank like sugar cubes.

Richie sensed she reveled in this, waiting for the sweet view of *Oh Shit* so many display after insistence of innocence vanishes. Slight-of-hand tricks and deception evaporate. Egos and bravado erased.

Not me.

He studied the photo. *It couldn't be. How did they get this shot?*

It depicted he and Sonny outside of The Tango, chatting like a few buddies on vacation. He recalled the night—an hour after the Martinez fight. He and Sonny waited on Benny.

The once solemn and reticent driver blabbed like a schoolgirl in junior high. "Got brought up with the wrong crowd. First it was tagging buildings, next thing I know, I'm running with Peter and Paul Fiorgi."

"Who?" Richie leaned against the wall and watched a pair of heavy bosomed brunettes seated at one of the patio tables giggle and throw flirtatious glances toward him.

"Couple of young toughs back in the day. Both dead now. Anyway, we always got into some shit. What about you? A few skeletons in your closet?"

"Not really. Been low key most of—"

"Richie?" Shaw tapped the photo, breaking the involuntary nostalgic trance.

"You gonna arrest me?"

"All depends." Campini's thick index finger thumped the recorder. "You gonna play ball?"

"What do you want?"

"Let's get something to eat. I've got a hankering for pulled pork. Deb, you hungry?"

"I could eat." Shaw opened the door and cocked her head. "Besides, I think the kid could use a little sustenance. We've gotta ways to go."

Richie grabbed the handle of the door. "Is now the time to ask for an attorney?"

Campini turned with a mocking frown. "You could. I wouldn't, though. You haven't heard the story."

"I don't want to hear it." Richie gripped the handle and began to push but stopped. The coyness irked him. Contempt dripped from every word of these assholes.

How much did they know?

"I think you do, Mr. Frezza. It's titled 'The Life of James Benussi: Special Investigator'. It's a doozy."

CHAPTER SIXTY-SIX

Timothy's Jeep screeched and hopped a median running perpendicular to Center St. A few onlookers swerved when he over corrected, slid across gravel, and braked in front of the sidewalk still roped in police tape.

In a whir, he jumped from the car. Glass bits crunched beneath the soles of his rubber training shoes, grinding louder as the steps quickened.

A patrolman from inside the diner came running out. "Excuse me, this is a crime scene."

"My girl works here. She's not answering her phone. Is she okay?" He bounced on his toes and looked beyond the cop to the diner.

"I can't divulge any information right now."

"Her name is Ruby. Is she okay?" He felt the vein on his neck pulse, bleeping with each quickened beat of his heart. "Tell me."

"Sir." The cop's hand rose, admonishing. "I cannot discuss anything. It is an ongoing investigation. Please calm down."

"Cut the shit." Timothy knelt beneath the tape but felt

the guy's arm around his neck. "Get off me. Let me through."

"Don't make me arrest you for obstruction."

Timothy swung his hip into the cop and launched the seemingly weightless man over his back. The guy thumped to the sidewalk and Timothy rushed to the open door.

Bullet holes pocked the ceiling of dining area. The mirror behind the bar had fallen in shards, and just the rubber backing pitted with dents clung to the wall. Broken dishes and debris covered the floor and tables.

A gloved woman echoed the same monotonous "crime scene" bullshit. Timothy heard it, but the words converged with the vibrating echoes within his head and produced indecipherable mashing sounds.

Reaching the end of the bar and peeking to the floor, all noises flattened. In an instant, the traffic noise outside ceased. The shuffling feet of crime scene technicians faded. Camera shudders snapped but made no noise. Spastic orders from investigators hit the air and died. All but one sense remained within him: vision. Clear and vivid sight.

An oblong puddle of dark maroon behind the counter lay flat across the rubber flooring. Red, vibrant, and still.

Then, he found his voice. And louder than any noise attempting to interrupt his train of thought, he screamed "Where is Ruby?"

The question repeated. Over and over. With hands rising and tears falling, Timothy yelled the question. His thunderous roars so loud the patrolmen from earlier pulled his weapon and barked orders. Timothy saw the mouth moving but heard nothing.

"Where is she?" Timothy repeated, his eyes drowned in water and a heavy sob escaped his gaped mouth.

"Hands behind your back." The patrolmen moved

closer, gripping the pistol in both hands. "I said hands behind your back!"

"Where is Ruby?" The screams now babbling, teary mutters.

"Put your fucking hands behind your back!"

"Please." His knees hit the rubber. He cradled his stomach, the aching like drumbeats within his body. "Where is she?"

The cop yanked Timothy's hands down to the small of his back and cuffed the wrists hard. A knee into his back forced him face down to the floor. Wrenching pain coursed through the injured hand. The questions continued, but now they came out half audible amid choking sobs.

"Sir, you're contaminating a crime scene. No more bullshit. We clear?"

Timothy relented and rolled over. "Just tell me."

"If I knew the name of the deceased, which I do not, I'd still not tell you. Understand? Do you?"

Timothy shook in the cuffs trapped beneath him now, the steel cutting into his skin and punishing the hobbled hand. "I need to make a call. Uncuff me, man."

"You sit right there."

"Please, it's a detective I met a while ago. I have information for him."

"Bullshit." The cop's teeth clenched. "I've had enough of you."

"Honest." Timothy rolled to his side and reached for his back pocket. "Just check my wallet."

"Oh yeah? What's his name?"

"Reese Campini."

"Huh?" The patrolman reached into Timothy's pocket and flung the wallet open.

“You see it?” He repositioned himself, now seated flat enduring the tug of the steel clasps. “His card?”

“Yes.” The officer poked out Campini’s card and clicked on his shoulder radio. “This is Cortez, badge number RC37932. I’ve gotta situation at the diner on Center Street.”

CHAPTER SIXTY-SEVEN

Campini dipped a fry in barbeque sauce. The bare plastic plate in front of him harbored a few stragglers and small chunks of pork. Hoping to rattle but not alienate the little twerp, he decided to slow the aggression. "Look, we're not interested in you. We know you're a pawn."

"Call me what you want, detective, but I'm not a rat." Richie sipped lemonade and sat back in the chair.

"You're whatever we say you are." Shaw twirled a toothpick in her hand.

Campini wiped at his mouth with a napkin then tossed it onto the plate in front of him. A toddler clumsily walked toward him, hand in hand with his mother. He grinned at the child. *One day you'll be one of us or one of them.*

"You want to cut me a deal, right? I get it. I've seen the movies, dude." The defiant little shit said the tough-guy line but fear painted his face.

"This isn't a movie, Mr. Frezza. The sooner you realize that, the better. Now, let me tell you how this goes down."

"I'm all ears." Richie circled the lemonade with his arms and sipped again.

"I have enough surveillance and testimony from Detective James Benussi to put you in a cell for the next fifty years. But doing that serves no purpose." Campini straightened in his chair and crossed his arms. "See, you're a small fry. You can be replaced tomorrow, and the ship still sails. What interests me, is Salvador Purelli slung on a gurney with potassium chloride running through his remorseless, evil veins."

Richie shifted in the booth. Shaw, seated in front of a half-eaten Mediterranean salad, offered a maternal smile. "We need to work together."

"I'm not a rat."

Campini chugged soda from the plastic cup, still smeared in a combination of hot and mild sauces. A million answers would have been better, given that Benussi's death complicated things. Without eyewitness testimony to corroborate the hours of surveillance collected, no State Attorney would dare go against Purelli and his prospective million-dollar defense team.

Motions to suppress evidence, motions to change the venue, motions to go fuck yourself.

It all played out in a vivid premonition. Supporting the hundreds of hours and thousands of pages of Benussi's undercover work required a living set of eyes with a solid memory and steel balls.

Campini's short leash complicated matters further. Captain Taggert's decree hung in his head like a chandelier covered in razor blades, cutting the inside of his brain. *Three months and it's over.*

"I need to take a piss." Richie scooted from the chair.

"Better not be thinking of running." Shaw rose but Campini extended a hand.

"That would be stupid," he said. "Are you stupid, Mr. Frezza?"

"Nature calls, man. You want to hold my dick for me, too?"

"I trust you. Bathroom is that way." Campini jabbed a thumb toward the hallway pasted in numerous Polaroid photos of previous customers chowing down on Ben's Famous Three-Pound Burger.

The kid moseyed toward the men's room.

"Take it easy." Campini's eyes jumped to Shaw. "If we go to trial without a person to corroborate the investigation's evidence and lose, the whole operation has been for nothing. More importantly, it meant Benussi died for nothing. We need to play nice and win him over."

"I get it." She forked a mouthful of salad and chased it with iced tea. "It's kind of sad he's the only hope we have."

"As far as Purelli is concerned, yes." Campini glanced toward the hallway. "If he doesn't cooperate, we'll have to settle for Bianchi getting strapped to the gurney."

Shaw blinked and wiped at her face. "Seems to be a pretty shitty parting gift, wouldn't you say?"

"Not my call. The Captain has me on a time frame."

"Then let's get this little bastard to talk." Shaw stabbed the salad with the fork a few times. "Benny, I mean Bianchi isn't the prize."

"Exactly." The men's bathroom door swung forward and Richie trudged through the opening. "All right, game face, now."

"Where's Sonny now?" Richie slipped back into his seat and slurped the remnants of the lemonade.

"It's not your concern." Campini popped another fry in his mouth. The toddler from before, now seated with barbeque sauce dripping from his nose and ears, tossed a salt shaker to the floor. *My guess is, you'll be one of them, kid.*

"So, what happens next?" Richie asked.

"We turn on the recorder and you tell me everything or—"

"If I say a word, I'm dead. You hear me? Dead. I'll take my chances."

"What chances are those?" Reese jabbed three fingers into the air. "One. You don't cooperate and we arrest you right now. Two. You don't cooperate, somehow beat this case, and Purelli kills you to tie up loose ends. Three. You run out of here right now, we track you down, and arrest you. Don't be stupid. We're you're only chance."

Shaw leaned forward and clasped Richie's hand. "As we speak, the SA is waiting for a response. I've got cuffs ready to go, Mr. Frezza."

"SA?"

"State Attorney. She's the one who decides who and what to prosecute. Basically, she can put your balls in a vice, or she can cut you a deal."

"What kinda deal?"

"Full testimony. Spill it all and also wear a wire. Get closer to Purelli. Work *with* us, and I'm sure State Attorney Cooper will pull some strings."

"I'm not a rat." This time the declaration came out flat and Campini sensed the confidence dwindling.

"Okay, then you're an inmate. And you'll be an inmate for another fifty years." Shaw gathered the photos and papers spread across the booth's table top.

"I need to think about it. This is my life we're talking about."

Shaw pressed. "These are your decisions we're talking

about too, Mr. Frezza. Choices you made. Choices have consequences."

"I need time. Give me a day."

"Take as much as you need." Reese knocked the table with his knuckles. "You can think it over at the station."

"You're not going to let me leave?"

"No way." Reese's lips lifted into a sneer.

You're my puppet now.

CHAPTER SIXTY-EIGHT

Shaw opened the interview room door and guided Richie to the steel bench of the metal table welded to the floor.

She placed a paper cup of coffee next to him. "I'll be back in a minute."

He turned from her and surveyed his new surroundings. A brown door cut a square of color into four walls of flake white. His eyes tracked to the coffee. Its steam vapors swirled like the ghosts escaping his vault.

They appeared in the traditional sense of the word. Transparent bodies without faces. Each took turns speaking, and the voices revealed the identities of which condemned soul had the floor. O'Leary's Irish accent opened the dialogue.

It's over. Man up and take the deal.

You deserve less, Harold chimed in.

No, Richie thought. *I'm not a rat. This is smoke and mirrors.*

You're a dead man walking, Cranswell said. The vapors solidified, and a skeleton formed. Next materialized the gaunt, pale face with the bullet hole—an onyx circle stamped into white and rotting skin. *Doesn't matter what you do. Either way, it's over.*

They don't have anything, Richie justified to himself. *I barely knew Sonny. What could they charge me with?*

Oh, I don't know, Cranswell mocked. *Murder. Accessory to murder. Extortion. Destruction of evidence. Tampering. Should I go on?*

Don't forget, being a little shit stain, too, Harold's voice shouted, though it came from Cranswell's formed mouth.

Can't prove any of it. My word against theirs, Richie countered.

Ha. So, those files of surveillance and photos can't put you at any scene? You think they'll take your story over a decorated investigator? Cranswell said. *The ego! C'mon, you twerp. Think! Stop acting stupid and think.*

O'Leary took center stage. His form now returned. Half a face atop a thick neck and broad shoulders. *You think these cops are letting you walk out of here? Take the deal. No more mistakes.*

You don't even exist. Richie cradled his head in his hands. *You're dead. All of you are dead. This is my life. Shut up.*

Cranswell's thumb and index finger formed a gun. *I say fight the man. Let em' know who is boss. Ha. Then spend your life behind bars. What a life. What a life.*

There must be some way. Richie slammed both hands to the metal table.

CHAPTER SIXTY-NINE

In an observation room thirty feet down the hall, Reese Campini and Deborah Shaw stood shoulder to shoulder.

A row of three monitors, each bolted into the wall and wireless, fed into the three active interview bays. The left screen presented a clean picture of room one in clear, colorful pixels.

Richie Frezza sat hunched over, his stare on the rear wall.

The two cops stood silent; their eyes glued to the screen. Reese focused on the kid's mannerisms.

"What's he thinking? I wonder. Seems kind of dazed." Campini tapped the glass of the screen. "Did we scare him enough?"

"He's cocky, I'll give him that. Maybe he knows our case depends on him?" Shaw's arms crossed beneath her bust.

"Doubt it. He's smug but young. Let him simmer for a while." Campini knuckled the glass again. "Is he talking to himself?"

"Crazy things happen in these rooms. I've seen perps

confess under their breath before. Too bad it isn't admissible in court."

Campini looked away from the screen. *Seen people commit suicide in these rooms, too. Hold on, Richie.* His cell phone buzzed. "This is Reese Campini."

"Dispatch connecting a call from Patrolmen Cortez. Shall I put him through?"

"Go ahead." The line clicked three times and burst static. "Campini here."

"Sir, this is Cortez. I have an issue over here at the diner."

"Ms. May's?" Campini nudged Shaw with a raised eyebrow.

"Yeah. A guy came in here, ran past me, and started asking questions. I was able to get him in cuffs, but he's got your card in his wallet and wants to speak with you."

"Gotta name, Cortez?"

"ID says Timothy Vietta. Mean anything to you?"

"I'll be there in fifteen minutes." He killed the call then looked to Shaw. "I've gotta go. We may have a break."

"You sure you don't want me to come along?"

"I'll handle it. Let this little worm squirm for a while." He checked the Bulova on his wrist. "Meet back here in an hour and we'll turn up the heat."

CHAPTER SEVENTY

The Impala parked behind Timothy's Jeep. He sat on the opposite side of the road, cuffed and stuffed in Cortez's squad car. He looked up through the window and Campini opened the door.

"Mr. Vietta, what are you doing here?" Mr. OCD draped his arm over the top of the door and peered into the cruiser.

"I need to know." Timothy wiggled in the metal braces, aware of its futility.

"Know what?"

"My girl. Is she alive?"

"Mr. Vietta, this is an ongoing investigation you have now compromised." Campini pocketed his sunglasses and knelt to reach Vietta's eye level.

"Please, just tell me if she's okay."

"I can't discuss anything. This is a crime scene."

"If one more asshole tells me, this is a crime scene, I'm gonna lose it." Bowed like a blow fish, he rolled his shoulders in an attempt to slip the cuffs. They clanked but held firm.

"Sorry you feel that way."

"I'll talk."

Reese's head perked up. "About what?"

"Everything." Timothy rolled his shoulder to his face, wiping the remnants of tears perched atop his swollen cheek.

"You had your chance to cooperate. I've got a much bigger fish on the line as we speak."

"I know a lot."

"If I need you down the road, we'll chat." The cop started to close the door and Timothy's foot swung to stop its momentum.

"Please. Just tell me. Is she dead?" He surveyed the ruin of the diner. A ghastly building of death. Lazy shadows danced across the decay as the sun's glow gave into the night's mask.

"I can't discuss an ongoing investigation." Campini hooked his arm and pulled him from the car. "Turn around."

"Please. Off the record?"

"Sorry, but it's the law. Kind of a big part of my job. Go home and get some rest, Mr. Vietta." He unhooked the cuffs and nodded to Cortez, who stood with both hands extended outward. "It's okay, Sergeant. I'll handle this."

Timothy crumpled and gripped the loose gravel, groveling in whimpers.

Campini knelt and patted his back. "I'm sorry, Thunderstorm."

"You don't give a fuck about me. All you care about is that badge and the power that comes with it." Timothy glanced up for a moment expecting to see a scoff or scowl from the detective.

Instead, Campini's lips pressed together in a tight line.

"Some things are more important than the job. I'm still human." He rose and yanked Timothy up with him. "Maybe I'm just desensitized to it. I see carnage every day, but that doesn't mean what you're feeling is lost on me."

"She's dead then?"

Campini shot a glance to Cortez. The patrolman bent below the perimeter tape and scaled the steps of the diner. He nodded but said, "I'm not at liberty to discuss an open investigation."

Timothy's mouth opened to cry out and his eyes widened to pour tears, but neither came. At this moment, with the travesty confirmed, sorrow sat down with its hands beneath its ass cheeks. Anger rose and growled, a bellowing and piercing howl shook him within. He felt its presence more vivid and amplified than ever before in his young life. It crisscrossed through his brain, pinging every nerve.

"Can I trust you won't go back in the diner? No more freebies, Mr. Vietta." Campini tapped the cuffs hanging from his belt.

"There's nothing in there for me anymore." Timothy wiped at his face with the injured hand. The scabbed scar had begun to flake and even out over the skin. He traced a finger over it. "I've got other places to be."

CHAPTER SEVENTY-ONE

"Can you talk?"

"Busy day, here. Lotta shit about to hit the fan," Benny replied into the phone. *Don't have time to play boyfriend right now.*

Five o'clock approached and thunderous claps descended from the heavens. The first line of drops fell a half mile north, masking the highway in a concrete color.

"I hate to say it, but more shit is coming." Deb's usual playful tone and flirtatious vibe nonexistent.

"What are ya talking about?" Benny flicked the wipers on and lowered the radio.

"You know Richie Frezza, right?"

"Yeah." Benny hated to confirm anything over the phone, but her manner interested him.

"He's in deep shit. So are you."

"This better not be a fucking joke." Benny honked at a grandma who adjusted her umbrella halfway in the crosswalk. "What are you talking about?"

"We've said enough on the phone. Meet me at my house."

Benny killed the call, honked again, and swerved past the woman, running a red light in the process.

Deborah Shaw lived in a neighborhood unlike The Trails. Outward appearances were important in this community. Manicured lawns divided by stone walkways hugged the road. Primped shrubs rounded the edge of identical yards leading to white screened porches. Each building, a two-story contemporary stucco structure, housed small families.

Backyard barbeques. Yard sales. A true piece of suburbia living—an annexed portion of land secluded from the stench of Ridgemont Cove's breath.

The neighbors—a conglomerate of lawyers, executives, doctors, and small business owners—were pleased to know a civil servant sworn to serve and protect lived within earshot.

Benny had been here before, careful to scope the street for nosy assholes with too much money and not enough responsibility.

The meetings were intimate and passionate encounters. He'd been on this couch plenty of times, but never clothed or sober. "Start from the beginning, Deb."

"I got called out to the 5-20 on Center street and I—"

"Lose the cop talk. What the hell is a 5-20? English, please."

"Sorry, baby." She put her feet on his thighs. "It means I was called in for the murder at the diner."

"Yeah." Benny rubbed her toes and felt the electricity complementing arousal. This couch had seen plenty of it, and he struggled to keep his hands from tracing her long legs and reaching the jackpot.

"So, while I'm there with my team, this young cop shows up. I recognized him, but I didn't say anything. Anyway, he comes up to me and starts talking about the crime scene. He seems real interested in what I'm thinking."

"Jesus Christ, get to the point."

"The point is this guy is Reese Campini."

Benny searched his memory. He knew most of the players in the department. That name meant nothing, a scary proposition considering Deb's tight scowl and locked eyes. "Who?"

"He's OCD, Benny."

"Are you fucking kidding me?" Benny pushed her feet to the floor then hunched over the small mirrored table in front of the couch. His wide-eyed and pale reflection stared back. "Might as well be staring at a ghost. This is bad."

"I wondered why a big-wig from the Organized Crime Department showed up." She stood from the couch. "Campini is the big time."

"How come I've never heard of him? I know anybody that's anybody."

"Most of his cases are classified. He runs the undercovers."

Benny's ears perked up to this. *Sonny's boss?* "Who got whacked at the diner?"

"That's why I called you." She plopped back onto the couch next to him, draping an arm across his neck. "Campini starts spilling the beans about this super covert investigation into Salvador Purelli. Turns out, the dead man at the diner is an undercover named James Benussi. You know him as Sonny. You were right."

"That rat fuck." *Under my nose for two years.* A dull thump traveled through his chest and up his throat. "If this doesn't get straightened out, Purelli will kill me." He pulled away from Deborah's grasp and stood. "You sure about this?"

"Yes."

"How do I know this ain't a double cross? What if you're playing both sides? Jesus Christ, what if they're watching us now?" He waddled toward the window overlooking the front yard and drew the shade back. The gray evening cast a charcoal color over the empty street.

"Calm down, baby. I've got some good news."

"Good news?" He turned to her. "This is serious shit, Deb. How do I know you ain't playing me?"

"If I was *playing* you, would I be telling you all this?" Her hands shot upward and a pitiful grimace crossed her face. "What could I gain?"

Benny considered this, but his mind refused to operate with the premise of common sense. *Trust no one. Not even her.* "Sonny knew enough to send me to Death Row."

"You're not going anywhere. Please, take a seat and listen." She caressed the empty cushion of couch with her hand.

"Prove it. How do I know for sure?"

"I played the good girl for years. You know what I got? Shitty pay, worse hours. Asshole men thinking a woman could never be a cop. Half of them trying to get in my pants and the other half trying to get rid of me. I'm done with the good guy side. You know this, baby."

"Still—" Benny's lips smacked together tight, and he shook his head, unsure of any truths at the moment.

"Wanna frisk me?" Widening her legs and setting them on the glass coffee table, she grinned. "Think I'm wearing a wire? I'll take my clothes off, big fella."

"I need a drink." Benny ambled into the kitchen. Dishes clanked and cabinet doors slammed.

"It's in the top cupboard." She called from the living room.

Benny located the bottle of Chianti. He slung a mouthful then filled the glass and walked out to her.

"Better, baby?" She'd removed the pants of her suit. Her legs, now a wide V, revealed silk purple panties he had chewed on before.

"Well, I'm glad you're so Goddamn calm. What's this good news then?"

"I'm the lead detective, so Campini unloaded it all. They've got your balls in vice, baby. There's a way out, though."

"What do they have?" He chugged from the cup and considered another pour.

"Hours and hours of documented wire taps. Benussi was mic'd up for two years. I heard some of this stuff. It could end *you,* but it's not what they want." Her hand caressed the couch again and Benny sat.

He tried to focus on the words she spoke but could only target the pink flesh accented by the purple lace of her underwear. He grasped her thigh. "Why should I not be worried?"

"They're hard on for Purelli and running out of time. The plug is about to get pulled."

"When?"

"A few months before they cut all the funding. Campini has to do something. Don't get me wrong, Reese will settle for you on Death Row, but I suspect the plan is to bring you in and turn you CI."

CI was one cop term Benny knew well. All mobsters did. *Confidential Informants.* They ended up with their tongues cut off and stuffed into their assholes. This wasn't an exaggeration, either. Benny had handled a few CI's in the past.

"I would never talk to the cops. Ever." He released his

grip on her and pushed a stray strand of hair back into place.

"I know, but Campini will try to stir up some nasty stuff for everyone. Like I said, there's a way out, baby."

Benny retraced the last two years. His initial meeting with Sonny Denardo replayed. The guy had hawked a few stereos from a warehouse for a joke cut. At the time, it seemed like an earner trying to pay homage to the old school mobsters. Now, it stung, the naivety overpowering like the cheap Chianti's vinegar aftertaste.

Shoulda saw it then. Too good to be true.

A few months later, a chance meeting at Moonlighters. Another coincidence.

Two Irishmen overstayed their welcome. Sonny busted some prick's mouth for disrespecting Candi. She vouched for him, telling Benny he'd always been a gentleman and never got out of line.

A man's man. No question.

A couple small jobs turned into bigger endeavors. A sit-down with the boss after. Soon, Sonny Denardo, a half-ass wise guy, is driving the Solano underboss around. Clean assimilation into the ranks.

Right under my fucking nose.

"We can fix it, baby." Shaw straddled him, grinding his groin and flicking her tongue on his neck.

He was lost in thought now, unaware of her growing animalistic moans.

It couldn't be, though. No way this cop infiltrates without a peep from one of the fifty contacts Purelli pays. No way.

There were far too many instances of unlawful activity to drape in the shadows of reasonable doubt. Murders, shakedowns, extortion, and corrupt gambling. Benny tilted the Chianti glass and swallowed the rest.

"What's my way out?" Benny blurted, shrugging her off and wiping at his neck.

"You know where I was earlier?" Shaw stood again, a hand pressed firm to her hip, and the other raised with a pointed finger.

"Where?"

"Speaking with Richie Frezza. He's in a world of shit, too."

Benny's head involuntarily shook. *Bad news getting worse.* Thoughts of Sonny's surveillance trumped the original reason Deb called. "Did he flip?"

"Not yet. I'm supposed to head back to the interview soon."

"Interview? I dropped Richie at the barbeque joint. You said it would be casual."

"It was. Kid got scared. Campini laid it on thick. Not much I could do. Hard to dispute the evidence OCD has collected. He hasn't agreed yet, but it's just a matter of time."

"How is this good news, Deb? You're talking in fucking circles."

"Money, honey. Deep pockets. Sonny's death destroys their case. The surveillance won't hold up in court. Purelli's got the cash to beat this. Won't even make it to a preliminary. Without those recordings and Benussi's case notes, they have nothing."

"But if Richie flips," Benny said, connecting the dots and shuddering at the thought of what may have to come.

"They need him to corroborate Benussi's case notes against you. With Richie's statement, they can put pressure on you. And I can't help if it gets there."

"I don't think the kid will. He won't squeal, Deb."

"You willing to stake your life on it? I can hold him downtown for another few hours. Campini will charge him after that. He's hungry and persistent."

"Charged for what?"

"All the stuff on those tapes. Last time I checked, and I did, the kid's net worth is six hundred dollars. No cash means public defender and a loss. But if he agrees to talk, they'll take him to protective custody. Nobody will know where he is then. Not even me."

"I don't think he's gonna talk." Benny felt his voice inflect in his throat, pouring from his mouth with an edge. "He's a natural."

"If he does," she said with a cautious tone, "it's going to be very bad."

Benny wiped at his face with a glare toward the kitchen hallway. "So, what? What do I do? Kill the guy?"

"Yeah, baby."

CHAPTER SEVENTY-TWO

The Impala snaked around the corner. Its taillights shined like rubies in the rising dark of the evening.

Timothy's wallet sat in his lap. He slid Campini's card from a slit in the leather and tore it into pieces. Its remnants scattered throughout the blacktop as a slight wind passed through.

Patrolmen Dickhead stood inside, sweeping the street with his eyes through the window. Some shards, still intact in the frame, jabbed out like teeth. He eyed Timothy with his hands planted to his hips, but said nothing.

Across the street, the Jeep idled with the driver side door still ajar. From within it, the lyrics of *Hotel California* carried atop the wind, but by the time they reached the curb Timothy sat on now, all but a mumbled whisper remained.

He pushed his slashed hand into the sweat pants, ignoring the discomfort. *That is all it is now, discomfort not death.* He emptied his pocket on the sidewalk. Four dollars, a single bronze key, and an individual pack of Advil—a neat pile of his only belongings.

A series of memories traveled through him.

Lighthouse Putt-Putt on a cool Friday night. Ruby, then wearing an idyllic and innocent face, wagered a kiss. She won, but they'd kissed anyway. Seventeen and in love with the world a black void but for the twinkling of the plastic lighthouse and Ruby's green eyes.

A car horn screamed in the distance and broke his trance. He peered over his shoulder to the near glassless window. Cortez's stare continued.

The memories cycled.

Annabelle. At sixteen months old, she figured out how to open the upper cabinet drawers. He came home to find silverware scattered throughout the kitchen. Knives, forks, and spoons lay on the hardwood floors of the farmhouse. Dread turned to anger. Anger became sympathy. An inspection for scrapes and cuts yielded nothing. They hugged and Timothy could remember how that one moment was the first time he'd ever felt true fear.

This memory washed-out to black and a boxing match shifted to focus. A grueling slugfest for all six rounds, but a unanimous decision declared *Thunderstorm* the victor. Unable to talk through the swelling of a cracked jaw and a cocktail of prescription painkillers, the first conversation with Benny had been one sided and encouraging. Promises of fame and fortune enthralled the twenty-something year old single father and broke schmuck.

This faded and the white hospital room appeared. Hand mangled. Ego broken. Demonic eyes and hissing warnings. Threats.

Eventually Lighthouse Putt-Putt faded in and a smile resurfaced on his face.

The snippets of memories repeated for twenty minutes before he stood and blotted them out. He considered going home and admitting defeat, living out monotonous days picking peppers. The most practical option, but Timothy never cared for the mundane.

A second choice could be the police department. A man with knowledge of the Purelli-run Solano Crime Family could offer enough intel to cripple the lower-level guys. If Campini didn't want the info, some hard-on would. But involving cops meant little revenge—and a need for vengeance would, no, *must* be quenched.

Joe represented a third option. Of all the people in Ridgemont Cove, Joe could be trusted and understood the carnage unfolding.

After contemplating each possible course of action, he decided none were viable. Inside the Jeep's center console, a Visa credit card sat atop some assorted change. A piece of plastic reserved for emergencies. And if this wasn't one of those, nothing would ever be.

The card had purchased three things. Last June, wisdom teeth had pushed through the upper gums of Timothy's mouth. The surgery had been invasive and caused his mouthpiece to fit awkward for three months. A year prior, a certain diamond ring purchase spiked the minimum dues. More recently, the card handled the bill for admittance and care in Ridgemont Cove Memorial.

He gripped the card and tapped it on the steering wheel. A piece of plastic for peace in plastic.

Hopefully, enough is left on this thing.

CHAPTER SEVENTY-THREE

Richie grew increasingly tired of the white walls and blank noise. A single drone of annoyance dripped from the vent near the corner to the left of the door. Just a monotonous hum and flaked walls. A clock hung on the wall stared back at him, its red second hand ticking up past the black stems pointing to the 5 and 11.

Still defiant and without cause, he retraced as much of the last month as his tired and weary mind allowed. Sonny wasn't there when Roger Cranswell died. Later conversations ensued but they wouldn't hold up in court. *Right?*

Then there was Harold and Georgie. Benny chopped Georgie's finger off and Georgie stabbed Harold afterward.

How do either of those fall on me?

Bryce O'Leary's death had been a two-man job. Richie and Lorenzo dropped O'Leary, and Sonny was nowhere near the scene or clean-up. Again, and regrettably, conversations took place in darkened bars and vacant lots, but names and locations were hushed.

Hear-say, right?

All of these events could be explained away, but *would*

there be a chance? The last month aged him by a year, but the span had been a wise-guy crash course. Embedded in the instruction was a solitary and frightening fact: people who go against them—*or was it us now*—disappeared into holes, were crushed and sent overseas, or simply tagged and dropped on a corner.

Okay, so I stand my ground? What then? Is Purelli supplying an attorney?

These thoughts kept his mind abuzz as his eyes traced the clock hand's revolutions. It twirled round and round a million times, it seemed.

How much longer?

CHAPTER SEVENTY-FOUR

Campini stewed, troubled by Vietta's current news and growing impatient with this little asshole in the interview room.

Be patient. A day at the office for me is another's personal nightmare. Walk the line and balance your feelings.

The monitor blinked and lost focus for a moment. Then, the pixels converged, presenting Richie Frezza seated at the metal table. He stared at the clock then to the door.

"Everything okay?" Deborah Shaw entered the observation room with two paper cups swishing black coffee.

"Yeah." He took one and sipped. "Think he's ready to talk?"

"No time like the present." Shaw's eyes diverted to the screen. "Been about three hours now."

Campini glanced to his watch. "That long?" He thought of his side trip to the diner then a call from his mother. "Worried," she had said. "You didn't look right last time I saw you."

Gee, mom. Thanks. "Where have you been?" Campini asked, eyes now on the screen.

"Had to step out for a minute. My mother is old and needy."

I know what you mean. "Let's go in for the kill." Campini sipped the coffee again.

"Ready when you are."

The clicking of heels caught his attention. He turned from the TV show that was Richie Frezza. Alaina Cooper, the State Attorney, pranced toward him in long strides clutching a briefcase in her jeweled hand.

"Detectives," she said as she approached. She stopped and stood with a hip extended out.

He flushed and offered a slight nod.

A trim and exotic brunette with a wide smile and pin-up figure, Alaina Cooper caught the attention of just about any man traversing the waxed marble floors of the courthouse, with Campini the rule and not an exception. Today the light blue blouse and sleek black skirt accentuated her caramel skin and fresh hazel eyes. The diamonds on her wrist seemed dull in comparison.

They'd become acquainted upon his arrival in OCD. Both similar in the way they had accomplished so much at such young ages, some of the older veterans around city hall had blackballed them. Nobody likes to meet their replacements, so the two stuck together through the adversity of being new, successful, and irritating to the "old guard". A mutual respect, and perhaps more, palpable and easy to detect when they spoke with one another.

"Can we talk in your office?" She looked past the two detectives and eyed the screen.

"Of course," he replied. "You know Deborah Shaw, right?"

"I believe we've met." She offered a dainty handshake.

In the elevator, he and Alaina chatted about a party

they were to attend. His eyes wandered from her heels to the hem of the skirt, capturing the tan lines and wondering how faint the skin became beneath it.

The elevator buzzed.

"After you." He extended a hand to the open hallway. She mimicked a curtsy and followed Shaw out.

Once in his office, Alaina plopped her briefcase on a vacant chair then spread a stack of files across the desk and flipped through the multi-colored tabs of the folders.

"I think you're slipping in your old age." Alaina opened a folder tabbed in red.

"What are you talking about?" He sat in his chair and propped his shoes to the desk corner.

"I'm talking about the fact that you have the wrong guy in a box right now." She retrieved another tabbed folder from the briefcase and perused a few pages inside. "Dead end, Reese."

"Who? Frezza? He's the one shot we have at closing this case."

Shaw sat in the chair next to the briefcase full of files and peeked at the labels. "You've been busy."

"I sure have, detective. Busy enough to know that Richie Frezza is a nobody." She leafed through the pages of the second file and pulled out a stapled stack of papers. "The kid with no priors? First-time offender? Low-level connect in the Solano crime family?" She dropped the documents in front of Campini. "This kid is the ace up your sleeve?" Her eyes flicked in blue flashes beneath long, thin eyelashes.

"He can corroborate Benussi's case notes. Nobody else is willing to talk, counsel." He smoothed his tie with his palm. "Do you have some magical witness in that satchel of yours?"

"Perhaps, I do, Mr. Campini." Alaina chuckled, revealing stark white teeth made brighter by the accent of dark rouge on her pouty lips. "My team and I have been pouring over Benussi's surveillance logs. I've had two law students running eight-hour shifts to read and listen to the last two years of his life. Thought we were up shit's creek."

"Thought?" Campini lowered his feet to the floor and set his elbows to the desk. "You got something?"

"Yeah, Reese, we've got something. The name Georgie Silva mean anything to you?"

"Vaguely." Two years of surveillance produced thousands of names and he did not have a bunch of do-good college kids tackling the grunt work. The last month had been a clusterfuck of information overload. An attempt to pinpoint the importance of Georgie failed. "I've got five open cases, a shrinking budget, and Captain Taggert chewing my ass like a meaty rib bone. Oh, and a dead operative in the city morgue. So, no. Georgie Silva means little."

"He's the man who murdered Harold Remnick." Her smile broke and the tone of her voice stiffened.

"Sorry. I didn't mean to snip at you." He rubbed his eyes then glanced to the window. "I'm tired."

"It's okay." She dragged the briefcase to the floor and sat, crossing her legs in a fluid dance. "Georgie should be in your room right now."

Campini struggled with the name. After hearing so much of Benussi's surveillance, trying to identify one particular perp amongst a sea of assholes and degenerates was akin to narrowing down a specific taxi lumbering down Broadway at five o'clock in New York City. "Not following you, Alaina."

"Let me explain. The best I can charge Richie Frezza with is poorly choosing his friends. Benussi's testimony and surveillance are full of juicy intel, but not a lot implicates the kid, who by the way, has the entire mob's payroll."

"The kid's a murderer."

"According to who?"

"James fucking Benussi."

"All hear-say. He didn't witness any murders. He heard Frezza's name after the fact." Alaina glanced to Shaw. "Would you consider that a hot lead, detective?"

"Nope." The detective leaned forward and clasped her hands together. "What if he talks about Bianchi? Shake the tree a little bit."

"Possible, but not ideal." Alaina turned to Campini. "Rolling on either Benny or Purelli is a death sentence. The kid would never make it to court."

"Look at you with all the answers." He sat back and ran a wide sweep through the crafted and gelled blonde hair atop his head.

"I'm here to help," she replied with a smirk.

"So, what's the move, counsel?"

"A guy like Georgie is the prime candidate to cut a deal. Benussi witnessed him stab Harold Remnick."

"So did Frezza. The kid's an accessory to murder." Campini's desktop phone rang. He lifted it then dropped it back into the carriage.

"But Georgie's a convicted felon with a rap sheet long enough it could supply toilet paper to this whole building."

Reese snickered at the joke. "So, what are you getting at?"

"I'm saying your number one priority should be finding Georgie. You can try to flip Frezza, but I'd prefer you track down this guy so I can charge him with first degree murder. My guess is he'll cut a deal. Good news for you and your case."

Reese frowned. *How could he have missed this?*

Alaina, seemingly sensing the embarrassment said, "If we can find Georgie and show him Benussi's testimony, he'll sing like a choir girl. It's perfect. Georgie doesn't know Benussi's dead and another felony on his record is automatic Life Without Parole."

"And if he talks—"

"Then we get Frezza in hot water. Once we have a real case against Frezza, we bring Benny in. From there, well, you know what we do."

"They'll all fall like dominoes," Shaw whispered.

"Exactly." Alaina scooped papers from Campini's desk with an assured and outright sexy tooth-filled smile.

"What about Frezza now?"

"State law says we can hold a person for questioning up to eight hours. Based on the logs I've read from your department; he's been here around four. Either get him to confess or kick him loose. You want my advice?"

"Absolutely, Ms. Cooper." Campini's eyes drifted down the blue blouse. The skirt rode a bit high from the crossed caramel legs. *No pale skin after all.*

She adjusted in the seat and flushed again. "We go and get Georgie, flip him like a burger, and then take them all down."

"Frezza knows about Benussi, though."

"Knows he's undercover or he's dead."

"Undercover."

"Well, that was stupid, Reese. Like I said, you're slipping."

"I thought it was the right move."

"Truth is, it doesn't matter. His case notes make it clear they were on to him. Hell, they may have ordered the hit. Detective Shaw, any leads on the case?"

Shaw shook her head. "We're waiting on ballistics and searching for witnesses. Nothing solid."

"I'm sure something will crack." Alaina turned to Campini. "Anyway, Frezza was going to talk to Purelli whether or not he was locked up."

"How do you figure?"

"He's got no family, Reese. He's allowed one phone call. Bet your ass the call is to the Solanos. If they didn't already know about Benussi, they would have found out, regardless. Letting Frezza go doesn't change anything. Besides, we let him out, find Georgie, and then bring him right back. We've got one shot at this. Let's do it right."

"But if we flip Frezza—" Reese stopped to formulate the right words, hoping to at least take credit for something.

"Unless you get a confession, which doesn't look likely, I can't prosecute. We need Georgie Silva."

Reese thought about Timothy and regretted the cold exchange outside of the diner. "I have another guy."

"Who?"

"Another Purelli victim with a score to settle."

"For now, find Georgie. The rest will fall in place."

CHAPTER SEVENTY-FIVE

The little slut State Attorney stalked out of Campini's office with her ass jutted in the air like a balcony. Campini's eyes followed the show and Shaw steamed in anger. *This guy needs to keep his prick in his pants and stay the course.*

"I still think Frezza is an option." She dragged her chair closer to the desk.

"You heard her." Campini reached below her eye level. Hinges of a drawer squealed and when his hand appeared again, it held a stress ball. He squeezed, whitening the knuckles of his manicured fingers. "Let's find Georgie Silva."

"So, we're taking orders from her now? Last I checked, this is our investigation."

"I've invested a lot of time in this." He switched the moldable ball to the other hand. "If the woman tasked with prosecuting the case says we need Georgie, then we need to get him."

"And Frezza?" Shaw cringed, scrunching her face. Black drifters formed in her eyes when they opened and she felt nauseous, tired. *Benny can't take much more suspense.*

The phone rang and Campini picked it up. He covered the mouthpiece. "Kick the kid loose."

She returned to the interview room.

"You're free to go." Shaw's watch read seven o'clock sharp. She jotted the time on a release form.

"Huh?" His neck sprang back in surprise and he stood. "You serious?"

"Sign here." She placed the form and pen to the steel table. "By doing so you are accepting release from the interview process, but also acknowledging that we can call upon you again if needed."

He flicked the pen across the document without reading it.

And just like that, Richie Frezza crept back into the wild. The kid sauntered down the steps of the department side entrance. She flipped open the phone.

Little time and high stakes, now.

"Yeah," Benny said after the third ring.

"Some things have changed." She watched the little gnat float from her grasp and turn the corner. "You available?"

"What has changed?"

"Not on the phone."

"I'm in a meeting. We'll link up tomorrow, okay?"

The line died, and Deborah Shaw fought the acidic climb of anxiety running through her throat.

CHAPTER SEVENTY-SIX

Streetlamps cast orange spheres on the black pavement of the road. Since being led up these very stairs four hours ago, the temperature had dropped fifteen degrees.

Bewildered and fearful of the unknown, but free to venture out into the world for at least one more day, Richie jumped the last three steps and cut right.

An arduous six-mile trek to Center St. awaited, though he had no interest in attempting the journey. If Deborah-whatever was still peering through his back, it was best to keep up appearances.

Head down and feet pointed toward Center.

His belongings were sealed in a plastic bag. The burner, four crumpled twenty-dollar bills, a pack of Trident and three keys attached to a bottle opener key chain. He ripped the plastic hard and freed the phone. *Benny won't believe how stupid these cops are.*

The phone rang seven times.

No answer.

CHAPTER SEVENTY-SEVEN

The sun blanketed the crisp Sunday morning in golden dew. Its rays reached far and high, even sprinkling specks of glow through the second-floor window of The Tango.

Benny turned from the view. "I spoke with my contact last night. She said things changed."

Purelli tapped his slender finger against the waxed cedar of the desk and said nothing. His black eyes bounced in their sockets from the window to the floor.

"Any thoughts?" Benny asked in hopes of some reaction. The boss was tight-lipped on most days. Today, a monk would seem like an auctioneer in comparison to him. The news of "Silent" Sonny, a crippling blow to the operation, rattled the boss. Awaiting a reply but recognizing the futility in such an endeavor, Benny stepped forward. "I'll find out. It'll work out. Could get messy, but we've been through worse, right?"

Purelli's blank expression remained. Not a flint of the eyes, a nod of agreement, or even a whisker moving beneath a pulsed jaw. Stone.

"She thinks the case is weak since Sonny is dead."

Benny plodded closer. His belt buckle rested on the edge of the desk. "I'll meet her later today and get particulars."

"Have we swept this place recently?" Purelli asked, the unflinching glare to the window continuing.

"Lorenzo did last night. Nothing."

Purelli retrieved a cigarette from the silver case. The flames of a struck match danced across the reflection in the window. "You trust this friend of yours?"

"She's a good broad, boss. She's crazy about me."

Purelli pulled on the smoke hard and then placed both elbows on the desk. "That's not what I asked, Benjamin."

"Yeah. I trust her."

The bustling of The Tango below shook the floor. Cooks, waiters, bartenders, and hostesses all cogs in a wheel and aids in the building of an empire. Their innocent roles an imperative tentacle of the organization. Make the cash and clean it. Funnel the fruits of misdeeds and degradation through a wholesome and innocent system. It had worked well for many years. Now, an infestation brewed. Rodents chewed the foundation of this enterprise. Worth dying for? *Yes,* Benny thought. *It may come to that now.*

"You trusted Sonny, too." Purelli clasped his hands. The cigarette trembled in his lips.

"We vetted him. You and I—"

Purelli's black eyes flared, accosting such a remark without the need of a voice.

Benny recognized the expression and stood back from the desk. "I'm just saying—"

"I know what you are saying." Purelli stood and tossed the half dead cigarette into the ash tray. "And did we, what is the word you used . . . vet. Did we vet Richie, too?"

Purelli's tone and newfound willingness to speak created a sunken stone in Benny's belly.

"Sonny's dead and Richie ain't a rat."

Purelli smirked but kept his lips tight.

A vibrating noise cut the silence. Benny reached into his pocket. RF highlighted the screen of the phone. "It's Richie."

"Let it ring."

"He called last night and now he's—"

"Could be a trap." Purelli dragged the cigarette and exhaled. His mouth formed an O and the whips of smoke came out in misshapen circles. "One dead rat and one in a cage."

"Let me talk to the broad. She'll clear this up."

"Not another word to this woman. We must assume the worst. Let her speak only."

"I understand."

The phone stopped buzzing and Purelli rounded the corner of the desk and stood square eye-to-eye. "I don't think you do, Benjamin." He slid his hand down Benny's cheek then gripped his neck. "I cannot, and will not, tolerate another mistake."

"I've been with you a long time." The boss's touch, a cold and dry sponge, sent shivers tramping through him. "You have my word. This will be cleaned up."

"You're my dear and oldest friend in this business." Purelli embraced him. He kissed each cheek then grabbed his shoulders.

Benny had never seen the man's eyes so black, empty. "I'll handle it, boss." He receded from the awkward grip, unsure how to interpret the intimate discussion. Old mob movies showed exchanges of cheek-to-cheek greetings, but that was a practice of the old-timers, a habit lost on the current regime until now.

"I trust if anyone can do it, it is you." Purelli turned his attention to the window. "Keep me informed, Benjamin."

Benny made his way back to the Cadillac. Lorenzo leaned against the passenger side, arms crossed, grimace prevalent. "Everything good?" He opened the passenger side door.

"Yeah."

Purelli's tone and accusations stung. Sure, Sonny and Richie came into the organization with clearance from Benny, but the boss had final say.

In a more legitimate company, HR brought candidates in, but the executives spearheaded personnel acquisition.

Not a lot of fucking difference, Benny thought. *Guess it don't matter anyway.*

The Solano Family didn't sell goods or services. Purelli didn't run board meetings like a high-priced CEO. The title of executioner better fit the job description. Benny chuckled, picturing a morbid business card.

Salvador Purelli
Solano Family Company
Executioner
PH: 555-DEAD EXT 187

The inward laughter faded and reality returned. An acrid shit storm bled dark, with Benny wafting through the debris alone. *Deb can fix it. She has to.*

"Where we headed, Benny?" Lorenzo adjusted the rearview mirror and stared into it. He picked at his teeth with a toothpick.

"The broad's house."

Lorenzo pulled the Cadillac into the street and headed north toward Shaw's house. Benny flipped the radio dial to

KSN News and sat back. Purelli's words on the forefront and breaking news relegated to background noise.

"How long you been seeing this girl?"

"On and off a few years." Benny flipped his phone open. He pulled up a text message menu and jabbed Shaw's number into the device.

Headin' to U.

"A cop, though? How'd it happen?"

"Just happened." Benny pocketed the phone then rotated the volume dial, hoping his new driver would take the hint.

"You trust her?"

"How many questions you got for me? Do I answer to you?"

"Sorry, I didn't mean nothing by it. Just wondering is all." Lorenzo tapped the steering wheel with his thumbs and brought his eyes back to the windshield.

The commercials of the radio faded, and the news program's opening jingle jumped through the stereo speakers.

A double murder at Ms. May's Diner on Center Street yesterday morning has no new leads. Police have not revealed much in the way of suspects, but the common theory among many reporters is the shooting was gang-related. One source close to the investigation has mentioned known organized crime members frequented the diner. Representatives of the police department refused to comment.

"Who are these sources? Goddamn reporters just make it up." Benny huffed and crossed his arms like a child refusing to back down to the request of a parent.

"They're right, though."

"It's gotta be Ms. May. I guarantee she opened her

mouth. First Sonny, and now this woman is talking. We gotta lot of work to do."

Lorenzo didn't respond.

The news channel continued to report other breaking headlines, but none of them discussed anything of interest to Benny. His mind drifted in and out, focusing and losing clarity like a camera shutter fighting obtrusive sparks of sunlight.

Purelli's attitude.

Shaw's second call.

Richie.

By the time more commercials began, the Cadillac parked in front of the walkway leading to Shaw's house.

"Keep your eyes peeled." Benny clicked the handle and forced the heavy door open. "We're targets now."

CHAPTER SEVENTY-EIGHT

"I'll take that one." Timothy stood in front of a glass case. Handguns and accessories pressed into foam looked up from the clear encasement. "The FNS."

"Good eye." The bearded owner said. A nametag pinned to his tie-dyed shirt plumping at the waist had Earl written across it in black cursive. "Great starter gun. Balanced, easy to clean."

"Expensive?"

"How can you put a price on safety and comfort?" Earl huffed with a wheeze and located a single brass key among a collection of others in varying sizes and molds. He pushed it into the lock on his end of the glass.

"Tough to argue with that. My credit card may struggle with the debate, though." Timothy watched Earl muscle the FNS from its cushion beneath the glass and raise it.

"All items are negotiable." The convict cut-out with long graying hair and smudged green tattoo sleeves racked the slide then released the magazine. He flipped it on his index finger in a smooth circle and extended the grip to Timothy. "I'll shoot ya straight. No pun intended."

How many times has he said that before? Timothy took it and slipped his finger to the trigger. He dropped it to his side. "It's light."

"Yeah. Add a full magazine, it gets a little manlier." Earl slid a clipboard across the glass and pulled a pen from a cup near the register. "Before we get to that, I'll need your ID and consent to run a background check."

Timothy placed the gun down to the glass and flipped the clipboard around. He scanned each page to find where a signature was required and flicked a few squiggly lines. "How long will it take?"

"The check?" Earl flipped the pages to ensure all signatures were in order. "I'll have it in seconds." He highlighted something on the paper and tossed the clipboard back on the glass. "Need your name, address, and social, bud."

"My bad. Just excited." Timothy filled in the missing information. "So, I'll need bullets too, huh?"

"When you come back to pick it up."

"Thought you said it takes seconds to get approval." He glanced up from the form. Earl had the FNS in his hand.

"The check takes seconds. You'll still have to wait the mandatory ten-day cool off period."

"You're kidding?" Timothy jotted the final digits of his social security number and slid the papers back to Earl.

"Safety issue, Mr."—he ran his finger across the top of the highlighted page—"Vietta. Can't have emotion getting the better of people. You don't mind waiting, do you?"

"Not at all." *Ten days. Twenty. Fifty. Doesn't matter to me. My mind is made up.* "We going to talk price?"

CHAPTER SEVENTY-NINE

She opened the door wearing a see-through robe and a glass of Chianti in hand.

"You're not on duty today?" Benny stepped in, pecked her cheek, and moved toward the living room.

"I'm off, my love. Hoping to get off, too." She winked and lifted the silk robe beyond her thighs.

"You never quit, do you? Kinda gotta shit storm brewing out there, Deb." He sat on the couch and eyed a candle burning on the coffee table. It spewed fragrant black wisps, canvassing the room in a rich scent of vanilla.

The shades, normally stretched to the side and clipped to the wall, were closed and fastened with yellow string. Daylight peeked through the crevice not covered by the drapes, but the house resembled an ancient tomb.

"We may have good news." Shaw cozied next to Benny and brought the glass of wine to her lips.

"Oh, yeah? I could use some good news today." He took the wine from her and sipped.

"I met with the SA. Her name is Alaina Cooper."

"And," he growled, irritated by Deb's habit of circling around the point.

"And she's got the case all shaken up."

"How?"

"Yesterday, I was in a meeting with her and Reese Campini."

Benny nodded and took another swig of wine. "The guy from OCD?"

"Yep." She licked her lips and Benny tipped the glass for her. "Apparently, Richie can't be charged and wouldn't talk."

"I knew he was a stand-up kid. So, we're in the clear?"

"Not exactly." Shaw cringed, pursing her lips.

"What now?" Benny wiped at his face. It felt hot and swollen. *Can't take much more of this shit.*

"Cooper, the SA, wants to go after somebody else. She thinks bringing him in would strengthen the case."

Benny's eyes widened, running his thick eyebrows into an arc. "Who?"

"Georgie Silva."

"Who?" He repeated, unable to grasp the name or its importance.

"Apparently, Benussi's case notes talk about a murder in a barn. Georgie Silva killed Harold Remnick in front of you and Richie."

The memory came back and slapped him across the face. Falling back into the couch, he tipped the glass of Chianti. It emptied in a final pour and warmed his throat. "You gotta be kidding."

"I wish I was. This guy is a multiple felon and Cooper thinks more than willing to cooperate. If you can get to him, it's over, baby."

"Everything is so fucked, Deb. I'm not sure what's going to happen."

"Here's what's going to happen. You send your crew or whatever to find this guy. Silence him, and tell Frezza to keep his mouth shut."

"I'm not worried about the kid. The big guy is, though. It's all a mess."

"One thing at a time, hon." Shaw swung her feet into his lap and propped her elbows on the arm rest of the couch. "Focus on Georgie. Any clue where to find him?"

"Last time was at some bar. A real shithole over in the slums."

"Okay, that's a start. Campini has a few months left before they pull the plug on this case. Get Georgie and then lie low. There's a light at the end of the tunnel."

"Gotta case the bar. Look out for the schmuck."

"We get him before they do and this all goes away, but we have to act fast. They have the resources and bodies to canvas the entire town and look for this guy. I'll try to keep up with them, but I'll need your help, too."

"We, huh?"

"Yes." Her toe traveled to his chin and scratched at the stubble. "I won't let anything happen to you."

Benny smiled. A real smile, not forced or for show, but genuine. *This woman loves me. Not sure why, but she does.* "I'll send Lorenzo now."

"Who?"

"My new driver." Benny nodded toward the shaded window. "Real mouthy prick, but a good earner. Takes orders and don't ask questions."

"Perfect. You think he can wait a few minutes."

Benny placed the empty glass on the glass coffee table and hunched over her. Their tongues flicked and the urge to slip his hands beneath the silk grew. *Business first. Play later*. He stood and headed for the door. "Soon. Let me get my guys set up for the day."

Shaw wrapped a hug around his waist from behind. "We're going to get through this, baby. It'll be me and you."

Benny turned, and they kissed again—a passionate exchange of saliva and sweat. Carnal. A symbol of love neither thought could exist but now did. A new beginning for them both.

"What do ya think of Barbados?" He swiped a fallen bang from her forehead. "Heard it's beautiful. Get past this shit and take a vacation."

"I'd like that, baby. I'll have to get a bathing suit."

"A few skimpy ones, I hope."

They kissed again and Benny pushed through the door —hankering for a hammock strewn between two coconut palms like a corny post card. A Mai Tai in one hand with Deb's ass in the other. A future shining, much like the sun over the white beach just days away. He could smell the salt breeze and hear the caws of birds flying overhead.

One little matter to worry about first, though. Find Georgie Silva and wipe the prick out. Then suntan lotion and sticky sand, baby.

CHAPTER EIGHTY

Lorenzo stood at the passenger door and opened it. Benny erased the small smile and barked, "Take me back to my house. I gotta picture there of this guy I need you to find. You know the biker joint on Kanter Highway?"

"Yeah." Lorenzo closed the door and swung around to the driver's side. Back in, he buckled the seat belt and shifted out of park. "Why, boss?"

"What I tell you about the questions?"

"Sorry. Just curious."

"I need you to find a guy there, okay? He'll show up sooner or later." Benny flipped open his phone and began plugging at it in exaggerated strikes.

"Mr. Purelli's order?"

"No, it's my fucking order." Benny's eyes widened, and he dropped the phone to his lap. "Just drive the car and do as you're told."

"No disrespect, Benny. I have other things to do."

"You telling me no?" The heavy brute shifted in the seat. His weight shook the idling Cadillac.

Lorenzo's hands rose, and he glared toward the open road ahead. "I've got other orders."

"You do what I say, capisce? Don't forget, I brought you into this business."

"My job can wait." His head drooped, and he guided the Cadillac onto Worthington Avenue. Benny adjusted the volume dial on the stereo.

He glanced to Benny, who now had the phone in his hands again, and turned in the opposite direction of his house. *Didn't see it.*

"And another thing, Lorenzo. New rule, when you're driving me, you don't speak unless I tell you to." Benny glanced out the window, a bewildered expression crossing his face. "You high or something? My house is back there. I told—"

"Sorry. I have to make a stop first."

"Where do you get the balls?"

"It'll only take a minute."

Lorenzo pulled the Cadillac into a backstreet entryway to an abandoned building and angled behind a privacy fence. The rear bumper extended a bit beyond the wall cover. He shifted into park and Lorenzo dropped his left hand beneath the side of his seat.

The pistol snagged onto the track of the chair and required a forceful tug. *Goddamn silencer.*

"You gotta lot of nerve, Lorenzo. You need an ass-whipping. Don't forget who the fuck I am."

"I need Richie's number."

"For what?"

"Orders are orders, boss. The number." Lorenzo brought the gun up. It trembled for a moment. *It's your time now.* He focused on the weapon, willing it to stifle and aim true. It did.

"Hey, take it easy. I'm just busting your balls. It's in my phone. Put the piece down."

"Sorry, boss."

"For what?"

"Give me the phone." The barrel of the gun rose to Benny's chest. "It's in your shirt pocket. Nothing stupid."

"Okay, okay." Benny complied and tossed the phone to Lorenzo then dropped his hand back to his lap.

Lorenzo noticed, aware of the Luger snug on Benny's hip. *Don't make this difficult.*

"Take it easy." Benny wore the face of a priest. Solemn but in control. He'd played the game a long time. "Put the gun away."

"Sorry, boss. I got orders this morning."

"I give the orders."

"Not anymore. What's that you always say?" Lorenzo kept the gun stable and the other hand's index finger jabbed at his temple. "Chain of command. I outrank you now."

"That slick son-of-a-bitch." Benny's round face whitened. An exhalation escaped from him, the sound like a ball deflating. "He's gonna whack me?"

"I'm sorry, boss. It brings me no pleasure." Lorenzo steadied the gun, fixing the barrel between Benny's furring eyebrows.

"Take it easy, take it easy." Pushing back to the inside panel of the door, Benny's hands climbed the air like he ascended an invisible ladder.

"I know you have the pistol on your left side. Don't think about it. For once, I need you to stop talking and listen, *capisce*."

"Yeah. Whatever you say." Benny reached into his waistband.

"By the handle. Don't try anything dumb or this will be painful."

Benny removed the Luger while holding his other hand up. He placed it on the console, grip facing forward.

Lorenzo snatched the gun and tossed it to the floorboard on his side. "My orders are to handle a problem. You're a problem, Benny. Too many mistakes."

"What mistakes?"

"Sonny. Richie. Your little cop girlfriend."

"Let me talk to him. I can straighten this out."

"Sorry, boss. He's got eyes and ears everywhere. This whole rap depends on you. You're the silver bullet. The one man with the knowledge." A pinging flare of pain crept across Lorenzo's back. The gun in his hand felt like it gained twenty pounds. He relaxed and propped the pistol on the center console. "If you start talking, we're in trouble. I'm not saying you would, Benny, but—"

"Orders are orders." Benny clasped his hands in his lap. "After everything I've done for him."

"Some sooner than others. Some more violent than others. But, in this business, we all check out." Lorenzo traced the contours of Benny's face with the gun. Steady and straight. No apprehension.

"So, this is how it ends? What are you waiting for? Do it."

"Sorry, boss. Mr. Purelli has a great deal of respect for you. He just wants to know if there are any unknown issues out there. Anything at all. Talk and it'll be one shot to the temple." Lorenzo lowered the gun and aimed at Benny's gut. "Stay zipped, it's three to the belly. It'll take twenty minutes. A painful twenty."

"I don't know anything else. Pull it."

"What about your lady friend?"

Dead-panned with eyes of fire, Benny said nothing and straightened the tight jacket. His gold cuff links reflected in the window, sending a light sheen down the glass. "Do what ya gotta do."

Lorenzo exhaled then pulled the trigger.

Pop.

The nine-millimeter slug crashed into Benny's stomach, sending quakes of flesh gyrating. His hand dropped to the wound in a vain attempt to pause the damage and he hissed with light gurgles, a foreign sound Lorenzo would remember forever.

The wound widened. Blood and chunks of flesh poured like mashed meatballs boiling in dark tomato sauce.

Lorenzo fired again.

Pop.

The gallbladder exploded, and this pain drove Benny's shoulders forward. The force knocked him toward the glove box of the Cadillac. Red chunks splattered the dash and windshield like a sadistic Rorschach test.

The silenced Glock 19 delivered its third round.

Pop.

Wheezes became muffled shrieks as Benny's throat expanded, overflowing with waste.

"It's funny. Never thought in a million years I'd be doing this." Lorenzo's head hit the backrest. Benny, fading now, opened his mouth to speak. Dark sludge dripped from his lips, painting his chin in streaks like warrior paint of the Indians.

"We've been doing this a long time, boss. I always wanted to move up the ranks. I figured if I could keep earning and prove my loyalty, the opportunity would present itself." Lorenzo reached across the console and sifted through Benny's suit pocket. He pulled the pack of cigarettes out and flipped the top open. "But when Mr. Purelli sent for me today, I couldn't believe my ears."

Hollow moans escaped from the dying man. A sorrowful and pathetic plea for one more chance to breathe clean air, smell pasta steaming on a plate or feel the wetness of a kiss.

Lorenzo lit the cigarette and cocked his head, resting his elbow on the console. "But then I remembered something you said a long time ago. This business is about colors. Red and green."

He tapped a button on the armrest of the door. The window lowered, and Benny's head dropped over the opening, obscuring all but a reddened chin. The gurgling sound intensified. A drawn-out raspy hiss followed. Benny's dying breaths.

"If it's any consolation, I didn't want this. And I'll do you a solid. Mr. Purelli doesn't need to know. It'll be our little secret, boss." Lorenzo tucked the barrel of the Glock beneath Benny's chin. "No more pain, my friend."

Pop.

He got out and circled to the ass of the Cadillac. He dragged the cigarette hard and flicked it across the gravel of the empty alley.

With a cautious glance to each side, he popped the trunk.

A plastic bag from the local hardware store contained the "clean" items. Putty, a brush, a bundle of rags and a small can of black paint.

Some bullets had passed through Benny and the door. He scooped out some painter putty and filled the holes then slathered the raw mess black. The rags caught the remnants of Benny's brains in their mesh grip. Crude and sloppy, but it didn't matter. *The prized Cadillac isn't entering a fucking auto show, now is it?*

Get it to Tom's Salvage and Tow undetected, the order had been. Five-thousand dollars later, the Cadillac and Benny would be reduced to a cube the size of a mini-fridge and loaded on a barge headed to China. On the way, after another greasy hand got paid, the container would slip off the ship and Benny Bianchi would literally sleep with the fishes. *It's like a bad movie. Ha.*

Lorenzo bagged the tools of treachery and tossed them in the trunk. He climbed in and tapped the window button. It rose beneath the weight of Benny's head, splashing dark chunks of what was once a criminal mastermind throughout the interior. Pristine leather drenched. Waxed woodgrain paneling stained. Now a hearse, the Cadillac shifted to drive and nosed toward Kanter Highway.

Benny's corpse swayed as the car changed lanes, bobbing and weaving like a fresh boxer in the first round. Lorenzo changed the news talk radio to catch the final minute of Billy Joel's *Innocent Man.*

"Sorry, boss. Bad joke."

CHAPTER EIGHTY-ONE

December 7th - 7:57 A.M.

Vietta slapped the plastic box with two interlocking tabs to the coffee table. He unclipped the latches and opened the case. He and Earl from Gold's Guns haggled about the price of the FNS for a minute or two ten days ago. Since he'd strutted out of the shop, very little else had crossed his mind.

The previous nine days were spent training, though the motive for such back-breaking work remained elusive. Since Ruby's murder, the urge to reenter the circuit had lessened with each day. Sweating and straining now offered a distraction from the guilt and shame, but an actual fight in the ring seemed impossible.

Marty offered the cot after the diner massacre and he accepted. Facing well-to-do parents, and looking into the face of a younger version of the angel he lost, proved too fresh a wound to heal. A festering and incurable open seam.

For nine days he slept at the gym, awaiting his purchase. Outside of Marty's, a shanty rodeo bar's music played like a soundtrack. On a few occasions, fights broke out and the reflection of police red and blues flashed in the small window above Marty's desk.

There was something about the way calamity aided sleep and halted the mind from wandering. Nomadic thoughts were unnecessary and often led to mistakes. Thunderstorm would make no more of those.

On this morning, the tenth day, Timothy sat in the quaint Belleview farmhouse fenced in by fresh seedlings of pepper plants, marveling at the sleek FNS - 9C compact 9mm semi-automatic pistol. The Visa had struggled to handle the purchase. After a box of ammo and three targets, a credit line of twelve dollars remained.

Maybe a Big Mac and fries later? It was worth it.

This gun held more power and might than clenched hands or lucid minds could ever possess. In a millisecond, it could change lives. *No, it would change lives.*

Admiring its tan grip and hammer forged stainless steel barrel, Timothy loaded twelve bullets into the magazine. The last few required a staunching effort and his hand throbbed after completing the job.

Twelve was excessive, but so was the hatred.

He pushed the mag into place and racked the slide. Earl's lesson this morning proved to be worth the extra twenty bucks and eighteen minutes of political banter.

With a flick of two recessed knobs on the top of the grip, a bullet jumped from the chamber. It landed on the coffee table with a loud thud. The rogue slug rolled beneath the table and Timothy reached with the scarred hand to secure it.

The television mounted to the living room wall flashed white and the melodic score teased a juicy morning story.

The news anchor, a pretty short-haired brunette in a burgundy jacket, grasped papers in delicate and manicured hands. She began:

Shocking news today.

CHAPTER EIGHTY-TWO

December 7th - 7:57 A.M.

Richie sat in the dank living room of the apartment. Rancid stenches, the remnants of week-old take out plates and unwashed linen, clung in the air like a fog.

A cold can of beans served as breakfast, though driving the soupy legumes downward had taken patience and discipline. The stomach wasn't built for such a nerve wracking and sodium filled combination. It could have been kerosene, and he'd have been none the wiser. On the television, commercials for cleaning products stacked one after the other, and Richie kept checking the oven clock. Three minutes until the morning news.

The previous nine days had yielded little excitement—the recollection a collage of tense moments and droll hiding spots.

After the police station, Richie made calls. Busy tones and automated voicemails became a lethargic lullaby of anguish and anxiety. Uncertain if the apartment was free of the law, he hitched a ride to the farm in search of Joe. His truck left fresh exit tracks in the dirt driveway and the barn's door stood wide.

A call to Knuckles Up ended with a robot prompting a message after the beep. Alone and afraid, the ghosts opened the vault. The chance of sleep, wherever it may be, a moot point.

The next morning, a call to Benny went unanswered. The day after, too. Hope that Purelli would reach out faded as the days passed. *Something* had happened, and it was consuming—an annoying tick in the spine like a reachable itch that couldn't be tamed. Then, the ghosts. *The fucking ghosts.*

Benny's disappearing act spelled trouble. Not since Richie had met the guy was there ever a day the two had not spoken. Now silence, a chilling and ominous quiet. A warning. Ridgemont Cove held little appeal. Benny remained mute, Joe didn't return calls, and Purelli hadn't reached out once.

So much for loyalty, right? One cop asks one question and the gypsies close up the tents and vanish into a cyclone of dust.

During the third day of this self-imposed vacation, Richie stumbled across an article depicting the shootings at the diner. *Two Dead in Suspected Gangland Slaying.*

Quotes in the story came from Ms. May, so for the moment, she remained intact and breathing.

The others? The newspaper didn't release names of the dead, but it offered solace for the "innocent lives" engulfed by the flames of tyrannical greed.

As the only civilian there besides Ms. May, Richie presumed Ruby had been the one engulfed.

Richie figured the other victim was Sonny, but an unlucky passerby may have been caught in the gunfire.

Either way, blood had flown. Vengeance enacted. Hatred bloomed.

Seven days of motel fees and meals wreaked havoc on Richie's finances. Advances of cash were bountiful once. Thick wads of green had been the reason it all started.

Make the dough. Save your mom. Do something with your life.

But nearing the ninth day of his relocation, wrinkled business cards and useless plastic filled the slots of his wallet. No choice but to head home.

He'd come back to Ridgemont Cove a few hours ago and ventured over to Knuckles Up. A deadbolt locked into place over the door's dual exterior handles shined in the sun's early fight. A handwritten sign hung from the doorknob. It read *Closed*.

Richie sat on the curb waiting for a glimpse of Joe's truck. Nothing. Subsequent calls ended in the robotic voicemail, though the gym phone's dull ring penetrated the locked entrance door. No movement from within.

From there Richie walked to Ms. May's Diner. A construction crew replaced windows and plastered gouging holes pocking the window trim. The sign in the window indicated a reopening was "tentatively set" for early December.

Richie then backtracked through the southern entrance of The Trails. The zombies glared with dull eyes. Squatters Row bounced with an early afternoon buzz. Fixes had. Money exchanged. Souls, if you could call them so, expiring and reincarnating in the bodies of people once dear but now a faded memory. Through the squalor, Richie pushed toward the apartment. Eyes looked down from balconies and hidden shades. With no strength to prepare a façade of invincibility, he let their stares pierce through. Without Joe,

Benny, and indirectly, Purelli, picking a fight seemed to be a losing proposition.

The boxing shit. It's a pipedream. A fantasy. *Maybe mom was right all along.*

A stack of newspapers piled against the apartment door. The key still worked.

Why wouldn't it, dumbass? Harold had sneered.

"Shut the fuck up," Richie responded to the voice in his head.

Though he'd never admit it, last night he cried himself to sleep. The ghosts had fun with that.

A flip of the light switch in the foyer produced a dim, yellow glow. Power meant an operating fridge. Breakfast would help. Unfortunately, the available edible food for consumption in the fridge was an unopened can of baked beans. Richie used a knife to slice the top open and took a seat in front of the television.

At eight o'clock, the familiar voice of Susan Teagan, a pretty news anchor for *Wake Up Ridgemont Cove,* appeared on the screen looking sexy in her burgundy jacket. Richie's impure fantasies halted, however, when she read from the papers on the desk.

Shocking news today.

CHAPTER EIGHTY-THREE

December 7th - 7:58 A.M.

Reese Campini stared at the familiar ceiling—a brown water mark shaped like a jagged sailboat a welcoming sight. The department's retirement party for one of the guys in the burglary division last night did a number on him this morning. The taste of margarita and sleep filled his mouth.

The last few hours of the shin-dig were a blur of half-cocked dance moves and slurred conversations. The extravagant spread of food had not been important at the time.

More margaritas please. I'll get a plate later.

Staring at the watermark with one eye still slumbering, the realization of too much courage and not enough sustenance added to the headache, already forceful and relenting.

A jabbing turn of the cement block, once known as his head, brought splinters of dull pain.

On his right, a woman slept. The covers draped from her torso down.

Dear God. Don't be Abbey. Anyone but that tramp. The guys would never let this one go.

Groggily, he turned. The pixels strengthened and gained definitiveness after a few exaggerated blinks. Stark black hair and tan, sun spotted shoulders.

Whew. Abbey's a blonde. Coffee skin. Wait a minute.

The faint scent of Chanel still traceable through the smell of sweat and dehydration lifted from the covers.

No way.

Three years had passed since they'd first met. Familiarity became flirting. Flirting led to sexual fantasies. With margarita still coating his throat and half-memories clogged by a massive headache, the fantasy existed in real-life.

Why didn't I eat last night? Jesus Christ, you got in, and you don't even remember it.

A droning sound on the nightstand interrupted the self-wallowing. The time was 7:59. The caller ID displayed *Taggert.*

"Hello." The word slid from his throat as if coated in wax.

"Turn on the news." The boss's voice, dry and rasped, seared Campini's eardrums. "Wake Up Ridgemont Cove".

Campini searched for help, hoping to all that was holy he'd remembered to stock a bottle of water. He opened the drawer.

Success. You smart bastard.

He chugged it. Saliva began its return and washed out the sawdust taste caught in his throat.

"Good morning, Captain."

"Good morning, detective. Turn the fucking news on."

He grabbed the remote from the nightstand and powered the television on. "What's this about?"

"Just watch and listen."

Campini searched through the channels and landed on

Susan Teagan wearing a stark, neatly pressed burgundy jacket.

She said:

Shocking news today. Police have confirmed the identity of the body found at Tom's Salvage and Tow. In a routine inspection three days ago, an odd smell was detected by a representative of an insurance adjuster. After further investigation, it was discovered that human remains were on the property. Initial reports have revealed the victim died of multiple gunshot wounds, and fingerprint identification has confirmed the man is Solano Underboss, Benny "Beans" Bianchi.

"Not good, hotshot," Alaina said. She'd risen in the bed and startled the open-mouthed Campini. The sheets clung to her bottom half, but her breasts lay bare and exposed.

Campini covered the mouthpiece of the phone. "How bad?"

"Bad. As in, done."

"Detective, you still there?" The coarse voice of Taggert cut into the earpiece.

"Yeah, Captain. Still here."

"My office. Now."

Campini tossed the phone to the bed. "Shit."

"I didn't know he'd been missing." Alaina covered her chest with the sheet and propped up the pillow scrunched against the headboard. "Did you?"

"Nah. Ever since Benussi's death, things have slowed. We've been on the hunt for Georgie." Campini scratched his cheek. The stubble of his two-day beard scraped his fingertips. "Not much activity from the Solanos. Figured Benny was hiding."

"This stings, Reese." Alaina glanced to the mirror on the

far wall. She smoothed hair strands jilted awry. "It's all on Frezza, now."

"Thought you said he was a dead end."

"We fight on. You said it yourself last night."

"I did?" Campini searched through the black mud filling his brain. Splotches of images from last night fought for clarity, but the headache and booze squelched any remembrance.

"Yeah. Benussi can't die for nothing. Frezza is all we have left."

Campini threw the sheets to the side. The smell of sweat and friction lifted from beneath the fabric. "I have to go."

He chugged mouthwash and threw on a sport coat and khakis. "Lock the door when you leave."

"So, we're not going to talk about—"

"Last night?" He swiped his keys from the bureau then slipped on his loafers from the party yesterday. "Later."

On a normal day, the commute from his apartment took the better part of twenty minutes. Today, he ignored menial things like stop signs and pedestrians. He reached the station in record time.

Barreling out of the Impala, he searched for relief.

A few ibuprofen and java would do the trick. Everyone these days had the magical hangover cure. Coconut water and cucumbers. Eggs and almond milk blended with cayenne pepper. Though young, Campini drank and medicated like the old-school. Steaming black coffee and two pills.

He stopped at the food truck in front of headquarters.

Jimmy offered a short gruff and held out the individual pack of medicine. Coffee steamed from a Styrofoam cup on the ledge of the bar.

"Bagel and cream cheese, right?"

"No time today. Keep the change." Reese flicked a five-dollar bill at the senile and half-blind man.

"I'll be damned."

"Be grateful, you old bastard."

Jimmy retorted with a quip, but Campini caught only the set-up and missed the punchline as he climbed the steps toward the door.

In the elevator, Benny's death report replayed in his mind. The squad had had a meeting just yesterday regarding the slim footage of the Solano underboss. Some assumed Benny skipped town and others believed foul play. Reese hoped for the former but believed the latter.

Confirmed now. Worst case scenario—kinda like banging the girl you've had crush on for three years and not remembering if you pounded it home like a porn star or lasted three seconds and splat a huge load into the sheets. Goddamn tequila.

He popped the ibuprofen and swallowed a large drought of the scalding black coffee. The burn ran the extent of his throat, masking the headache for a moment.

The elevator opened, and he swiped the key card. Behind the reception desk, Taggert's secretary spoke into the phone and waved a lazy finger toward the glass door. *Not good.*

He pushed through and meandered the hallway decorated in the portraits of former captains. Mustachioed, white and wrinkled men with eyes leering at his every step.

The current captain's door stood ajar and Campini poked through.

Behind the desk, Taggert sipped from a mug with RCPD etched into the front. "I'm sure you understand why you're here." The captain motioned for him to sit in the empty chair nearest him.

"I've got an idea, Captain." Campini sat, unbuttoned the sport coat and clasped his hands on the edge of the desk.

"Good. Here's the short version. We're ending Firecracker."

"Captain, I—"

Taggert's hand rose and shook. The other flipped through a stack of papers stapled into a file folder. "We can't justify the cost or manpower anymore."

He saw this coming but was still shocked the last twenty-three months were a colossal waste of energy. Of the five operations funded for the OCD, Firecracker had the most potential to hit pay dirt. Losing it in this fashion, with the finish line in sight, stung worse than the scalding coffee and massive margarita-induced hangover. "So, it's over?"

"Yeah. Bianchi's gone. I've read all about Georgie Silva and Richie Frezza. Dead ends, detective. We cannot spend the money or resources attempting to turn either. And if we could, it guarantees nothing. Benussi's surveillance is rock-solid against Bianchi. Flimsier than a used condom against Purelli."

"The bad guys win again."

"For now."

"I still have the other open ops. Maybe we can catch a break and link one to Purelli."

"No, Reese. The funding is being pulled completely."

"What?" The hangover vanished. The burning sensation in his throat evaporated. "What are you talking about?"

"OCD will be absorbed by Special Case Unit. They'll move forward with the investigations under their budget. You'll be reassigned to Homicide."

"I'm being demoted?"

"It's not a demotion. It's budgetary." Taggert smacked the pile of papers in front of him with a frown. "We can still pay your salary, but your crew will be reassigned. I want you on the Blonde case. You're a great detective. You can help us with it."

"What do I know about serial killers? I catch mobsters."

"You haven't caught anything, detective." Taggert's voice strengthened. "Solve the Blonde case, and then maybe, maybe, I'll consider you for SCU."

"We have an enormous amount of evidence on the entire Solano Crime Family. I just—"

"Let me stop you there. This is not a negotiation. Firecracker failed. I'm going to deal with the aftermath." He jabbed his thick thumb into his chest. "It's over. Report to Homicide."

"Benussi is dead for nothing. Purelli walks away clean, laughing in our fucking faces."

"This is a battle. The war isn't over. Nobody is untouchable. The intelligence Detective Benussi gathered will be used one day in a court of law to fry the bastard. It just won't be today."

"You're the boss." Defeated, Campini stood and brought his eyes to the window.

Belleview peeked from within the melded colors of landscape in the distance. Somewhere out there, Purelli started the day. Ordering murders. Advising logistics for drug deliveries and pick-ups. Extorting an old man like Jimmy.

The phone in his pocket buzzed flat.

Probably Alaina.

"If police work was good guys vs. bad guys, I'd have your back on this." Taggert's reflection in the window twiddled a pen in his hand. He then turned in his chair and began perusing a file folder. "You know there is so much more to it. We rely on money just like the criminals we chase. It's not fair, but it's true."

Reese's fierce stare continued through the window. *Just poke your head out for a second, you sack of shit. I know you're out there.*

"We're paid by the people to protect the people," Taggert continued, rising from the desk and saddling up shoulder to shoulder. "Purelli is just not a public concern. I'm sorry your case has to end. I am. God knows I've caught enough flack for it on my end."

"So, what's next?" The headache returned, but it wasn't the remnants of twelve margaritas. Shame swept through him. Utter failure. Each dry thump a reminder of unaccomplished goals and foolhardy promises broken.

"You'll be partnered with Deborah Shaw. She's been informed of this development as well."

"So, I'm just a badge on the street."

"It's not personal. You did your best, and sometimes, it isn't enough. Get to Homicide. It's a fresh start. Find your partner and solve the Blonde case. Clear?"

"Yes, sir." He could spend thirty more minutes pleading, but had no argument worth presenting.

In the elevator, he pressed the button for the lobby. The phone buzzed again, and he pulled it from his coat pocket.

The screen indicated a recorded voicemail. He clicked the replay button, and the automation stated, "You have one message."

Reese then heard:

It's Deborah Shaw. I won't be in the office today. I left an envelope in my mailbox at home. 3247 Sherry Street. It's for you because you're the only one who will do the right thing. At least, I hope that's true.

I know this doesn't make any sense. I have to be careful. I'm not sure how far or wide his reach goes. Taggert may be on the take. Hell, it may go higher. I don't know. If things were different, we'd make a good team, but this isn't going to play out, I guess. I was a good cop once. I made a choice and now I have to make another.

Anyway, I'm rambling now. I tend to when I'm scared. And, Reese, I am very scared. Just please pick up the envelope. It may be the one thing you need to end Firecracker. I hope it does. This town needs a change. You can be the one to do it.

CHAPTER EIGHTY-FOUR

Ten days ago, Deborah Shaw watched Benny get into the Cadillac and drive off with Lorenzo. It was the last time they touched. Calls weren't returned. And before the broadcast, she knew her poor Benny was gone, though accepting it proved to be straining.

Needling hope stirred within her. It burrowed deep like a mole and gnawed. There was a chance.

Then, the stupid bitch Susan Teagan read from a stack of papers. Calm and emotionless, the cunt told her poor Benny died. *It can't be. Barbados and Bacardi were right around the corner.*

When Teagan shuffled the papers and began some benign report on a judge caught fucking a schoolgirl, the sadness set in. Then the tears. So many tears.

While they devised a plan to keep Benny out of the electric chair, Purelli planned an execution of his own.

He's always one step ahead, Benny had said on more than one occasion.

How could they have not seen it?

Trust and honor, maybe? That didn't exist in a world of

monsters, even though Benny was one of them. Backstabbers were the most likely to be stabbed.

We should have seen it coming.

The real threat Purelli had to worry about was Benny. Getting to Georgie and silencing Frezza meant little to the Don. *Always one step ahead.* Just kill your most trusted underling without as much as a tear. *Loyalty? No, savagery.* Barbaric monsters without remorse.

Poor Benny.

Shaw wiped a few straggling tears and began writing. She addressed the first letter to her mother Beverly. It expressed gratitude in peaceful and eloquent cursive strokes. Deborah recalled how the men of the family scoffed at the notion of a woman joining the police force. Beverly Shaw told little Deborah to ignore the naysayers.

Be stronger than the critics and humbler than the supporters, she'd said.

Shaw finished the letter with the quote and signed it, *Lil' Deb, your shining star.*

Her attorney Cecil Banks received the second letter. Within these pages, Shaw wrote her Last Will and Testament. All belongings would be divided between remaining family members. With no children or husband, the majority of assets would go to Beverly. Her father, a degenerate gambler who chugged beer from morning to night, would receive a small sum to help liquidate outstanding debt. The small portion allotted couldn't cover it all, but as Shaw saw it, would be a kind final gesture. The man did, after all, create her.

The third letter, a painstaking, emotional address to Reese Campini, came last. Though vested completely with the darker side of Ridgemont Cove, she still respected the work of hard-nosed and ambitious detectives. This, among other compliments, built the first page.

It took four full subsequent pages to describe her tumultuous liaison with Benny "Beans" Bianchi. It began with their first meeting in a dark, seedy bar in Sharpton. *No, he wasn't the most handsome or dashing man to strut through a bar, but the charisma and bravado had been intoxicating,* she wrote.

She recounted, at length, their conversations.

Tight-lipped at first, the relationship blossomed, and Benny's trust grew. Writing this part required discipline and a few extra glasses of wine.

Also, she revealed the most recent criminal activity Benny was privy to. Admitting her knowledge did not encompass all "Beans" involved himself in, Shaw felt Campini could use any and all intel at his disposal.

The Irish murdered Detective James Benussi and Ruby Miller in a counterattack related to the new kid Richie. In the pages, she detailed the murders of Harold Remnick and Bryce O'Leary.

Purelli would look to clean up all other messes, and as a liability, a murder contract had been ordered for her, no doubt.

I will not go by his hand, she wrote, scribbling in erratic swoops now as the wine worked its magic.

A few paragraphs pieced together a pattern of behavior Purelli displayed.

Her writing began to deteriorate, the letters melding into splotches. *You're probably aware of it, but I figured being honest, clear and forthcoming is something you deserve.* She poured a new glass of red.

The final paragraph discussed Lorenzo, the new driver, and revealed he was the last person she'd seen with Benny.

She jotted hard during this portion, ripping a hole through the sheet.

Anger bubbled as she penned the man's name.

The closing lines pleaded with Reese to look into the driver, the final piece of the puzzle. *Purelli's not invincible. Find the right coward to flip. Lorenzo can corroborate much of the evidence Benussi collected. If you want Purelli, that murderous asshole is the key.*

With the letters sealed, and Campini's tucked into the mailbox of 3247 Sherry Street, she dialed her new partner, but the call went to voicemail.

She placed a red wicker chair under the dangling rope. She purchased it for a tree trimming job a few months back.

Lee Clark, a heavyset neighbor with a pot belly and penchant for wearing tank-tops, had wrapped the thick branches and guided them away from the house. His brother Rodney then cut them. The green stains splashed into the rope when the tree branches sliced open and were still ingrained in the thick twist of the twine.

The rope is too long.

She stood on the chair and grabbed the lifeless end. Shaw ran the stretch of the rope through the small slat in the cross beam of the loft. A crude fashioning, but the rope itself would not be the focus later on.

With a few last drops of Chianti, she scanned her living room and brought the glass up for a final sip. *Chores finished.*

Shaw steadied on the chair and turned toward the front door. She encircled her neck with the noose. The loop tightened and the snug scratch of the line tickled.

Pleasant memories are savored. Her mother's words created a collage in her mind. Standing on the chair with a strangling rope, Shaw tried to recover the best memory locked away.

A childhood sleepover?

Thanksgiving dinner when Uncle Mike got drunk and dropped the bird right before the family sat down at their plates.

Jonathan Winslow cupping her breast at the varsity football game and licking her neck—the first time she'd been moist from a man's touch.

What about graduation of the Academy when daddy saw the dream realized?

Strong and important memories.

Which should be last?

Her feet shuffled off the chair. Benny Bianchi appeared with a smile.

CHAPTER EIGHTY-FIVE

He reached Shaw's house at ten in the morning after navigating through a few traffic stalls. The eerie voicemail from the elevator resounded louder in his head than the rock station blaring through the speakers.

I was a good cop once. This town needs a change. You can be the one to do it.

He parked the Impala in the driveway behind Shaw's state issued cruiser and grabbed the thick envelope from the mailbox. Before opening it, he knocked on the front door and waited with an occasional glance around the neighborhood.

Anybody would do. A nosy neighbor. Dog walker. The fucking postman.

People tended to talk, and if anybody could provide information, it would be helpful. *Nothing.* A crypt of expensive houses and manicured lawns.

He ran through the call logs of his phone and dialed Shaw. *Nothing.*

Another violent knock jilted the doorknob. *Nothing.*

Dropping from the stoop, he walked the perimeter of

the house. All windows were locked with blinds drawn and closed. A side gate led to a small backyard, but the door inside the small screen enclosure refused to budge, its inner latch snug in its home.

He dialed Shaw again.

"C'mon. Pick up the phone." He spoke to the sky with little conviction. Heavy air and silence simmered. "Pick up!"

It rang dully and then reverted to the automated voice-mail message.

Back in the Impala, he ripped the envelope to find a stack of notebook paper trifolded. At first glance, it appeared to be the nonsensical rambling of a jilted lover. But then the names and descriptions connected, and the words formed clean sentences presenting a brave confession of Shaw dancing on both sides of the law. Admittance of treason, though in some way, a love letter suited for the Lifetime channel.

He wanted to despise the traitor, a saboteur of many cases, including Firecracker. But the words were sharp claws, digging and maiming splinters.

Pain lifted from the notebook paper and he understood Shaw's complete and utter despair. Its energy lived within each stroke of cursive. Course spots on the paper caught his attention. Dried wet areas. *Tears*.

After finishing the letter, he unhooked the handheld radio from the dashboard. "Dispatch, I need a bus and back up to 3247 Sherry Street."

He put the letter back into the envelope and pushed it behind some other documents in the glove box. The words were too valuable to share just yet. He flicked the button of his holster and freed the service revolver then sidestepped to the front door. Now the occasional glances were fearful and stern.

A gun fight would be surprising, but years of training programmed all cops to assume the worst.

An old lady on the bus struggling to rise and ring the bell is a drug dealer. The girl on the pink bike with streamers flailing in the wind just robbed the gas station. Some four-eyed geeks in the library, anonymous and plain faces, researched ways to locate arsenic.

Assume the worst.

Stupid, sure, but expectations kept cops alive. In this case, the expectation was death, and after a heavy kick through Shaw's door, that's what he found.

CHAPTER EIGHTY-SIX

The first snow of the season fell in thin clusters this Thursday afternoon. Through the window, Joe's pickup caught the white sprouts and glistened. "I've made up my mind."

"Wisconsin?"

"Yeah. Wisconsin." Joe filled the sweating glass with Jim Beam and shook the ice.

"I guess you got your reasons. Just never thought you'd leave this place." Marty's thick tenor poured from a frown.

"I've had enough of *this* place. It's too dangerous."

"Why? The Solanos?"

"Benny's dead." Joe drank again, gulping. "Just a matter of time before they knock on my door. I've spent a lifetime paying for my mistakes. As soon as it's behind me, I make one more, old friend."

"What would they do?"

Joe limped toward the window. The bar across the street sat dormant, its tinted windows reflecting the sun's descending crawl. Another gulp from the glass sent fire down his throat. "I know a lot more than I should, Marty. It's *who* I know."

"The kid?"

He didn't respond and didn't have to. Although Marty was a whack-job and struggling with post-traumatic stress disorder, more than a few marbles bounced around up there. Joe pulled the rolled papers from his pocket and laid them on the edge of the sparring ring. "It's yours if you want it."

"I don't think I can afford it. Besides, I've got my own gym right here. Why would I need two?"

"Don't worry about the money. I'll sign it over to you for pennies on the dollar. I've got a solid base of customers. You'll just need to hire someone to run the day-to-day. It's a gift more than anything."

"I appreciate the generosity, but who would I hire?"

"That's the beauty of it. Whoever you want. The place is either yours or I sell it. I'd rather give it you."

"Can I think about it?" Marty flipped through a few pages. "A second location could beef up the business checking account, but this is your legacy."

"I'd rather forget it all." Joe finished the remaining drops of bourbon with another glance outside. Gravel spun beneath tires and the Jeep popped into view. "I'm hitting the road in a week or less."

Timothy exited the Jeep and traveled the stone walkway clutching a small canvas bag. The door swung open a moment later and daylight raped the gym's dark shroud.

"Marty? You here?"

"Timbo?" He stood from the ring's ledge in a shake. "What's going on?"

Timothy nodded to Joe who extended a hand.

"Hey," the young fighter said with a firm grip, "glad you're both here. I can use some help on something. What's this all about?" He pointed to the papers on the ring and then dropped the canvas bag to the floor.

"Joe's selling Knuckles Up," Marty said.

"Really?"

"It's time to move on, Thunderstorm." Joe said. "What's in the bag?"

"A gun." He knelt and unzipped the duffel. Joe recognized the shape of the casing being lifted from it.

"You bought a gun?" Marty's teeth clenched and his brows arched. He reached for the bottle.

"Yeah. I was hoping you could show me how to shoot." Timothy pulled the gun from its plastic case. "I figure you still got the skills. Maybe hold off on the bourbon."

"Tell me you're not thinking of doing something stupid." Joe took the pistol in his hand and slid the rack.

"It's protection only." Timothy's lie died in the air, and Joe didn't bite. "You see the news yesterday?"

"Yeah." Joe handed the gun to the youngster then hobbled past.

"That why you in a rush to get out of here?"

"It's part of it." Joe motioned for a refill from Marty. He shook the bourbon in the ice then sipped.

"Well, I can't just leave." Timothy wiped the gun with his sleeve and placed it back in its case. "My life is here. My daughter is here. If they come for me, at least I'll have a chance."

Joe fought the sarcastic comment bubbling within his throat. If they wanted Vietta dead, the little pistol wasn't going to matter. He stood with cane in hand and shot a frown to his old war buddy.

"I can show him a thing or two," Marty said with a nod. "It'll be safe."

Joe finished the whiskey and slammed the cup down on the canvas of the sparring ring. "You boys have fun. I'm hitting the road."

"Hey," Marty called after him, "if I buy your gym, can I rename it?"

Joe turned with a smile. "Sure. If you buy it, do whatever the hell you want. What's on your mind?"

"I was thinking Thunderstorm Title Boxing."

Timothy looked up from the duffel bag. "Huh?"

"You wanna job, Timbo?"

"It's gotta nice ring to it." Joe opened the door. "Let me know. Like I said, it needs to happen fast."

Back in the old pickup, Joe cranked the engine and fiddled with the heater. He glanced back at the gym. Maybe Marty's marbles had escaped and rolled out. Death knocked on Timothy "Thunderstorm" Vietta's door. Pistol or not, Purelli was coming for him.

Coming for us all.

CHAPTER EIGHTY-SEVEN

The news of two days ago debilitated him. The woman on the television spoke the words in clear, robotic phrases, but Richie's mind struggled to connect the syllables.

Benny is dead? No. No way. It's a mistake.

Disbelief became reality after the second news cycle kicked in. Then, unsure why, Richie locked the exterior doors of the apartment.

This morning, for the first time in a month, his mother's bedroom door opened, and Richie sequestered within it, sitting in the far corner. From this position, the window Georgie Silva escaped from mocked him.

Who would have killed Benny? A rush of lightheadedness filled Richie's vision with stars. *The Irish?*

"*Who else?*" Cranswell asked.

Richie's head shook. *But if they were responsible, why was the body found at Tom's Salvage and Tow?*

Because we're smart. O'Leary took the stage now. The top of his head flapped up and down with the words, revealing a pulsing and leaking brain.

No, Benny's death was an inside job. Richie stood, and

he paced, his legs trudging the floor. *If Benny Bianchi is expendable, what am I?*

A dead man. Harold shoved O'Leary from the vault and raised his arms. *Just like me, pal.*

It doesn't make sense. "It doesn't make sense." Richie peered through the window. A trio of zombies trekked toward the Row. *Why kill Benny?*

Loose ends. O'Leary's accented voice simmered within.

"No." Richie's voice shook him from the invisible conversation with the ghosts. He spoke to his reflection in the window. "Benny would have fixed this. Purelli wouldn't take him out. It must be the Irish. Yeah, payback tenfold for O'Leary."

With eyes puffy and thick like wet cement, he backed away and slid on the bed. The scent of his mother lived on the sheets and he nestled into the pile, inhaling the memory.

A loud knock at the front door startled him. He started toward the window. *A clean getaway.*

Another booming knock.

"Open up, Richie."

Tiptoeing through the living room, he reached the foyer window and drew the vertical blinds back an inch. Through the slit, he could make out the profile of a short, balding Italian man. The trademark penny loafers solidified the identification.

"Richie, I know you're in there. Open the fucking door." Purelli's puppet Lorenzo knocked again.

He returned the blinds and measured the options.

Run and live today.

Hear Lorenzo out. Maybe I've got it all wrong?

Or, I answer the door and eat a bullet. Dead at nineteen with forty-three dollars in my pocket.

"We gotta talk." Another thick pounding of the door shook the hinges inside.

Richie unlocked the door and propped it open, ensuring the eye hook fastened snug. At the time of installation a few years back, the extra lock served as a security measure. Mom felt safer. Now, assuming a flimsy hook screwed into cheap plasterboard served any real purpose seemed childish and immature.

"What's going on, Lorenzo?"

"Get dressed. I'll be in the car."

"Where are we going?"

"Get dressed, kid. I'll explain on the way. We're late." Lorenzo retreated to an unfamiliar black car snuggled to the curb. Richie closed the door and slumped to the floor.

Better get to it. Don't want to keep the boss waiting, Roger Cranswell said.

"I don't take orders from you!" The yell resounded within the foyer, anxiety seizing through his body in step with the vibrations bouncing off the walls.

I believe he's cracking up, Harold said. *Matter of time now. Hey, I got an idea. Run. Ha. Run through the window, little boy. Run, Run, Run.*

"Shut up. You don't exist. I'm in control. I'm in control." The vault closed but the murmurs of the dead permeated within Richie's mind.

They were talking. Mocking. Planning their escape and jubilation, they waited for the final bullet to end it all.

"Not today." He yelled to the empty apartment. "I'm not done yet. You hear me, you sick fucks! I'm not done yet."

Slithering up the wall, he shuffled back toward the bedroom. He obeyed orders like a good soldier and threw on some clothes.

Wear black, huh. O'Leary cackled with glee, the mouth of his half-head widening.

Richie ignored the slight in his mind and gripped the doorknob. *I'm in control.* He slammed the door behind him and jumped the steps.

"Hop in." Lorenzo leaned over in his seat and nudged the passenger door open. "On a time crunch here."

"Let's go." Richie slid in, his eyes on Purelli's puppet and hands balled in anticipation. *One wrong move, I'll break your fucking face.*

"The boss is waiting." Lorenzo shifted to drive and pulled out in front of a delivery van trolling by.

"The Tango, then? Any idea what this is about?"

"Nope." He flipped the radio dial. The melody of violins and harps filled the car.

Ten minutes later, they pulled into the back-parking lot of the restaurant. Lorenzo parked and killed the volume. "He's upstairs."

"What am I walking into?" Richie hoped the relationship he'd built with Lorenzo may have created some level of trust. After all, the O'Leary hit was the product of both of their efforts. Murder, like sex, connected participants beyond basic cordiality. "I'm okay, right?"

"Get out of the car and go talk to the man. We all got orders. I followed mine, so you obey yours."

He studied Lorenzo's eyes in hopes of uncovering something, anything.

"You waiting for an invitation, kid? Go."

Richie popped the car door open and scaled the twisting steps leading to the upper level. He entered the hallway through the back-service door and stopped dead at the threshold. An unfamiliar man posted in a chair from the lounge downstairs leaned against the door of Purelli's office.

"You, Frezza?" The goon said, half asking but seemingly aware of his name, regardless. He stood, revealing a full five inches hidden from his sitting posture.

"Yeah."

"Lift your shirt and take off your shoes."

"I'm not wearing a wire."

"I'm sure you're not. Nobody would be that stupid. Lift your shirt and take off your shoes."

Richie obeyed, and after a quick rummaging and pat down, the man twisted the door handle. "He's waiting for you."

Purelli lounged behind the desk. A lit cigarette jabbed between his fingers snaked smoke in thin twirling tornadoes.

"Sir?" Richie stood in the doorway, frozen.

"Good morning. Please, come in. Take a seat."

Richie complied, measuring his steps into the room, as if mines covered the floor. He sat on the couch, peering through the blanket of smoke obscuring most of Purelli's face.

"Sorry about the search out there." He pointed to the door. "You can never be too careful. And believe me, these are uncertain times."

"I understand."

"Good." Purelli dragged again and blew rings to the air. They died and climbed like phantoms in a horror film. "Tell me, how have things been?"

"Honestly, a little, well, uncertain." Richie slumped.

"Yes. Much has happened. I understand you spoke to the police a few weeks back."

Richie's posture stiffened like a board had been nailed into his spine. "I didn't say anything. You have my word. I would never—"

"I trust you, son. I cannot say the same for others, but you, I believe you. What did the police ask?"

Richie paused before answering, unsure of complete honesty's benefits. "A bunch of questions."

"Such as?"

"About O'Leary. They also showed me some photos and surveillance logs."

Purelli smashed the cigarette into the geode ash tray. He pushed out from the desk and joined Richie on the couch. With legs crossed and hands clasped, he resembled a grandpa on vacation more than a demon from Ridgemont Cove's bowels. "What were these surveillance logs about?"

"Well—" Richie paused, realizing his proximity to Purelli. A rash of shivers traveled his arms. "They had pictures of Sonny. Only, it wasn't him. They said Sonny's real name is James Benussi, and he's an undercover cop. Is that true?"

"We had our suspicions. What else did they say?"

Richie flung both hands in the air. "If I didn't cooperate, they'd come after me, but I would never talk, Mr. Purelli."

"I know. If you had, we would not be sitting here right now." Purelli pat Richie's knee. "So, they just let you go?"

"Kinda. I sat in a room for a while. Then out of nowhere, this lady cop, Shaw I think her name was, comes in and releases me. I don't know what happened. After all the talk about the things they had on me, they let me walk out. As soon as I was free, I called Benny, but he never answered."

"You did very good, Richie."

"What about Sonny? Where is he?"

"He's dead."

"Dead?"

"You were not aware? Yes, as I said, much has

happened. He and a waitress were killed in the diner attack."

Richie remembered the newspapers from hotel hopping in Belleview. He'd assumed Sonny was killed, but the confirmation was a clean and punishing uppercut. With Sonny and Benny no longer breathing, Richie represented the sole survivor from the crew. *I should have jumped through the window when I had the chance.*

"It's a terrible thing about the girl," Purelli continued, the trite black eyes shimmering beneath the gold-rimmed glasses. "But Sonny's death is a gift."

"How so?"

"You know what makes the rat such a vile creature, Richie?"

Accustomed to the mobsters' overuse of rhetorical questions, he awaited the answer.

"They have been known to carry up to 50 different diseases at one time. One bite, and you can contract typhus and meningitis." Purelli's nose scrunched as if the stench of a rotting corpse invaded the room. "But what's worse, they sneak out of their little hole and bite you while you sleep." He mimicked a snapping jaw with his fingers. "There is no room for them in this world. They are disgusting, dishonorable little pests. Sonny was a rat. A lowly, disgusting rat. I'm glad the Irish killed him."

"The Irish?"

"We believe so."

"And what about, um, Benny?"

"The Irish as well. Benny was a good man. We will find out what happened and plan accordingly."

Richie shifted in the seat, calculating the next words. "Why Benny? Doesn't make sense." Richie hoped the casual question didn't offend.

"They took it too far. Dishonorable creatures. No better than a rat. Now, we must regroup. And our vengeance, will not be one or two men. It will be an extermination."

Richie's head filled with the swirl of ghosts. The full vault a painful and continuous headache. A war would prove to be too much. "Mr. Purelli, the cops are watching me. I'm sure of it. They're gonna come sooner than later."

"Law enforcement is a concern every day. Their prodding does not change the direction of this family. A family you are part of. Benny is gone. Lorenzo will take his place. And you, my young friend, will be a Solano soldier. When the war is over, and it will end with our victory, you will be welcomed into this thing of ours."

"I'm just a boxer. It's all I've ever wanted."

"You are so much more. I have plans for this organization. For you. This is a violent business. To earn your stripes, you need to draw blood." Purelli's hand tapped Richie's knee. "Are you ready to realize how great you can be?"

CHAPTER EIGHTY-EIGHT

Two days ago, Campini kicked in the door and discovered Deborah Shaw sagging from a thick triple-twine rope like a sordid ornament.

Death didn't shock him. Corpses strewn throughout the streets of Ridgemont Cove acted as rules and not exceptions. Wide bullet wounds, deep stabs revealing cream-colored bone fragment and poisonings blotting the white from protuberant eyes made up an average Friday. All seen and investigated. *It's the job.*

Shaw, however, was different. "A horrific experience," medical examiner Jenny Kasper had commented with narrow eyes and a soft tongue.

The fall from the chair had not snapped the neck. In many hangings and executions of the past, a long drop created enough momentum to ensure a cervical fracture. When that happened, the hanged person would be rendered unconscious and the resulting quick death felt dignified. Unfortunately for Shaw, this had not been the case.

In her hanging, the short drop from the chair did not

provide the necessary force needed to complete the execution. Kasper reported the cause of death as asphyxia, or in this case, inadvertent self-strangulation. Shaw's pale face and dark purple tongue, hanging like a ripe eggplant, indicated a merciless demise.

The left eye bulged from the socket and both eyes were yellowed and filled with blood, the result of the capillaries in her face exploding. Her body, upon examination later, bloated from the heart's inability to send blood through the carotid arteries to her brain. In all, she died in a horrid fit of choking.

At what point, if at all, does someone enduring such pain regret stepping from the chair?

Did she try to halt the suicide, or was her intention so profound, that suffering through the pain felt right? Campini chewed on these questions during the drive to Belleview.

We'll never know.

Forty-five minutes later, the Impala idled in Timothy's parents' driveway. Shaw's letter rested in his lap, the pages turning with crisp wisps every other minute. The reading solidified the plan. A plan, incredibly, requiring the assistance of Thunderstorm. Shaw's tragic and disturbing death made this possible.

He read her words about the man named Lorenzo. Benussi's case notes detailed quite a bit of information, but he doubted Shaw's assertion of Lorenzo being a hot lead. This ruse would not include the newly appointed underboss of the Solano family. The plan required finesse and trust. Risk, too.

Timothy's white Jeep sat in the driveway a few yards in front of the Impala's fender. The make and model, along with the license plate number, confirmed this.

Before he'd made the drive, he conducted his research. A thick manila folder lay open on the front seat—a neat little package of Vietta's life. He sifted through the file for two hours last night and learned a few interesting facts about the kid. One of the most fascinating tidbits regarded a recent purchase with a Visa.

A customary exercise during Operation Firecracker, Campini plucked recent gun purchases in Ridgemont Cove on a monthly basis. As OCD's commanding officer, temporary access to the state database had been approved. Although the investigation's termination took effect as soon he walked out of Taggert's office, his credentials still worked.

The search revealed Vietta purchased an FNS compact pistol twelve days ago. This meant the gun had been in his possession no more than two.

The job taught lessons every day. One lesson almost all investigators learned was simple to understand. People buy guns for two reasons.

You procured a gun if you were ready to defend what was most precious to you or willing to take what was most precious to others.

Vietta purchased the gun on the same day he left him outside of the battlefield known as Ms. May's Diner. Revenge, an understandable emotion for Timothy to feel, took hold outside the tomb of his beloved.

Campini exited the car, tucked Shaw's letter into his coat pocket, and marched toward the house. A tractor in the distance darted across the field. A flattened grass track bent down the slope, likely left by a vehicle leaving.

Perfect.

He climbed the porch steps and knocked. The door cracked open and half of Timothy's face appeared. "What took you so long? I've been watching you out there for a while."

"Can I come in?"

"For what?"

"Let me in for a minute."

Timothy swayed the door inward and led Campini to the small living room annexed on the right side of the house. "What can I do for you, detective?"

"I just wanted to talk is all. How's the hand?" He glanced around. A family portrait hung above a stone fireplace. In it, a prepubescent Timothy smiled, his features soft and bright.

"You drive all this way to ask about my hand?"

"Not the only reason." On the mantle above the lit fire, three separate photos of the same toddler in pigtails sat in a row. He plucked one from the shelf. "She looks just like you."

"First the hand, now my daughter? You writing a documentary?"

Campini returned the frame with a chuckle. "I've got some information from a reliable source. Could be useful for a man with a vendetta like you."

"Vendetta?" Timothy reached over and straightened the picture. "I'm not looking for trouble."

"You're not? My experience tells me when a man buys a gun, he's either searching or waiting for trouble. What's your motive, Thunderstorm?"

"How do you know?"

"I'm a cop, Tim. I've got my ways."

"Can you ever just shoot me straight? You're always pulling your tough-guy cop act."

"I am a cop. How would you like me to act?"

"See, there's the problem with you. Walking around

with a shiny badge and thinking your shit don't stink. Talk to me like I'm not an asshole." Timothy's eyes flared and Campini sensed a few more ill-placed words may crumble the plan.

"Okay. Let's start over."

"You came here to talk, right? Then talk. Cut the bullshit."

"You're right." Campini sat on the couch and unclipped the gold badge from his belt. He tossed it up. It clicked off the glass and landed upside down on the table's edge. "Today, I'm not a cop."

"What kinda game you playing, man? I've got things to do." Timothy scoffed and shook his head. He traced the scar on his hand.

"No game." Campini slapped Shaw's crumpled letter next to the badge. Timothy eyed it and sat on the arm of the couch opposite of him.

"What's this?"

"This is the last thing Detective Deborah Shaw ever did with her life." He flattened the pages and uncurled the corners.

"Who?"

"Shaw was the lead detective on the double murder at Ms. May's."

"So." Timothy grunted, crossing his arms. "You here to remind me my girl is dead?"

"Not at all." Reese slid the letter across the table. "She left this for me before she hung herself. It's a confession."

"She committed suicide. Why?"

"She was in love with Benny. Can you believe it?"

"I don't care, man. Get to the point or get to the door."

"Just hear me out," Reese countered, his tone revealing a slight hint of irritation. "She was convinced the Solanos killed Benny, and she chose to end this life in her own way. It was a matter of time before Purelli ordered a contract." Campini cracked his knuckles on the table, each pop a darting echo. "It's admirable in a way."

Timothy picked the pages up in both hands. "What's to admire? She's dead. Like a lot of other people."

"I've read it nine times and looked for half-truths and inconsistencies, but there are none. I've crossed referenced dates and meetings. It all checks out."

"Okay." Timothy flipped the page and read for a moment. "You still haven't explained why you're here."

"This letter was addressed to me. It's like a blueprint of how to get the bastard."

"Why you?"

"Because," he ran a hand across the stubble of his chin. "she knew I was willing to finish this thing and my case would be destroyed with Benny's death."

"As far as I'm concerned, I'm glad he's dead. Hope Frezza and the rest of those assholes get it to." Timothy scrolled through the final page. "Why are you showing me this?"

"Let me start from the beginning." Campini grabbed Shaw's letter and tucked it back in his coat. He retrieved the badge and surveyed it like a doctor would a patient's chart. "This thing used to mean something. I was proud to wear it. Now, I'm not sure it's worth the cheap tin and plated gold it's made from."

"Shit, man. You're a lot different from the last time I saw you."

"Yeah. Sometimes I wonder." He clicked the badge back in place on his belt. "Anyway, do you remember Sonny?"

"Benny's driver?"

"Yeah. His real name was James Benussi. An undercover operative of the OCD. He infiltrated the Solano Crime family and Purelli's crew about two years ago. I've got thousands of pages and hundreds of hours of surveillance. A few things about you are in there, too."

Timothy looked down at the carpet. "What happened to him?"

"Shot and killed twelve days ago outside of Ms. May's Diner. The Irish shot it up in an act of revenge. They killed what they thought was a mobster and destroyed the diner to send a message. Ruby was an accident, though. I'm sorry to say it so crudely, but you deserve the truth."

"What were they getting revenge for?"

"Bryce O'Leary. Murdered one day before his fight with Richie Frezza. Benny confided in Shaw and she told me." Campini tapped the coat pocket harboring the letter. "Richie and a man named Lorenzo set up the O'Leary murder."

"Why are you telling me all of this? You're a cop. You've got your evidence. Go get these assholes. Lock up Frezza, Lorenzo and Purelli."

"I told you. Today I'm not a cop. It doesn't matter, really. Shaw's letter is as worthless as Benussi's surveillance. The people who are capable of corroborating are either dead or in the wind. My case has been closed and I've been assigned to a different unit."

"Well, sounds like we're talking in circles then. If the case is dead—"

"I have a chance." Reese nodded to Timothy's scarred hand laid flat on the coffee table.

The fighter's expression soured, and he stood from the couch. "Oh, I get it. You need me to testify? Forget about it."

"None of Benussi's surveillance links Purelli to

anything. The only hope I had was getting a man named Georgie Silva to testify against Richie and Benny. Then, turn Benny informant."

"So even if you found Georgie or flipped Richie, it won't matter?"

"Purelli's got too much money and pull to face a fair trial. No state attorney will touch the case. It's career suicide."

"I'm sorry about your friend." Timothy stirred the fire with a poker and slid the cage in place. Embers danced behind the sheath. "I remember the dude. Always liked him. This thing has killed people we both care about, but I've got a daughter. I make one squeak, and she's in danger. Purelli ain't afraid to murder a toddler, as far as I'm concerned. And if I can help it, he won't be killing my daughter."

"We want the same thing. Aren't you tired of losing? I know what you want."

"You're a cop again, huh? And what is it you think I want?"

"Revenge. It's why you bought the gun. You want them to pay, right?"

Timothy said nothing and drew a glance out into the yard.

Campini followed his trance. An enormous oak's arms swayed in the wind. A tire draped in snow hung high from a thick, slanted branch. "But if you try to do it your way, you'll end up dead or in jail."

"So, what do you suggest?"

"Let's do it my way."

CHAPTER EIGHTY-NINE

Richie scaled the final step and cut toward Lorenzo's car. The new underboss sat in the driver seat with his hand out the window.

Snow's faint descent from earlier now a steady trickle. Richie slid in to the passenger side. "He says you know the plan."

"Yeah." Lorenzo brought his arm back in the car and kicked the engine of the car on.

Richie fastened his seatbelt and exhaled deeply, feeling the nerves from this morning evaporate like the snowflakes hitting the windshield. "If you knew I was okay, why didn't you say anything?"

"Just wanted to see how you reacted, kid." Lorenzo whipped the car in reverse and grinned.

"Scared the shit out of me."

"Yeah, but you kept your composure. Never show what you feel in this business."

Richie shuddered. Benny's words pouring from Lorenzo's mouth. *Is this how it goes? One dies and another slides in. Same demeanor. Same backhanded advice.*

The vehicle turned down a side street running parallel to The Tango and cut through a vacant alley. "This is a night job." Lorenzo pulled his glasses from the console and perched them in place. "You got any black clothes?"

"At my house. You think this is a good idea, man?" Purelli's parting words rung in his ears. *This is a violent business. To earn your stripes, you need to draw blood.*

Lorenzo turned onto Worthington Avenue. "Let's take care of all the preparation. This hit is big, Richie. Much different than O'Leary."

Much, much different, O'Leary whispered. Richie's eyes scrunched and pain drove into his forehead. The vault's steel door closed tight. He could taste the metal. Its scent filled his nostrils. Gunpowder, too. He was back there. O'Leary's head splitting in two like a log being prepped as firewood. The blood . . . so much blood.

Shake it, Richie thought. *There's work to do and stripes to earn.* "We sure Beckett will be at the shop alone?"

"Yeah. We've been doing homework while you've been on vacation."

"What if he's not?"

"That's why we're both going." Lorenzo braked sharp behind a truck, forcing Richie's seatbelt to contract. "If there's two, three, or four it doesn't matter. We go in and handle the Irish once and for all. I'm surprised, rookie."

"What do you mean?" Richie turned to glimpse a snarl forming on the mobster's face.

"He's putting you on hit this big, this fast. Shit, took me years to get that kind of opportunity. The big guy likes you, kid."

"Opportunity? We're talking murder, man."

"This business is about colors." The truck ahead

crawled forward and Lorenzo shifted in his seat. He rotated the wheel to navigate a right turn. "Red makes green."

Our vengeance will be an extermination.

Richie's skin-popped with goosebumps. This wasn't the Wild West. Two guys couldn't take on four or five. "He's armed though, right?"

"Wouldn't you be? What's it matter? This asshole killed the waitress and blasted your friend's diner. Time for a little payback. We go in quietly, catch him off guard, put six in his chest, and then get the hell out of there."

"What happens after?"

"What do you mean?"

"After he's dead, who takes over? At some point they'll come after us, right?"

"Yeah, but this is the life. Kill or be killed. Besides, word on the street is Beckett's guys have been looking for you. Good thing you laid low after all the shit hit the fan."

"Looking for me? Why?"

"Eye for an eye." Lorenzo shoved a finger into Richie's chest. "In this case, boxer for a boxer."

Bryce, you hearing this? Seems a bit simple, huh? Cranswell propped the vault open with a grunt and its door flung forward.

I don't know what to believe anymore, the dead boxer said.

I know who not to believe. This kid is toast. Pack your bags, boys. We're heading home. Harold tugged at the knife lodged in his throat. It spurted dark slime, gurgling like a shallow brook.

The vault closed.

Worthington Avenue and Center Street intersected ahead. A left led to Ms. May's and Knuckles Up, but a right and small detour through the park ended at the loading dock.

Just a month ago, Richie dreaded the jog to Imperial Fish and Game. Now, alone with Lorenzo and game-planning another murder, the smell of fish carcasses and seaweed would be welcomed. Encouraged, even.

Lorenzo turned left. The yellow police tape outside of Ms. May's was gone and the windows intact once again. A crew of three men repainted the trim of the building. Richie squinted and peeked inside, but he saw nothing.

Next came Knuckles Up. It looked the same except for the "Closed" sign in the window. Richie couldn't blame Joe, but it would have been nice to say goodbye.

In three minutes, after Lorenzo steered through the narrow alleyways winding to the back of The Trails, Richie stood outside the apartment.

"Just black clothes? Nothing else?"

"Let me come in with you. Gotta take a piss anyway."

Both climbed the stoop and Richie nudged the front door open. The stale air slapped the men in the face. Richie tried the light switch, but it clicked up and down hopelessly.

"Keep the door propped open, the lights are off." Richie walked into the foyer and tried a different light switch. Darkness, still. He fumbled toward the separating wall of the kitchen.

"Can't see anything." Lorenzo's voice floated from behind.

With the blinds drawn, the foyer bled pitch black except for a thin sliver of white coming from the open front door. The apartment darkened behind the kitchen wall, and Richie bumped into a cabinet.

Then a loud thud.

"Lorenzo, keep the door open." He pushed forward, measuring each step. "Lorenzo?"

His eyes failed to adjust to the dark. Using the countertop as a guide, Richie grasped the handle of the refrigerator.

A single click then echoed in the muted black.

A gun.

He moved toward the cabinets to the left. A top sliding drawer held a few menacing knives.

"After O'Leary, I figured I was on to bigger and better things." Lorenzo's voice came from the foyer, but each word's volume gained weight. "Been in this crew for six years. Just a Goddamn errand boy."

"Put the gun away. You don't have to do this." Richie fumbled toward the drawer of knives. He grasped the corners and handles of various cabinets, counting in his head. *Was it two or three drawers from the left?*

"That changed, though." Soft footsteps traveled the foyer and then lightened.

Living room carpet, Richie thought. *Where is the fucking knife drawer?*

"I get to make my bones. Started with Benny, but there's one more name on my list."

A blinding white muzzle blast fractured the dark momentarily, followed by the grunt of a gunshot.

The drawer handle reflected for a nanosecond, but its shining ray disappeared.

Falling, liquid leaked from Richie's thigh. A wild grasp in the dark caught the handle of a drawer. It jammed at first but followed the weight of Richie's body to the ground.

A second shot. Wood chips from the cabinet fractured and ripped through his cheek. His hands traced the ground, scanning the cheap linoleum floor of the kitchen blindly.

"It's over, kid. Come on out. I'll make you the same deal as Benny. Quick and painless."

Richie grasped steel, but thick wetness halted the grip. "I'm not dying today. Not by you."

"One way or the other, kid, I'm completing the list." Lorenzo's voice now echoed in the kitchen.

He's close. Richie's clasped the blade of a knife, sending a stinging streak through the inside of his hand. Ignoring it, he attempted to crouch. The left leg mocked him and disobeyed.

The footsteps scuffed tile. A shadow, lighter but still pitch, stood at the separating wall's trim. Richie shifted the blade to the other hand, grasping the handle. It slipped in the blood.

It's your only way out. Hold the knife, Richie.

"Just like I told Benny," Lorenzo said, "Orders are orders."

If this fucking leg cooperates for three seconds, I may get out of this alive.

Crouching again, and mere feet from the shadow, he sprung up and forward. "Well, here I am." In midair he swung the blade. The handle jolted in his hand as the knife plunged into what he hoped was Lorenzo.

A blinding muzzle flash erupted and a carnivorous bite followed. Richie felt the skin of his neck sear and twinge.

He landed on the floor, still clutching the knife. Syrupy goo dripped down the handle, intertwining between the knuckles gripped tight.

Aching and now tearing, heavy breaths escaped his mouth, a monotonous series of exhalations.

Then a garbled wheeze preceded a wet cough. It had not come from Richie, and panicked, he toppled onto

Lorenzo, not seeing but feeling the man's presence. The knife rose and fell in sweeping, violent thrusts.

Was it worth it, Richie? Do you have all you've ever dreamed of? Cranswell mocked.

The grip weakened, but the knife's force came crashing down.

Blood sprinkled Richie's face with each jab of the point. "No. No!"

Harold barged in with a loud chuckle. *Isn't this funny? We've had some memories in this kitchen, huh, bud? I wonder what Benny would think about this. Kinda funny, ain't it?*

"It's not funny. It's sick." The knife's blade drove deep into the mass on the kitchen floor, a sinister squishing sound complementing each thrust. The dark masked the massacre, but Richie's stomach turned, imagining what it looked like. Each stick ripped wet slices. Open gorges of raw meat. And as much as he wanted to stop the onslaught, he was certain if the slick and throbbing hands tired and relented, Lorenzo's gun would burst again.

Tears now poured, carrying the hatred and shame of the past weeks.

O'Leary appeared. His head still split into two. Now he wore white boxing gloves and a green mouthpiece. Jabbing and ducking, splashes of blood flying from the huge opening Lorenzo created two weeks ago.

Through the mouthpiece he mumbled, *you cheated again. You weren't supposed to make it out of here. You're always slipping by, aren't you? You're a coward.*

Richie's hand grew numb and he no longer felt its arc of destruction.

In the air. Into Lorenzo. In the air. Into Lorenzo.

"I know. I'm sorry. I don't want it anymore." The knife

slipped from his grasp and clipped to the floor. Exhausted, Richie fell over, trembling in tears of pain and guilt. "I can't do it. I just can't."

The vault closed then opened again, and this time new figures appeared. Benny sat in the Cadillac wearing a tuxedo and gold cufflinks. The pockmarks of his face invisible. Sonny, masked by wide sunglasses, draped his meaty arms over the steering wheel—his mouth sewn shut in crisscross strands like laces of a shoe.

It won't end, kid. We're part of you now, Benny said, the familiar chuckle intact.

"It has to. I'm sorry. I'm so sorry for it all."

It's just business. You knew from the start how this thing of ours works.

"I didn't want it."

Of course, you did. You're a natural.

Richie Frezza screamed as long and as hard as his throat and lungs would allow.

Fatigue overcame the adrenaline, and his eyelids drooped, shutting the vault with a thud.

Silence now. Complete black.

CHAPTER NINETY

Reese Campini plucked the newspaper from its plastic sheath. Thick stacks of Christmas shopping season fodder spilled out and fell to the floorboard of the Impala.

Outside of the cruiser, Vito Marzetti screamed into a cellphone.

No rush. Purelli would be at The Tango today, regardless. According to Shaw's letters, he was there on all Mondays—the day of restaurant delivery service. Apparently, the meticulous and careful wise guy refused to allow anyone to sign documents bearing his name.

So, Vito could yell into the phone for another hour. It didn't matter. *In fact, the longer the suspense, the better the reward.*

He folded and tossed the paper on the dashboard and glanced at the file Alaina prepared earlier this morning. Within it, a crisp printed complaint placed in front named Salvador Purelli in the assault of Timothy Vietta. It wasn't an arrest warrant, unfortunately, but it would have to do. He knew the contents of this file wouldn't put a needle in Purelli's arm, but it would warrant the man's attention.

Flipping through the file, he smiled at the grainy photos from the hospital surveillance cameras. Purelli outside of Timothy's room. The mobster leaving. The photos were useless a month ago, but now they contained firepower. Ammunition in a machine gun prepped to fire and shred all in its path.

Marzetti struggled with the handle, and after a brief tug-of-war, opened the passenger side door and climbed in. "I can't stand women."

"Problems with the ladies?"

"Not ladies. *Lady*. My Goddamn ex-wife. The stupid bitch doesn't understand I'm a cop, not a doctor. She thinks I should be paying more child support. More? Half my check goes to her every month, and last time I saw her, she had a brand-new wardrobe and the kids were bitching about their school supplies."

"Glad I'm not you." Reese shifted the car into drive and pulled from the department's lot.

"Tell you one thing. Take it from me. Don't ever get married."

"I'll write that down when I get a chance."

Marzetti buckled his seat belt. "Anyway, where we headed? It's been a while."

"The Tango."

"Purelli's joint?" Marzetti wore the dumb look of his. It usually accompanied a rhetorical question. "For what?"

Campini tossed the file into his partner's lap. "We're gonna have a little chat with our old friend."

Marzetti sifted through the documents and offered shallow grunts and utterances. "So, the boxer wised up? He'll testify? Not like it matters, anyway. Purelli will kill him before the trial, probably."

"Maybe, but for the first time, I've got something real

enough to rattle his cage." He checked the mirror and switched lanes, entering the highway ramp. "I want him to know I haven't forgotten."

"Aren't you supposed to, though? Wasn't Firecracker shut down?"

"Yeah. I'm in homicide now. This guy's a murderer, right?"

"You don't quit, do you?"

"Never."

They rode in silence. Marzetti flipping the pages of the file and him gripping the wheel, absorbing the excitement permeating within.

This is it. He's going down. Finally.

Campini took the exit a minute later and inched toward a red light. In the distance, the roof of The Tango punctured the sky.

Marzetti rummaged through the papers and chuckled. "We'll be chasing this guy for years. He's got more money than God and better guns, too."

"Things change." Campini tapped the steering wheel with extended thumbs from each hand. "Nobody's untouchable."

"This is Ridgemont Cove, Reese. As far back as the twenties, Solanos have used it as their personal playground. That's not changing."

The light turned green and Reese punched the gas with force, annoyed by his partner's unwillingness to believe.

Soon he will. Everybody will. Today is the beginning.

The two detectives, different men with separate values and interests, rumbled toward Purelli, the monster of Ridgemont Cove.

It was time.

CHAPTER NINETY-ONE

Salvador Purelli sat with a phone nudged between his ear and shoulder. The line rang nine times then clicked off. He dialed the number again with the same result.

Lorenzo had not checked in after his assignment yesterday. A few contacts in the RCPD proved to be useless, too. None were aware of his whereabouts, but all could say he was not in custody or in the morgue. *Could they be trusted?*

A knock.

"Do your job, Vinny."

The door opened partially, and Vinny's head peeked through.

He paid the guy one thousand a day to sit outside and keep everyone out. *Add him to Lorenzo's list.*

"There's a cop here to see you, boss."

"I'm busy." Purelli drew his black eyes down to a delivery invoice in need of a signature. The door swept open and two men in suits pushed through.

"Get un-busy. We need to speak."

The younger of the two strolled in like a celebrity clutching a file folder in one hand. Vinny muscled forward but Purelli raised a hand. "Gentlemen, good morning. What is it we need to discuss?"

"I'm Detective Campini and this is my partner, Vito Marzetti." The young one jabbed a thumb to his left. "We're with the Ridgemont Cove Homicide Department."

Purelli recognized the name from a conversation with Benny about Sonny. *This is the puppeteer.* "Please, take a seat."

"Actually, this is time sensitive. I need you to come with me, Mr. Purelli." Campini flicked his fingers on his wrist.

"Am I under arrest?"

"I have a written complaint from Timothy Vietta. You know, the man you stabbed at Ridgemont Memorial."

"Nonsense. Contact my attorney if you wish to converse legal matters. Regretfully, I have a very busy schedule, Mr. Campini." He forced his eyes to a leather folder and sifted through arbitrary receipts from last night's till.

"That's *Detective* Campini."

The self-assured policeman plopped the file on the desk and leaned forward, placing both palms down next to it. "We're here to discuss a brutal assault. There is no time later."

"Preposterous. You have been misinformed."

Campini flipped the file open and snatched the top photo. He placed it in front of Purelli. "Is this not you at Ridgemont Cove Memorial?"

Is this the best they have? Clueless, arrogant cops. "I know many people. There are times when people grow sick or are injured. I always drop by to lend my support. This does not make me a criminal."

The detective's temples pulsed. "Here's the deal. You can come down and discuss your involvement in this alleged assault and clear your name, or I can get my team up here with a search warrant. They'll turn this place upside down for the next eight hours. What's it going to be?"

"A search warrant? For a civil complaint, detective?"

"Yes, Mr. Purelli. We'll take a look at your calendars, emails, and speak with people downstairs to ensure nothing of this matter has been talked about. Also, we'll search for the weapon and dust the soles of your shoes."

"My shoes?"

Campini plucked a photograph from the folder. "The assailant in the case stepped in blood and left us a pretty track. Size ten and half. I'm curious, what size shoe do you wear?"

"Now detective, I'm curious." Purelli reached into the silver case atop the desk. He tugged a cigarette from it and struck a match. "Why didn't you just come with a warrant in the first place?"

"Out of respect, I don't want to pull eight of my men down here to search this place if you have nothing to hide. I'd rather just speak with you man-to-man. We can clear it up in an hour."

"What else do you have in the file, detective?" He dragged and blew the fog toward the middling annoyance.

"Vietta's statement. More photos."

A bluff. The footprint is a doctored photo to be sure. These cops grasp at every straw imaginable. Purelli flicked the matchstick into the ash tray. "I am not going to your station, detective. However, I will oblige in some capacity. How about you and I talk alone? We have many things to discuss, as I am sure you are aware."

"You're not making this easy, are you? Tell you what. Let's have a cigarette out back. It's a beautiful day."

"Indeed," Purelli agreed and picked up the silver case. "Vinny, get my lawyer on the phone."

"Marzetti," Campini said with a glance over his shoulder, "run around front and hop in the car. I'll be there in a minute or two."

"After you." Purelli extended a hand toward the hallway.

The cop didn't move. "We go together."

"As you wish." Purelli moved toward the door and offered a cigarette from the case. "Tell me, what are you really here for? You cannot think this little ruse is going to work."

The detective matched his strides down the narrow corridor and jabbed the unlit cigarette between his lips. "You got my man killed. I want you to know I haven't forgotten."

"Not sure what you are referring to."

"Sonny, or should I say, James Benussi. You know damn well what I'm referring to."

"Ah, Sonny. Yes. He was a driver for an associate of mine. I met the man a handful of times." Purelli grasped the knob of the exterior door and spun it. A rush of frozen air invaded and the back stairwell appeared.

"You've got an answer for everything, don't you?" Campini spat with a glare.

They descended the first flight of steps. The sun peeked through a few feathery clouds, its rays clinging to the frozen metal stair case.

Purelli grabbed the gold-rimmed glasses from his shirt pocket and slid them on, squinting in the early daylight. "In my line of work, you have to have all the answers."

At the landing of the stairwell, Purelli offered the detective the matchbook.

"At some point, we all go down." Campini struck the match and brought the flame to the dangling cigarette.

"Do you want to know why I entered this profession, detective?"

"What you call a profession, I call against the law, but go ahead." He dragged the cigarette then flicked the matchstick.

"I was born in Palermo. My father was a shoemaker, spending ten hours a day sewing soles to the bottom of shoes. For twelve years the man worked for pennies. And finally, when he had saved enough to put my mother and me on a ship sailing to America, he could not afford a third ticket." Purelli chuckled. *It seems like a lifetime ago, now.*

"Poor planning, huh?" The cop grinned and exhaled a cloud.

"Yes. We left. Two years later my mother tells me he is dead. I was nine. I made up my mind right there, detective. I would never be a disgrace like my father. I would leave my mark on this world. Good or bad, when I die, people will remember the name." Purelli inhaled deeply, sucking in the chill. "I wonder, will anyone remember you?"

"Perhaps, they'll remember me as the man who locked you up." The detective's posture stiffened.

"For this business with Vietta? *Ridicolo.* If you attempt to pin this nonsense on me, I will cut your heart out."

Campini dragged at the cigarette again then flicked it. It crashed to the street and sparks erupted from the tip. "Mr. Purelli, threatening an officer of the law is a serious offense. I'd suggest—"

"I suggest you stop this little game." Purelli's tone transformed into a hiss, the song of a python nearing its prey. "You're just a guest in *my* town. When I say the word, you disappear." He snapped his ring finger and thumb together.

"So, we're doing this hard way?"

"Go get your warrant if you wish. I have nothing to hide." He swiveled and stepped toward the staircase.

A shadow crossed though the daylight then—a grim apparition moving from behind the dumpster nudged against the fence of the parking lot.

The first shot crashed through the right lens of the gold-rimmed glasses and tore open the orbital bone. Its velocity snapped Purelli's head and neck backward, a violent thrashing of skin and muscle.

CHAPTER NINETY-TWO

Campini grabbed at his service revolver, but a second gunshot pierced the air. This shot struck the cop's right shoulder, throttling and spinning him one-hundred and eighty degrees in the air. The velocity of the round trucked him to the back wall of the restaurant and dislodged the gun from his grasp. Landing hard on the opposite shoulder, he clipped his head on the concrete. It bounced, creating clusters of blinking lights.

A thick welt formed, obscuring his vision on the left side.

The third shot clanked off the wall, and shards of broken stucco rained down. Campini craned his neck to see Purelli's face.

A dark red mass oozed from the socket of his right eye, dripping fierce and unrelenting. A hissing sound, delicate and weak, escaped from his throat. It became a slight breath and then evaporated.

Reese inspected his chest and neck for wounds, moving the good arm across his body. Satisfied the shot wasn't life threatening, he looked to Purelli once more.

Salvador Purelli lay still and wide-mouthed, the remaining eye glassy and black.

CHAPTER NINETY-THREE

Timothy reclined in the musty chair. Its ripped cushions near the arms now whittled down to the plastic and the seat creaked with every movement. It stunk like stale nicotine. Originally, he planned on tossing it in the dumpster, but after a test run, the chair earned its keep.

Gives the place character.

It was one of the few things Joe hadn't packed. When the keys were delivered and the office door unlocked, the chair and a poster of Joe's glory days were still in the back office, but every other personal belonging floated around somewhere in Wisconsin.

The only additions Timothy brought were a digital clock, a framed photo of Annabelle, and a clunky file cabinet from his father's storage shed. He wasn't sure what to put in it, but his father's enthusiasm of his son's new legal and mature profession was hard to deny.

You're a businessman now. You gotta keep your files safe.

Still empty, it at least filled up some space in the barren office. Beside it, the poster of Joe "The Giant Killer" Gallant hung flat, tacked in with a few finishing nails.

When Timothy shook Joe's hand for the final time, he assured him the poster would remain untouched as a tribute to his legacy. Joe had scoffed audibly, returning the generous honor with a dead-panned stare. That expression popped up whenever Timothy thought of the old man.

A knock interrupted the recollection.

"Come in."

The door swung inward and Campini stood in the doorway. His hand, slung in a wrap beneath a light blue suit jacket, clutched a thin folder. "Good morning, Mr. Vietta."

"Mornin'."

"How are things coming along?" He crept into the room and shut the door. His eyes, like all eyes granted access into the office, drifted toward the poster.

"Getting used to it. Kinda new at all this."

Campini nodded like he understood the ins and outs of running a boxing gym with one hand. "How's the paw?"

"Hurts a little."

"You'll pull through. I know you will. Listen, I was hoping we could talk for a minute."

"What about?"

"A few things. You got time?"

"Yeah. Not here, though. Have you eaten breakfast yet?"

"I could go for a bite."

The two men walked toward the front entrance and skirted past the sparring ring, still a disheveled slab of canvas and multi-colored ropes. It was the second thing on Timothy's list behind figuring out how to turn a profit.

Mikey, the young fighter he'd met during Joe's final weeks as owner, jumped rope in the stretching area and smiled as Timothy and Campini strolled by.

Thunderstorm raised a closed fist. "I'll be back in twenty. Hold the fort down, kid."

The two men stepped through the door and into the December morning. The hinges squeaked, and the weather stripping swayed from the slight breeze.

Number three, fix the door.

Red and green wreaths dotted entranceways throughout the block, and the fresh smell of spruce filled the air. Though cold, the day wasn't bitter, and for the first time in a long while, people other than flesh walkers and pill-pushers navigated the sidewalks.

A few people die and the entire town seemed to mourn and then escape the shell of fear and possession. The Solano family had been fractured, and the citizens knew it. Not just a person here or there was aware. The entire town, an entity in itself, breathed lighter and shared a collective smile.

Timothy traced his finger across the etching in the glass. *Thunderstorm Title Boxing.* Campini lit a cigarette and scratched at the slung arm.

Timothy noticed and nodded. "How's the shoulder?"

"It hurts like hell."

"You got lucky, huh? Coulda been deadly." Timothy walked ahead and Campini fell in with the brisk pace.

"Lucky for me." A laugh pushed fog from his mouth.

"Dangerous job you have there, detective." Timothy joined the cop in cracking up.

"I distinctly remember telling you to hit my bicep. It's the meatiest part of the arm."

"I was aiming for your bicep. Lucky I hit your shoulder."

"Shitty aim, Thunderstorm. Stick to boxing."

"I'm just glad I didn't kill you."

"Me too."

They turned left and headed toward Ms. May's Diner; a nook Timothy grew fonder of with each passing morning. He loved the woman and her cheap breakfast. Hot coffee and a breakfast plate for four bucks?

Sold.

"So, is everything good? Any problems I need to know about?" Thunderstorm caught his reflection in the window of a vacant building. Refreshed and renewed it seemed.

"No worries." Campini dragged at the cigarette. "I'm the one with problems. I had to fill out an incident report. Got interviewed for five hours. Then they got me in counseling. Can you believe it?"

"Counseling? For what?"

"It's protocol. If you're shot or you fire your weapon in the line of duty, the department makes you talk to this asshole with 'Dr.' in front of his name. He asks stupid shit like 'How are you feeling?' and 'Are you angry?' Total waste of time, but I have to play the part."

"What part should I be playing?"

"Nothing. You're not even on the radar, Thunderstorm. I gave the investigators a description."

"Who are they looking for?"

"Short, fat guy with red hair. They're not looking for you. All the Irish pricks have their assholes puckered up, though. I guarantee the Italians strike back."

"Italians? Who's left?"

"Freddy Solano is still alive. He's in prison, but it's only a matter of time before he brings new blood into the city."

Timothy frowned. These last few days had been pleasant. The town glowed in freedom. Shop owners kept a few more coins in their pockets. But soon, if Reese was right, it would all change. "Out with the old and in with the new, huh?"

"It'll be all out war."

They reached Ms. May's Diner. The fresh paint and clear glass left no reminder of the brutality of weeks past. The sidewalks had been pressure washed and repainted, but both men knew of its sacrifice.

"Right there," Campini said, pointing to a slice of the sidewalk.

"What?"

"That's where it happened." He puffed the smoke and then stomped it out. "Benussi's last moments."

"He died a hero," Timothy offered, surveying the cop's eyes gathering mist.

"*We* know that. Nobody else does."

Timothy searched for a response, but the diner's door popped open.

"Well, I'll be." Ms. May stood in the entrance and flashed an approving smile. "This makes five mornings in a row."

"Glad to be back." Timothy entered first and shrugged the cold from his coat. "I'm going for the record."

"I believe that it is twelve. You can do it. The normal spot, hon?" She winked and led them to a booth near the rear window. A server, not as pretty as Ruby, tossed a few menus on the table and walked back toward the kitchen.

"Being back here reminds me of Frezza." Campini fell into one side of the booth and picked up the menu. "I must have sat in here a total of twenty hours watching the gym."

"What happens with him?"

"Spread him with jelly, he's toast."

The waitress returned with two mugs, steam hovering above the brim.

Campini offered a shrug, and she trotted away. "All jokes aside, he's facing twenty-five to life as soon as he gets transferred from the hospital. I'm going to drop in tomorrow and have a chat with him."

Timothy nodded and turned toward the bar. In the last five mornings, the world blotted out and Ruby stood behind the countertop sorting silverware or pouring mugs of coffee. And in these moments, she existed alone. Today the picture lost clarity, and Timothy worried it was a sign of progress. *Revel in the moments but move forward.*

"Look," Campini continued, "a deal is a deal. If you want, I can get you close to him. We can end it for good."

He shook the thought of his dead. "Nah, let him rot."

"Probably for the best, anyway. We should switch our focus."

"We? Are *we* partners or something now?"

"*We* have to be." Reese slid the file toward Timothy. "Take a look."

Timothy glanced around the diner and propped the cover up. An old mugshot of Patrick Beckett scowled at him.

"You serious?"

"Yeah. We're not done yet."

"Shouldn't we lie low for a while? It's only been a week."

"What's the difference? One way or another, we finish this, Thunderstorm."

"No difference. I just want to be smart about it."

"We talked about this, right?" Campini shot a glance toward a couple seated at the high-top and lowered his voice. "All these guys are going to die. You said yourself. We got one of em'. Let's get this Irish prick, too."

"You don't think it's too soon? I mean, two bosses.

Seems a bit crazy. Besides, didn't you just say the Italians are gonna strike back?"

"It's perfect. They'll get the credit."

"But the Italians will know it wasn't them who did it."

"So? Let the gangsters hash that part out. We've got work to do."

Ms. May returned, and he flipped the folder closed. She jotted their breakfast order. Campini asked for bacon and eggs. Timothy ordered an omelet.

"So, fellas, anything exciting to look forward to today?" She tucked the notepad into her apron and slid a cylindrical sugar canister across the table.

"Just the usual, ma'am. Catching the bad guys." Campini ignored the sweetener and sipped the black. He drew a vacant glance toward the front window.

"And you?" Ms. May's eyes cut to Timothy whose scarred hand tapped the closed folder in front of him.

"Today? I'm wide open."

CHAPTER NINETY-FOUR

Richie's eyes muscled open with strain, like glue had fastened the lids together. Vision returned in the form of a striking white ceiling. So bright, it pierced the retinas of the born-again eyes. Machines whirred and beeped. A bandage ran the length of his neck, and when he did perk his head up, the new eyes saw a leg propped on a suspended gurney —the limb bandaged and throbbing.

A television bolted to the wall across from the bed showed the local morning newscast. He attempted to swivel his neck to each side, but it wouldn't cooperate. Straining to move it further than an inch to the left or right sent a stream of continuous pricks across his shoulder.

Again, viewing the television, a headline flashed across the screen: No new information in gangland slaying that takes the life of Salvador Purelli. Police have reported no suspects in custody.

Susan Teagan went on to report: "*Salvador Purelli, known capo and reputed leader of the Solano Crime Family, was killed last week. The brazen, daylight attack also resulted in an officer being shot in the shoulder, but his injuries are minor. We have no word as to why the officer was with Mr. Purelli. We'll keep you updated as information is received. While investigators have no leads on either the murder of Benny Bianchi or Salvador Purelli, the eyes of law enforcement will be focused on Patrick Beckett. With the Solano Crime Family crippled in the last few weeks, Beckett, the assumed leader of the Irish organized crime syndicate, will look to gain control over all the Ridgemont Cove underworld rackets."*

"Crazy news, eh?"

Richie jolted in surprise from the voice and groaned as the fire of pain rushed across his neck and shoulders.

"I would have bet a million dollars the Italians would have won the war. Shows what I know," the voice continued.

Ignoring the pain, Richie coerced his body to cooperate and swiveled in the bed.

"Wh—" Richie began, but his throat closed. The base of his neck tingled, bringing an alarming realization to the forefront. *I can't speak.*

"I know. You have lots of questions, huh?"

Richie glared at Reese Campini. He wore a powder blue suit. The right coat sleeve draped over a black sling, holding the man's arm at a right angle.

"The assholes who took out Purelli almost killed me, too. Doctor said a few inches to my right, and this slug is driving into my throat. Hell, I'd be in here right next to you, assuming I would have lived at all. It's a small price to pay, I suppose."

Trying to speak through chunks of dry mass at the base of his tongue, Richie lay stupefied at the energy it expended.

"Do you know where you are?" Campini used his

untethered hand to sweep the air. "You're at Ridgemont Cove Memorial. Do you remember anything this past week?"

"I-I . . ." Richie's mouth closed. The struggle to form words too painful to attempt.

"Let me fill in the blanks. A call was made. Neighbors heard gunshots coming from your apartment."

Lorenzo's attack in the dark surfaced within his memory. Apparently, the shot hadn't missed.

Campini dragged a chair to the bedside and sat. "You took two slugs. Gotta give you respect. Hit twice and still managed to kill Lorenzo Cantu. Holy shit, what a bloody mess. You sliced him up something terrible."

Richie managed to nod to the leg suspended in the air.

"Oh, right. So, you got one in your leg,"—Campini pointed to the lifeless limb hung like dying fruit in a haphazard basket—"and one grazed your throat. My guess is that's why you're being so coy."

Richie clenched his teeth and leered at the cop's mockery. Uncontrollable rage rose within. He lunged forward but was thrown back. Steel dug into his left wrist. A handcuff secured him to the railing of the hospital bed.

"I guess I need to explain that, too." Campini reached for a crumpled bag on the bedside table and sifted through it. He pulled Richie's Timex watch from the depth of the brown sack. "Does the name Georgie Silva ring a bell?"

Richie's jaw tightened. Benny's words radiated. *Nice touch, kid. You're a natural.*

"We were able to track him down. He told us a hell of a story. Now, I already knew you were a murderous piece of shit because of Benussi's surveillance, but to have Georgie willing to talk helps. I guess with Purelli, Benny, and Lorenzo dead, snitching carries little risk."

Richie lunged again, though this attempt feeble and exhausting. The handcuff connected to his wrist jangled, and the cool steel sent vibrations up the shoulder.

"You criminals are all the same." Campini patted the cuffed wrist. "Tough talk, weak walk. Anyway, Georgie confirms you and Benny were behind the murder of Harold Remnick, but even with his statement and Benussi's case notes, we wouldn't feel confident charging you." He leaned in, nose-to-nose. The scent of spearmint and a dash of cologne drifted in the sterile hospital air.

"Then your little battle with Lorenzo happened." Campini twirled Richie's cheap watch with his index finger. "You know what's great about a crime scene? As soon as a crime is committed, we have probable cause to search the premises." The cop smirked, raising both hands as if to say *wouldn't you know it?*

Richie shook in the bed and flailed, uttering weak grunts through his trapped throat. The steel cuff dug into his skin, breaking it open.

"And you wouldn't believe what we found taped beneath a dresser drawer."

Richie yanked the cuff again, noticing the dripping red and understanding the futile attack. No amount of groaning or sheer will could overcome the steel or damage taken.

"Ah, you do remember. See, we've got Georgie's ID card. He told us you took it, and Benussi noted it in one of his briefings, but without it in our hands, we couldn't prove it." Campini's blue eyes narrowed. "Until now. Physical evidence, buddy. Far more powerful in a court of law. Do you know what this means for you?"

Nineteen years on this earth ended in just six weeks. Death would be easier and less painful. More humane than what was to come.

"You're fucked. As soon as you're well enough to leave here, we'll be escorting you across town to RCPD and booking you for murder and conspiracy."

Tears attempted to drop, but Richie had none left. No amount of crying could undo the past. He struggled again with his cuffed hand.

Campini wiped at the screen of the Timex. "It's broken. Stopped at twelve-twenty-one." The smirking cop stood from the chair and rubbed at his slung arm. "I have to be honest. Figured you'd have a Rolex, big baller."

Richie squirmed and violent wracking shards of pain enveloped him.

"Maybe it's good you saved some money, pal. You're going to need every penny. With what you're facing, it would be wise to hire the best lawyer available."

"I . . ." Richie began, but the other words refused to roll from his tongue.

"Save it for the judge." Campini tossed the watch and it landed beneath Richie's slung leg. He walked out of view and then the door clicked shut.

The handcuff clanked against the bed railing. The steel was real. There was no coming back from this. Tears formed in minute portions but were weak, dripping like a clogged faucet.

A live report crossed the small television. Susan Teagan communicated with a reporter framed in a box in the upper right-hand corner of the picture. A pretty blonde stood in front of a familiar stoop Richie had scuffed down many times before.

The reporter said: *"Good news for the citizens of Ridgemont Cove. Weeks after a devastating shooting took the lives of two, Ms. May's Diner is back in business. For the last five days this quaint nook has given holiday shoppers a reprieve from the cold to go along with world famous apple pie. It's a new beginning for a storied business here in our home."*

The screen trolled a panoramic view of the neighborhood and then zeroed in on the diner, clean and painted. Ms. May stood at the front door wearing a waitress uniform. Clipped above her left breast was a name tag with Ruby written in cursive.

The reporter and Ms. May started an interview, and Richie felt the first true tears drip.

With pity in his heart, he forced the vocal cords to cooperate. "I am so—"

The apology died in his throat.

ABOUT THE AUTHOR

Joshua Widerman (J. Davis) currently lives in Jupiter, FL with his wife, Brinley, and two children.

His stories are gritty and action-packed, revolving around the challenges of making difficult choices and enduring the consequences.

Professionally, he is an instructional coach and spends his time teaching students to embrace the importance of education and communication.

In his free time, he enjoys spending time with his family, rooting for the LA Rams and sneaking out for a quick tennis match.

You can visit J. Davis here: jdavisauthor.com

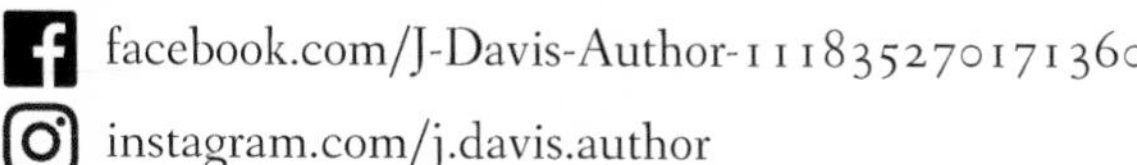
facebook.com/J-Davis-Author-111835270171360
instagram.com/j.davis.author

Made in the USA
Columbia, SC
23 May 2020

98123846R10331